Nice DRAGONS FINISH LAST

The first in a new series from the author of The Legend of Eli Monpress,

RACHEL AARON

Prologue

It was a very ugly house.

Two stories tall with a cheap yellow stucco finish and a roof sagging under the weight of the mismatched clay tiles, it stood alone in the vast expanse of the Nevada desert at the end of a long road meant to hold a hundred more just like it. But the second housing bust, or maybe the third, had nixed that plan, and years of bank ownership had left the property in limbo. With no landscapers to fight it back, the desert had moved in to reclaim the land, slowly covering the PVC pipes and pre-poured cement driveways until only the lone McMansion remained, sticking out of the sandy waste like a monument to terrible civic planning.

By contrast, the car crunching to a stop on the cracked asphalt at the road's end looked like a visitor from another world. Dark, sleek, and covered in black chrome with windows so tinted they would have made driving impossible in the days before computers took over the roadways, the sedan was a showpiece for its owner's wealth and importance, and the men who got out were exactly the sort you'd expect.

There were three of them, all dressed as nice as their car, but while the first two were so piled with muscle it was a miracle they'd managed to cram themselves into the designer suits currently straining over their shoulders, the third was of normal human proportions. Seeing this, one would expect him to be the most heavily armed, if only for compensation, but he carried no weapons at all. Just a single strand of long, brown hair wrapped around his first two fingers with a golden dowsing pendant dangling at the bottom, its pointed end jerking toward the ugly house.

"She's here."

The bigger of the two suited brutes pursed his lips and stared up at the house's dark, dusty windows. "You sure? Looks empty."

The man with the pendant made a sound of absolute disgust. "Of course I'm sure."

The big man shrugged off the implied *you idiot* and turned to his over-muscled accomplice. "I'll take the front. You go 'round back in case she bolts."

The other thug nodded and jogged off, pushing his way through the skeletons of the long dead bushes that divided the front of the property from the back. Meanwhile, the leader strode across the parched yard, up the rickety stairs to the scuffed front door. He tried the knob first, just in case. When it didn't turn, he put one hand on the concealed stun gun at his hip and began pounding on the weathered door with the other.

"We know you're in there, sweetheart!" he bellowed, slamming his fist down until the chipped paint was falling like rain. "Last chance to do things the easy way. You make us come get you, you ain't gonna like it."

He paused his beating to listen for a response, but the only sound was the night wind, and he turned back to the man with the pendant.

"She's in there," the smaller man snapped, stomping up the stairs to stand shoulder to huge shoulder with the thug on the rotting welcome mat. "I got this hair off her father's coat before we tossed him, and material links are never wrong." To prove his point, he held up the golden pendant, now straining at the end of the long brown hair like a tied-down missile. "It has to be her, and she has to be here. Just break it down."

The big man shrugged. "You're the mage." He lifted his trunk of a leg. "Mind your fingers."

The mage snatched his pendant back just in time before the door splintered under the big man's boot, the deadbolt and the lower left corner ripping clean off. Two more kicks took down the rest, and the thug stepped through the now-empty doorway with a menacing grin on his face. "Knock, knock, princess!"

A smaller crash echoed from the rear of the house, and the third man, the one they'd sent around back, yelled, "She's not in the kitchen!"

"You look around down here," the big thug ordered, turning toward the stairs. "I'll take the top. Remember, we got free reign to rough her up, but nothing permanent until Mr. Magic there confirms we've recovered the goods."

The mage shot to his full height, his face almost black with rage in the desert moonlight. "For the *last time*, my name is not—oh, never mind. Just get on with it."

The big man didn't seem to care about the mage's anger, though he did shoot a pointed look at his feet, which had yet to cross the house's threshold. "You coming?"

"A mage never enters another mage's house uninvited," the smaller man said stiffly. "Even when the mage in question is dead." He glanced around the faded foyer with a cringe. "This was Aldo Novalli's house. Lord knows what he left lying around."

The two big men inside froze, their scarred faces suddenly nervous, and the mage rolled his eyes. "Just go. Aldo's or not, there's nothing in there that could possibly be worse than what Bixby will do to us if we don't catch that little thief."

The mention of their boss's name had the desired effect. Both thugs immediately got to work with no further backtalk, opening closets and turning over furniture as they began their search.

The inside of the ugly house was little nicer than its shabby exterior, but far, far stranger. The scuffed walls were covered in old fashioned bookshelves packed to the edges with wire models of theoretical magical structures and even a few actual paper books on a wide variety of arcane subjects. The wooden floors in the living room and den were marked over in a rainbow of interlocking spellworked circles. Most of these were unfinished, but there were plenty of completed spells mixed into the mess, including one painted in purple in a continuous line along the crown molding that was making the mage on the porch particularly nervous.

"Well?" he called.

"Ain't no one here!" the big thug shouted from the second floor. "Someone's ransacked the bedrooms, took a bunch of stuff. Hundred bucks says she bolted before we got here."

The mage cursed under his breath and looked at his pendant again. Sure enough, it was still straining toward the house, the tiny golden weight pulling on the brown hair so hard, the strand cut into his fingers. He glanced at the thugs, who hadn't suffered any horrible curses yet, and then over his shoulder at the sleek car that would be driving them all to their deaths if they returned to the boss empty-handed.

In the end, the devil he knew won out. With a deep breath and a prayer to the god he hadn't bothered since high school, the mage followed his pendant through the splintered door into the house.

He stopped again the moment his foot hit the floorboards, holding his breath, but there was nothing. No curse, no trap, no spike of power. Just the smell of old drywall and casting chalk. With a long, relieved sigh, the mage lifted his pendant high. At the end of the brown hair, the golden pendant began to jerk wildly, almost yanking out of his fingers in its frenzy to get to the back of the house, and the mage broke into a grin.

"This way."

The two thugs shrugged and fell into step behind him as the mage strode confidently through the scribbled over living room and down a small hallway that led to what had once been the house's chief selling point: a whimsical hexagonal dining room. There was no dining going on now, however. Though clearly once present from the dents left in the carpet, the dining room table had been removed, leaving the room empty except for an enclosing circle of cheap, erasable whiteboards that had been propped over the windows, their faces covered in spellwork barely visible over the stains left by years of constant marking and erasing.

This normally would have given the mage pause—it was never a good idea to walk into an enclosed space with unknown spellwork on the walls—but the pendant was yanking wildly now, and he bounded into the room like a hunting dog finally cornering the fox.

"Here!" he cried triumphantly, grabbing the edge of the threadbare carpet and yanking it up with a flourish. "She's under—"

He cut off, the carpet falling from his fingers. He'd lifted the rug expecting to find a trap door to a basement, or even a storm cellar. Somewhere a girl could hide. But there was no door or hidden panel beneath the carpet. Just the dusty floor and a neat ponytail of long, brown, gently curling hair held together by a pink hair tie before the strands ended in a jagged, uneven fringe where it had been chopped off the base. That was as far as the mage's observations got before he smelled something burning.

His head jerked up just in time to see the markings on the surrounding whiteboards singe themselves into the plastic. The spell he'd seen painted on the crown molding was smoking too, the letters and symbols burning into the wood as magic flared in the air.

"Go!" the mage shouted, dropping his pendant as he turned and charged for the door. "Get out now! It's going to—"

The blast cut him off, echoing through the desert like cannon fire as the ugly house exploded.

***

Across the empty street, a young woman stepped out from behind the ruins of the failed subdivision's unfinished pool shed. The hot wind from the growing house fire whipped the ragged ends of her chopped off hair straight into her eyes. She pushed them back with purple-paint-smudged fingers, scowling at the tell-tale wetness that came away as well.

"Don't cry," she whispered angrily, scrubbing her eyes again. "Don't you *dare* cry."

She was still working on that when the fire reached the house's furnace. The second explosion was even louder than the first, blowing out the building's entire northern face and sending a corner of the ugly house's roof flying straight into the men's fancy car.

The sight of one of Bixby's expensive cars crushed under a smoldering hunk of support beams and clay shingles was enough to make her feel a little better. She watched it burn for a few more satisfying seconds, and then she turned her back on the inferno that had been her childhood home and ran across the empty lots to the failed subdivision's lone dumpster, and the dilapidated sedan she'd hidden behind it.

The old car was so over-packed, it took her several seconds to clear enough space to squeeze her body into the driver's seat. Even the dash was piled with bags and boxes, and she couldn't see out her back window at all. But while the rest of the car looked like a promotional shot for an episode of *Magical Hoarders*, the passenger seat was empty except for a glittering ball the size of a large grapefruit.

At first sight, the ball appeared to be made of solid gold. On closer inspection, however, it became clear that the sphere was actually glass: hollow, ancient, paper-thin glass gilded on the inside with a gold leaf pattern so dense, it looked like a solid, shimmering wall. The combination of glass and gold leaf was as fragile as it was beautiful, and it was protected accordingly by a nest of tissue paper that was itself tucked inside a towel-lined basket and lashed to the passenger seat by both the seatbelt and a half-dozen strips of duct tape. But for all the care the girl had clearly put into packing the delicate golden orb, the glare she shot it was anything but gentle.

"You'd better be worth it," she grumbled, scrubbing again at the tears that refused to stop coming as she started the car.

It took three tries before the old engine actually caught, and longer still before the dashboard booted up. For once, though, the car's age worked in her favor. It was too old to have integrated augmented reality, which meant she could still drive it manually whether the computer was up or not. Good thing, too, because she'd already made it all the way to the end of the subdivision by the time the screen above the gearbox finally flickered to life.

"Destination?" the hollow voice of the GPS wheezed.

"Detroit Free Zone," the girl replied, wincing at the blinding glare of the burning house in her side mirror. "Fast."

That last command was pure wishful thinking, but the computer did its best. "Calculating fastest route," it announced sedately.

The girl okayed the first suggested route as soon as it came up, tapping her fingers anxiously on the steering wheel as the auto-drive took over, rolling them out of the crumbling subdivision and onto the dark highway just in time to avoid being seen by the flashing emergency vehicles coming over the horizon from the other direction.

And back in the subdivision, unseen in the dark and the smoke, a pigeon flew out of a nearby juniper bush. It was a common city pigeon, completely out of place in the desert, but it flew like it owned the smoky sky, riding the hot updraft from the roaring fire to the top of the smoke pillar before circling back around to follow the girl's fleeing car into the night.

Chapter 1

"**G**et up."

Julius woke with a jump, toppling off the slick modern couch. He landed face down on hard white carpet, smacking his knee painfully on the corner of his sister's abstract coffee table in the process. When he reached down to clutch his smarting joint, his sister kicked his hand away again with the pointed toe of her black leather flats.

"I have to be at the hospital in thirty minutes," she continued as she marched across the room to yank open the hanging blinds. "That means you need to be out of here in ten. Now get moving."

Julius rolled over and sat up, squinting against the bright ray of sunlight she'd sent stabbing across her ultra-fashionable, ultra-expensive apartment. "Good morning to you, too," he said, furtively rubbing his injured knee, which was still throbbing.

"Try afternoon," Jessica snapped. "Honestly, Julius, it's nearly five. Is this when you got up at home?" She turned with a huff, walking over to the marble breakfast bar that separated her immaculately white kitchen from the other immaculately white parts of her apartment's open floorplan. "No wonder Mother kicked you out."

Mother had kicked him out for a whole host of reasons, but Julius didn't feel like giving his sister any more ammunition, so he spent the energy he would have used explaining himself on standing up instead. "Where's your bathroom?"

She stabbed one perfectly manicured nail at the hall, and he shuffled as directed, though it still took him three tries before he found the right door. The others led into beautifully furnished bedrooms, none of which looked to be in use.

Julius sighed. Two guest bedrooms, and she'd *still* made him sleep on the couch. But then, Jessica had always been very conscious of where she stood in the pecking order, which was usually directly on top of Julius's head. The only reason she'd let him sleep here at all was because he was her brother, and the consequences for not helping family were dire. In any case, it wasn't like he was in a position to complain. When you found yourself shoved off a private plane into a strange airport at dawn with nothing but the clothes on your back, you took what you could get.

He found the bathroom and showered as fast as he could only to get right back into the same faded T-shirt and jeans he'd slept in, because what else was there to wear? He didn't even have a toothbrush, and he wasn't about to risk Jessica's wrath by using hers. In the end, he had to settle for mostly clean, raking his shaggy black hair into some semblance of order with his fingers and wishing he'd had a chance to get it trimmed before his life had gone down the drain. Of course, if he'd had any advanced warning of last night's personal armageddon, he wouldn't have wasted it on a haircut.

By the time he emerged into the living room again, Jessica was dressed for work in a pants suit, her long, blond-dyed hair pulled back in a tight French twist. She sat in the kitchen, perched on a silver barstool like a model in an interior design magazine as she sipped coffee from a minimalist white mug. Naturally, she hadn't made any for him.

"Here," she said when she saw him, shoving a sleek, black metal rectangle across the marble countertop. "This is for you."

Julius's breath caught in amazement. "You got me a phone?"

Jessica rolled her brilliant green eyes, the only family feature they shared. "Of course not. Unlike you, *I* know how to be a dragon, which means *I* don't give out freebies just to be *nice*." She hissed the last word through sharpening teeth, letting a bit of her true nature show before resuming her human mask. "It's from Bob."

Julius snatched back the hand he'd been reaching toward the phone. Bob was his oldest brother and their dragon clan's seer. He was also insane. Presents from him tended to explode. But the phone looked normal enough, and Julius had already been kicked out of his home and dropped in a strange city without a dollar to his name. Really, how much worse could today get?

He picked up the feather-light piece of electronics with tentative fingers. Cursed gift or not, this phone was much nicer than the old one he'd been forced to leave behind. As soon as the metal contacts on the back touched his skin, the phone's augmented reality system blended seamlessly into his own ambient magic. After a second's calibration, the air above the phone flickered, and a 3D interface appeared. He was still getting used to the beautifully designed, almost unusably small icons floating above his hand when a flashing message appeared directly in front of his face, titled THIS IS WHAT YOU WANT.

Hesitantly, Julius reached up to tap the floating message. The moment his finger passed through the icon, a short paragraph appeared, the glowing letters hovering seemingly in thin air.

My Dearest Brother,
Sorry I didn't warn about Mother's incoming Upset. I foresaw it last year and simply forgot to tell you due to other VAST AND SERIOUS events currently unfolding. To make it up to you, I've taken the liberty of preparing the proper credentials for your new Life in the Big City. I can

only hope it's all still valid, seeing how I'm putting this phone in the mail to you four months before you'll need it, but We Do What We Must. I've also set you up with some money from my private hoard to make the transition a little easier. Try not to spend it all in one place!

Hearts and kisses, your infallible and all-knowing brother,
Bob

PS: I almost forgot to give you your advice for the day. You must be a GENTLEMAN above all else, and a gentleman never refuses to help a desperate lady. You're welcome.

Julius read the message twice before setting the phone back down on the counter. "If he knew to mail me a phone four months before I needed it, why didn't he just tell me Mother was going to kick me out instead?"

"Because he's not really a seer, idiot," Jessica replied, setting her empty mug down with a clink. "He can't *actually* see the future. He's just insane. You know how old dragons get." She slid off the barstool with a huff. "Honestly, his only real power is his ability to convince Mother that his stupid antics are all part of some huge, incomprehensible scheme that's going to help her defeat the other clans and become queen dragon of the world."

Julius didn't know about that. From what he'd seen, Mother believed in Bob completely, and she didn't do anything without good reason. Of course, it was hard to tell what was really going on across the enormous distance he kept between himself and the more powerful members of his family. That was Julius's entire life strategy, actually—stay out of the way of bigger dragons—and up until last night, it had worked perfectly. More or less.

He sighed and grabbed the phone again, putting his finger through the glowing accounts icon as soon as the AR interface came up. Whatever the actual status of his sanity, Bob was indisputably old. Old dragons couldn't help storing up vast piles of wealth. If Bob was giving Julius money from his own private stash, then maybe...

His fledgling hopes crumbled when the balance appeared. Ninety-eight dollars and thirty-two cents. Bob had given him ninety-eight dollars and thirty-two cents. That was barely enough to get him through half a week back home. It probably wouldn't last him a day in a big city like the DFZ.

Julius slumped against the breakfast bar, staring blankly at the miles of shiny white superscrapers and animated ad-boards looming beyond Jessica's floor-to-ceiling windows. What was he going to do?

And how? His life back home might not have been great, but at least he understood it. Now he was uprooted, lost, tossed into the biggest city in the world with nothing, and he couldn't even change into his true form and fly away because of what his mother had done.

That thought made him more depressed than ever. He'd been trying his best not to think about what had happened last night, what had *really* happened, but there didn't seem to be much point in avoiding it now. He'd have to face facts sooner or later, so he might as well get it over with. It wasn't like things could get any—

His phone rang.

Julius jumped, jerking the phone up so fast he narrowly missed cracking it to pieces on the underside of the counter. Jessica jumped as well, and then her green eyes grew cruel. "I can guess who that is," she said in the sing-song voice he'd hated since they were hatchlings.

"It might not be her," Julius muttered, though that was more desperate hope than any real belief. After all, there were only two people who could plausibly know this number, and Julius didn't think he'd be lucky enough to get Bob.

Jessica clearly didn't think so, either. "Much as I'd love to stick around and witness you get chewed to bits, I've got work," she said cheerfully, grabbing her bag off the counter as she strolled toward the door. "Don't touch my stuff, and don't be here when I get back. Oh, and if she decides to kill you, make sure you don't die in my apartment. I just got this carpet installed."

She tapped her heel on the white carpet before walking into the hall, humming happily to herself. As soon as the door closed, Julius sank onto her vacated stool. He propped his elbows on the counter as well, shoring himself up as best he could. Finally, when he was well supported and out of ways to put off the inevitable, he hit the accept call button like a man ordering his own execution and raised the phone to his ear.

"Well," crooned the sweet, familiar, smoky voice that never failed to tie his insides in knots. "If it isn't my most ungrateful child."

Julius closed his eyes with a silent sigh. "Hello, Mother."

"Don't you 'hello, Mother' me," she snapped, the click of her long fangs painfully audible through the new phone's magically enhanced speakers. "Do you know what time it is?"

He glanced at the clock. "Five fifteen?"

"It is exactly nineteen hours since you left my company. *Nineteen hours*, Julius! And you never once thought to call and reassure your poor mother that you were alive and had found somewhere to stay? What is wrong with you?"

Julius could have reminded her that it was her fault he was in this position in the first place. She was the one who'd barged into his room at midnight and ordered him to get out without letting him grab his phone or his money or any of the tools he needed to make the call she was angry about not receiving. But burdening Bethesda the Heartstriker with facts when she was in a rage was only slightly less suicidal than contradicting her, so all he said was, "Sorry."

His mother sighed, a long hiss so familiar he could almost feel the heat of her flames through the phone. "This is harder on me than it is on you, you know," she said at last. "But you gave me no choice. Something had to be done. All your brothers and sisters are getting along splendidly. Even Jessica managed to work her doctor nonsense into a position of power. She'll be running that hospital in five years. But *you!* You are *hopeless*. If I hadn't watched you hatch myself, I'd doubt you were a dragon at all."

She'd told Julius as much almost every day of his life, but for some reason, the insult never stopped smarting. "Sorry," he said again.

His mother went on like he hadn't spoken. "You're not ambitious, you don't make plans, you don't try to take things over. It's like you were born with no draconic instinct whatsoever. All you've done since I let you out of training is hide in your room, avoiding the rest of us like the plague."

He'd always thought of it more as avoiding jumping into a pool of hungry sharks, but he knew better than to say so. "I wasn't bothering anyone."

"That's exactly the problem!" Bethesda roared. "You're a dragon! Dragons don't worry about *bothering*. We *demand*, Julius, and the world *gives*. That is the rightful order of things. I thought if I left you alone, your instincts would kick in eventually, but it's been seven years and you're as bad as ever. Clearly, something in that head of yours is broken beyond repair, and I don't have the patience to wait any longer."

He swallowed. "I—"

"Twenty-four-year-old dragons should be out making names for themselves! Not living at home with their mothers! People are beginning to *talk*, Julius. I had to do something. "

"So you decided to seal me?"

The second the words were out of his mouth, Julius's stomach, which was already clenched to the size of a marble, threatened to vanish entirely. But there was no taking it back. The horrible truth was out, and, in a raw, painful way, it felt good to hear it spoken. So, since he was a dead dragon anyway, he kept going.

"Why, Mother?" he asked. "You wanted me to be a dragon, so why did you lock me into *this*?" He waved his hand down at his lanky, too-skinny human body before he remembered she couldn't see him, which only upset him more. "Why did you send me away? Why did you send me *here*?" He shot a panicked look at the forbidding wall of superscrapers outside the window. "This is the DFZ. They kill dragons on sight here. If I'm—"

He cut off with a choked gasp as his mother touched the seal she'd placed at the root of his magic. She might be hundreds of miles away, but he could still feel her claws in his mind, the sharp tips pressing painfully on the wound she'd made nineteen hours ago when she'd cut into his soul and locked him away from his true nature. It was only for a second, but by the time she let him go, Julius felt like he'd been sliced open all over again.

"That's better," his mother said, her words punctuated by the clink of gold coins as she shifted her position. "Honestly, Julius, do you even listen to yourself? Complain, complain, complain, when all your life you've been coasting, never even considering the position that puts me in."

He hardly thought that being sealed from his powers and stranded in the one city in the world where dragons were illegal was a frivolous complaint, but he couldn't have said as much even if he'd dared. His mother was on a roll, and there was no stopping her now.

"You don't even know what I suffer for this family!" she cried. "Every day, every *hour,* our enemies are looking for ways to cut us down. The other clans would like nothing better than to see the Heartstrikers brought low, and you're helping them! Being a disappointment within your own family is one thing, but can you imagine what would happen if the rest of the world found out that my son, *my* son, spends his days locked in his room playing video games with humans? *Humans,* Julius! And you don't even win!"

Julius began to sweat. "I don't see—"

"That is exactly the problem!" she yelled, making his ears ring. "You *don't* see. If one of your siblings was doing something I wanted them to stop, I'd just threaten their plans or thwart their ambitions, but you don't *have* any of those. You don't have *anything,* and so I was forced to take the only thing I could."

She touched his seal again as she said this, and suddenly, Julius couldn't breathe.

"You are the worst excuse for a dragon I've ever seen," she snarled. "But even you still need to actually *be* a dragon. So if you don't want to spend the rest of your soon-to-be very short life as little more than a trumped-up mortal, you'll listen closely to what I'm about to say."

She released him after that, and it was all Julius could do not to flop panting on to the counter. But showing weakness would not improve his mother's mood, so he forced himself back together, breathing deep until he could trust his voice enough to say, "I'm listening."

"Good," Bethesda replied. "Because I've fought too long and too hard to get where I am to be made a fool of by my youngest child. I really should have eaten you years ago, but a mother's hope springs eternal, so I've decided to give you one last chance. A final opportunity to make something of yourself."

Julius didn't like the sound of that at all. "What am I supposed to do?"

"You're a dragon," she said flippantly. "Be draconic. Take something over, destroy one of our enemies, win a duel, capture an advantage for our clan. I don't really care what you do, but you will do *something* to make me proud to call you my son before the end of the month, or I will do to you what I did to my other under-performing whelps."

Julius didn't need the snap of her fangs at the end. His blood was already running cold, especially when he realized today was already August 8th. "But…that's not even four weeks."

"Think of it as a trial by fire," Bethesda said sweetly. "You'll come out of this a real Heartstriker or not at all. Either way, you won't be an embarrassment to the clan anymore, which makes it a win-win for me, and we all know that's what really matters."

Julius closed his eyes. Trial by fire. How excessively draconic.

"I can hear you moping," she warned. "Don't be so defeatist. That's exactly the type of behavior this little exercise is supposed to correct. And sorely as I'm tempted to let you dangle, I'm not throwing you out completely on your own. It just so happens that your brother Ian has some work he's agreed to let you take on, a little jump-start to get you going on the path toward respectability." Her voice turned rapturous. "Now *there* is a dragon, and an excellent son."

Julius frowned, trying to remember which brother Ian was. He had the vague recollection of an icy demeanor and a calculating smile, which probably meant Ian was one of those plotting, ambitious siblings he normally stayed far, far away from. Of course, if Mother liked him, the ambitious part was a given. Bethesda never loved her children more than when they were trying to engineer each other's downfalls.

"I already sent him your information while you were whining," she continued. "He should be contacting you soon. And Julius?"

He fought the urge to sigh. "Yes, Mother?"

Bethesda's voice sharpened until the words dug into him like claws. "Don't fail me."

The call cut out right after that, but it took Julius a full thirty seconds to unclench his fingers enough to set the phone down safely below Jessica's never-used collection of copper cookware. When it was out of harm's way, he dropped his head to the cold marble counter with a thunk. He was still lying there when his phone buzzed again with Ian's terse message to meet him at a club halfway across town in fifteen minutes.

* * *

In the end, he had to take a cab.

He couldn't afford it, not really, but there was no other way to keep Ian's deadline, and Julius wasn't about to get himself eaten by his mother because he was too cheap to hire a taxi. It ended up being a good choice, though, because the drive across the elevated skyways gave him his first real look at the Detroit Free Zone in the daytime.

Not surprisingly, it looked exactly like it did in the pictures: an impossibly clean city on the banks of the Detroit River with blindingly white, thousand-floor superscrapers rising from a beautiful, whimsically spiraling lattice of elevated skyways held high off the ground by huge concrete pillars. Pressing his face against the car window, Julius could catch glimpses down through the gaps at Old Detroit, the ruined city that still lay beneath the new one like a rotting carcass, but not enough to see anything interesting. No packs of death spirits or ghouls or any of the other horrors that supposedly terrorized the Underground. But while that was disappointing, the DFZ's other most interesting attraction was impossible to miss.

Rising from the blue depths of Lake St. Clair, Algonquin Tower looked like a spire made by gods to hold up the sky. Even here in downtown, a good ten miles away, Julius could still make out the sweeping curls of stonework that made the two-thousand-foot tall granite pillar look like an endlessly swirling waterspout instead of static rock. Supposedly, there was a leviathan that lived underneath it, but even without the giant sea monster, the tower was a fitting and undeniable reminder of who ruled Detroit, and why.

When the meteor crashed into Canada in 2035, sending magic surging back into a world that had long forgotten such things existed, human mages weren't the only ones who had reawakened. The sudden influx of power had also roused spirits of the land forced into hibernation by almost a thousand years of magical drought. They'd woken with a vengeance, too, but none so much as Algonquin, the Lady of the Lakes.

Even now, sixty years after magic's return, people still talked about the night Algonquin rose to sweep the Great Lakes clean. Her purifying wave had come from nowhere, washing away centuries of pollution in a single night, and most of the cities that lined the Great Lakes with it. No place, however, felt her wrath like Detroit.

While other cities were merely flooded, Detroit was nearly swept off the map. Those who survived claimed Algonquin's wave had been over a thousand feet, a black swell of all the poisons dredged up from the bottom of the Detroit River and the bed of Lake St. Clare that she'd emptied on the city without quarter, crushing buildings and drowning millions in the process.

When the flood waters finally receded, Algonquin had claimed the ruins of Detroit as her own, and with the rest of the world still reeling from the return of magic, the U.S. government hadn't been able to tell her otherwise. From that night on, Detroit, Michigan became the Detroit Free Zone, an independent territory of the United States and the only city anywhere governed by a spirit. Algonquin had wasted no time changing the rules, either, dumping almost every law on the books, especially those limiting business and immigration, and she'd refused to regulate the new practice of magic at all. The resulting sorcery research boom had made the DFZ one of the largest, wealthiest, most magical cities in the world. It was also the most dangerous, especially for him.

For reasons Julius didn't know, but could easily imagine, the Lady of the Lakes hated dragons with a passion. His kind were tenuously accepted in the rest of the U.S., and ruled outright in China, but in the Algonquin's city, where everything from drugs to guns to prostitution was legal, dragons were strictly forbidden. Even small ones like him fetched bounties in the millions. He had no idea why his mother had decided to force him to "be a dragon" in the one city where doing so would automatically make him a target, but at least it gave Julius a reason to be happy about the seal. Awful as it was not to be able to fly or breathe fire or stretch his tail properly, he didn't have to worry about accidentally revealing his true nature and getting killed for it. So, that was something.

He'd barely finished this exercise in extreme positive thinking when his cab pulled to a stop beside a crowded, elevated square lined with trees, fountains, and high-end restaurants. *Very* high-end restaurants, the sort with unpronounceable names and dress codes that involved jackets. Julius looked down at his own ancient green T-shirt and slightly singed jeans with a sigh. The part of him that was still trying to stay positive pointed out that he should be glad he'd at least been wearing a shirt when his mother had burst into his room, but the rest of him just wanted to get this over with.

The automated cab had taken its fare out of his phone's account the second it reached the requested destination, so Julius got out of the bright yellow, driverless car without looking back. It took him a few minutes to push through the crowd of fashionable professionals and the tourists taking pictures of them to the address Ian had given him; a slick club/restaurant hybrid with tinted glass doors and no name at all, just a picture of a tree laser etched into the windows.

As expected for such a high-end establishment, the first set of doors was just for show. The real doors were inside a dimly lit foyer guarded by three cameras and a doorman. Normally, a human wouldn't have worried Julius too much, but this one was clearly packing some augmented implants—human arms just didn't get that bulky without medical help—and he didn't look shy about using them.

Considering how sorry he looked right now, Julius fully expected the bulky doorman to pick him up by the fraying neck of his shirt and toss him right back out into the square. From the expression on the man's face, he clearly wanted to do just that, but when Julius gave his name, the doorman simply pushed open the leather-covered inner door and told him that his party was waiting at the back.

After the bustle of the crowded square, the inside of the restaurant was shockingly silent in the way only real money could buy. Even the silverware didn't seem to clink as Julius wove his way between the white clothed tables and high-backed booths. The place smelled rich, too, a deep, subtle mix of hardwood, leather, truffle oil, and other things his sensitive nose wasn't cultured enough to recognize.

The VIP area was in the far back corner, separated from the rest of the restaurant by a wall of malachite-beaded curtains. Julius pushed them open with only a slight hesitation, pointedly ignoring the well-dressed couples who turned to gawk at him as he looked around for his brother.

He didn't have to look long. He might not have been able to place Ian's name earlier, but now that he was here, he spotted his brother at once. He also saw why their mother was so fond of him.

From the first glance, it was obvious that Ian was a dragon's dragon. Even dressed in a black suit sitting in a black booth, he effortlessly overshadowed the well-dressed men with their jewel covered women and thousand dollar bottles of champagne like a panther lounging in a flock of peacocks. Julius, on the other hand, felt a bit like a mangy dog as he slid into the leather booth across from his brother and dipped his head in greeting.

Ian did not return the gesture. He just sat there, regarding Julius through slitted, Heartstriker-green eyes before letting out a long, vexed sigh. "What on earth are you wearing?"

"What I had," Julius replied irritably. "I didn't exactly get time to pack."

"So I heard," his brother said, tilting his head forward so that his perfectly tousled black hair swept down over his dark brows, enhancing his speculative scowl. "There's been quite a bit of talk going around about what you did to send Mother into such a rage. I don't think I've ever heard of her sticking one of us on her private jet for a cross-country trip in the middle of the night before."

Julius started to sweat. Heartstriker gossip, about *him*. Just the thought made him twitchy. The only thing worse than being beneath a dragon's interest was being the target of it.

"Sending you away was a good sign, though," Ian went on. "Normally when she goes on the warpath, she just eats the parts she likes and tosses what's left into the desert for the vultures. She must really believe you can be rehabilitated if she didn't kill you outright."

Julius supposed that was a comfort. "She threatened to do it."

"Bethesda has threatened to kill all of us at one point or another," Ian said with a shrug. "It's how she mothers. That doesn't mean she *won't*, of course. A weak dragon is a liability to the whole clan. The real challenge is, how do we make her start seeing you as an asset instead of a disappointment?"

Julius shifted his weight on the buttery leather seat. He had no objections to what his brother was saying, but the *we* part made him decidedly nervous. He didn't know Ian at all personally—he was the sort of powerful, popular sibling Julius normally steered well clear of—but if he met their mother's definition of a good son, then he'd rather hang himself with his own tail than help a family member for free. "What do you want?"

Ian smiled. "You," he said. "For a job. It just so happens that I've come across an intriguing opportunity for someone with your…unique talents."

Julius had no idea what that meant. "So you want me to do something?"

"Yes," his brother said crisply. "For money." He shot Julius a skeptical look. "Do you understand how a job works?"

"No, no, I get that part," Julius grumbled. "I just want to know what you want me to do before I agree to do it." Because the list of things he wouldn't do for money was very long and included a number of activities most dragons would do for fun. Of course, being one of those dragons, Ian missed his point entirely.

"Don't be stupid, Julius," he said, picking up his drink. "Mother's the only reason I'm bothering to speak to you at all. Naturally, then, it follows that I won't be asking you to do something she'd object to, especially not *here*. I know you've spent your adult life as far under a rock as possible, but even you must understand that doing anything remotely interesting in Algonquin's city would bring Chelsie down on both our heads, and we can't have that."

His casual mention of Chelsie put Julius even more on edge than his talk about Mother. Chelsie was one of their oldest sisters and the Heartstriker clan's internal enforcer. Julius had only seen her from a distance at family gatherings, and even that had felt too close for comfort. Mother might rant and rave and threaten to skin you alive, but most of the time, it was Chelsie who actually wielded the knife, and unlike Mother, you never heard her coming.

"Do you think Chelsie's here in Detroit?" Julius whispered.

Ian shrugged. "Who knows? Bethesda's Shade is everywhere. It might as well be the family motto: 'Watch what you say. Mother's in the mountain, but Chelsie's right behind you.'"

He chuckled like that was a joke, but even Ian's too-cool front wasn't enough to keep the fear out of his voice. Not that Julius thought less of him for it. *Every* Heartstriker was scared of Chelsie.

"So, what's this job for, exactly?" he asked, eager to get back on track and out of this conversation before saying Chelsie's name too many times summoned her. Instead of answering, though, Ian's eyes flicked to something over Julius's shoulder. Before Julius could turn around to see what, his brother leaned back in the booth, his body relaxing until he looked lithe and limber and confident as a cat. But while his posture was suddenly almost obscenely casual, his whispered voice was sharp as razor wire.

"Too late to back out now," he said. "Sit up straight, and whatever you do, don't stare. You don't want to embarrass yourself any more than is inevitable."

Julius was opening his mouth to ask whom he was going to be embarrassing himself to when she was suddenly there, appearing beside their table without a sound. And even though Ian had warned him, Julius couldn't help himself.

He stared.

Chapter 2

She was a dragoness. Of that there was no question. Even in human form, she radiated danger of the casually cruel, playful kind. She was not, however, a Heartstriker. Julius didn't know his entire family by sight—only his mother could do that—but he was pretty sure he'd remember someone like this.

She was beautiful, of course, but as a snow leopard taking down a stag was beautiful. Every feature, from her pale, pale skin to the white blond hair that slid over her bare shoulders in a snowy stream to the razor-sharp nails at the ends of her elegant fingers, was cold and otherworldly. Even her smile was deadly, the sort of delicate half smirk ancient queens must have worn when ordering slaves to fight to the death for their amusement. But what really got Julius was the calculating look in her ice-blue eyes as she gave him the speculative once-over dragons always performed when sizing up newcomers. *Player or pawn?* it asked. *Tool or threat?*

For Julius, the assessment was over in an instant. He could almost feel the word "pawn" being affixed to his forehead before the female dismissed him completely and shifted her gaze to Ian. "This is the one you told me of?"

Her accent was as cold and strange as the rest of her, a mix of Russian and something much, much older. Ian, of course, seemed completely unaffected. "My brother, Julius," he replied, gesturing with his drink.

"Julius," the dragoness repeated, her accent slicing off the J so that his name came out more like Ulius. "He is one of your youngest brothers, then? Or did Bethesda clutch again while I wasn't paying attention?"

Ian and Julius winced in unison. No Heartstriker liked to be reminded of their mother's ridiculous naming system, or the reason such a thing was required. Most dragonesses who chose to dedicate the enormous amount of magic required to bring new dragons into existence laid no more than two clutches of eggs in their entire lives, usually with five hundred years or more in between. Bethesda had laid ten, once with fewer than fifty years between broods. This fecundity had made her something of a legend among the other dragon clans, and to help her keep track of her unprecedented number of children, she'd named each clutch alphabetically. A names for her first, B for the second, and now finally down to J. At least the new dragoness hadn't called their mother

Bethesda the Broodmare, or Ian and Julius would have been honor-bound to attack, and that wouldn't have ended well for anyone.

"No," Ian said crisply, setting down his drink. "We're still on J. But as you can see, he's decidedly non-threatening. No guile I've witnessed, but I'm led to believe he's not an idiot. Just soft."

"Soft?" The dragoness said this the same way a human would say *leprous*.

"Non-aggressive," Ian clarified. "But clever in his own way, I think. And if he fails, my mother will kill him, so motivation won't be an issue."

Julius knew better than to offer his opinion to this summation. He was used to powerful dragons talking about him like he wasn't there. Still, he didn't like the way the female was eying him now. Family would threaten him all day, but no Heartstriker would risk Bethesda's wrath by actually killing him. This foreign dragon, on the other hand, was studying him like she was trying to decide which of his organs would make the best hat.

"I think you may be right," she said at last. "He will do well enough." With that, she sat down next to Ian and turned to Julius like she hadn't just been ignoring him for the last few minutes. "I am Svena, daughter of the Three Sisters. Ian assured me you will be of assistance."

She paused like she was waiting for a reply, but Julius couldn't manage more than a choking sound. The Three Sisters were among the oldest and most powerful dragons left in the world. They were so magical, legend had it that they'd created their eggs one at a time using only their own power, no male consort needed. The offspring of this unconventional arrangement, all daughters, were in turn some of the most mysterious and feared dragons alive, which meant that Julius was sitting across the table from, at minimum, a thousand-year-old dragoness who was also one of the Heartstriker clan's sworn enemies. The Three Sisters *hated* Bethesda, and as far as he knew, the feeling was mutual. What was Ian *doing*?

He glanced at his brother to ask just that, but Ian was shooting him a lethal caliber version of the *shut up and play along* look. So, with effort, Julius turned back to the dragoness, who he now knew for a fact could turn him into a gooey puddle with a snap of her fingers, and plastered what he hoped was an obliging smile across his face. "What kind of assistance did you have in mind?"

She pursed her pale lips. "It is a delicate matter. My youngest sister, Katya, has run away from home. I want you to bring her back."

Julius blinked. "You want me to find your sister?"

"Not *find*," Svena snapped—a literal *snap* of her too-white teeth that gave Julius the distinct impression Svena didn't spend much time in her human form. "I know *where* she is, but she is being headstrong and difficult. I have indulged her as long as possible, but I cannot afford to do so any further. Unlike your clan where a dragon might vanish for years before someone notices, there are only twelve of us. If our mothers discover Katya's absence, things will become difficult. I need a neutral third party to stop her foolishness and bring her home before this happens."

She was very good at keeping her voice haughty and superior, but Julius had been appeasing bigger dragons his whole life, and he'd become very good at picking up subtle changes in tone. Between her cool disinterest and the not-so-subtle digs at his family, Julius could just make out the faint trace of real worry in Svena's voice. Whether that concern was for her sister or herself when her mothers found out, he wasn't sure, but what he really wanted to know was, "Why me?"

"Because you're a failure," Ian said with a superior smile. "And you're sealed. Katya's running from her sister because she knows she cannot defeat Svena, but you're another story. Unlike us, you're completely benign, a non-threat, which means you alone will be able to get close to Katya without causing her to bolt."

"And do what?" Julius asked. "Even if she doesn't run from me, how am I supposed to convince a—" powerful, magical, likely centuries older than him and still in possession of her true form, "—dragon to go home when she doesn't want to?"

Svena waved her hand dismissively. "You can't. If Katya could be convinced of anything, she would never have run in the first place. You only need to get close enough to put this on her." She reached out as she spoke, placing something on the table with a soft clack. When she removed her hand, Julius saw it was a thin, silver braided chain. "There's a binding spell woven into the metal," she explained. "I created it specifically to placate my sister, but it must touch her skin to work, and I haven't been able to get closer than a kilometer to Katya since this nonsense started."

Julius stared at the chain glistening like frost on the white tablecloth, heart sinking. He had no interest in getting tangled up in another clan's family drama. He especially didn't want to trick a runaway into going back to a home she clearly wanted to escape. As someone who'd seriously considered running away himself dozens of times, tricking this Katya out of her freedom and forcing her back into the kind of situation that would make a dragon flee felt unspeakably cruel, but what was he supposed to do? Argue against his qualifications as a failure?

"This is a great opportunity for you, Julius," Ian said, his voice calm and rational and completely not open to negotiation. "You've gotten an unfortunate reputation for being softhearted over your short lifespan, but there's still time to turn yourself around. Mother has entrusted me with your rehabilitation, but if you insist on being lazy—"

"I'm not lazy."

Julius regretted the words as soon as they left his mouth, but he didn't try to take them back. Backpedaling would only make him look even weaker, and anyway, he *hated* being called lazy. Staying alive in their clan was a full time job for someone like him, because Julius wasn't just the youngest Heartstriker, he was also the smallest. Big dragons like Ian never understood just how much work it took to fly under the radar in a family of magical predators with a sixth sense for weakness and a pathological need to exploit any opening just because it was there.

Speaking of which, Ian was already watching him, his calculating eyes weighing Julius's hasty words as much for what they didn't say as what they did. "So resentful," he said. "But you have no one to blame but yourself. The fact that I didn't even know your name until this afternoon perfectly illustrates your complete and utter failure to be an asset to anyone. That you are alive today is due entirely to our mother's magnanimity, and since we both know how fickle *that* can be, I suggest you stop making a spectacle of yourself and consider your next words very carefully."

He didn't even need to add *because they might be your last.* By the time Ian finished, the threat in his voice was like a noose around Julius's neck. Beside him, Svena was observing the back and forth with the sort of bored impatience of a sports caster watching a veteran boxer taking on a volunteer from the audience.

That was how Julius felt, too—punch drunk, completely overpowered and outmatched. He still didn't think it was right, and he knew he'd regret his actions, but Ian had his back against the wall, and they all knew it. So, with a heavy sigh, he reached out and scooped the silver chain off the table, shoving the unnaturally cold metal into his pocket as quickly as he could. "Where can I find her?"

"I have word she's going to a party tonight," Svena said, reaching into her silver-spangled clutch purse to pull out a sleek, expensive phone. "Some kind of gathering for human mages." She paused. "You *can* still do magic, can't you? Your mother didn't seal that as well?"

She hadn't, but then, she hadn't needed to. Unlike humans, who drew magic from the world around them, dragons made their own. But while J clutch had been one of Bethesda's more magically inclined broods, Julius hadn't been keen on the idea of competing with his cutthroat siblings in an arena where it was perfectly acceptable to banish your rivals to another dimension. He'd learned the basics he needed to survive, but everything else he knew about sorcery, draconic or otherwise, could probably fit on a small note card. Not that he was going to admit that to Svena, of course.

"No problem," he lied. "Where is it, and when should I show up?"

Svena looked down at her phone to find the information. Beside her, Ian met his eyes across the table and mouthed, *good job*. Julius nodded and quickly lowered his head over his own phone, trying not to look as nauseated as he felt when Katya's information, including pictures, movement notes, and Svena's practical instructions on where and how to deliver her runaway sister's unconscious body once the deed was done, popped up on his screen.

Sometimes, he really, really, *really* hated being a dragon.

***

Thirty minutes later, Julius was sitting at the club's bar, ignoring the bitter and expensive cocktail Ian had bought him as a fancy way of saying *get lost* while he finished his "discussion" with Svena, and he wasn't feeling any better. Thanks to the information Svena had given him, he'd had no problem finding the party Katya was supposed to attend tonight. Getting in, however, was another matter entirely.

From the listing on the DFZ's public mage forums, it seemed the gathering was being hosted by a circle of shamans, human mages who did their magic with the help of spirits and natural forces, something Julius decidedly was *not*. Despite Ian's dismissive assurances that his little brother was "good with humans," he had absolutely no idea how he was going to convince a bunch of secretive mages to let him into their exclusive magic-nerd night. He wasn't actually sure how Katya had gotten in since dragon magic was entirely different from the human variety, though considering Svena's "little sister" was a thousand years old if she was a day, she probably had her ways.

Julius's ways, on the other hand, were decidedly more limited. Not surprising considering who ruled it, the DFZ was packed with spirits. The presence of so many powerful allies gave the local shamans a decided home-field advantage. With so much magic at their fingertips, a good shaman might be able to spot his true nature even with his mother's seal, and then he'd be in real trouble. What he needed was a mage of his own, someone who actually understood how this stuff worked and could act as cover, but where was he going to find a mage on short notice in an unfamiliar city who would be willing to work on credit until Ian paid up?

He was still puzzling over this when he felt the telltale prickle on the back of his neck that meant someone was watching him. Probably Ian preparing to call him back to the booth so they could "discuss his plan," or maybe Svena with some last-minute advice/threats. But when Julius turned around, it wasn't a dragon watching him at all. It was a woman. A human woman sitting at one of the small tables by the door.

She got up the second he made eye contact and started straight for him, cutting through the expensively dressed crowd like an arrow with him as the target. Julius thought frantically, trying to remember if he'd met her before. It was true he knew a lot of humans for a dragon, but that was only over the internet. Face-to-face contact was limited to the residents of the New Mexico desert town his mother's mountain complex supported, and this girl definitely wasn't someone from home. She was sure acting like she knew him, though.

As she got closer, Julius's confusion grew, because she looked like she belonged in this club about as much as he did. Her combination of sparkly silver vest, long-sleeved white shirt with dramatic, oversized cuffs draped over chunky plastic bracelets, and tight black pants tucked into glossy black, calf-high leather boots reminded him of an old-school stage magician. It wasn't unattractive, especially not on her. She was actually very cute in a warm, human way that was a relief after Svena's chilling beauty. Still, her getup definitely didn't fit in with the rest of the club's too-cool aesthetic, and her hair was patently ridiculous.

The thick, dark brown strands had been chopped into uneven chunks ranging from almost buzz-cut short in the back to chin-length wisps around her face. It was uneven over her ears as well, with longer strands trailing down at odd places, like she'd pulled her hair back and chopped it off in a mad panic. She didn't *look* crazy, though. Just determined as she walked up and slid between him and the stool on his left, leaning one elbow on the bar so that she was directly in his field of vision.

Under normal circumstances, a pretty girl coming at him out of nowhere would have sent Julius into defensive retreat. Today, though, half-panicked already and stuck in survival mode, he stared straight at her, holding his ground out of sheer desperation as he breathed deeply to catch some hint of the trap this had to be. When he didn't smell so much as a whiff of draconic power other than the chain in his pocket, though, he said, "Can I help you?"

"No," the girl said, flipping her hand with a flourish. "I can help you."

A white card appeared between her fingers, and Julius jumped before he realized he hadn't felt any magic. It had been sleight-of-hand that produced the card, not a spell. The paper itself, however, told another story.

Marci Novalli, it read. *Socratic Thaumaturge, MDC. Curse breaking, magical consultation, warding services.* Below that, a smaller line proclaimed, *No job is too big or too small! References available upon request.*

A mage, he realized dumbly, staring at the card with a growing sense of dread—an impressive feat, considering just how large his dread had grown today already. But a mage appearing out of nowhere at the exact moment he realized he needed one? If that wasn't a set-up, then he was his mother's favorite son.

He leaned away from her offered card like it was poison. "Sorry. Not interested."

"Just hear me out," the girl said, closing the distance he'd just put between them. "I can understand if you're apprehensive about mages. You're under a very nasty curse."

Julius blinked. "Excuse me?"

"The curse," she said, gesturing at him. "It's all over you. I can't imagine how you must be suffering, but you don't have to worry any longer. I have a lot of experience in curse breaking, and I'm very gentle. Give me an hour and I'll have that thing off you no problem."

Julius stared at her, uncomprehending, and then it dawned. She was talking about the *seal*, the one his mother had put on him to trap him in his human shape. After that, it was all Julius could do not to burst out laughing, both at the notion of a mortal mage breaking his mother's seal in an hour and how Bethesda would react if it actually worked. He glanced at the girl again, just to make sure she wasn't kidding, but her expression was deadly serious, and all he could do was shake his head.

"I'm afraid my curse isn't the sort you can remove," he said. "Thank you for offering, though." That last bit came out surprisingly heartfelt. Her unexpected sales pitch was the nicest thing anyone had said to him all day.

The girl stared at him a moment, and then her shoulders slumped. "Well, do you have anything else you need done? Wards? Spirits banished? I can show you my portfolio."

She'd started pulling a binder out of the enormous black messenger bag on her shoulder before she'd even finished the question, and Julius fought the urge to sigh. *Humans.*

"I'm good, really," he said, putting up his hands. "You don't have to show me anything. I'm not interested."

The girl stopped short, and then she stuffed the binder back into her bag, her face falling in utter defeat. "Sorry," she muttered, flopping down on the barstool beside him. "I'm not normally so..." She waved her hands as she searched for the word, making the chipped silver glitter polish on her nails sparkle in the club's low light. "Car salesman-y," she said at last. "It's just that I *really* need the work. If you have anything magical you need done today, anything at all, I'll give you a huge discount. I swear I'm completely legit. I'm fully licensed in Nevada, actually, but I'm new in town and, frankly, getting a little desperate. So if there's any work you need a mage for, just say the word. If not, I'll stop bothering you."

Julius opened his mouth to say sorry, he had nothing, but the words stuck in his throat. The girl was looking at him so earnestly, and that word *desperate* kept rolling around in his head. Bob had told him to be a gentleman and help desperate women. Of course, Bob had also once told Julius that he would have dinner with a phoenix on his birthday.

Turning away from the human, he pulled out his phone and reread the seer's message, but he hadn't made a mistake. There was the warning from his maybe-insane, maybe-future predicting brother who'd mailed him a phone loaded with a Detroit ID and money four months before he'd needed it, and here was the desperate woman said brother had told him to help, and now Julius had to make a decision.

On the one hand, years of well-honed paranoia told him for certain that this was a trap. No one's luck was good enough to have a random mage walk up and offer her services at the exact moment she was needed. Far more likely was that this Marci Novalli was working for someone else from the Three Sisters who didn't want Katya found, or maybe another clan entirely. If he took her offer, he'd be playing right into the clutches of his family's enemies like the idiot failure his mother always said he was. On the other hand, though, rejecting her meant he'd be going against his brother's advice, and therein lay the quandary. Unlike most of his family, Julius didn't think Bob was crazy, or, at least, not *only* crazy. He wasn't sure if his brother actually saw the future, but Bob definitely saw *something*. Trouble was, Julius wasn't sure which side this particular warning fell on: the crazy or the something. He was still trying to figure it out when the girl slid off the barstool.

"I'm really sorry to have wasted your time," she said quietly, looking down at her feet as she adjusted her bag on her shoulder. "Thank you for listening, and I hope you have a nice—"

"Wait."

The girl looked up in surprise. Julius was surprised, too, because he hadn't thought he'd made up his mind yet. But while he still wasn't sure if the mage was a trap, a vision of Bob's unsettled mind, or some combination thereof, he had come to a decision. The *sorry* had been the deciding factor, but the *thank you* had sealed the deal. Julius couldn't remember the last time he'd heard those words from anyone's mouth except his own and, trap or not, he couldn't let the person who said them just walk away.

Of course, now that he'd stopped her, he had to come up with something to say.

"Marci, right?" he asked, clearing his throat as she sat back down on the stool. "Can you do illusions?"

"Absolutely," Marci said, counting off on her fingers. "Area, personal, spatial, full sensory immersion, though I'll need a day to set that last one up if you want it on something bigger than a ten by ten square."

Julius didn't know enough about human magic to gauge whether that was good or not, but Marci certainly sounded like she knew what she was talking about. "I guess it would be a personal illusion," he said. "On me. But I'd rather not explain it here. Do you have somewhere else we could talk?"

Marci nodded and hopped to her feet. "I'll need my workshop to do a credible illusion anyway. We can discuss terms on the way over. Would that be okay?"

Julius glanced over his shoulder, but his brother and Svena were still sitting in the VIP area with their heads together, and he was loath to interrupt. Really, though, he saw no reason to deal with Ian again at all. He had the chain, he had the information about the party, and now he had a mage to help him get inside. If he moved quickly, this whole mess could be over by midnight.

"That sounds great," he said, smiling at Marci as he slid off his own stool. "Let's get out of here."

***

Getting out of the club was much simpler than getting in. Rather than running the gauntlet past the augmented bouncer, Marci led them out a side door and down the alley, away from the tree-lined square and its well-dressed crowds. Then she led them down *from* the street, descending a long set of cement stairs from the elevated skyway.

"I swear I'm not taking you off to mug you," she said as they walked away from the evening sunlight and the bright glow of the Upper City's ubiquitous halogen street lamps. "It's just that you don't have to pay for parking down here."

"No worries," Julius said, glancing around. Even with his dragon sealed, he wasn't terribly worried about a human mugging him, and he was far more interested in his first look at the underbelly of Old Detroit.

Going below the skyways was like entering another world. All the brilliance of the Upper City—the fancy tree-lined square, the towering superscrapers, the elegant curving roads full of luxury cars and computer driven taxis—was like a model sitting on a table, and underneath it, an entirely different city thrived in the dark.

After all the stories he'd heard, Julius had expected Underground Detroit to look like a war torn ruin, but this looked more like Shinjuku in Tokyo. The buildings, many of them apparently dating from before the flood given the high water marks on their second stories, had been completely renovated to hold as many shops as possible. Every window seemed to have at least two signs hanging in it, and the combined glare of all the neon, back-lit plastic, and flashing LEDs, actually made it brighter down here than it had been up top in the sun.

If there was any organizational system, Julius couldn't see it. Bars, restaurants, and theaters shared walls with banks, private schools, and massage parlors in a chaotic jumble. Some establishments didn't even bother making divisions, advertising salon services and gambling at the same time. Even the buildings themselves were mismatched. Some, the short ones, looked like the normal office buildings and strip malls they must have been before Algonquin had built an entire other city on top of them. Others, ones that had collapsed and been completely rebuilt in the years since the flood, or the ones that had been too tall to fit under the skyway's eighty foot clearance and had been cut to fit, reached right up to the ceiling, using the huge cement base of the Upper City in place of an actual roof.

The chaos continued on the ground as well where food carts and semi-permanent kiosks competed with cars for room on the ruler-straight grid of the old roads. Trash and advertisements and people were absolutely everywhere, crammed into every nook and cranny and selling everything under the sun to anyone who was willing to pay regardless of age. The only breaks in the madness were the enormous, city-block-long cement support pillars that held up the skyway overhead, but even these were plastered with billboards advertising everything from concerts and exotic pets to drugs and pay-as-you-go augmentation clinics. Just trying to wrap his brain around the chaos of capitalism gone crazy was making Julius feel overwhelmed and dizzy, but most astonishing of all were the people.

Back in Arbor Square, the crowd had been ethnically diverse, but still so uniformly wealthy and well-dressed that they'd all blended together. In the Underground, though, there was some of everything: ethnicity, class, religion, occupation, *everything*. It was like some power had swept the world, picked people at random, and dumped them all here. It was nothing short of extraordinary, and Julius almost fell down the stairs in his eagerness to get a better look.

"First time below decks?"

Julius winced and glanced up to see Marci grinning at him over her shoulder. "That obvious, huh?"

"You are gawking a bit," she said, slowing her pace until they were climbing down side by side. "Not that I'm judging, of course. I was shocked too, my first time."

"It's actually a lot nicer than I'd thought it'd be," Julius admitted, nodding down at the young, excited crowd waiting to get into a five-sense theatre. "I'd always heard, you know…"

"What? That the whole place was a giant slum of rotting buildings and desperate characters straight out of a corporate dystopia? Oh, don't worry, there's plenty of that, too. This is actually one of the tourist areas the DFZ Visitor's Board pays to keep colorful and edgy, but not so scary that outsiders won't spent money."

Julius looked over at the brightly colored, music playing, fully automated gun, alcohol, and party drug vending machines that lined the landings of the stairwell. "*This* is the tourist area?"

Marci spread her arms wide. "Welcome to the DFZ!"

A proper, crafty dragon would have shut his mouth after that and kept his ignorance hidden, but Julius was curious, and this seemed kind of important. "What about security? I mean, I know everything is legal here, but isn't this kind of excessive? How can so many corporations have their headquarters in the DFZ if there are vending machines selling drugs to tourists only fifty steps down from Arbor Square?"

"There's plenty of security," Marci said. "It's just reserved for people with money, spirits, and fish. Especially fish, actually. Life's great here if you live underwater."

He arched his eyebrows in question, and she pointed over at a giant yellow hazard sign posted on the nearest support beam. Julius hadn't noticed that particular billboard amid all the other advertisements, but now that Marci had pointed it out, it was impossible to miss the giant wave crest logo of the Algonquin Civic Corporation followed by a list of substances that you were not allowed to dump into the water system and the horrible punishments that awaited anyone who did, written in a world tour of languages. There were more signs when they reached ground level with similar warnings against littering and burning illicit materials, but nothing for human on human crimes like theft or assault, which made a pretty clear statement about the Lady of the Lakes' priorities.

"I see what you mean," Julius said, stepping closer to Marci as they pushed into the teeming, noisy crowd that smelled strongly of sweat and human at bottom of the stairs. "Crime here must be ridiculous."

"It varies," Marci said, turning them down a side street that, while still crowded, at least had breathing room. "If you stay in areas where people can afford to pay their police fees, it's not bad at all. If you go where they can't, well…better not to do that."

Julius nodded silently. Now that they were actually down in it, he could see the glitz of the tourist area was only on the surface. The main streets were full of vendors and tourists, but the side streets were packed with a very different crowd. Humans in filthy clothes sat together against the buildings, their eyes glassy and empty. Others waited on corners, watching the crowds of tourists like predators eying a herd. Every now and then, one of them would duck off only to come right back with a purse or shopping bag tucked under their arms. Julius shook his head, rolling his eyes up to the sooty black underbelly of the elevated highway that served for a sky in this place. "Why do people put up with it?"

He'd meant that to be a rhetorical question, but Marci answered immediately. "Opportunity. The Lady of the Lakes might care more about fish than people, but this is still the Magic City. There's no immigration office, no background checks. Anyone can come here with nothing and try to make a new life. That's a powerful draw, and there are a lot of jobs here, especially if you aren't too squeamish." She shrugged. "I think of it as a gamble. The DFZ is dangerous and unfair and full of weird magic, but if you're willing to brave the risks, you can win big."

"Or lose everything," Julius countered, eying a line of drugged out humans taking refuge behind a dumpster, several of whom were children. "I don't know. It seems kind of like a step back."

"Maybe," Marci said. "But it is what it is, and the city's held on this long, so something must be working."

"I suppose," Julius said, but only to be polite. Honestly, he didn't see how a city ruled by an ancient spirit who clearly didn't care at all for human life, where the rich lived literally on top of everyone else, and you had to pay a fee just to call 911 could be anything other than a dystopia. He didn't want to rain on Marci's enthusiasm, however, so he kept his mouth shut, sticking close to her side as they walked away from the bright, jangly tourist area into a slightly quieter, more residential part of the crowded Underground.

"So," Marci said, smiling at him. "I probably should have asked you this way earlier, but what's your name? Unless you want this to be a secret contract, of course. Again, not judging."

"Not *that* secret," he said, laughing. "And my name's Julius."

She nodded. "Julius what?"

Julius faked a cough to buy himself time and grabbed his phone in his pocket, popping up the AR display only he could see right through the fabric of his jeans. It still took him a few seconds of fumbling before he was able to navigate the new menus to see what last name Bob had put on his residence ID. "Quetz," he read, gritting his teeth. "Julius Quetz."

"Quetz?" Marci repeated incredulously.

"Short for Quetzalcoatl," he explained, letting the phone go with a huff. "It's an old family name." And Bob's idea of a joke. Or at least, Julius hoped it was a joke. There was no other reason a sane individual would think using the name of the most infamous feathered serpent ever to terrorize the Americas as a cover alias for a dragon in hiding was a good idea.

"Wait, you shortened your *last name*?"

Julius missed a step on the uneven sidewalk, eyes wide. Was that not something humans did? "Um," he stalled. "It was too hard to spell?"

That explanation seemed to fly, because Marci nodded. "I see. It's too bad, though. I think Quetzalcoatl would have been a pretty awesome last name." She shrugged and flashed that infectious grin of hers at him again, stopping to put out her hand. "Well, Julius Quetz, I'm happier than you can know to be doing business with you. And speaking of which, I hope you don't mind signing a standard U.S. contract. As I said, I just moved here, and I haven't had a chance to get my DFZ paperwork in order, such as it is."

Julius shook her hand after only a slight hesitation. He was about to tell her a U.S. contract would be fine when Marci turned around and walked over to the dusty car parked on the sidewalk beside them. It was a beat-up old junker that looked a good ten years older than Marci herself, but it wasn't until she walked around to the trunk and started wiggling the key—a metal key, not a wireless fob—into the ancient lock, that Julius realized this was *her* car.

With that, the last of his fears that Marci was a trap set by another clan vanished. If there was any draconic trait even more universal than their love of plotting, it was snobbery. No dragon, no matter how cheap or desperate, would be caught dead using a human who drove a car like this. With that settled, though, there was only one question left. Why had Bob set him up with *this* mage?

He was still wondering when Marci finally got the trunk open. "I normally charge a flat hourly fee plus expenses," she said, pulling out a stack of slightly creased papers. "But I promised you a discount, so I'm cutting my rate in half and waiving my retainer." Closing the trunk again to use its hood as a writing surface, Marci crossed several clauses off the top of the contract with an expensive-looking marker she'd pulled from her pocket. Once it was all marked through, she wrote in the new rates by hand before giving the contract to Julius. "Is that okay?"

Julius took the pages with trepidation. He couldn't remember the last time he'd seen an actual physical contract, let alone signed one. The paper felt odd, too, almost tingly. "Is there a spell on this?"

Marci's eyes widened. "Oh, I'm so sorry, I forgot to mention that. Yes, a minor truth spell, just the usual security against falsification. It's all on the up and up, though, see?" She pointed at the top of the page where the paper had, indeed, been notarized by the State of Nevada Magic Commissioner's Office. "Nothing nefarious."

Julius studied the seal for a moment, and then he glanced through the rear window of her car at the backseat, which was packed high with bags and boxes. There'd been boxes in her trunk as well. Clearly, Marci Novalli had left Nevada in a hurry. He wanted to ask why, but he wasn't exactly in a position to pry, and with the discounted rate she'd written down, he was getting her services for almost nothing.

He felt kind of bad about that, actually, but he needed a mage, she needed work, and a paper contract would keep his name out of any databases that could come back to haunt him. So, before he could second-guess himself into paralysis, Julius took the pen she offered and signed his first name on the dotted line. *Only* his first name, since the truth spell would have outed his last as a fake. Marci arched an eyebrow, but she didn't comment as she signed her own name on the line below.

"You won't be disappointed," she promised as she snatched the paper up, tucking it into a plastic envelope, which she then slipped into one of the many pockets of her shoulder bag. "Now, what kind of illusion did you need tonight?"

"Well," Julius said, walking around to the old car's passenger side. "I need to get into this party."

Marci's eyes widened in astonishment, and then, to his surprise, she blushed, her whole face turning bright red. "What kind of party wouldn't let you in?"

He tilted his head curiously. "What do you mean?"

"Nothing," she said quickly, hurrying around to the driver's door to unlock the car. "It's just, you don't look like the sort of guy who has trouble getting in anywhere, if you get my drift."

Julius didn't, but Marci was still blushing for some reason, so he didn't push the issue. "Not this one," he said, getting into the car. "It's some kind of exclusive mage thing, and I'm not a mage."

"Say no more," she said, tapping a destination into the flickering console that passed for an autodrive in this relic of a vehicle. "We'll have you looking magical in no time. What kind of mage do you want to be?"

Julius winced as the car sputtered like an asthmatic old dog, but it made it out of the narrow parking space and down the road without dying, and he eventually relaxed into the threadbare seat. "What are my options?"

Marci's enormous smile caught him completely off guard, but he had plenty of time to recover as she passionately recited the seemingly endless variety of magical vocations, with commentary, that he could choose from.

Chapter 3

Considering the sorry state of Marci's car, Julius expected her to drive them somewhere truly scary, like one of those hourly Underground motels where they always found the body in DFZ crime movies. He was pleasantly surprised, then, when her route took them out of the dark undercity altogether, driving north away from the water and the skyways into one of Detroit's few surviving historic neighborhoods.

By some miraculous happenstance, the old University District had avoided the worst of Algonquin's initial wave. There was still visible flood damage on the rotting telephone poles, but most of the area's quaint brick and stone houses with their odd little towers and arches were still intact. Unlike the heavily renovated buildings of the packed Underground they'd just left, though, there were no shops or vending machines or noisy crowds. There didn't actually seem to be anyone out here at all.

After experiencing the oppressive, cave-like atmosphere of living below another city first hand, Julius thought people would be fighting tooth and nail to live out here where there was still sky and fresh air. The moment Marci had driven them out of the shadow of the skyways, however, the crowds had shrunk to a trickle. Even stranger, most of the nice houses here seemed to be abandoned. Some had even been grown over entirely by yards turned wild over years of neglect, which didn't make any sense at all.

"Why is this place so empty?" he asked, glancing in the side mirror at the cliff-like edge of the two layered city behind them. "We're only fifteen minutes from downtown, and there's so much space. Why isn't it all one giant suburb?"

"Those are all on the south side," Marci said. "I mean, if you want to see the corp towns, I can totally take you later, but no one builds that stuff up here."

"Why not?"

She looked at him like he was joking and pointed out his window. When Julius turned to look, though, he didn't see anything but the same collapsing houses that had prompted him to ask the question in the first place. He was about to ask again when he spotted a glimmer of silver above the rooftops, and he realized he'd been looking too low.

About a hundred feet behind the houses lining the street on his right, a chain link fence topped with razor wire rose high into the evening sky. This far away, it was almost invisible, but now that he was staring straight at it, Julius could feel the faint hum of magic coursing through the air like electricity. "What is that?"

"Reclamation Land," Marci said. "All the area east from here until the skyways pick up again by the shores of Lake St. Clair is designated for spirits. It's sort of like a refuge. Spirits live a very long time, which makes them kind of curmudgeonly. A lot of them haven't adapted well to modern life after the comet woke them up. Some people say that's the real reason the Lady of the Lakes took Detroit in the first place; she wanted to give her fellow spirits somewhere safe to adjust to their new world. Personally, I think that's giving Algonquin way too much credit for selflessness, but the Reclamation Land does seem to be a legitimately safe space. Humans aren't even allowed inside unless they work for the Algonquin Corporation."

Julius looked at the fence again. He couldn't see any spirits beyond it—just collapsed houses surrounded by trees and open fields—but after Marci's story, he could feel their power stronger than ever. The magic here smelled of wild places, of forests and water and mountains. Magic like this did not belong so close to a city, and yet here it was, layered over the rundown homes and overgrown lawns like a blanket of wet snow.

"Anyway," Marci went on. "That's the reason this strip of land hasn't been developed. None of the big companies wanted to build this close to the spirits, and no one else can afford to live here. The lots are spaced so far apart that there aren't enough people to split the fees for roads, trash, and cops down to an affordable level, and that's not even counting the wards you'd need."

"Wards?"

"That fence is to keep *people* out." Marci said, nodding at the Reclamation Land border. "The spirits don't mind it at all. Plus, look at all this open land. Trees and grass and open ground attract supernatural activity everywhere, but this close to Algonquin, the pull is super charged. If you wanted to live in one of those houses, you'd practically need a mage on staff just to keep your property from being overrun."

Julius leaned away from the car door. "Overrun by what?"

Marci laughed. "Everything. Spirits, magical animals, feral dogs—you name it, it lives out here. I actually chased a water nixie out of a guy's bathtub just this morning in exchange for breakfast. I should have charged him, but he was such a nice old man, and he was clearly dead broke anyway. It worked out okay, though. He made *really* delicious pancakes."

Julius was about to ask if chasing away spirits was how Marci made her living out here when the car's automated route ended. Marci took over with a jerk, grabbing the steering wheel for the final turn into the driveway of a house that left him speechless.

"It's only temporary," she said quickly. "And it's not nearly so bad on the inside."

Julius nodded dumbly, staring out the window at the ruin that had once been a Tudor style brick mansion.

If the neighborhood's other houses were in decline, this place was nearing the bottom of a nosedive. Technically, it was two stories tall, but the top floor was caved in completely, the collapsed roof utterly overgrown with ivy. The bottom level didn't look much better. The brick was cracked in several places, and one corner of the foundation was sinking, causing the whole structure to tilt. Given the state of the roof, it was probably even worse on the inside, but Julius couldn't tell for sure since every window was blocked by huge, dusty piles of boxes and furniture pressed right up to the glass. Apparently, whoever had lived here before Marci had had a serious hoarding problem.

The lot was just as bad. Though clearly once a fanciful garden full of benches, stone paths, and cutesy statuary, the side and front yards were now a jungle of ornamental plants gone wild. Bushes ten feet tall battled elephant-sized tufts of pampas grass for every inch of arable land, devouring the poured cement garden statues of cupids and angels until all that remained were their weather-stained hands reaching up out of the vegetation like victims of the Blob. And then, of course, there were the cats.

Julius didn't normally see cats. Felines of all types had a natural nose for magic that could sense a dragon a mile away, sealed or not. Here, though, there were cats *everywhere*. Maybe they were too muddled by the thick magic of this place to notice his arrival, or maybe they just didn't care, but everywhere Julius looked, there they were, hiding in the overgrown bushes and peering out through the ivy of the collapsed roof. Still more watched from the house's dusty windows, their eyes bright with feral wariness as they followed Marci's car around the back of the house where it eventually rolled to a stop in front of the collapsing back porch.

"I can see why you were desperate," Julius said as they got out of the car.

"Yeah, well, a roof's a roof," Marci grumbled, walking around the tree sized azalea bushes to the dug in cement stair that led down to the house's basement, scattering cats as she went. "Mrs. Hurst was my first customer when I got into town. I took care of a spirit that was giving her trouble, but she didn't have the money for my fee. We were still working it out when her son heard about the incident and sent his mother a plane ticket to come live with him in Chicago. So, since she wasn't going to be here anymore, the old lady said I could stay rent-free in lieu of payment until they sold the house. Free was about my price range at the time, so I took it. Not exactly the Ritz, I know, but something's better than nothing, right?"

Not always, Julius thought, casting another skeptical look at the house's sagging foundations. He didn't want to be insulting, though, and it wasn't like *he* was going to be living here, so he followed Marci down the steps and into the basement without a word.

Given the state of the house above, he'd braced for the worst, so Julius was shocked when he stepped through the basement door into a neat, well-lit space. It was still a basement with a cement floor and ground-level windows set high on the cracked brick walls, but unlike anything else he'd seen in this place, it was immaculately clean. Or, at least, part of it was.

The basement was as huge as the house above it, but only half of it was nice. The half by the door was bordered by a strip of yellow plastic caution tape covered in spell scribbling. On their side of the plastic line, it was a clean, orderly space that smelled faintly of artificial lemon. On the other side, it was chaos.

Beyond the line made by the yellow tape, filthy, sodden trash lay in huge piles. Julius couldn't even see far enough back to spot the stairs that led up to the house itself. His view was blocked by mountains of discarded boxes, old clothes, broken furniture, stacks of old magazines, and cats. Uncountable cats, their eyes gleaming from the shadows as Marci clicked on the tall parlor lamp sitting on top of the mini fridge in the corner.

"Don't worry," she said, nodding at the caution tape. "The cats can't get through the ward. It keeps out the smell, too. You would not believe what this place was like when I got here."

Julius believed it just fine. "Free or not, why would you live down here?"

If he'd thought better of it, he wouldn't have put the question quite that way. Fortunately, Marci didn't seem offended.

"It fit my needs," she said with a shrug. "My father died suddenly Tuesday night, and I ended up having to move in kind of a hurry. I haven't had time to pick up my Residency ID yet, and I don't have a stable source of income, which makes it kind of hard to get a lease even in the DFZ. I've just been trying to roll with the punches and make do."

She'd certainly done that, Julius thought, looking over the tiny island of order and cleanliness she'd carved from the vast, disgusting sea of trash and cats. In addition to the mini fridge and the lamp, she'd acquired a couch and a gigantic wooden wardrobe that looked like it might contain Narnia. There was also a large, open square of floor off to the side that was covered in chalk casting circles, which he assumed must be her workspace. Not bad at all for someone who'd only been here…

"Wait," Julius said. "*Tuesday*? Like, three days ago?" When she nodded, he cursed himself for an insensitive idiot. "My condolences for the loss of your father."

Marci's face fell for a split second, but then she was right back to business, throwing open the doors of the huge wardrobe to reveal, sadly not fur coats and a snowy forest with a lamppost, but a neatly organized collection of magical paraphernalia, which was far more useful at the moment. "Thanks," she said. "I miss him a lot. But hey, at least I haven't had time to dwell on it, right? Hard to be sad when you're under an endless siege of cats."

Her voice was bright and cheery, but Julius's ears were tuned for dragons, and he could hear the falseness of her words clear as a bell. But it was neither his problem nor his place to call out her deception, so he let it go. He had to, anyway, because Marci was shoving an intricately carved wooden box into his face. "Hold this a sec."

He did, using both hands when the box proved much heavier than it looked. It was also vibrating slightly, the little motions making the paper seal on the lid flutter like a flag in a high wind. Julius grimaced and moved the box to arm's length. Family competition aside, this sort of creepiness was the other reason he'd stayed away from serious magic.

"So," he said as Marci climbed up into the wardrobe to grab a meticulously labeled box of multicolored casting chalk off the top shelf. "You're from Nevada?"

"Las Vegas," she said proudly. "My dad and I used to have a magical solutions business there."

That explained her card. "What kind of solutions?"

"All kinds," Marci said. "Though we specialized in curse breaking. Las Vegas is a vengeful town, and that makes good business for both sides of the curse market." She paused. "I was also going to school at UNLV for my doctorate in Thaumaturgical theory, but I had to quit when my dad died."

"That's too bad."

She shrugged. "Nothing to be done. It was probably for the best, though. I was getting tired of the limits of academic magic."

The false ring in her voice was back again when she said this, and again, Julius ignored it. He didn't think she was lying outright this time, more like telling only half the story. That was still enough to make him uneasy, but considering he hadn't told her a hundredth of his story, it was far simpler to just let it lie. He kept his mouth shut as he followed her over to the interlocking magical circles she'd drawn on the cement.

"Give me a moment to redraw these and we'll get started," she said, grabbing a dry mop from the corner and using it like an eraser, scrubbing the circles off the cement with a few deft strokes.

"What was wrong with the old ones?"

"Totally inappropriate initial casting parameters," Marci said, putting the mop away and selecting a fresh piece of gold-colored chalk from the box she'd pulled out of the wardrobe. "Is this your first time watching Thaumaturgy in action?"

This was his first time watching a human cast anything, but before he could say as much, Marci charged right ahead.

"Thaumaturgy is the best form of magic," she said in the bright, excited tone of someone getting a chance to explain something she truly loved. "It's the process of using logical spell notation to create detailed instructions that tell the magic how to behave. Watch, it all starts with a circle."

She grabbed a metal folding chair leaning against the wall and taped the stick of chalk to its leg. Before Julius could ask why, she unfolded the chair halfway, stamped the back leg down, and then, using the half-folded chair like a protractor, she touched the foot with the chalk taped to it against the cement floor and spun the chair like a top, drawing a perfect circle. Julius watched, dumbstruck. Apparently, Marci Novalli's ability to make do extended to all sorts of things.

"There," she said, setting the chair back against the wall. "Now we have a place for the magic to gather before we use it, sort of like a holding tank." She looked up expectantly, which Julius took as his cue to nod. This earned him a brilliant smile and the resumption of the impromptu lesson. "So, now that we've got a place for the magic to pool, it's time to put down the instructions that will tell it what to do."

She retrieved her chalk as she said this, kneeling at the circle's edge to begin writing a line of Greek symbols, numbers, and abbreviated words along the inner curve. "I use Socratic notation because it's the most precise and I like it the best, but there are several other spellwork languages that all do basically the same thing. The idea is to create a progressive series of algorithms that tell the magic how to behave, kind of like writing a computer program. Once the spellwork is finished, all I have to do is pull the magic through the circle and *voila*, the spell is cast." She glanced up at him. "Speaking of which, have you decided what kind of mage you want to be?"

He considered the question. "Well, it's a shaman party, so probably a shaman of some sort. Preferably something quiet." Because if anyone actually tried to talked to him about magic, he'd be revealed as a fraud in no time.

Marci thought for a moment, and then bent back over her circle. "I've got a good one," she said, clicking chalk across the cement floor in deft strokes. "Just let me get it down and we'll be golden."

Julius nodded and settled in to wait, watching in fascination as Marci worked. He'd always thought of magic symbols as just that: random mystical shapes that controlled magic. Now that she'd explained what those long lines of spellwork actual did, though, he was surprised to see it really did look like code. Parts of it even looked almost readable. He was about to kneel down for a better look when something cold brushed against his leg.

He jumped before he could stop himself and glanced down to see a large, fluffy white cat. And then he jumped again, not just because this cat was inside the ward where cats weren't supposed to be, but because this cat's body was *transparent*. It was glowing, too, shining with its own strange, blue-white light, almost like a—

"Ghost!"

He looked up to see Marci kneeling with her hands on her hips and a furious scowl on her face. "You know you're not supposed to bother customers," she said firmly, pointing at the far side of the basement. "Go on! Get out of here!"

The transparent cat gave her a disgusted look and stalked off toward the couch. He turned his back on them when he got there, silently grooming his paws like this relocation business had been entirely his idea.

"Marci," Julius said, very slowly. "Why do you have a ghost cat?"

"Technically, he's not a ghost," Marci said, going back to her spellwork. "That's just his name. He's actually a death spirit. You probably noticed Mrs. Hurst had a bit of a cat problem?"

Julius glanced over at the wall of reflective eyes peering at them from the shadowy mountains of trash on the other side of the yellow plastic ward. "I noticed."

Marci shook her head. "Nice old lady, but way too soft-hearted. She told me she couldn't stand to turn away strays but never had the money to get them fixed, so naturally the house began to fill up. They've had the run of the place for years, which sadly means a lot of dead cats hidden in the garbage, and dead bodies bring death spirits."

Julius looked at the transparent cat sitting on the couch with a cold shudder. "You're saying *he's* the job you did for the lady who owned this place? The one you traded for free rent?"

"Yep," Marci replied. "I was going through the public job boards when I saw this listing from an old lady who swore that a ghost cat was trying to kill her. I don't normally take crazy jobs, but no one else had answered it and I needed the money bad, so I told her I'd come over and check it out. When I arrived, I found Ghost there sitting on top of my future client's chest. He'd nearly sucked her dry by that point, and I ended up having to bind him just to make him detach."

Julius recoiled. "That's horrific."

"You're telling me," Marci said, laughing. "I had to dodge furious cats the whole way in, and that was before I knew I'd be doing a binding."

"But *why* did you bind him?" Julius asked. "Why not banish him?" He didn't know much about human magic, but he knew binding was a serious commitment that tied spirit and mage for life. That didn't sound like the sort of thing you did on the fly with something as openly hostile as a death spirit.

"I thought about that," she said. "But if I banished him, he'd just come back again and bother someone else. Besides, he's a bit of a rare specimen. It's been hypothesized that cats have more natural magic than other domesticated animals, but this is the first time I've seen or heard of a death spirit specific to the species. He'll be a great thesis topic if I ever get a chance to go back and finish my doctorate."

Julius stared at her, mouth open, an expression that was rapidly becoming his default around Marci. "You mean you bound a *death spirit* to yourself for all time on the off-chance you can write a paper about him if you go back to school?"

"Well, he's also pretty useful," she said, brushing the chalk off her hands as she stood up. "When I can get him to obey, that is. Would you hand me the box, please?"

Julius did as she asked, silently handing her the shaking wooden box he'd brought over from the wardrobe. The soft rattling stopped when Marci broke the paper seal, and she reached inside to pull out something long, black, and slightly ridged, like an animal horn. "What's that?"

"Chimera tusk," Marci said proudly, holding the black object out for him to see. "And before you ask, it's from a licensed humane farm in Canada. I don't buy from factory mills. It taints the magic."

Julius hadn't been about to ask, mostly because it had never even occurred to him there would be chimera farms in Canada. He was, however, suddenly feeling very uneasy about this spell. "Why do you need a chimera tusk?"

"Well, I don't *need* it," Marci said, placing the tusk squarely in the center of her palm. "But it takes a lot of magic to do two illusions thick enough to trick a room full of mages, and since I'm pretty sure you don't want to stand around here all night waiting while I pull down that much power manually, I thought I'd employ an outside source. Think of it as using a battery." She looked down critically at the tusk in her hand. "Besides, this one's getting kind of old. Better to use it up now than wait and risk losing potency, you know?"

"I'll take your word for it," Julius said. "But why are you doing two illusions?"

"Because I'm coming with you." Marci gave him a sideways look. "What? You didn't think I'd let you go alone, did you?"

"Well," Julius began. "I—"

"You're my client," she said, clearly appalled. "I can't let you just go in without backup. What if you get dispelled? Also, and please don't take this the wrong way, but you talk like a total null. It doesn't matter how good a cover I slap on you, you'll be outed in a second if you don't have someone standing by to feed you lines."

Julius couldn't argue there. "I'd be happy to have you along, but I still don't understand why you need a disguise. You're already a mage."

Marci's eyes widened like he'd just called her a dirty name. "Weren't you listening? I'm a *Socratic Thaumaturge*. You know, logical thinking, repeatable results, known best practices, all the tenets of *real* sorcery? We're sneaking you into a *shaman* party. Shamans consider themselves artists at best, spiritual gurus at worst. Most of them just throw magic around and hope it works out. There probably won't be a single person in that place who could write out a spell in proper notation if their life depended on it. They'll take one look at my personal magic and know what I am for sure. The real challenge will be masking my well-maintained aura in enough random nonsense that they don't see the good stuff underneath."

"I didn't mean to insult you," Julius said quickly. "I'm sure your way is better, but theirs can't be all bad. I mean, they might not do magic the way you do, but there are a lot of shamans around." Including a guy he'd been in a gaming guild with last year who'd been really decent, if a little odd. "They must be doing something right, or they wouldn't keep getting work."

Marci made a face. "I guess you could say that shamans are better at casting on the fly. Thaumaturgy does require some set-up time since we're not just, you know, *making things up* as we go along. For the sort of illusion you need, though, Thaumaturgy is waaaaaay better."

Julius had the feeling Marci would claim Thaumaturgy was better for everything, but he was perfectly ready to let it lie. "I'm lucky you found me, then."

She rewarded him with a beaming smile as she placed the bit of chimera tusk into the middle of the meticulously marked chalk circle. "Ready?"

Julius nodded and stepped into the circle where she indicated. He felt the hum of her magic as soon as his body crossed the chalk, an intense vibration that sang like a tuning fork against his bones before fading to a pleasant buzz.

Marci put her hands on his shoulders and moved him around until he was standing directly over the bit of tusk in the center. "I'm going to start pulling magic through," she warned him, stepping out of the circle. "You might feel a little pressure."

He took a deep breath. "Go for it."

The words were barely out of his mouth before the chalk circle flared up like phosphorus. Magic landed on him at the same time, nearly sending him to his knees.

The sudden panic at being buried by foreign magic almost caused Julius to throw it off with his own. He stopped the reflex just in time, clutching his magic tight and breathing through the pressure until it felt more like a wave than a landslide. When he was sure he could take it, he opened his eyes again to find Marci giving him a funny look.

"Did you ever get tested to see if you could be a mage?" she asked, moving her hands through the air between them like she was conducting an invisible orchestra. Every time she moved, another line of the notation she'd written on the floor lit up, and the magic pulled tighter around him. The process felt uncomfortably like being tied up, and it took Julius several seconds before he got himself together enough to shake his head.

"Maybe you should. You have a surprising amount of natural magic. Your curse seems to be warping it, though. I've never worked with magic that feels like yours." She gave him a concerned look. "Are you *sure* you don't want me to try breaking it? Because that can't be healthy."

"Positive," Julius said. Now that he'd felt Marci's magic, he was more sure than ever that she couldn't break his mother's seal. Their magic was just too different, and trying would likely only end up with

Marci getting hurt, not to mention blow his cover. That said, the seal was actually working out astonishingly in his favor right now. It was much easier to let Marci assume that his magic felt odd because of a curse and not because he wasn't actually human.

She didn't look happy with his answer, but she didn't press again. She just kept working until, at last, she lowered her hands, and Julius felt the magic lock around him like a buckle clicking into place. "All done," she said with a proud smile. "What do you think?"

Julius looked down... and saw he was exactly the same. "Um, did it work?"

"Of *course* it worked," Marci said. "If anyone looks at your magic, you'll look like a rock. That's what I made you, a stone shaman: flat, boring, and naturally silent. Will that do?"

He blinked and looked again. He saw magic naturally as a dragon, so he'd never bothered learning how to do it as a human. It turned out to be surprisingly difficult, but if he squinted, he could just make out the haze of Marci's magic hanging over his own like a golden curtain, and the more he looked at it, the more he saw that she was right. He *did* look like a rock.

"I thought I'd go for a badger shaman, myself," Marci said, motioning for him to step out of the circle. "Something nice and nasty no one will want to mess with."

As she bent down to rub out the end of the spellwork notation and rewrite it for herself, Julius stepped back a bit to focus on getting used to the weight of Marci's illusion. To his surprise, it was actually fairly pleasant once he'd adjusted. Dragon spells tended to be as sharp as their fangs, but Marci's magic was soft and thick, like a heavy blanket.

He was just starting to settle into it when a flash of light caught his attention, and he looked up in time to see Marci lower her hands with a thrust that blasted the chalk circle at her feet into a cloud of dust. "There," she said, turning around. "What do you think?"

She didn't look terribly different, but her short brown hair was now black with two white stripes, just like a badger. She'd also changed out her sparkly vest for an illusion of a long duster that looked decidedly homemade and replaced her boots with sandals that tied up her feet with rainbow ribbons. "I think the shoes are bit much."

"Then you clearly don't hang out with many shamans," she said, wiggling her toes, which were also rainbow-painted. "I'm positively sedate. Now let's get out of here. We're already ten minutes late."

Julius cursed under his breath. Between cats and ghosts and costuming, he'd completely lost track of time. Fortunately, Marci was ready to go in three minutes, though she insisted on stopping to lock the basement door behind them. This seemed pointless to Julius since the wooden door was so rotted he could have pulled the lock out with his hand, but when he saw the flare of a ward settling into place as she turned the key, her insistence on locking up suddenly made a lot more sense. It also made two wards of Marci's he'd seen, counting the yellow tape, and he was ready to bet she had more he hadn't noticed. This, in turn, made Julius wonder just how many thousands of dollars worth of magical work Marci had sunk into making her cat hole livable. It didn't seem worth it to him, but then, he wasn't in her situation. When magic was all you had, magic was what you used.

"How long do you think it will take us to get there?" he asked as they climbed back up the short run of stairs to the driveway.

She glanced at the address. "It's over on the river by Belle Isle, so about twenty minutes." When Julius winced, she added, "Don't worry. It's a shaman party. Those never start on time."

He sincerely hoped she was right. He also hoped Marci's car would make it. All the cats watched as they drove away from the rotting old mansion, and though Julius couldn't be sure, he swore he saw Ghost sitting on top of the chimney, staring after them with gleaming blue eyes. Creepy as that was, though, dealing with a dead cat spirit felt like a vacation compared to what he was supposed to do next.

He slipped his hand into his pocket to make sure Svena's silver chain was still there. It might have been his imagination, but the links seemed to jump up to meet his fingers, the metal still cold as frost even after an hour against his body heat. He snatched his hand back immediately, fingers curling into a fist. He *really* didn't feel right about this, but then, he never felt right when he was doing the sort of things dragons were supposed to do. It wasn't like his opinion mattered, anyway. If he didn't chain and return Svena's little sister as ordered, Ian would report his failure, and then Mother would make a chain out of Julius's intestines, which put a definite damper on any plans to buck the system. It was hard to hold the moral high ground while also trying to hold in your innards.

That lovely mental image made him sigh, and he leaned his head on Marci's window. He was being ridiculous. So what if the idea of cornering a runaway dragon and delivering her unconscious body back to the clan she feared made him feel lower than dirt? He should be focusing on how to appease his own family so he could remain alive and uneaten, not worrying about his conscience. Real dragons didn't have consciences, anyway. His certainly hadn't done him any good.

"What's wrong?"

Julius jerked his head up to see Marci staring at him. "Excuse me?"

She bit her lip and looked back at the road. "You just made a really sad sound."

He looked down at his lap, embarrassed. Great, now Marci thought he was pathetic, too. "It's nothing," he lied, sinking lower.

"Do you want to talk about it?"

Her quick offer caught him off guard, but not nearly as much as how desperately he wanted to take her up on it. If she'd been a dragon, such a question would have been an obvious play for information. Of course, if she'd been a dragon, she wouldn't have asked if he wanted to talk in the first place. She would have demanded.

But Marci wasn't a dragon, and she wasn't ordering him to do anything. He didn't even think she was fishing for secrets. She was just being politely concerned. Being nice. Humans got to do that, and Julius was so tempted to take her up on the treasure she'd just unwittingly offered him that he actually started thinking up excuses for why spilling his troubles to her would be a forgivable offense.

In the end, though, he kept his mouth shut. Eager as he was to confide in someone who wouldn't use every word against him later, revealing clan business to a human was a quick way to get that human killed. Fortunately, being inoffensively quiet was a survival skill Julius had perfected long ago, and he set himself to staring out the window, studiously ignoring the concerned glances Marci shot him whenever she thought he wasn't looking.

***

Considering the rates most mages demanded for their services, Julius had expected the party to be up on the skyways with all the rest of the money. Instead, the address took them back into the Underground, but not the flashing tourist part this time. Though clearly once a nice neighborhood by the water, nearly all of the original buildings were now gone, replaced by large brick warehouses built to serve the massive riverside casinos overhead.

"You're sure it's *below* the casinos, not in them?" Marci asked, eying the lower levels of the huge hotels that poked down through the suspended skyway like tree roots reaching for the real ground below.

"This has to be it," Julius said, though even he wasn't feeling so sure himself. Other than the warehouses, the only other things down here were the massive blocks of prefab tenements built to house the armies of workers who kept the big hotels above them ticking over. There were a few crowded family style restaurants and a cheap chain grocery store, but nowhere a bunch of mages would throw a party, and definitely nowhere he'd expect to find a dragon. Still, according to the listing Svena had shown him, this was the place, so he went ahead and told Marci to find somewhere to park.

The address itself turned out to be for a large warehouse right on the river. Julius didn't want to risk scaring off his target, so he had Marci to park in an alley one block down so they could case the place first. When they approached the warehouse itself, though, Julius realized he needn't have bothered.

Apparently, this "exclusive mage party" was about as exclusive as a frat kegger. Every door, window, and loading bay in the warehouse had been thrown open to let in the night wind off the water, and music was thumping so loud, Julius could feel the bass through the sidewalk. They walked right in through the front without challenge, and while Julius wanted to attribute this to Marci's excellent illusions, he had the feeling that he could have crashed through the roof as a dragon and not turned a head.

"It smells like an Amsterdam canal in here," Marci yelled over the music, batting at the smoky air in front of her face. "What are we doing at this party again?"

"Looking for someone," Julius yelled back. "I'm going to go check the back. You stay here and try to blend in. I'll message you if I need help. What's your number?"

"I don't have a phone." When Julius gaped at her, she raised her hands helplessly. "What? You need a Residency ID to get a phone in the DFZ, and I don't have one yet. I'm working on it."

Julius heaved a deep sigh. "Just stay here, then. I'll be back soon."

He waited until she nodded before moving away, breathing deep as he walked to see if he could pick out the sharp, metallic scent of another dragon. Unfortunately, smelling anything through the overwhelming mix of river, humans, and pot smoke turned out to be impossible, so Julius began searching the old-fashioned way. Fifteen minutes later, he'd found two people who claimed to be dragon shamans, one white-haired young woman who called herself a human dove, and zero actual dragonesses. He was starting to worry Katya wasn't here at all when he felt a tap on his shoulder.

Julius whirled around, furious and frightened that he hadn't noticed someone sneaking up on him, and came up nose to nose with a tall, youngish human male with long hair and a pleasantly goofy grin plastered across his face.

"Welcome to our party, newcomer rock-man," he said, offering Julius a weird half bow. "I'm Lark, albatross shaman and the head of the local circle here on the waterfront. Are you interested in joining our communion with the spirits of the land and such?"

It took Julius several seconds before he remembered what kind of mage he was supposed to be. Deciphering the rest of the greeting took a good bit longer. "Wait," he said at last. "If you're an albatross shaman, why is your name Lark?"

The young man threw up his hennaed hands. "Don't get too caught up in labels, my brother. That way lies madness. You gotta just *be* with the magic inside you, ya know?"

Julius nodded blankly. Marci's rant about shamans was starting to make a bit more sense now. "Well, if you're the leader, maybe you can help me. I'm looking for a friend. Her name is Katya."

When the shaman shook his head, Julius pulled out his phone and brought up the picture Svena had given him. The moment he saw it, Lark's eyes brightened. "Oh! You mean Katie. You just missed her, man. She and the gator left ten minutes ago."

Julius stared at him. "Gator?"

"Ross Vedder, alligator shaman," Lark clarified with a wink. "They set up together last week. Great couple, really. Hilarious."

That description was so undragonlike, Julius wasn't sure they were talking about the same Katya. "Do you know where they went? I really need to find her."

Lark shrugged and pulled out a surprisingly nice phone of his own. When he got it close to Julius's, another picture of Katya appeared in their shared AR with the name KATIE beside it. In it, a happy Katya was smiling wide and hugging an equally ecstatic-looking Lark at a party just like this one, and her blatant joy hit Julius like a punch to the gut.

"Ross and the rest of his peeps have a commune downstream," Lark went on, sending a map location to Julius's phone. "Real nice setup, very 'one with the powers of the place' vibe. They're doing some absolutely amazing work restoring magical ecosystems down in the pipes. I've been trying to get something similar going up on the old Ambassador Bridge for us bird types for years, but we're kind of hard to manage. You'd think we'd flock better, right?"

Julius waited impatiently for him to stop laughing at his own joke before asking. "And you're sure she's at this place?"

"Who can be sure of anything?" Lark said sagely. "But I'm pretty sure. She said she was going home for the night, and that's their home. Ergo, et cetera."

Julius glanced back down at the address Lark had sent him. It wasn't much, but it was the best he was probably going to get. "Thank you."

"My pleasure to be of assistance to any creature," Lark replied, clapping Julius on the shoulder. "Hey, you wanna drink? We got a full bar out back. Liquid, herbal, and nitrous, what's your pleasure?"

"No thanks," Julius said, ducking out of his grip. "I've got to go find my…" He paused, trying to think of an acceptable title for Marci. "Companion," he said at last. "Maybe later."

"Suit yourself, Mr. Rolling Stone. We'll be here all night if you change your mind." Lark pressed his hands together. "Namaste!"

Unsure what else to do, Julius returned the gesture before pushing back through the crowd to where he'd left Marci. When he reached the door, though, she was nowhere to be seen. This sparked a minute of frantic searching before he finally spotted her standing with a crowd of people in the corner, watching a man in some kind of tribal costume spin a halo of fire over his head.

Julius walked up behind her and leaned down to speak into her ear. "Let's go."

"Just a second," she said. "I want to see if he's going to blow himself up." She scowled at the costumed man, who was currently waving his arms in a frantic motion as he tried to maintain the roaring ring of flames. "That is *not* how you cast that spell."

Julius grit his teeth. "Come *on*, Marci."

She heaved a long sigh and followed him out of the warehouse. When they were safely down the street, he filled her in on what Lark had told him.

"You mean we missed her by ten minutes?" Marci groaned. "That's *so* unlucky."

"Luck has nothing to do with it," Julius said. It never did with dragons. "We need to find the alligator shaman. If she's still with him, tonight won't be a total—"

He never got to finish, because at that point, Marci vanished from his side with a gasp. Julius whirled around a split second later…and found himself staring straight down the silenced barrel of a gun.

Chapter 4

Oddly enough, Julius's first thought was that the pistol, a souped-up next gen Colt .45, looked oddly small. A heartbeat later, he realized he was mistaken. The pistol was normal-sized—it was just being held by an absolutely enormous man. His other hand, equally huge, was wrapped around Marci's face, smothering her mouth and holding her tight against his chest with her feet kicking a good foot off the sidewalk.

"Easy there, buddy," the big man said, wagging his gun in Julius's face like a tsking finger. "This here is a private matter, none of your concern."

Marci made an angry, muffled sound against the man's palm. The thug squeezed in reply, cutting off the noise and her kicking in one move. When she was quiet, the man smiled and shifted his eyes back to Julius. "You just go on about your business and won't be no trouble." He tightened his finger on the trigger. "Now walk away."

Julius looked at the gun, and then at Marci, who was staring at him above the man's fingers, though not in fear or desperation, as he would have expected. Instead, she was looking straight at him like she was trying to tell him something. Julius was still trying to figure out what when the magic she'd used to disguise him as a rock shaman exploded in the big man's face.

The thug flew backwards, his scream echoing down the alley before cutting off with a crash as he slammed into the brick wall of the warehouse across the street. His gun went off at the same time, firing harmlessly into the dark. He also dropped Marci, who landed in a coughing heap on the dirty pavement.

Julius was at her side in an instant. "Are you all right?" he cried, pulling her to her feet. When she nodded, he moved on to the next most important question. "What was *that*?"

"Backfire," Marci replied, her voice thick and slurring, almost like she was drunk. "Couldn't cast with him tryin'a crush my skull, so I backfired our illusions at him." She turned to grin triumphantly at the man now lying unconscious on the other side of the alley. "At'll teach him to grab me!"

The question *why did he grab you?* had already formed on Julius's tongue when he saw the thin trickle of blood coming out of Marci's ear. "You backfired yourself, too, didn't you?" When she lifted her shoulders in careless shrug, he grabbed them. "*Marci!*"

"Was worth it," she slurred. "He had a gun in your face."

Julius blew out an angry breath and tightened his grip on her shoulders, using them to steer her firmly toward the car. He'd find out what was going on later, when they were safe. For now, he just wanted to get out of—

He stopped short as two shadows, big ones, stepped out of the loading bay at the alley's dead end. There were footsteps behind him, too, and Julius glanced over his shoulder to see three more men had moved to block off the street, trapping him and Marci in the middle. Since this part of the Underground wasn't covered in neon, the light in the alley was awful, but even stuck in human form, Julius's eyes were sharp. He could clearly see the lumpy shapes of guns tucked inside the men's dark jackets. He was trying to decide what to do about that when Marci yanked out of his grasp.

When he snapped his head around to see why, she was shaking herself like a dog. When she stopped, the glassy look was gone from her eyes, and she stepped into what would have been a fighting stance if she'd had a weapon in her raised hands. "Don't worry, Julius," she said softly. "I got this. Just stay back. I'll protect you."

"Protect *me*?" he said just as one of the men blocking off their exit raised his voice.

"Don't even think about it, Novalli!" the big stranger bellowed, the words bouncing like buckshot down the alley. "You can't blast all of us and you know it. So be a good girl and come quietly and we won't hurt your boyfriend there. Mr. Bixby wants a word with you."

Marci's whole body went stiff at the name *Bibxy*, but she didn't drop her hands. If anything, she looked more deadly than before, even with the trickle of blood that had now worked its way down from her ear to stain the white collar of her shirt. But while Julius knew she was a mage and absolutely not to be underestimated, she was also human. Human and hurt, facing down five armed men, all of whom had a good six inches and at least a hundred pounds on her, and she was doing it to protect *him.*

That thought did something to Julius's insides. It twisted him over, rearranging priorities he'd thought long settled. The cautious thing, the right thing, would be to step back and let her do as she liked. After all, said a voice that sounded very much like his mother's, she was only human. Why should he risk himself for a mortal? Especially here, in the Lady of the Lakes' territory where any slip-up would bring Chelsie's wrath down on his head, or worse, the Lady's down on his mother. That was a situation Bethesda would find deathly inconvenient. Julius's death, specifically.

That horrifying thought should have settled everything. For almost all the years he could remember, Julius's survival strategy had revolved around avoiding situations that would give his mother a reason to kill him. Now though, he didn't want to stay out of the way. Maybe getting kicked out of home had fatally skewed his better judgment, or maybe he'd finally hit his limit for belly-crawling to creatures more powerful than himself, but when Julius looked down the alley, he didn't see an inconvenience for his family. He saw big, thuggish, idiot humans threatening *Marci,* the person who'd shown him more kindness, compassion, and help in the last hour than he'd experienced in twenty-four years of life. Marci, whom he'd already started thinking of as his ally, maybe even his *friend*.

It was a terrible excuse. Friendship was as undraconic as generosity. But then, as everyone liked to remind him, Julius never had been much of a dragon. And that was funny, because when he clenched his fists and stepped up to stand beside Marci, Julius felt more draconic than he had in a long, long time.

"Can you handle the two behind us?"

Marci jumped at his whisper so close to her ear. "I'm pretty sure," she whispered back. "Why do you—"

Julius was gone before she finished. His true form was sealed and he was woefully out of practice, but it didn't matter. He was a dragon, they were human, and that was enough. Before the three men at the end of the alley even realized he was gone, Julius was behind them with his hand on the crown of the biggest human's skull.

With surprise on his side, one push was all it took to slam the thug's face into the street. The big man went down like a tree, and Julius paused just long enough to kick the gun out of his hand before turning on the remaining two.

He'd fully expected to find them gawking, or maybe fleeing in terror, but these men were clearly professionals. By the time he turned, they'd recovered enough to swing their guns back toward him. But Julius was getting back in the swing of things now himself, and he hadn't lived this long as the smallest dragon in his clan by being slow.

The men had barely raised their weapons before he was in front of them. He dropped down at once, sweeping the first man's legs out from under him with a fast kick that sent the large human sprawling backward, slamming the back of his skull against the street with an extremely satisfying crunch. Julius didn't wait to see if the man would recover. He was already closing in on the lone survivor.

By this point, the last man standing had actually managed to get his gun up and aimed at Julius's chest, but the shock of Julius's inhuman speed seemed to have made him forget how to use it. Normally, this sort of fear-induced paralysis would have been enough to make Julius stop. Unlike the rest of his siblings, he didn't enjoy scaring people. This time, though, stopping didn't even cross his mind. This man needed to be scared almost as much as Julius needed to be scary. After years of being labeled a failure because he refused to participate in the cruel, cutthroat power games that absorbed the rest of his family, it felt amazingly good, right even, to finally be a dragon in someone's eyes. *Especially* since he was doing it to save a friend, rather than crush an enemy.

He approached slowly, giving the long-buried animal part of the man's brain time to understand that he was facing an apex predator. The more the man shook, the slower Julius went, using the steady crunch of his footsteps like a hammer to drive the fear deeper until the thug was trembling so badly he fumbled his weapon. Only then, when the man had lost his gun and looked ready to lose his lunch as well, did Julius finally grab him.

The thug screamed, fighting like a cornered animal. But strong as fear had made him, it still wasn't strong enough. With a sharp-toothed smile, Julius lifted the frantic man up by his collar and flung him into the wall across the alley. The man bounced from the impact and fell flat on his face, and though he was still breathing, he made no move to get up again. When Julius was sure he'd stay that way, he turned to check on Marci only to find her standing exactly where he'd left her.

That couldn't be right. He'd ended his fight fast, true, but not *that* fast. She should have moved at least a little. But then he saw the men he'd left to her at the far end of the alley, and everything became clear.

When he'd last seen them, the two men had been standing with their guns drawn. Now, they were both down on their knees, grabbing at their necks like they were trying to pull something off. Marci, meanwhile, was standing with her arm thrust out, holding something in her outstretched fist that was glowing like a floodlight. As Julius got closer, though, he saw it wasn't actually in her fist, but on it. The glowing object was one of her bracelets, a chunky, pink plastic ring he hadn't paid much attention to before. Now it was lit up, though, Julius could clearly see the tight lines of spellwork on the inside of the inch-wide band pulsing like a heartbeat, and every time they flashed, the men at the end of the alley scrambled harder.

By the time he'd made it back to Marci's side, both men had fallen over, their faces purple from lack of oxygen. Marci's own face was red with effort, but her expression was triumphant as she finally released the fist she'd been holding.

"What did you do?"

She jumped foot into the air when he spoke, and then jumped again when she turned around and saw the three men he'd defeated sprawled across the alley. "Christ," she panted, eyes jumping back and forth between the bodies, the cracked wall, and Julius himself. "What did *you* do?"

"I asked you first," he said, tilting his head at the men she'd choked unconscious—or maybe to death. He wasn't close enough to tell for sure. "I thought Thaumaturges didn't cast spells on the fly?"

"We don't," Marci said, sticking out her arm to display her line of thick plastic bracelets, all of which, Julius could now see, had inner bands that were absolutely covered in spellwork. "This one's my own variation on the force choke. An oldie but a goodie, and very effective."

He gave her pink bracelet an appreciative smile before looking back at the men she'd downed. "Are they dead?"

She shook her head. "Murder is illegal even in the DFZ, and I try not to rack up too many felony charges my first week in a new town."

Julius couldn't help it. He started to laugh. Marci laughed too, leaning on him for support in a familiar way he found both comforting and startling. He couldn't remember the last time anyone had touched him with trust or affection. She didn't seem to realize she was doing it, either, because she jumped off him again just as suddenly a few seconds later, cheeks flushing.

"Sorry," she said. "I'm, um…" She looked around at the body-strewn alley as though seeing it for the first time, and the flush of color drained from her face. "Wow," she whispered, running her hands through her choppy hair. "I am really sorry about all this. Thank you very much for helping me."

"Any time," Julius said, and then stopped in surprise at how much he meant it. "It was nice to help someone," he added when the silence had stretched too long. "Though, of course, I would like to know why a group of armed men attacked you."

"They're from Vegas," she said. "But I never thought they'd chase me all the way up here, and I especially didn't think they'd find me." Her expression turned bleak, and she started wringing her hands together so hard he worried she'd wring them off. "Again, I'm really sorry about this. Like, really, *really* sorry. I guess you'll want out of our contract now?"

"Why would I want that?" he asked, looking around. "Though we should probably get out of here."

She nodded. "Fleeing the scene is definitely the smart criminal thing to do."

The words were clearly meant to be a joke, but Marci's delivery was oddly flat. Everything about her right now seemed off, actually, though whether it was from the shock of the fight or the backlash or some combination thereof, Julius wasn't sure. Whatever the reason, she was wobbling so badly he had to step in, sliding his arm under her shoulders to keep her from going down.

"Thank you," she whispered, leaning tentatively on him as he helped her to the car.

"You're welcome," Julius said. "Though I *really* wish you hadn't backlashed yourself. I'm no magical expert, but isn't that how mages kill themselves?"

Marci snorted as he lowered her into her seat. "It'd take a much bigger spell than that to kill me. Though I will admit I hit myself a bit harder than I anticipated. It's been a while since I lost control of my magic enough to get backlashed flat out like that. I'd forgotten how much it sucks. But I didn't exactly have time to be picky since that bastard had a gun in your face. Of course, if I'd known you were secretly a ninja, I wouldn't have been so worried." She looked back at the men he'd taken out. "How did you do that, anyway? I've never seen anyone move that fast."

Julius thought back to the years of training every Heartstriker underwent before being allowed out into the world at seventeen, not to mention his overwhelming biological advantage. Neither of those explanations would work for Marci, though, so all he said was, "My brother's into martial arts and extremely competitive. I picked up a few things during my time as his punching bag."

That wasn't exactly a lie, but Julius shut the door before Marci could ask any more questions. Fortunately, her car was behaving itself. It started on the first try, and Marci grabbed the wheel straight out, skipping the autonav in favor of getting them out of the alley and away from the downed thugs as fast as possible.

When they'd put several blocks between themselves and the scene of the crime, she slowed to a more reasonable speed and slumped over the dash with a long sigh. "I'll waive the fee for today, of course. I know it's no proper thanks for saving my bacon, but it's all I can afford right now."

Julius thought of her horrid basement apartment and shook his head. "I can't let you do that. You did the job I hired you for. I'm happy to pay." Her full rate, he decided, just as soon as Ian paid him.

Instead of being happy, though, Marci's jaw tightened. "Let me buy you dinner, at least. I know a good place."

"It's really okay."

She turned to him with a cutting look. "Julius, you saved my life. You have to let me do *something*."

"You're going to keep working for me, right? That's something." Potentially a big something, because they still had to chase down Lark's lead on Katya and her alligator shaman. Marci, however, did not look appeased.

"That doesn't count!" she cried. "You can't let me pay you back by doing work I was going to do anyway!"

Julius shifted uncomfortably. Honestly, he didn't want Marci paying him back at all. Trading debts was what dragons did, but Julius had helped her because he'd wanted to, and it had felt like freedom. Given the chance, he'd do it all over again for that feeling alone. But that wasn't a line of logic a human would understand, so Julius decided to give in. Just a little.

"I'll accept dinner," he said. "But only if you tell me what that was about."

Marci suddenly looked much less eager. "You're sure you want to know?"

Julius shrugged. "I don't mean to pry into your business, but believe it or not, I don't normally get into back-alley brawls with strange men."

"Well, if anyone deserved breaking your 'no slamming people into walls' streak over, it would be Bixby's idiots."

"I only got half of them," he reminded her. "You did the other. Credit where credit is due."

Marci laughed. "If by 'credit' you mean 'assault and battery charges,' then I guess you're right." She shook her head and turned to flash him a warm smile. "You know, we make a pretty good team."

Julius felt that smile all the way to his toes. By the time he'd recovered, she'd turned away to fiddle with her car's GPS, muttering under her breath about skyways and satellite uplinks and idiots who built cities on top of other, perfectly good cities.

In the end, she gave up and drew the route by hand, laying down a path that took them into the city's industrial south west. Julius had no idea what she was trying to get to down there, and he didn't ask. He was too busy enjoying the novelty of the words *we* and *team* to care about anything else as they sped away from the grim alley, following the river south as the moon began to rise.

***

Considering they were driving away from the lake and Algonquin's tower and everything that was generally considered the heart of the DFZ, Julius had fully expected the city to get scarier, but it actually did just the opposite. The further they drove south along the river, the more corporate and uniform everything became. Instead of old buildings renovated into massive shopping centers, the Underground in this part of the city was filled with parking decks and massive housing units that, while nicer than the ones they'd just left by the casinos, were still bleak, utilitarian bricks of poured cement broken up only by railed walkways and tiny glass windows.

If you looked past that, though, the area actually reminded Julius far more of traditional suburbs than the DFZ Underground you saw in the movies. There were chain restaurants and coffee shops and shopping centers with parking decks full of mid-range cars and corporate buses shuttling people up to the massive offices on the skyways overhead. If it wasn't for the fact that the whole place was basically a cement brick built under a giant bridge, it could have passed for anywhere in America once you overlooked the camera drones and armed private security patrols.

Since she'd driven them down here, Julius expected Marci to turn them into one of the huge chain restaurants, but she didn't even look at them. She just kept driving until, eventually, they drove right out of the Underground and into the dense factory district that butted right up against it.

Before, when they'd driven out of the city, it had been all open space and plants and strange magic. This time, it was a very different landscape. In a deal that had brought dozens of multinational corporations to the DFZ, Algonquin had ceded the entire south western corner of her city to the new technology of magical fabrication. Even now, fifty years and two monetary overhauls later, the vast majority of the world's magically integrated consumables—five sense projectors, the mana contacts on phones that made AR possible, even enchanted paper like the stuff Marci's contract had been printed on—was still made in the massive factory complexes that had transformed what used to be the city of Dearborn, Michigan into a bleak landscape of monolithic, windowless buildings and canyon-like roads.

Huge at it all was, though, the factory park definitely didn't seem like the sort of place you'd find a restaurant, and the longer Marci drove, the more uncomfortable Julius got. "Um," he said at last. "Are you sure this is the right way?"

"Positive," Marci replied. "I looked this place up on my way over before I had to chuck my phone. Best rating in the city."

Julius didn't see how a restaurant could survive out here, let alone be good, but he was even more curious about why she'd had to chuck her phone. He was dying to ask about a lot of things, actually, but he forced himself to wait. This job was already much more complicated than he'd anticipated, and as much as he wanted to push his lead on Katya, he wasn't ready to charge recklessly forward without solving Marci's puzzle first. Besides, he hadn't eaten anything since he'd gotten off the plane this morning, and now that she'd reminded him about food, eating suddenly seemed much more important than following a tip that might well be the start of a wild goose chase. Or wild dragon chase, in this case.

Fortunately, he didn't have to wait much longer. Despite the seemingly endless wall of identical industrial complexes, there were actually several smaller business squeezed in between the factories wherever there was room. Marci's restaurant was one of these, a squat wooden shack built right up against the wall of a factory that made enchanted glass for AR displays. According to the back-lit sign, it was a BBQ joint. According to Julius's nose, however, this place served greasy, sauce-covered heaven.

"We're lucky it's between shifts," Marci said as they got out of the car. "I tried to come here yesterday, but the factories had just let out, and the line was around the block."

Julius could see why. Despite the delectable smell drifting out its screen door, the inside of the restaurant was barely big enough to hold twenty people. It was empty now, though, and he took advantage of that to get them a prime booth in the corner that put his back to the wall and gave him a good view of the front door.

"Order whatever you want," Marci said as she plopped down across from him. "Everything here is fantastic."

Julius bit back a grin as he picked up the one page laminated menu. Marci had no idea the trouble she was inviting, telling a dragon to order whatever he wanted. Hungry as he was, though, he was determined not to use more of her clearly limited funds than was absolutely necessary to make her feel better. So when the waitress came out of the tiny kitchen to take their order, Julius kept it small, just two plates of pork, three sides, a half order of cheese fries, a basket of cornbread, and a banana pudding.

Marci's eyebrows were nearly up to her chopped-off hairline by the time he finished, but she didn't comment as she ordered her own dinner of a pulled-pork sandwich and a beer. When the waitress asked her what kind of beer, Marci shrugged and told the girl to surprise her.

"Honestly, I don't even like beer," she confessed as the waitress vanished back into the tiny kitchen. "But a day like today demands a drink."

Julius couldn't argue with that. "So," he said, resting his elbows on the red checkered tablecloth. "Do you want to start, or should I?"

Marci waved her hand. "Fire away."

"Who is Bixby?"

"One of my dad's old clients."

The anger in her voice was all the hint Julius needed. "Bixby was involved in your father's death?"

Marci sighed, but the waitress returned with their drinks before she could answer. "It's more complicated than that," she said when they were alone again. "Dad was one of the first wave of mages born after the comet. He never had a formal magical education because there wasn't any such thing back then, but he taught himself how to break curses, which was a booming market in Vegas at the time. Business was good when I was younger, but my dad was very bad with money, and soon we were in a lot of trouble."

She took a long swig of her beer, then made a face and set the bottle aside. "I didn't actually know how much trouble until I was thirteen. That was when my mom got fed up and left us, and I learned that Dad was up to eyeballs in debt thanks to his moocher family and terrible money skills. I'd also tested positive as a mage by this point and enrolled in the best private magic school in the area, so there was that to pay as well." She heaved an enormous sigh. "My dad was so proud of me. He would have cut off his right arm before he took me out of class. He was desperate, and Bixby knew it."

Julius rolled his water glass between his palms. "I'm guessing Mr. Bixby isn't exactly a legal sort of person?"

"I'm sure some parts of his business are legal," Marci said. "But he definitely leaned more to the shady side. He knew my dad needed money, so he proposed a racket. Bixby's mages would curse someone, and then my dad would use the good name he'd built up over the years to come in and break it for an exorbitant fee."

"They wagged the dog," Julius said.

She nodded. "It didn't seem so bad at first. The debts were getting paid and money was coming in again, but Dad was miserable. He had this thing about being a hero, rescuing people from evil magic, that sort of stuff. It was the whole reason he got into curse breaking to begin with, and turning that mission into a scam was killing him. He hid it from me while I was a teenager, but as soon as I found out, we started working on an exit strategy. I was just an undergrad at the time, but I already knew enough to work with him on expanding the legal parts of his business—the wards and magical consulting and so forth. The idea was to get away from curse breaking and Bixby all together, but just when I thought we were clear, Bixby wouldn't let him go."

Her shoulders slumped as she spoke, like she was sinking into the table. "He threatened to have Dad arrested. There was more than enough evidence to convict him, and Bixby had cops on the take as well. Dad knew it, too, so he folded and went back. I tried several times to get him free over the years, but every time, Bixby would come up with some threat to make Dad stay until he finally hit his limit."

"What pushed him over the edge?"

"I don't know," Marci admitted, taking another drink. "But last Tuesday morning, he marched into Bixby's office and threatened to expose the whole operation unless Bixby paid him the final amount he was owed and let him go. But Bixby isn't the sort of man who responds well to threats. He told my dad to try it and see what happened. Of course, I didn't know about any of this until I came home from class that afternoon and found my dad packing up the house. He said we were leaving that night."

At this point, Marci's expression turned so sad, Julius was amazed she didn't start crying. "What happened?"

"We fought," she said, eyes on the table. "You have to understand, I always knew Bixby was bad news, but I didn't know *how* bad. I didn't know my dad's life was in danger, and I was only twenty credit hours away from finishing my doctorate. If I'd known what was really going on, I never would have argued, but he wouldn't tell me anything. He wanted me to leave school, just dump my *whole semester*, and run away with him."

She stopped, pressing her palms over her eyes, but Julius didn't push. He just sat there, waiting, until Marci continued. "I stormed out. I knew it was a childish thing to do, but I was just so *angry*. When I came back an hour later, he was already gone. I never saw him alive again."

She did start crying then, little sniffles she quickly hid behind a long sip off her beer. "Sorry," she whispered, wiping her eyes.

"Nothing to be sorry for," Julius said, handing her a paper napkin.

She took it without a word, wiping her eyes. "It just all happened so quickly. I left for the DFZ that same night, and I've been running ever since. I don't even know where I'm running to anymore, other than away." She balled the napkin in her fist and shot him a watery smile. "Some professional I am, huh?"

"Professional doesn't mean superhuman," Julius said quickly. "And for what it's worth, I think you've done amazingly well considering what happened. I have no complaints at all about the work you've done for me, and it was my pleasure to send a few thugs packing on your behalf. Good exercise, too. I haven't done anything like that in years."

He finished with a wide smile, but Marci was staring at him in wonder, like she was seeing him for the first time. And then, without warning, she smiled back. A warm, radiant, open smile he wasn't quite sure how to respond to. Fortunately, the food chose that moment to arrive, and they both seized on the distraction.

As Julius's nose had predicted, it was all delicious. He wolfed his first plate down while Marci was still putting sauce on her sandwich, but the second took him much longer. By the time he was ready to start on his sides, Julius was astonished to find he was full.

"Eyes bigger than your stomach?" Marci asked.

"Guess so," Julius grumbled, trying not to sound as upset as he felt. Apparently, even his appetite was limited to a human scale now, which meant he'd lost food *and* flying to his mother's seal. That realization almost made him weep. He *loved* eating.

There was no point in wasting good food, though, so he offered his untouched sides to Marci. She took them gladly, eating the fries so quickly he started to wonder when she'd last had a proper meal. But as he watched her eat, the story she'd told him circled around and around in his head, and the more he thought about it, the more he realized the ending didn't add up.

"Marci?" he asked, leaning on the table. "Can I ask you a rude question?"

She shrugged. "Go for it."

"If your father wronged Bixby and died for it, why is Bixby still after you?"

Marci looked down, poking at the fries left in the basket. "I know a lot about his operations in Vegas."

"We're a long way from Las Vegas," Julius said. "Not to say your knowledge isn't valuable, but unless you've got material evidence against him that could be used in a court of law"—he paused until she shook her head—"I don't understand why he'd send men all the way up here just to hush you up." Maybe he did have a plotting draconic talent in him somewhere, because the more Julius thought the situation out from Bixby's angle, the less sense it made. "And the fight," he continued. "The man who grabbed you could have just as easily broken your neck instead, but he didn't. They clearly wanted you alive. Why?

Do you have information Bixby wants? Something to do with your father, maybe?"

"Not that I know of," Marci said, keeping her eyes locked on the fry she was stabbing into a glob of cheese sauce. "My best guess is that this is about pride. Bixby always made a huge deal about how no one who wrongs him gets away with it. That's probably why he's putting in so much effort to catch me. If he lets me run, other people might start thinking they can get away, too."

Now *that* Julius could understand. Dragons were just the same. Unfortunately, pride was a much more troublesome enemy than greed or fear. If Bixby was determined to make an example of Marci, he couldn't be reasoned with and he wouldn't give up, not until his ego ran out.

Considering what Marci had said so far and his own observations of Bixby's penchant for employing giant, suited men to do his dirty work like he was the villain in a crime drama, Julius didn't see that happening any time soon. If it had been any other human, he would have said she was screwed. But Marci was clever and resourceful, and she had him now. As she'd said, they made a good team, and Julius was determined to hold up his end. So long as he was here, Bixby wouldn't touch a hair on her head.

Just thinking that made him feel worlds better, and he gave Marci a reassuring smile. "Don't worry, we'll figure something out to get him off your back. In the meanwhile, the DFZ's a very big place."

"And his goons will think twice about taking us on after the beating we gave them," Marci said proudly, tipping her beer bottle toward him in a one-sided toast.

Julius wasn't at all sure about that, but he liked how prominently and confidently she included him in her plans. In fact, he liked the idea of being Marci's competent partner so much more than being Bethesda's failure that he didn't even rush her as she slowly worked her way through the rest of his food.

"So, that's my story," Marci said between mouthfuls. "What about you? Where are you from?"

"New Mexico," Julius said, which was the truth. "I just arrived in the DFZ this morning, actually."

"I knew you were green," she said with a chuckle. "Though I couldn't tell if you were new to the city or just to the Underground. Where are you staying?"

"I hadn't figured that out yet," he confessed. "I also came here on a family emergency, and I haven't had a lot of time to get the details straightened out."

"Family emergency, huh? Is that why you're looking for that girl?"

"Sort of," Julius said. "My brother asked me to find her." And pleasant as this was, they really needed to get moving on that.

He pulled his phone out of his pocket to pay their check quietly, because despite Marci's insistence that she was buying, she didn't have a phone. No phone meant no electronic bank account, and he wasn't going to sit here and wait while the register validated every piece of cash she handed them. But when he clicked on the AR to check his account, a message was waiting for him.

Duck.

That was it. The sender was listed as Unknown Caller, but Julius had no doubt who was behind it. What he didn't know was if Bob wanted him to duck *now*, or four months from now.

Just to be safe, Julius dutifully dropped under the table, motioning for Marci to do the same. She obeyed instantly, crouching down on the padded bench. They stayed that way for a good thirty seconds before Julius got up again with a sigh.

"What was that about?" Marci asked, looking over her shoulder.

"Sorry," he said, glowering at the message. "I think my brother is confused."

"Oh," she said, brightening. "The one looking for the girl?"

"No, another brother," he said, standing up. "Come on, we'd better get out of here."

"How many brothers do you have?" Marci asked, following him to the counter.

"Too many," Julius grumbled, paying for dinner with the last of the money Bob had given him and hustling Marci out before she realized what he'd done.

They'd nearly made it back to the car when the hairs on the back of Julius's neck begin to prickle. He looked over his shoulder, eyes darting to find who was watching him, but the street was deserted.

He forced himself to walk normally to his side of the car, only half listening as Marci berated him for stealing her chance to pay for his dinner while he focused on his nose. He'd always been better at smelling than listening, but no matter how deeply he breathed, he caught nothing out of the ordinary. Just the chemical smell of the factories, rust from Marci's car, and the warm scent of delicious barbecue mixed with the faint reek of oil from the truck yard across the street.

He shook his head with a sigh, trying and failing to stomp down on the instinctual urge to run for cover. But then, why should his body calm down? Between his mother, Bob's cryptic messages, guns shoved in his face, and Ian playing games with powerful females from other clans, he'd had enough stress today to last a lifetime. A little jumpiness was a perfectly natural reaction. It didn't mean there was actually someone sneaking up behind—

A hand grabbed his shoulder.

Julius nearly jumped out of his skin, but the hand kept him in place, four knife-sharp nails pressing into the tender hollow just beneath his collar bone as a cold, soft, female voice whispered in his ear.

"Hello, brother."

And that was when Julius knew for a fact that he was dead.

Chapter 5

"**T**ell your human to wait and meet me in the alley on the left," Chelsie said, her claws digging deeper into his flesh. "Now."

Julius nodded, but the hand on his shoulder was already gone, vanishing as suddenly and quietly as it had appeared. He didn't bother turning around to look after that. The sidewalk would just be empty, and Marci was already leaning over to give him a funny look through the passenger window. "Julius? Are you okay?"

"Just realized I forgot something in the restaurant," he said quietly. "Give me two minutes."

Marci nodded, but he was already backing away, trusting his feet to find their own path as he walked back to the barbecue shack's screen door. When he knew Marci couldn't see him anymore, he darted to the side and down the alley as Chelsie had instructed.

It was a tiny, dark, dirty place, a gap between factories barely wide enough for a car to squeeze through. The narrowness hadn't saved the walls from being covered in advertisements, though. Posters covered every inch of the brick as high as a person could reach, mostly for the seedier kinds of services people loitering in alleys would find attractive. But while he found directions to thirteen different massage parlors just off the wall in front of him, he didn't see any sign of Chelsie. He was starting to panic that he'd gone down the wrong alley when he suddenly felt someone standing right behind him.

The light here was bad even for dragon eyes, but Julius had made it a point to stay as far from the Heartstriker's family enforcer as possible. As a result, the glimpse he got through the gloom when he whirled around was the best look at Chelsie he'd ever managed.

Oddly, the first thing that struck him was her height. At five eleven, Julius had always assumed his human form was the shortest of all Heartstrikers, but Chelsie was only a hair taller, and that might have been from her boots. What she lacked in stature, though, she made up everywhere else. Everything about her—her lean body packed into black, no-frills carbon-weave body armor, her short, ink-black hair, the long sword sheathed at her hip—spoke to her purpose as the Heartstriker's bogeyman, but the scariest thing of all was how closely she resembled their mother.

It would have been hard for an outsider to see. Other than the family's trademark green eyes and her high cheekbones, Chelsie's physical resemblance to Bethesda the Heartstriker was limited. Her skin was darker, her cheekbones sharper, her body smaller and more compact. If Bethesda was a resplendent queen, Chelsie was a well-honed knife. Both were deadly, however, and Chelsie's murderous glare was so like their mother's that Julius had already backed himself up against the far wall before she could open her mouth.

"Well, well," she said at last, her voice as cold and soft as the year's first frost. "I never thought I'd have to pay *you* a visit, Julius." She paused, tilting her head like a hawk considering the mouse trapped under its claws. "You know why I'm here, of course?"

Julius swallowed, mind racing. On the surface, Heartstriker family rules were simple: don't do anything that made Mother angry. But what Bethesda took offense at varied according to her mood, the day, the political situation, and who was doing the offending, which was *exactly* why Julius had tried so hard to keep his head down for the last seven years.

When he didn't answer, Chelsie narrowed her eyes. "One hour ago, six men in an alley by the river—ring any bells?"

Julius's heart began pounding so hard he grew lightheaded. How did she know about that? The alley had been empty. Of course, just because he hadn't seen her didn't mean Chelsie hadn't been watching. She'd already proven she could get right on his back without him noticing a thing. But just because she *could* follow him around didn't explain why she *would*. Chelsie had the entire Heartstriker family to worry about. Julius was no one, the underperforming runt of Bethesda's youngest clutch. It didn't make any sense at all for her to be watching him, not unless she really did watch everyone. But that was impossible. No matter what the rumors said, no matter how old and powerful and all-knowing Chelsie was supposed to be, there was just no way she could *actually* watch all of Bethesda's children all the—

"I do."

Julius's whirling thoughts screeched to a halt, and Chelsie gave him a slow, cruel smile. "I don't actually read minds," she said, her nails tapping idly on the wrapped hilt of her sword. "But then, I don't need to. You all make the same face when you start thinking, 'There's no way she can do it,' but I'll let you in on a family secret." She leaned in, her neon-green Heartstriker eyes bright with malice as she dropped her voice to a whisper. "I am *always* watching. I watch every single one of you conniving little lizards. I watch you every moment of every day so that the second you set one claw over the line, I'll be there to *cut it off.*"

Julius flinched as she finished, and Chelsie straightened back up, crossing her arms over her chest with a satisfied look. "Now that we're clear on that point, let me explain what you did to trigger this little visit so we never have to see each other again."

He nodded, breathing heavily. "I shouldn't have attacked those men," he said quickly. "I understand that. I should have stayed out of the human's business and—"

Chelsie's eyes narrowed, and Julius snapped his mouth shut. When it was clear he wasn't going to try and talk again, she continued. "If I came after every idiot Heartstriker who got into a street brawl, half the clan would be dead by now. I also don't care what mischief Ian has you up to in his hopeless courtship of that Three Sisters ice snake Svena, who, for the record, is going to chew him up and spit him out like a piece of gristle. I'm not even terribly concerned that you showed a bit of tooth and claw in the DFZ. Everyone does that from time to time. *My* problem, Julius, is that you left *witnesses*."

Julius opened his mouth to explain, but Chelsie grabbed him first. Faster than he could react, faster than he could even see, she wrapped her hand around his throat and slammed him into the wall, scattering the layers of old advertisements in a rain of tattered paper.

"Six humans went into that alley with you," she snarled in his face. "And when you left, six humans were still alive. Do you know what that is, Julius? That's a *mess*. And when a Heartstriker makes a mess, it's my job to ensure they never. Do it. Again."

Her fingers squeezed tighter with every word, choking him by inches. Just when Julius was sure he'd suffocate, Chelsie let go, dropping him in a heap on the dirty asphalt.

The coughing fit hit him a second later. Julius rolled to his knees, clutching his throat until, after what felt like hours, his breathing returned to something like normal. When he looked up again, Chelsie was looming over him, a black shadow outlined by the lone factory floodlight five stories overhead.

"Poor little Julius," she cooed. "You're so *nice*. You don't want to hurt anyone, don't want to get into trouble. But you're not in the mountain anymore, whelp, and there's no more room for nice. From this moment forward, if a human who's not under your direct control sees you doing anything that might make them think you're not what you seem, you kill them. Not knock out, not threaten, *kill*. Do you understand?" When he didn't answer at once, Chelsie slammed him back into the wall with her booted foot. *"Do you understand?"*

"Yes," he wheezed.

She released him, and he slid back to the ground. She let him lie there a second before turning away with a little huff that was a perfect copy of the sound their mother made when she was particularly disappointed. "I can't believe I'm having to explain something as basic as witness elimination. No wonder Mother kicked you out. I assumed she was exaggerating, but now I think you might really be the worst dragon we've ever had."

Julius had heard this many, many times. He'd heard it in every variation imaginable, and he usually shrugged it off. It was always easier to go back to his room and bury himself in something better—a videogame, a book, a movie, homework for an online class, whatever was at hand—than to try to defend himself. Now though, he didn't have a room to retreat to. He was stranded in an alley with his back literally against a wall, and he was so, so sick of being talked down to, the words just burst out.

"Maybe I don't want to be a good dragon."

Chelsie stopped, turning back to him with blood-chilling slowness. "Excuse me?"

He pushed up to his knees, wiping the dirt from his face with trembling hands, though whether the shaking was from anger or fear, even Julius didn't know. "So far as I can tell, 'good dragon' is just another name for coldblooded sociopath," he said. "No friends, no trust, no love. Why would I ever want to live like that? It's not like any of you good dragons are happy."

The taunt echoed down the alley, and for one heartbeat, Chelsie's cold expression morphed into a mask of pure rage. As he saw the anger flaring in his sister's eyes, Julius knew this was it. This was his death. When Chelsie was done, they'd be finding pieces of him all over the DFZ. But just as he was making peace with his final end, Chelsie's anger vanished, covered up in an instant by the usual haughty disdain most dragons wore when looking down on him.

"Oh, Julius," she said, her voice pitying. "You are so young. Too young and far too exposed to sentimental human idiocy to understand what it truly means to be a Heartstriker. But you will learn, little whelp, or you will break. Either way, consider this your first and only warning."

She crouched down as she finished, her face hovering over his like she was going to bite off his head. When she spoke again, her voice was barely more than a breath.

"You make one more mess," she whispered. "You set one talon out of line, make one ounce of trouble for our family in this place, and you won't have to worry about being a good dragon any longer. Because I will end you, right then, right there. You won't even see it coming, and no one except your little human girlfriend will mourn you. Nod if you understand."

Julius nodded, and Chelsie's lips curled into an icy smile. "Good boy," she murmured, straightening up. "And on that note, I hope you didn't need any of those humans, because they're fish food now."

He swallowed against the bile that rose in his throat and ducked his head. Of course she'd killed them. Chelsie was a C, one of two surviving children from their mother's third clutch, which meant she had to be seven hundred years old at least. She'd probably killed more humans in the name of 'cleaning up messes' than Julius had met in his entire life. He didn't even care that Bixby's goons were gone; he just couldn't get the image of Chelsie casually breaking the unconscious men's necks before tossing them in the water out of his head. By the time he pulled himself together enough to look up again, the alley was empty.

After his first shaky attempt at standing landed him back on knees, Julius used his hands to pull himself up the wall until he was back on his feet. He brushed off his worn jeans and shirt as best he could, but it was hopeless. His clothes had been ratty to begin with, and life in the DFZ was proving to be too much for them. Still, he took the time to make himself as presentable as possible and not like he'd just gotten kicked around an alley before heading back to the car.

To his enormous relief, Marci was right where he'd left her. He hadn't actually realized how scared he'd been that she'd leave until he saw her sitting in the front seat of her car, examining something round and golden under the cabin light. From this distance, it looked kind of like a gilded softball, or maybe an oversized Christmas ornament. Whatever it was, she shoved it back into her bag when she heard him coming, leaning over to push open the passenger door for him instead.

"What happened?" she cried, eyes flicking over his disarrayed clothing as he sat down. "You look like you got mugged! Are you okay?"

"No," Julius said, forcing himself to sit normally instead of collapsing, which was what he really wanted to do.

"No, you're not okay, or no, you didn't get mugged?"

Yes, Julius thought. "No, I didn't get mugged," he said, pulling his phone out of his pocket to pull up the address Lark had given him for where Katya was supposedly shacking up with her shaman. "It's not important. We need to get mov—"

He froze. Two new messages from the Unknown Caller had arrived on his phone while he'd been in the alley with Chelsie. One looked like a copy of the first message, just the word *duck,* but the final message was new.

"Goose," Julius read, staring at the glowing letters. "Duck, duck, goose."

"What are you talking about?" Marci asked.

Julius didn't answer. He just leaned forward and banged his head against the scuffed dash. He brought it down a few more times for good measure before sitting up again. "I don't know," he said tiredly, waving his fingers through the hazy sphere of augmented reality above the phone's screen to delete both of Bob's messages forever. "I don't understand anything. I'm terrible at this, apparently."

Marci looked more confused than ever. "Terrible at what?"

Being a dragon, he wanted to tell her. Being a scheming lizard who didn't need to be reminded to murder witnesses and understood cryptic messages from crazy seers. And right then, he wished Marci actually was his human girlfriend, because he could really use a hug.

"It's nothing," he muttered, leaning over to type the address Lark had given him into the car's autonav. "Let's just get this over with."

Marci didn't look convinced, but to Julius's relief, she didn't ask any more questions. She just let the car pull them into the dark, canyon-like streets between the factories, back toward the city.

***

When his retrieval team failed to check in, Bixby ordered the rest of his employees to cancel their evening plans. They were going to Detroit.

"*All* of us?" cried the mage he'd hired to replace the one the Novalli girl had blown up. "To the *DFZ*? But—"

Bixby's second, Oslo, cut the man off with a wave of his huge hand, saving his life. Not that that was why Oslo had done it, of course, but the mage was too new to recognize when Bixby was in killing mood. If his ignorance got him shot, Oslo was the one who'd have to find them another replacement mage on short notice, and if there was anything Oslo hated, it was doing more work than was absolutely necessary.

"I want this taken care of fast and right," Bixby went on, leaning forward on his desk as he swept his eyes menacingly over the hired muscle crowding his normally spacious office. "I don't care what you spend, I don't care who you piss off, and I don't care what you break. I just want that overhyped golden grapefruit back in Vegas in time for the drop-off tomorrow night, and I want that little thief delivered to my office trussed up like a pig."

Oslo sighed and removed his hat to wipe a white handkerchief across his smooth shaved, and completely dry, head. It was his favorite stalling technique when he wanted to say something he knew his boss wouldn't like, so Bixby wasn't at all surprised when his second finally said, "I know you're pissed, sir, but if you don't mind me asking, what's all this with the girl? Aldo was the one who stole the thing from you in the first place, and he's been coyote food for days now. It don't matter how much money you throw at this, it's gonna take a miracle for us to get your stolen property out of the DFZ and back here before the deadline. If we have to worry about the girl, too, I don't think we can—"

"Oslo," Bixby said, drumming his fingers on the arm of his leather chair. "There are times when you're paid to think and times when you're paid to do what I tell you. Guess which one this is?"

Oslo put his hat back on with a sigh. "Sure thing, boss. Thief trussed up like a pig. Got it."

"And no killing," Bixby said, jabbing his finger at his men. "Rough her up, scare her, cut off her arms, I don't care, but she keeps breathing or you all don't. Got me?"

When Oslo nodded, Bixby waved his hand. "Good. Now get out of here. I'm expecting a phone call."

Actually, his phone call had been scheduled for two hours ago, but this client never called on time. If it had been anyone else, Mr. Bixby wouldn't have tolerated such behavior for love or money, but this client was his seer as well as his buyer, and real seers were a lot harder to replace than mages.

Now that the marching orders had been given, Oslo jerked his head, and the room cleared out. When his men were gone, Bixby messaged his numbers guy to start moving money into the operational budget. Out-of-town work was always more expensive than one expected, and Bixby didn't want Oslo to have any excuses if this fell through. He also sent notes around to his Detroit contacts to make sure no one up there took offense when Oslo's war party rolled into their territory. He'd covered nearly half the DFZ before his private phone finally began to buzz in his pocket.

Bixby set the sleek black device on his desk. The no expense spared enchanted glass picked up the phone's AR at once, throwing the incoming message up like a marquee in the air in front of him.

Having trouble, are we?

Bixby grit his teeth. This was another of his seer's obnoxious peculiarities. The bastard set the call times, but never actually phoned. He only messaged, and none of Bixby's hackers had ever been able to crack the number behind the Unknown Caller ID.

If the man's predictions weren't air tight every time, Bixby would have cut this nonsense off at the throat ages ago. Instead, he tapped his hand on the desk's glass surface, bringing up the glowing virtual keyboard to type his reply. Since he was alone, he spoke the words out loud as he typed them, just to make himself feel like he was still in charge of this conversation. "It's being taken care of. We'll have everything in time for the pick-up tomorrow."

That's not what I heard.

Bixby almost put his fist through the glass. He checked his temper at the last second, closing his eyes instead with a deep breath. When he opened them again, several more messages were hanging in the AR.

Poor little Bixby, time's running out. Of all the predictions I've made for you, every single one has come to pass, except the last. You're courting your own death with this incompetence.

"Screw you!" Bixby yelled at the floating letters, but his fingers were shaking as he began to type his reply, because the seer was right. From the moment the first mysterious message had come into his life last year, everything the seer had predicted had come true exactly as promised, and Bixby had become very, very rich. But this latest prediction was the only one that really mattered, because the last thing the seer had told him was the story of Bixby's death, and the role Aldo Novalli's daughter would play in it if he couldn't get her contained.

"I'll find her," he growled as he typed. "You think I don't know how to catch runners? Even if my men don't get her in time, I've been in this business for thirty years. I've had real assassins die just trying to get into my building. There's no way I'm going down to some little mage girl no one's ever heard of."

Save your bluster, the seer replied. *You think you can rattle your saber and scare the future into doing your bidding like one of your hirelings? How absurd. Time is a river. It flows on and on with no care or notice for those caught in it. But while you can see nothing but the water around you, I have the ability to look downstream. I can see all the possible paths the future might take, and while even I cannot say for certain which way the water will bounce when the time comes, I can tell you without doubt that there is not one single possible future in which you survive past midnight tomorrow without the Novalli girl in your custody. Not a single one. Do I make myself clear?*

Bixby let out a long, angry breath. "I'm working on it."

The reply came instantly. *Work harder. I've made you a rich man in many ways, Mr. Bixby, and I can make you richer still. I've even told you how to save your pathetic life, but you have to pay the price. I want my Kosmolabe. If you do not have my merchandise at sundown tomorrow as promised, the Novalli girl will be the least of your worries. I will contact you again tomorrow at six. See that the news is good.*

Bixby slammed his hands on the desk, cutting off the AR with a curse. There was no point in replying after that. Once the seer posted the time of their next conversation, the current one was over, and any other messages he sent would be ignored. Being hung up on like this made him crazy, but there was absolutely nothing he could do about it. The fortune teller was the only person in the world he couldn't squeeze. He didn't know where the seer lived, he didn't even know the jack off's name. The best he could do was put the whole thing out of his mind and get back to work, and he was attempting to do just that when his phone buzzed again.

He grabbed it at once, but it wasn't another message from his seer. It was Oslo.

"Why are you bothering me?" Bixby snapped when the call connected. "You idiots can't even be at the airport yet."

"Sorry, boss," Oslo said. "I thought you'd want to know this. I just got a call from my mole in the DFZ dispatch office. One of Algonquin's water patrols found our guys face-down in the river."

Bixby cursed loudly. For a supposedly sweet little nerd of a PhD student, Aldo's daughter was turning out to be much more of a killer than he'd expected. "Was it her?"

"Don't know," Oslo replied. "Someone with a lot of magic scrubbed the bodies clean before dumping them. Real professional work. Seems our girl got herself some protection."

That made Bixby pause, but then he shook his head. "This changes nothing. Protection or no, you do whatever you gotta do to get Novalli and her golden ball back here ASAP or I swear to God, Oslo, I'm going to kill the lot of you."

Normally, that was an idle threat, but not this time. This time, Bixby was deadly serious, because if he didn't stop Aldo's girl from playing her part in the seer's prediction, he wasn't going to be around to regret shooting his entire organization. He was going to be dead.

Oslo must have heard the truth in his boss's voice, because he turned meek as a lamb, "Yes, sir, Mr. Bixby. Will do."

Bixby nodded and hung up, spinning around to stare out the window overlooking the glittering Vegas strip. Normally, the sight of so much easy money was guaranteed to make him smile, but not tonight. Instead, his eyes went to the mountains, looking north and east over the desert toward the double layered city on the edge of a lake where his wannabe death was running free, completely oblivious to the hammer she'd just brought down on her head.

***

An hour later, back in Detroit, Julius was about ready to give up.

73

They'd gone straight from the restaurant to the address Lark had given them only to find a parking deck. No apartment, no house, nowhere a dragon could possibly stay, just a gated six story deck that served as a commuter lot for the office complex on the skyway above them.

Julius knew that last part for certain because he'd climbed all the way up the spiral stairs to the top street level on the off-chance Marci's GPS had gotten the vertical location wrong, but there was no mistake. This was the address the albatross shaman had given him, and unless Katya was hiding under one of the forgotten sedans in the back, she wasn't here. No one was at this time of night, and now Julius had a problem.

It was one he needed to deal with in private, though, so he left Marci with the car and walked across the street to call Ian. When his brother didn't answer, Julius hung up and called again. Finally, on the third try, the ringing stopped, and Ian's excessively put-out voice growled in his ear.

"This had better be to say you have her."

"Well I don't," Julius snapped, slumping against the pole of a streetlight that probably hadn't worked since the turn of the century. "We got into the party, but she'd already left with some guy before we arrived, and—"

"We?" Ian interrupted.

"I had to bring in a mage to help," he explained, suddenly nervous. "A human."

Julius hadn't actually considered what Ian would think about Marci's involvement, mostly because he hadn't thought this job would take long enough for her to learn anything she shouldn't. Apparently, though, hiring a human mage to find a missing dragon was nothing out of the ordinary for Ian, because all he said was, "Continue."

Julius cleared his throat. "As I was saying, the host told me Katya left early with a human shaman, but the address he gave me was bad, and now I have no idea where she is."

"So find out."

"How am I supposed to do that?" Julius cried. "In case you forgot, I was kicked off a plane into this stupid city not twenty hours ago. Going to a party to pick up a lost dragon is one thing, but it takes *money* to play detective, which is something I don't exactly have a lot of at the moment. So unless you're ready to give me an advance on my payment, we're going to have to call this a wash for tonight, because I've got nothing."

It wasn't until ten seconds into the long pause that followed that Julius realized what he'd done. He'd lost his temper and yelled at his brother. His *older* brother, who was doing him a huge favor by letting Julius work a job to convince their Mother he deserved not to be eaten.

Before he could apologize for the outburst, though, Ian said, "Why, Julius Heartstriker, you *almost* sounded like a creature with a spine just then."

Julius blinked. "Um, thank you?"

"Unfortunately, I've already given you everything I'm willing to," Ian went on, talking right over him. "I'm not running a charity here. I hired you to fetch Katya, practically handed her to you on a platter, and if your failures have squandered that opportunity, I don't see how that's my responsibility."

Julius closed his eyes with a stifled hiss. *Don't get mad,* he reminded himself. Ian was the one who'd be reporting his progress to Mother, and Julius desperately needed him to give her a good one since Chelsie had undoubtedly already told Bethesda about his screw-up with Bixby's goons. He was a little surprised he hadn't gotten a call about that yet, actually. Surprised and relieved, because talking to his mother always put him in an abysmal mood, and if there was ever a time he needed to stay positive, it was now.

"I don't think I'm being unreasonable," he said when he could trust his voice again. "You're in business, Ian. You know you can't get something for nothing. I'm not even asking you to pay me extra, just give me some working capital so I can—"

"No," Ian said, his voice hard. "The deal stands. I pay you when you get the dragoness. If you need additional resources to complete your task, then I suggest you stop whining to me for handouts and figure out a way to get the money yourself. Go take some from a human or something."

Julius stared at the phone in horror. "Are you telling me to mug someone?"

"Well, I would hope you could come up with something more elegant than brute force," his brother said. "But mugging will do in a pinch, yes."

"No!" Julius cried. "I'm not going to start robbing random humans! That's *terrible!*"

"Julius," Ian said dryly. "That is what our kind has been doing for thousands of years. Where did you think the contents of Mother's treasury came from? Donation boxes?"

He hadn't quite thought of it that way, but Ian wasn't finished. "You see, this is exactly why your life has come to this sorry state of affairs. You are simply unwilling to do what needs to be done."

Julius was unwilling to believe they were actually having this conversation. "I don't think my failure to cross the 'petty crimes against innocent people because your brother is too cheap to give you an advance so you can do your job' line qualifies as a summation of my existence."

"Actually, I think it sums it up quite nicely," Ian said, his voice growing irritated. "When are you going to understand that this isn't about the money? It's about you growing some fangs and finally learning that there's no place in our world for *nice*. Nice dragons finish last, *if* they finish at all, and we have no room for losers in this family. So stop whining, get yourself straight, and get me some results, or I call Mother, and we cross one more Heartstriker off the roster. Do you understand me, little brother?"

Julius closed his eyes with a ragged breath.

"I'm waiting."

"Yes," he growled.

"Good," Ian said, his voice smooth as silk again in an instant. "I'll be expecting word of your success by tomorrow."

Julius almost choked. *"Tomorrow?* But—"

"You're a dragon," Ian said. "Figure it out." And then he hung up.

Julius lowered the phone with a muffled curse, kicking the dead street lamp as hard as he could. The metal pole rang like a gong, startling a small colony of bats that had taken up residence in the broken light fixture. It also startled the pigeon perched on top of the ancient NO PARKING sign directly above Julius's head.

The bird took flight with a frantic spate of flapping, sweeping so low its tiny talons almost caught Julius's hair before it found its wings and flew straight up into the dark, vanishing through a crack in the skyways high, high overhead.

Chapter 6

Meanwhile, high atop a superscraper in the Upper City, far from the dirt and tawdry worries of the world below, Svena, White Witch of the Three Sisters, Terrible Serpent of the Sibirskoe and, once, in a moment of youthful indiscretion, the Savage Protector of Ljubljana, lay reclined in Ian's enormous bed, regarding her newest lover through slitted eyes.

Said lover, however, was not looking at her. Ian was typing messages into the AR keyboard of his phone, an activity that had occupied his attention ever since he'd hung up on his whining puppy of a baby brother. But where a younger, less secure dragoness would have been deathly insulted by such divided attention, Svena did not mind. As the second daughter of her own clan, she understood the demands of having to report on the doings of absurd younger siblings, and anyway, the lull in their activities gave her a chance to enjoy the view.

And what a view it was. All dragons were pleasing to look on in their human forms, but Svena had always secretly considered the Heartstrikers a breed unto themselves. There was just something intoxicatingly exotic about their warm tanned skin, sharp, haughty features, and straight, ink-black hair that brought to mind equatorial climates and golden cities full of cowering humans who still remembered their rightful place. Even Ian's eyes reminded her of bright green jungles, and this was just his mortal disguise. After hearing tales of Bethesda's beauty for the last thousand years, Svena was perishing of curiosity to see if the Feathered Serpent's glory had bred true in her son, enough that she'd actually asked him to change for her as they'd lain together in the aftermath. A request that Ian had refused, the clever little snake.

"I see what you are doing," she said when he finally put down his phone. "You are teasing me. You think if you do not show me your feathers, curiosity will drive me back to your clutches."

Ian leaned across the silk sheets to kiss her bare shoulder. "Naturally."

She arched an eyebrow, and Ian gave her a serpentine smile. "If I wasn't sure you could see through such a shallow ruse, I would not have pursued you in the first place. Fortunately for me, knowledge of the bait's true nature does not lessen its temptation." His smile widened. "Of course, considering how much you enjoyed being in my clutches, perhaps I didn't need to bother with bait at all."

He reached for her as he spoke, but Svena slid away at the last moment, rising from the bed with a languid stretch. "Arrogant creature. You talk very big for a hatchling not yet out of his second century."

"You deserve no less," Ian said, lying back on the bed to watch her. "A little youthful arrogance would serve you well, Svena, and you know it. That's why you agreed to come home with me in the first place."

She picked up her discarded dress off the floor and pulled it over her head. "Are you a seer, then, to predict what I do?" When he didn't reply, she turned to face him and let her human form recede. Not fully, not even enough to change size. Just a hint, an icy whisper to remind him of the force he was daring to taunt. "Do not presume to know my mind, little dragon. Perhaps I only wished to see for myself if you were as wanton as your mother."

For a moment, Ian's green eyes flickered. That surprised her, but then, she'd never met a Heartstriker who could stand to hear his mother's name impinged. A prideful idiocy, Svena had always though, and a pointless one. With ten clutches from ten different fathers in barely a thousand years, Bethesda the Heartstriker's honor was an impossible thing to defend.

"My mother is my mother," Ian said, lifting his chin with a look of such arrogance, Svena's breath caught in delight. "A great and powerful dragoness who commands the largest dragon clan in the world. When the magic faded centuries ago, your mothers fled beneath the Siberian ice, sleeping and hoarding their power out of fear. *My* mother adapted, and now that magic has returned, she is already moving to make this world her own. It's true she isn't an ancient power, but no power lasts forever, Svena. By the time your mothers wake, they will find themselves forgotten, and Heartstriker will be the name all the world fears."

Svena regarded the young dragon in the bed with a new eye. "I was wondering when your true colors would show," she said softly. "Is this why you invited me here? To spew Heartstriker propaganda? Or are you Bethesda's lure? A tasty morsel to tempt me into a mating flight so she can add another clutch to her army?"

Ian rose from the bed in one swift motion and stalked forward to stand right in front of her. Given the age difference between them, Svena was certain she was the larger dragon, but in their human forms, she and Ian were the same height. Yet another reason she'd accepted his suit. Svena despised being looked down upon.

"Just because I respect what my mother has built does not mean I'm bound by her plans," he said quietly. "Not when there are so many other, more tempting options available."

Svena flashed him a predatory smile. "Does that mean you wish to turn traitor?" she whispered, reaching up to run her nails over the smooth shaved line of his jaw. "Poor Ian, we're not interested. Our clan is full up. And in any case, you'd make me a very bad sister."

"The last thing I wish to be is your sister," Ian replied, fearlessly leaning into the knife-sharp tips she'd pressed against his skin. "But there are more things in this world than siblings and parents, Svena."

She removed her claws from his face, waiting for him to finish, but all Ian gave her was a long smile before turning away.

"For an ancient and wise dragoness, you think very small," he said, walking over to retrieve his robe from its hook inside his expansive closet. "I may not be the oldest or the strongest of my clan, but I am, without question, the most ambitious of all Heartstrikers, and my plans for you go far beyond anything our mothers could dream."

It had been so long since anyone had dared to play a game like this with her, Svena was forced to take a moment to make sure her voice didn't betray her excitement. "And what would these fantastical, undreamable plans entail?"

Ian chuckled, a low, delightful sound. "For that, you'll have to come to me again. Tomorrow night. I'll send a car."

"Clever snake," Svena whispered, wagging her finger at him.

She was enjoying this game far more than she'd expected to when she'd accepted his bold offer at the restaurant. Being around so much raw ambition brought back old dreams she hadn't considered in many, many years, and Svena couldn't help thinking that perhaps Ian was right. Perhaps the centuries *had* made her complacent. Her eyes lingered on Ian's silk-clad back as he walked to the sidebar to pour himself a drink. Maybe she did need someone young and hungry to remind her what it meant to be a dragon.

But while she was now certain she'd take the lure he offered and come again tomorrow, Svena saw no reason to tell him that. Ian wasn't the only one who could play this game.

With a coy smile, she walked over and turned around, motioning for him to zip up the back of her dress. Ian obliged, his fingers skimming over her skin so lightly she knew he was doing it on purpose, and she liked that knowledge even more than his touch. Oh yes, this would be a fun game indeed.

When she was presentable, Svena gathered her purse and coat from the couch where she'd flung them and walked out without a word, leaving Ian to stare after her and wonder. Only when she was safely ensconced in the private elevator coming down from his penthouse at the top of one of the DFZ's most prestigious superscrapers did she allow her coy smile to broaden into a real one.

As ordered, her limo pulled up the moment she stepped into the lobby. She swept past the bowing human doorman and into her softly lit vehicle without pausing, but it wasn't until she'd settled into the dove-gray seat and the car began to pull away that she realized she wasn't alone.

"Enjoy your evening?"

Svena's body went still as a cobra's before the strike. Only her eyes moved, flicking to the front of the limo, where an amazingly beautiful woman lay sprawled like an ancient queen across the car's rear-facing seat. She was as tall as Svena, her skin just as pale, but unlike Svena's icy blond, this woman's hair was true white, framing her face like a river of snow. But then, Estella was the oldest of them all. It only made sense that she'd go white first.

Despite her dramatic appearance, however, her older sister had yet to actually look up from the crumbling paperback in her lap. That was not unusual. Estella had read a book a day since the invention of the printing press. Centuries ago, when she and Svena had still been close, Estella had confessed that she didn't even like most human writing. She did, however, like surprises, and novels were the only stories where a seer didn't know the ending before it began.

"Svena," Estella said again, her voice sharpening as she turned a page. "I asked you a question."

"And I am deciding whether or not it deserves an answer," Svena replied, hiding her nervousness behind cold indifference. "If you are merely prying into my affairs, then we have nothing to discuss. But then, perhaps you are here because you wish to compare notes? Did you not enjoy a Heartstriker once?"

That was a very sore subject, and Estella closed her book with a snap. "I think there has been a misunderstanding. I instructed you to enchant that chain and give it to the Heartstrikers because I foresaw it would lead to the return of our darling baby sister. I do *not* recall suggesting that you continue the acquaintance to the point of absurdity by consorting with the spawn of Bethesda the Broodmare. And not even one of the famous ones. Honestly, Svena, couldn't you have done better than an *I*? Isn't she only on J?"

"I do not recall requesting your opinion on my private dalliances," Svena replied icily, folding her arms over her chest. "Why are you in my car, Estella? I thought the entire reason behind sending me to the DFZ after Katya was so that you wouldn't have to lower yourself by entering Algonquin's little experiment personally. What changed your mind?"

Svena posed the question more out of habit than any real expectation of receiving an answer. Even if Estella did deign to explain herself, her reasons wouldn't make any sense. Seer logic was only decipherable by other seers. Therefore, Svena wasn't surprised at all when her sister dropped her paperback into her purse and placed her hands on her knees, announcing in her usual cryptic voice, "You begin to fade."

"Sounds lovely," Svena said, leaning over to check the limo's automated control panel. "Do I get to enjoy this fading now, or is this my ten-year warning?"

Her only answer was silence, and she looked up again to find her sister staring at her with an intensity that suddenly made this conversation very, very serious. "Now is not the time for games," Estella said. "I came here because your future is vanishing from my sight."

Svena pressed her hands into the seat to hide her growing nervousness. "Vanishing how?"

"It started as soon as you left," the seer said, touching her slender fingers to her forehead. "Bits and pieces at first, but now whole decision trees have passed beyond my reach. I didn't even see Bethesda's brat sneaking up on you until it was too late."

Svena fought the urge to sigh in frustration. "So what does that mean? Am I dying?"

"Death would be better," Estella said bitterly. "I would much rather you be dead than let him take you from me."

Svena didn't bother to hide her scorn at such a notion, or her bared teeth. "No one takes me. I am the White Witch of the Three Sisters, feared on seven continents. I am no one's prey!"

She finished with a roar, but Estella was already shaking her head. "This is not a battle you can fight. Not when you debase yourself so willingly before that pretty whelp of a dragon, listening gladly while he pours poison in your ear against our mothers, against *me*."

Svena narrowed her eyes. "I hope you are not questioning my loyalty to our clan."

"I don't need to," Estella said. "You already have."

Centuries of experience kept all signs of shock from Svena's face, but nothing could silence the sudden pounding of her heart. Seer or no, there was no way her sister could know thoughts Svena had barely considered herself, and yet Estella was glaring at her as though she'd already turned traitor.

"You are approaching a crossroads, little sister," Estella said, leaning forward. "I saw it coming many years ago, but I could never foresee its outcome. Now, at last, I know why. I am being blocked. Another seer has entered the game, and *you* let him in. You took the Heartstriker's bait. You let yourself be played!"

"That's absurd," Svena scoffed. "I would never—"

"You will!" Estella snarled, her ice blue eyes flashing in the dark car. "I know you, Svena. I've known you all your life, that which you've lived already and that which is yet to come. Of all our mothers' daughters, you were always the most ambitious. You fought tooth and claw until you stood at the head of the world's most-feared clan, second only to myself and our mothers. I always admired you for that, but even a dragon can reach too high." She flashed her sister a deadly smile. "It would be a great shame if you were to lose all you've fought for because you believed the empty promises of a handsome young dragon and his grasping clan."

Svena's nails bit into the seat beside her, puncturing the soft leather. "I do not appreciate threats."

"Oh, but it's not a threat," her sister said innocently. "It's a warning, and a courtesy. I can no longer foresee if you will be clever or foolish, so I am forced to tell you what you should already know."

"Because you think I will be foolish?" Svena growled.

"Because I think you will be fooled," Estella growled back. "There is no path worthy of the daughters of the Three Sisters save the one *I* lay out. I am both the eldest and the seer. I *always* know best. You would do well to keep that in mind."

Svena met her sister's icy glare cold for cold as she reached over and stabbed her finger against the limo's command console. The car pulled over at once, sliding through the skyway's night traffic into a quiet corporate park. The second they stopped moving, Svena threw open the door. "Get out."

Her older sister exited the car without another word, the sharp heels of her delicate white stilettos clicking against the pristine sidewalk. It wasn't until her sister was completely outside that Svena realized she didn't actually know where they were, but any regrets she might have had about kicking her sister to the curb in a strange city vanished when she spotted a second limo waiting just around the corner, its door already open.

Svena fought the urge to sigh. Of course. Estella was a seer—of *course* she would know exactly when and where she was going to be tossed out and make preparations accordingly. The only real surprise was that Svena hadn't seen it coming. Nothing in this world ever turned out anyway except exactly as a seer wanted.

Like she could read her mind, Estella chose that moment to turn, her lips curling into a cold smile as she slipped her purse over her shoulder. "Remember that, Svena," she said, her voice haughty. "No matter how it may seem, no matter what you do, I *always* come out on top in the end. But while your arrogance suggests otherwise, hope is not yet lost. You have not vanished completely from my sight, which means the future can still be changed. All you have to do is be sure that, when the time comes, you make the right choice. Will you promise me that, little sister?"

Svena's answer was to slam the door. Her limo pulled out a second later, peeling away from the little park so fast, Svena never had a chance to see the beautiful man with the absurdly long jet black hair and bright green eyes watching the drama play out from a park bench just a few feet away.

Estella was not so unobservant. Long after her sister's car had vanished, she stood on the curb, watching the man with the sort of intense, focused hatred mortals simply did not live long enough to achieve. The man, in turn, smiled wide and patted the empty spot on the bench beside him.

With a glare that could have frozen the whole of Lake St. Clare, Estella turned on her heel and marched to her limo, slamming the door behind her. A second later, her car shot down the street after her sister's, passing the man on the bench so fast, the rush of wind sent his long hair whipping into his face. He brushed it back again with a grin and put out his hand to provide a landing spot for the pigeon who'd just flown up through the tiny gap in the skyway below.

"Well," he said as the bird settled on his fingers. "Isn't that interesting?"

The pigeon tilted its head inquisitively, but the green eyed man simply kissed its soft feathers and set the bird down on the bench beside him, freeing his hand to pull a phone out of his pocket. It was an old keyboard model from before the return of magic, a veritable antique without even the most basic AR, but the lack of modern accouterments didn't seem to bother him. He simply scrolled through the enormous contact list until he reached the Js, selected a name near the bottom, and began to type, humming the bridge of a song that wouldn't be composed for another ten years as his fingers moved unerringly over keys that had long since been worn blank.

***

"Come on," Julius muttered, tapping his foot as Lark's phone rang and rang and rang. When the shaman's voicemail kicked in, he hung up and started the cycle over. Again.

After ten calls failed to garner even one answer, he was forced to admit defeat. He didn't know if Lark was deliberately ignoring him or if the shaman was simply too drunk and/or stoned to answer his phone. Both were possible. Honestly, though, he wasn't even sure why he was bothering. It wasn't like Lark had given him a bad address on purpose. The shaman had probably just passed on the information Katya had given him, and no dragoness on the run would be stupid enough to give a human her actual location. The real question was, how stupid was Julius for thinking she had?

Pretty stupid, he decided, pacing back and forth on the cracked sidewalk. And dead. Very, very dead. It was almost midnight already. Even if he pushed Ian's deadline to the absolute limit, he had less than twenty-four hours to find a dragon who didn't want to be found in the DFZ. He wasn't sure he could pull that off even with unlimited money. On his current budget, it was downright impossible, but if he didn't get *something*, he was done for. So what was he going to—

"Julius?"

He stopped pacing with a jerk and looked up to see Marci standing tentatively on the curb a few feet away, her hands clasped in front of her. "Are you okay?" she asked. "You've been over here for a while."

Julius rubbed the back of his neck. He supposed she did deserve an explanation, especially since he wasn't going to be able to pay her the way things were headed, what with him being dead and all. Then again, who knew? Marci was clever and resourceful. Maybe she could help?

The idea of pulling a human he liked as much as Marci into his problems made Julius feel a little ill, but he didn't know what else to do. So, with a deep breath, he told her the truth. "I'm in trouble."

"I figured," she said with a sympathetic smile. "That parking deck was supposed to be your missing girl, wasn't it?"

Julius nodded. "If I don't find her by tomorrow, I..." *will be declared a failure and eaten.* "I won't get paid."

"Which means I won't get paid either," Marci finished, putting two and two together. "Okay, what are our options?"

He stared at her, astonished. "You're not mad?"

Marci shrugged. "Hazard of contract work. Sometimes things fall through, and getting mad about it doesn't do anyone any good. Besides, it's not like you're trying to screw me over, right?"

"Of course not," he said, horrified, which made her grin.

"See? Nothing to be mad about. I'd much rather spend my energy trying to save the job in any case. So, ideas?"

Julius didn't answer. He was too busy savoring the wonderful astonishment at being treated like a partner instead of an idiot and a failure. "I have several ideas," he said at last. "But they all require money."

"Most things do," she said with a sympathetic sigh. "What's our operating budget?"

"About two dollars."

Marci giggled. "Funny. Really, though, what is it?"

Julius shuffled his feet awkwardly. "I wasn't making a joke."

She froze, the grin vanishing from her face. "You weren't?"

He shook his head.

"You don't have any money?"

He shook his head again.

For several moments, Marci just stood there, mouth opening and closing like a fish. "But," she got out at last, "you were in Arbor Square. *Everyone* in Arbor Square has money!"

"I was just there to meet my brother to get this job," Julius said. "Come on, you didn't really think I belonged in a place like that, did you? I mean, *look* at me."

He waved his hand at his ratty T-shirt and jeans, and Marci began to sputter. "I thought you were wearing that *ironically!*" she cried. "You know, one of those 'I'm wearing comfortable clothes because I'm too cool to care how rich I am' guys." She covered her face with her hands. "I can't believe this. How were you planning to pay me?"

"After my brother paid me," he said. "I never meant for things to get this bad. This job was supposed to be over at the party!"

Marci flopped against the lamppost with a hopeless sound, and Julius felt all the warmth she'd just given him drain away.

"I'm sorry," he said softly. "I never intended to mislead you."

"I know, I know," she muttered, staring up at the dark. "It's just...this is always my luck, you know? Only I could bluff my way into one of the most exclusive restaurants in the DFZ and come out with the only client in the whole place who wasn't loaded." She shook her head with a bitter sigh before pushing off the streetlight. "Par for the course, I guess. Okay, sorry, pity party over. So how much money do you think we're going to need?"

Julius stared at her. "You're not leaving?"

She snorted. "Come on. Just because you aren't actually a secret millionaire doesn't mean I'm going to abandon you. First, we still have a contract, and second, you kind of saved my *life*. If I left you now, how would I live with myself? That said, of course, I don't actually have any idea what we're going to do. As you might have noticed, I haven't exactly had a lot of luck making quick cash in the DFZ."

Julius didn't have any immediate ideas either, but knowing that Marci wasn't going to throw him over made him more hopeful than he'd felt in years. He was trying to figure out a way to tell her as much that wouldn't make him sound like a desperate loser when his phone buzzed.

He'd actually forgotten he was holding the thing until it began to vibrate in his hand. For a soaring moment, he thought it was Lark calling him back, but when he glanced down at the AR, it wasn't a call at all. It was a message from the Unknown Caller.

J,

A little bird told me you could use some help, and since I am of an extremely Helpful Nature, I have sent some your way. No need to thank me, A Good Deed Is Its Own Reward. Also, I already cleaned out your room back home and sold everything to cover the costs. Family first!

Yours etc., B

His face must have looked awful by the end, because Marci's hands came up in her battle stance. "What?! What's wrong?"

"My brother is sending me some help," he said, reading the message again.

"Oh." Her arms fell back to their natural positions. "That's nice of him."

"Nice isn't the word I'd use," Julius grumbled. "My brother's a bit...eccentric. His idea of what's appropriate can be a little off." And dangerous, or obnoxious, or both. That said, Bob *had* given him a phone pre-loaded with money and IDs yesterday, which definitely counted as useful. Maybe lightning would strike twice?

He checked his balance, just in case, but it still read two dollars. Not money, then, but what else could Bob have meant by costs? And surely his brother hadn't been able to sell off *everything* in his room already. Julius had only been gone a day. He glanced back down at the call button. Maybe he should phone his mother's housekeeper and check?

Before he could do anything, though, an enormous crash echoed through the dark, making them both jump. It sounded like someone had dropped a dumpster from five stories up. For several seconds, all Julius could hear was the ringing in his ears, but then he caught the unmistakable scrape of claws on asphalt, followed by a loud and horribly familiar shout.

"*Julius?*"

Oh no, he thought, cringing. No, no, *no*. He was going to *kill* Bob.

"What is that?" Marci said, looking all around.

"The opposite of help," he growled, shoving his phone into his pocket. "Stay here, I'll be right back."

"But—"

"Stay here," he said again. "Please."

Marci did not look happy, but she did as he asked, standing right on the edge of the curb as Julius jogged across the street and around the edge of the parking deck into the alley where he'd heard the crash.

Sure enough, when he rounded the corner, a man was standing under the alley's lone working orange street light. He was exceptionally tall, almost six and a half feet, with a classically handsome face and military short black hair. He was pulling on a shirt when Julius spotted him, his bulging muscles flexing like he was a model in a protein shake commercial as he tugged the thin, tight cotton over his head. Thankfully, the bottom half of him was already clothed in dark jeans, though he'd probably only put those on first so he'd have somewhere to hang the enormous sword currently sheathed on his belt.

He must have heard Julius coming, because his bright green eyes locked on him as soon as his head was free of his shirt, and he lifted his sculpted chin in greeting. "'Sup?"

Julius covered his face with his hand. "Please," he groaned. "*Please* tell me you didn't just fly here."

"Only from the airport," the dragon said, leaning down to pull on his socks. "Cab fares in this place are murder."

He started shoving his feet into a pair of black motorcycle boots next, and Julius dropped his hands with a sigh, wondering why he'd expected anything different.

With shoulders like an orc linebacker and an air of absolute confidence that Julius would never in a million years be able to match, his brother Justin came from the opposite end of the Heartstriker gene pool. They shared the family basics—black hair, high cheekbones and, of course, the green eyes—but otherwise they could have been strangers. This was especially odd because Justin and Julius were full brothers, hatched from the same clutch only minutes apart. But where Julius had come out as the runt, Justin had shot straight to top, as evidenced by the sword at his hip.

The black-sheathed blade was a larger version of Chelsie's, one of five Fangs of the Heartstriker given only to Bethesda's deadliest weapons. But while Justin's battle prowess was unquestioned, Julius couldn't help wondering sometimes if the rest of his brain hadn't quite caught up yet.

"Justin," Julius said, as calmly as he could manage. "You can't just fly around in the DFZ. Do you *want* Chelsie to gut you?"

"She'd have to catch me first," his brother replied with a smug smile. "You look terrible, by the way."

Julius decided to ignore that comment. "What are you doing here? I thought you were in China."

"I was, but then I heard Mother kicked you out, so when Bob sent me a ticket to the DFZ, I thought I'd come lend you a hand."

Julius's stomach sank. "You heard about that in China?"

"*Everyone's* heard about it," Justin said. "There's actually a betting pool going for how long you'll last." He arched a dark eyebrow. "You know, a little gratitude wouldn't be out of order. I did just fly halfway around the world to come help you."

Julius sighed. "Thank you. But—"

"You're welcome," Justin said, slapping his hands together. "Now, who are we killing?"

Julius was opening his mouth to say they wouldn't be killing anyone when he heard soft, quick footsteps in the street behind him, and his blood went cold. *Oh no,* he thought as Justin's eyes darted to the mouth of the alley. Not *now.*

But, of course, Marci chose that moment to walk around the corner. She stopped with a gasp, her hands flying to her mouth just as Justin's fell to the hilt of his sword. For a second, Julius thought his brother was going to attack first and ask questions later, but Justin did nothing of the sort. He did something much worse.

"Well, well, well," he said an innuendo-laden voice loud enough to be heard for blocks. "Is that *your* human?"

And that was when Julius began praying that Chelsie *was* watching, because a quick death from behind was starting to sound very nice indeed.

Chapter 7

"**S**he's surprisingly hot," Justin went on, nodding in approval. "Good job, Julius. Didn't know you had it in you."

Julius flashed Marci an apologetic look before grabbing his brother and yanking him down with a strength he'd never known he had. "She's not *my* human," he whispered frantically. "She's *a* human, and she's helping me. She also doesn't know what we *are*."

Any sane dragon would have gotten the hint after that and shut up. Justin, of course, paid no attention whatsoever.

He pushed out of Julius's hold and walked down the alley, coming to a stop in front of Marci with his legs apart and his hands on his hips like a draconic Conan the Barbarian. "You, girl," he said. "What's your name?"

Marci shot a nervous glance at Julius, which he couldn't return thanks to the palm he was currently slapping against his forehead. "Um, I'm Marci Novalli."

Justin nodded like this was acceptable and stuck out his hand. "Justin, Knight of the Mountain and Fifth Blade of Bethesda. You know, you don't look half bad for a human."

"Thanks? I think?" Marci said, shaking Justin's offered hand like it was an unexploded land mine. "I'm guessing you're Julius's brother?"

"His *older* brother," Justin said pointedly.

"By two minutes," Julius snapped, cutting between them before this situation could finish going from bad to worse and move on to catastrophic. "Sorry, Marci, can I borrow Justin for a sec?"

She backed off at once, putting her hands up with clear relief. "All yours. Sorry I interrupted. I'm just going to go back to the car. You guys reconnect or whatever."

Justin watched her walk away with an appreciative ogle at her backside. "You have unexpectedly good taste," he said, turning back to Julius. "But do you really have time to be playing around with humans? Mother's going to eat you soon if you don't start showing some initiative."

"I'm working on it," Julius said. "And Marci is an integral part of that, which is why you need to *shut up* before you get her killed."

"What are you so worked up about? Lots of dragons have humans. Just keep her on a tight leash and you'll be fine."

Julius closed his eyes, wishing he could close his ears. This was *exactly* why his brother couldn't stay. Five minutes with him and Marci would have to be stupid not to guess the truth. Of course, given five minutes, Justin would probably manage to insult her so badly she'd be ready to turn them both in to Algonquin for the bounty. Julius half wanted to turn Justin in himself already, but while he wasn't feeling it at the moment, Justin was usually one of the few brothers he actually liked, which was why he decided to nip this in the bud as nicely as possible.

"Listen, Justin," he said in a calm, measured voice. "I really do appreciate you coming all this way to support me. It means a lot, but this isn't your kind of operation. I'm doing a delicate job for Ian, and—"

"What job?"

It would be more work to put Justin off than to tell him, so Julius quickly explained the situation with Svena and Katya, going to the shaman party, and how he'd come to be standing in front an empty commuter deck in the middle of the night.

"So let me get this straight," Justin said when he'd finished. "A human gave you a false address, and you let him get away with it?"

"It's not like that," Julius said quickly. "I don't think Lark did it on purpose. Katya probably just gave him a dummy address to keep people off her trail. She *is* on the run."

"No excuse," his brother growled, popping his knuckles. "He lied to us, he has to pay. I say we go back there and squeeze him until something useful pops out."

"I'm not doing that!"

Justin gave him a disgusted look. "Why? Because it's not *nice*?"

"Because it would be pointless," Julius said. "Look, if Lark was trying to trick me, he's long gone by now, and if he wasn't, then he doesn't know anything more than he's already said. Either way, hunting him down isn't going to help. We don't need violence, we need a professional who knows what they're doing. There are guys who make their living tracking people who don't want to be found. I know one, actually."

"That's convenient," Justin said. "What's his clan?"

"He's not in a clan. He's human, one of my old gaming buddies."

Justin rolled his eyes. "What is it with you and humans?"

"I *like* humans," Julius reminded him. "Anyway, he might be able to get us a lead on Katya using the picture Lark gave me. I just need to get some money together for his fee and—"

"Wait, wait, wait," Justin said, putting up his hands. "You're going to *pay* him?"

Julius blinked. "Of course. He's a professional."

"He's a *human*," his brother snapped. "Humans serve us. Get that through your skull. You're a Heartstriker, a *dragon*, an ancient and fearsome predator. You should be making people fall at your feet for the honor of doing your bidding, not *paying* them, and definitely not letting them lie to you without repercussions." He turned away with a huff that sent a thin line of black smoke curling from between his lips. "This is exactly why Mother kicked you out, you know."

"Well, what else am I supposed to do?" Julius cried. "Fly around bellowing for Katya to come out and fight me?"

"You could go back to that party and start shaking down humans," Justin said. "She's supposed to be with an alligator shaman, right? Someone there knows him, so stop being a pushover and go make them talk."

Julius paused. Going after the alligator shaman wasn't such a bad idea, actually. Still. "I'm not going to interrogate a bunch of drunk mages," he growled. "No one's going to be intimidated by a *sealed* dragon any—"

A loud, pained squeal shot through the air, making both brothers jump. Justin recovered immediately, but Julius was still reeling when he whirled around to see Marci standing beside her car. Her right arm was out in front of her, like she'd just finished throwing an underhanded pitch, and the first bracelet on her wrist was glowing like a spotlight in the dark. That was all Julius caught before he started to run.

He got halfway across the street before he remembered to drop his speed to a believably human rate. He still made it to Marci's side in seconds, hands up and ready to take on whatever it was they were fighting. But there were no goons waiting in the shadows when he reached her, no armed thugs threatening to attack. Instead, Marci jogged over to the curb and bent down to grab something black, furry, and unmoving out of the storm drain.

"What is that?"

The sharp question made him jump, and Julius looked up to see Justin standing right beside him. Naturally, he wasn't winded at all from the run, though he did look a little disgusted by the thing in Marci's hand. For once, the brothers were in agreement. From what Julius could make out, it looked like Marci was holding a rat the size of a terrier, but no rat he'd ever seen had fangs like that. Or five beady eyes, all of which were still twitching as Marci hoisted the thing aloft like a prize fish.

"It's a crater vole," she announced proudly. "I've never seen one this big!"

Julius recoiled in horror. "And you're *touching* it? I thought they were poisonous."

"Oh, very," Marci said. "Why do you think I roasted it first? Well, microwaved, to be precise." She nodded to the first bracelet on her wrist, a blue plastic ring which was still steaming slightly. "The

Thaumaturgical code of safety and ethics forbids the use of magical combustion in urban environments, which eliminates most combat fire spells. So I created a variation on the college staple 'No-Microwave Microwave' spell that does basically the same thing, only without the actual fire part."

Julius gaped at her. *"Why?"*

"Because the microwave spell is horribly underutilized as a mere cooking charm," she replied authoritatively. "As you see, the weaponization possibilities of a spell that instantly boils water particles *inside* organic matter are potentially—"

"No, no, I understand that part," he said. "I meant, why did you randomly kill a crater vole?"

Marci blinked at him. "For the bounty, of course. Crater voles are an invasive, non-native species. DFZ Animal Control pays three dollars for every one you bring in."

"Hold up," Justin said, stabbing his finger at the smoking mutant rat in her hands. "You killed that thing for *three dollars*?"

"Hey, three dollars is three dollars," Marci said, hefting the heavy carcass as she walked back to her car.

Justin stomped after her. "But three dollars isn't even worth the drive to turn it in. Why not go after the bigger bounties?"

"Because I don't want to die," she answered, grabbing a trash bag out of her trunk and shoving the dead vole inside. "And maybe three dollars isn't worth it to *you*, but when you're broke, you can't afford to leave money just waddling around on the side of the road."

Julius heard the rumble of his brother's reply, but he wasn't actually paying attention to the argument anymore. He was too distracted by the storm drain Marci had yanked the crater vole out of. Specifically, he was staring at the deep cuts in the pavement around the drain's metal grate.

From across the street, you couldn't see them at all. Standing directly over the storm drain, however, the grooves were impossible to miss, and obviously man-made. This was no natural cracking. Someone had deliberately cut a thin line around the edge of the drainage grate with a cement saw. It wasn't until he'd squatted down for a better look, though, that Julius understood why.

"Marci," he called. "Can you come over here, please?"

He heard a trunk slam, and then the loud slap of Marci's boots as she stomped over. "I can't *believe* that jerk is related to you. And where does he get off wearing a *sword*? What century does he think this is?"

Julius wasn't touching that question with a ten foot pole, so he changed the subject instead, pointing down at the cut in the pavement and the thin copper strip covered with etched markings he'd spotted at the bottom. "Is that a ward?"

Tirade forgotten, Marci squatted down beside him, squinting through what Julius suddenly realized was probably very bad light for a human. "I think it is," she said. "But it's a really weird one."

"A shaman ward?" he prompted, holding his breath.

She nodded. "Without question. No Thaumaturge would be caught dead putting down notation that sloppy."

He could have hugged her. "This is it!"

She gave him a strange look. "This is what?"

"Lark didn't give me the wrong address," he said, pointing at the storm drain, which was located directly in front of the parking deck, right where Lark's address said it would be. "They're not in the Underground, they're *underground*. The shamans we're looking for are in the sewers! Right here!"

Now that he said it, it all made perfect sense. Where else would an alligator shaman live in a city like this? Lark had even said they were living in the pipes. If that was right, then maybe Katya *was* here. Maybe he wasn't dead after all!

"Why are we staring at a drain?"

Julius jumped at the sound of Justin's voice, but even that couldn't bring down his newfound good mood. "Justin, look!" he said, hopping to his feet. "We found them!"

Justin gave the old grate a distasteful look. "The crater voles?"

"*No*, the shamans. The people we're looking for." He moved closer, dropping his voice to a whisper only dragon ears could hear. "The ones Katya's hiding with."

Justin's eyebrows shot up. "That was easy," he said, breaking into a grin. "How do you want to do this?"

Something about the way he said that made Julius decidedly nervous. "What do you mean?"

Justin heaved an enormous sigh and wrapped his arm around Julius's neck, dragging him away from Marci. Normally, Julius would have been grateful for his brother's unusual thoughtfulness in not blurting things out where she could hear. Right now, though, he was too busy trying not to choke to pay proper attention.

"What are you doing?" he gasped when his brother finally released him.

"Keeping you from screwing up," Justin snapped. "You can't go in the front door. That's where all the traps are."

Julius stared at his brother in astonishment. "*You're* worried about traps?"

"No, but I'm not the one who's sealed, am I?" He crossed his massive arms, looking Julius up and down. "This isn't some mortal you're chasing, idiot. You can't just show up at a dragon's stronghold and expect to negotiate like equals. She's not going to listen to a thing you say while she's in her lair, surrounded by her troops."

If this had been a dragoness like Svena, or any of their own sisters, that would have been a good point, but Julius didn't think his brother had the right of it this time. "I don't think it's like that," he said. "We're not assaulting the Three Sister's ice palace. The humans down there probably don't even know Katya's a dragon."

"That doesn't mean she's not going to act like one," Justin said, glaring over his shoulder at Marci, who'd been steadily edging closer to them in a not-so-subtle attempt to eavesdrop. When she got the hint and backed off again, he continued. "Look, it's very simple. All we have to do is sneak in and take out her humans before she knows what's up. Then, while she's reeling, we take her down. Once we've got our boots on her neck, she'll do whatever we want."

Julius suddenly felt queasy. It wasn't that he thought Justin's plan wouldn't work, but taking out a commune full of the sort of mages who hung out with Lark felt…wrong. And then there was Katya herself, who was on the run from her clan, which was to say, ruthless hunters who thought like Justin. Two dragons busting into her safe haven to put their boots on her neck would terrify her, and no one fought harder than a cornered, terrified dragon. That would be a real shame, too, because given the humans she'd chosen to hang out with, Julius had the feeling Katya wasn't a fighter. He had no idea how to explain all that to Justin in a way his brother would understand, though, so he tried another approach.

"I don't think we need to do that," he said, keeping his voice reasonable, rational, and completely without challenge. "The whole reason Ian picked me for this job was precisely because I wasn't someone Katya would consider a threat. If we go in guns blazing—"

"We don't have guns."

Julius sighed. "Fine, if we go in like *dragons*, she's just going to bolt, and then we'll have to hunt her down all over again. But if we go in nicely and give her the chance to see us as allies instead of enemies, we might not have to fight at all."

Justin stared at him. "Really? That's your plan? Talking?"

Not knowing how else to answer, Julius nodded, and his brother threw back his head with a hiss.

"You know, Julius, this is your entire problem. You waste all your time thinking up ways not to fight instead of ways to win. Let's say

94

Katya does agree to chit-chat. It isn't like she's going to just change her mind and go back to her family because you ask. What were you going to do then, genius? Knock her on the head and wave goodbye to her mages on your way out?"

Julius had to fold his fingers in a fist to keep them from going to the chain in his pocket. That *had* been the plan, more or less, but hearing Justin spell it out like that, especially after his own arguments for negotiation, made him feel like a big fat hypocrite. His brother must have seen it, too, because Justin went straight for the kill.

"I didn't come all the way over here to help you play nice," he growled. "If this job was actually about getting the Three Sisters' runaway back, they would have sent someone competent. But they didn't, because it isn't. It's a test. A challenge to see if there's actually a dragon under that scrawny frame of yours, and I'm here to make sure you don't screw it up."

Julius swallowed. "I know that. But I'm supposed to do what Ian—"

"Screw Ian," Justin snapped. "He's using you. So forget him, and forget his stupid plan. You don't show Mother how great a dragon you can be by exploiting the fact that no one thinks you're a threat. You need to *be* a threat, so here's what we're going to do. We're going to walk down the street to the next storm drain over and go in from there. We'll find a way into Katya's hiding place from the side, where her defenses aren't as strong. Once we're in, we'll smash her humans before they know what's up and force her to submit. When it's over, Ian will have his lost dragon back, the Three Sisters will be reminded that Heartstrikers are not tools, and you'll come out looking like a dragon to be feared at last. Trust me, Mother will love it."

Julius had no doubt that Bethesda would, in fact, *adore* such a blatant show of ruthless force. There was a reason Justin was one of her favorites. Julius, on the other hand, didn't like it at all. "I don't think—"

"I don't care," Justin said. "It was your stupid way of thinking that got you into this mess in the first place. My way is going to get you out. Do you want your wings back or not?"

Julius closed his eyes with a silent curse. This whole thing felt like it was spinning out of control. Much as he hated to admit it, though, Justin did have a point, and it wasn't like Svena's plan to trick and chain her sister was any better. Seeing that, why not trade a distasteful plan that used him like a tool for one that at least made him look fearsome and ruthless in his mother's eyes? Other than the part where he didn't particularly want to be fearsome or ruthless, or kill a bunch of human mages who probably had no idea that the woman they were protecting was actually a dragon, or—

"You're taking way too long to think about this," Justin said, slapping him on the back hard enough to bruise. "Come on, let's go."

He walked away before Julius could protest, marching back to the car where Marci, who'd apparently given up trying to overhear, was attempting to stuff a few more things into her already massively over-packed shoulder bag. Julius followed a second later, doing his best to reason away his rapidly ballooning sense of impending doom.

So Justin had bulled him into doing something he didn't want to do. What else was new? His brother meant well, and he really did seem to be genuinely trying to help, which was more than Julius could say for the rest of his family. The fact that his plan didn't feel right didn't mean a thing. Nothing properly draconic ever felt right to Julius. But however bad Justin's plan to make him look like a ruthless dragon seemed, it couldn't possibly be worse than getting eaten by your mother for not being one, right?

That logic sounded solid in his head, but Julius still couldn't shake the feeling that he was about to do something he'd regret. A feeling that only got worse when Justin started jogging down the street toward the next closest storm drain, yelling over his shoulder for them to get a move on.

***

"I want it stated," Marci said, grasping her bag tight as she stared down the gaping hole beneath the storm drain's cover, "just for the record, that this is a terrible idea."

"Duly noted," Julius muttered, peering into the dark in an attempt to see the water he could hear rushing below them.

"I mean it," she went on. "I don't care what your idiot brother says. Going into the DFZ sewers is a stupid, reckless, horribly dangerous thing to do under any circumstances, but going down at *night* is just suicidal. Haven't you ever watched *Sewer Hunters: DFZ?*"

Julius hadn't, but he could guess well enough. "Let's just get this over with quickly."

"Why'd you let him talk you into this, anyway? This is your job, not his."

Julius didn't know how to reply to that in a way Marci could understand. *He's bigger than me*, or *he's what I'm supposed to be* weren't explanations that would fly with a human. In the end, he settled for a half truth. "It's just easier to go along when he gets like this. Justin's very stubborn."

"*I'm* stubborn," Marci said with a snort. "He's a runaway freight train."

"We'll be fine," Julius insisted, albeit with more confidence than he felt. "You're a great mage, and Justin's tougher than he looks. Also, we're not going into the sewers. We're going into the storm water system, which should be pretty clean thanks to all of Algonquin's water regulations. And anyway, it's not like we have to go far." He nodded back toward the warded storm drain, only half a block away. "Surely we can survive walking a hundred feet underground."

"Well, I still think it's a stupid risk," Marci said. "There's a reason all the DFZ's sewer work is done by automated drones. Magic rises from the ground, and thanks to Algonquin, Detroit's ground has more of it any other city on the planet. Not all of that power is friendly. Why else do you think everyone who can afford to lives up on the skyways?"

Julius could think of several reasons, but he was tired of arguing. "You don't have to come with us if you don't want to."

"No way," she said, shaking her head. "I said I'd stick with you and I will. I just want to get all this out now so I can say 'I told you so' later when we get eaten by a Balrog."

Despite everything that had happened, Julius couldn't help smiling at that. "I can't believe you know what a Balrog is."

She gave him an arch look. "Who doesn't? I mean, really."

"A ball-what?"

Julius and Marci both turned to see Justin standing behind them, his hand resting casually on the hilt of his sword. "If you nerds are done yakking, can we get a move on? I've got other things to do tonight."

Marci's face pulled into a snarl, but before she could rip into Justin as she so clearly wanted to, the dragon jumped into the storm drain and vanished. A few seconds later, a loud splash echoed up the pipe as he hit the water below.

"Drop's only about twelve feet," he called. "Hop on down."

By this point, the look on Marci's face had gone from deadly to deathly. "I can't hop that."

"Neither can I," Julius said, pointing at the metal ladder that was bolted to the side of the drain pipe. "There."

The sight of the slimy rungs only made Marci's eyes go wider, and for a second, Julius was sure she was going to bolt. Instead, she took a deep breath of the stale, Underground air and sat down on the drain's edge, slowly feeling out the ladder with her feet. Too slowly for Justin, apparently.

"Get a move on, woman!" he bellowed up the pipe.

"I'll move when I'm ready!" she bellowed back, clutching the ladder for dear life.

"I'm very sorry about him," Julius said quickly. "He doesn't mean anything by it. My brother's just a jerk sometimes."

"Only sometimes?" Marci grumbled, glaring down the pipe at Justin's head like she wanted to drop something heavy on it.

In the end, though, they made it down, landing safely in a cement spillway that was much larger than Julius had expected. The ceiling was high enough that even Justin could stand up straight, and since it was the end of summer, the water flow was barely more than a trickle, leaving plenty of dry space on the sides to walk. But despite the roomy proportions and the Lady of the Lakes' strict water regulations, it was still a storm drain. The runoff water might have been relatively cleaner than in other cities, but it still stank, and every surface was covered in bugs and black slime mold glistening wetly in the light of the LED flashlight Marci had pulled out of her bag.

"Lovely," she said, using the light to send the bugs skittering before training the beam on Justin's back, already twenty feet ahead of them down the tunnel. "Does that man even know the meaning of the word patience?"

"If he does, I've never seen it," Julius said, catching Marci when her foot slipped on the spillway's slick floor. She flashed him a quick smile that made him feel slightly less guilty about getting her involved in all this and started carefully making her way after Justin.

"You know," she said, stepping high over a puddle where the trickle of water had caught and pooled on a knot of trash, "there's no guarantee we'll be able to get into whatever this place is from down here. If I was living in the storm water system, I'd consider the below-ground entrances much more dangerous than the street level and ward them accordingly, if I didn't just brick them over."

Julius nudged a rat skeleton out of their way. "Are the things down here really that bad?"

"Not all of them," Marci replied. "But think of it like this. The DFZ is full of magic, and magic attracts magical creatures. That wouldn't be so bad if the DFZ Underground wasn't also one of the world's densest human populations, but it is, which means all those magical animals are competing with people for space. Usually, this is where the government would step in and balance things out, but this is the Detroit Free Zone. Animal control is an outsourced, free market system, just like everything else."

"You mean the bounties?"

She nodded. "People pay the Animal Control office, and they pay freelancers per head—small amounts for minor annoyances, and big pay outs for the really dangerous stuff. It's not actually a bad system most of the time, but the whole thing breaks down when you get into areas where the cost and trouble of killing the animal is more than the price you get for its head."

"I see," Julius said. "So the hunters don't come down here because it's too much risk for the reward, and as a result, the pipes have become a safe haven for magical nuisance animals."

"Bingo. It's like roaches running under your fridge because they don't want get stepped on. Only these roaches are enormous, man-eating, and sometimes fire-breathing."

He grimaced. "What a lovely picture."

"Welcome to the DFZ!" Marci said with a laugh, hopping over a particularly smelly pile of washed up plastic bags.

Julius was digging out his phone to look for pictures of the sort of stuff they could expect down here when the slime-coated pipe they'd been following suddenly merged into a much larger spillway that was actually filled with water. Fortunately, some long-dead contractor had thought to build a metal walkway into the wall above the waterline. Justin was already on it, perched on the edge of the rusting metal like a giant, overly aggressive bird. He pulled Marci up one-handed when she came into arm's reach, and then did the same for Julius, plucking him off the ground as easily as he'd pull a weed.

"We have a problem," he announced once they were both safely above the water. "The mages we're after should be straight ahead."

"And?" Julius prompted.

His brother's answer was to point further down the way they'd been walking, which, thanks to the T-intersection of the pipes, meant he was now pointing straight at a cement wall.

"Oh," Julius said. "That *is* a problem."

"I'd cut through it," Justin said. "But it looks load-bearing, and you two are kind of squishy. We need to find another way around."

Julius sighed and glanced down at his phone, but the AR display came up blank. Apparently, even the DFZ's municipal wireless couldn't reach all the way down here, and GPS completely useless when there was twelve feet of pavement and dirt between you and the satellite signal. In any case, the map would have only shown roads, not the water system below them. Julius was about to use this as an excuse to tell his brother they should call the whole thing off and go knock on the front door like he'd originally suggested when Marci spoke up.

"I have an idea."

Justin and Julius both turned to see her digging through her bag.

"We're looking for a commune of mages, right?" she asked, handing her flashlight to Julius.

"Right," he said slowly, taking the light.

"Well, lots of mages means lots of concentrated magic, and if it's magic we're looking for, I think we could try *this*." She pulled her hand out of her bag with a flourish, holding up the golden, grapefruit-sized orb Julius had seen her examining in the car after his dust-up with Chelsie. Back then, it had glittered like a golden ornament. Now, it sparkled like the noon sun on a waterfall in the brilliant glare of the LED flashlight, throwing little golden dots all over the waterway's dark stained walls.

"What is that?" Justin asked. "A golden disco ball?"

"It's a Kosmolabe," Marci said, her voice giddy with excitement. "An ancient tool used by mages, the *first* mages from back before magic faded, to detect and identify other dimensions."

"Why would we need that?" Justin said with a snort. "We're already in the right dimension."

Marci must have been amazingly excited, because she didn't even look annoyed. "Ah," she said. "But Kosmolabes find those other dimensions by detecting their ambient magic. It's been theorized for decades now that a properly trained mage, given enough power, could open a portal to another dimension. No one's actually tried it yet, though, because there's no way to know what would be waiting on the other side. The wall between our world and the other planes is simply too thick for us to see through. We could be opening a hole into the vacuum of space, or into a star, or into a completely new environment we can't even imagine. That's where the Kosmolabe comes in."

She stuck the ball directly under the flashlight, making it shine painfully bright. "You see the pattern on the gold leaf under the glass? It acts as an amplifier, reacting to the natural vibrations of magic on a molecular level that's supposedly a thousand times more sensitive than anything a human can feel. Sort of like a compass, only the needle points at magic instead of North. I've been dying to try it out!"

"Uh-huh," Justin said, crossing his arms over his chest. "Still waiting to hear why I should care."

"You should *care* because we're looking for a heavily warded community of shamans," she said hotly, leaving the implied *you moron* thankfully unvoiced. "And if the theories are correct and the Kosmolabe *is* like a compass, then that sort of magical density should act like a magnet."

"I see," Julius said. "They'll pull the needle right to them. That way, even if we have to go off course, we'll always know which direction the mages are in."

"Yes, *thank* you," Marci said, giving him a beaming smile. "At least someone here gets it."

Justin rolled his eyes, but Julius moved in for a better look at the golden ball. This close, he could actually see the points in the tiny golden patterns twitching, exactly like little needles. "That's amazing. I've never heard of a Kosmolabe."

"They're incredibly rare," Marci said. "Even back when mages were thought to be common, not many places had the sophistication needed to make one, and once the magic dried up, the knowledge was lost all together." Her face fell. "Most magical learning was, actually. The only reason we know dimensional connection is even possible is because Kosmolabes exist. We're only beginning to rediscover just how much we lost during the magical drought, and we still don't know why the magic went away in the first place. Thankfully, we have our ancestor's tools to help us figure everything out again." She smiled down at the golden ball in her arms. "This one's a Persian Kosmolabe. They're supposed to be the most accurate, and the most delicate. It's a miracle this one survived so perfectly intact. It might just be the last fully functional Kosmolabe remaining in the whole world."

"Uh huh," Justin said. "So why do you have it?"

Marci jerked at the question, then she relaxed, shrugging with the sort of careless flippancy that was the hallmark of someone about to tell a whopping lie. "My dad gave it to me. Anyway, like Julius said, this Kosmolabe should be able to guide us right to our target. Once I figure out how to use it, of course."

"You mean you haven't tried it yet?"

Marci lifted her head high. "Well, *obviously* I haven't had the chance to test its ability to find missing mage colonies, but there's no reason it shouldn't work." She looked down, peering into the golden patterns like she was trying to read her future in a crystal ball. "Actually, I think I've got something already. Follow me."

She got to her feet and set off down the walkway, her boots clacking on the metal grate. When Julius stood up to follow, though, Justin grabbed his shoulder.

"You sure about this?"

"No," Julius said. "But coming down here was your brilliant idea, remember?"

"I'm not talking about the sewers. I'm talking about the part where your human just lied to us."

Julius blinked. He hadn't actually thought Justin would pick up on that. His brother didn't usually do subtleties, but then, Marci was a pretty awful liar.

"She probably only lied because you asked her such a nosy question," he said. "Anyway, it's not my business where she got her Kosmolabe. All I care about is how Marci does her job for me, and so far, she's been excellent. When it comes to magic, I trust her completely."

His brother snorted. "You're gonna get yourself killed thinking like that. Blind faith makes a terrible leader."

"It's not blind faith," Julius said. "I trust Marci. She's my…"

Justin went after his hesitation like a bull after a red flag. "Your what?"

"I trust her," Julius said again.

Justin crossed his arms over his chest. "Why?"

Because she was his friend, and because she trusted him back. But Justin was too much of a dragon to understand that, so Julius said nothing, which of course, his brother took entirely the wrong way.

"Oh, no," he groaned. "You're not having a thing with her, are you?"

"Of course not," Julius snapped. Not that having a thing with Marci would be *bad*, but… "I just trust her, okay? Leave it alone."

He stomped away, leaving his brother to follow. For a moment, the metal walkway was silent, and then, with a long sigh, Justin jogged after him. His brother quickly matched and then beat his pace, leaving Julius to run alone behind him through the dark.

***

Thirty minutes later, the Kosmolabe had led them up, down, and over more disgusting, slime-covered, bug-riddled pipes and tunnels than Julius ever wanted to see again in his life. Even Justin was starting to look a little green. Marci, however, was practically skipping in delight, all her earlier fear completely replaced by the dazzling sparkle of the Kosmolabe.

"It works!" she cried yet again, nuzzling the golden ball with her nose. "I knew you would work, you beautiful darling!"

"Works nothing," Justin snarled, shaking something unmentionable off the toe of his boot. "We've been walking for half an hour, and we still haven't seen so much as a Keep Out sign."

"It works perfectly well," Marci said. "It's not the Kosmolabe's fault your mages decided to hide in the one drain that apparently doesn't connect to any of the others."

"But why do we keep going *down*?" Julius asked, stepping over a stagnant puddle. "It would be one thing if we were going in circles around a fixed point, but we're not. We just keep heading lower."

Marci shrugged. "That's where the signal goes." She tapped her heel on the dank cement floor. "There's an enormous magical concentration right below us. It has to be our mages. Nothing natural could generate pressure like that. I mean, just look at it."

She held the Kosmolabe out for them to see, but while the gold leaf flecks were indeed all waving like tiny flags in a storm, they didn't seem to be waving in any particular direction. Julius imagined it would look different if he focused on seeing the magic instead of the physical reality, but since physical reality was the one that was going to soak him with disgusting water if he slipped, he kept his attention on the real world.

"Okay," he said with a sigh. "So we're closing in. What's the plan when we get there?"

He directed the question at Justin, partially because he needed to know, and partially to prevent his brother from snipping at Marci again. He'd taken to playing peace-keeper for the last quarter hour just so he wouldn't have to hear them bicker, and he'd quickly discovered that the key to keeping harmony between his mage and his brother was to keep each of them focused on their respective jobs. Fortunately, both Justin and Marci were highly distractable when it came to their areas of expertise.

"Recon comes first," Justin said, drumming his fingers on his sword hilt. "We need to know what we're up against. Once we've got that, we make a battle plan from the information and proceed from there." He glanced back at Julius. "I'll do the actual fighting, of course. The way you're panting like an old woman, you'd probably just give yourself a heart attack."

"I am not panting like an old woman!" Julius protested, albeit breathlessly. This hike through the pipes had been a lot more exercise than he was used to. "I'm just a bit out of shape."

"I can't tell you ever had a shape to start with," his brother said, giving him a caustic look. "Seriously, what happened to you? You used to be the fastest of all of us, but I think even Jessica could run circles around you now. Did you completely stop training when you exiled yourself to your room?"

More or less, Julius thought with a sigh. He'd hadn't liked combat training even back when he'd been relatively good at it, and once he'd turned seventeen and his clutch had been declared ready to enter the world, he'd seen no reason to continue. This was especially true living at home since the nature of combat training meant it had to be done in the same gym used by the exact hyper-competitive, aggressive older siblings he'd hidden in his room to *avoid*. Before he could think of a more flattering way to explain his lapse to Justin, Marci's voice rang out down the tunnel.

"Found it!"

Justin was moving at once, racing down the pipe and around the corner Marci had turned. Julius followed hot on his heels... and nearly crashed into him when he rounded the corner to find both Justin and Marci standing right on the other side. They were perfectly still, staring at what appeared to be a black wall. A second later, though, Julius saw it wasn't actually a wall at all. It was a precipice.

Beyond the cement lip, the sewer fell away into a space so huge, Marci's flashlight couldn't penetrate the darkness to find the edges. Julius couldn't even guess how big the room beyond must be, but what really bothered him was the smell. The air here was still, far too still for such a large space, but the draft that did reach him had a cold, oily thickness to it that he didn't like at all.

"What's down there?" he asked, covering his nose.

"No idea," Marci said, glancing at the golden ball in her hands. "But the Kosmolabe says our target is dead ahead."

She pointed straight down into the inky dark, and suddenly, Julius was more certain than ever that this was not something they should be doing. "I—"

"There's a ladder right here," Justin interrupted, reaching out to grab the condensation-beaded metal ladder bolted to the wall beside the ledge. "Let's go."

Julius grabbed his brother's sleeve. "I don't think we should go down there," he whispered, deliberately pitching his voice too low for Marci's ears. "I don't like the smell of this place."

"You don't like anything," Justin said. "It's part of being a wuss."

Julius ignored the insult and tightened his grip. "I mean I *really* don't like it." Even just standing on the edge, he could feel the strange, oily power of the darkness below coating his lungs with every breath. "We shouldn't do this."

His brother smacked his hand away. "Enough. Stop being an embarrassment and come on." With that, Justin grabbed the metal ladder with one hand and swung out, pivoting like a hinge to land on the nearest rung. The moment he was steady, he clamped the insoles of both his boots against the ladder's side rails and let go, sliding down the ladder into the blackness.

Marci watched him vanish with a look of grudging respect. "Fearless, isn't he?" she muttered, stowing the Kosmolabe back in her bag.

"I think it's more that his arrogance has created a shell so thick, no fear can get through," Julius replied, reaching out to grab the disgustingly slick, cold ladder. "Let's get this over with."

It took them forever to reach the bottom. Not because they had particularly far to go—the seemingly endless drop ended up being only about thirty feet—but because Marci's pace down the ladder was only slightly faster than glacial.

Julius didn't blame her in the least. This place looked like a pit into the abyss even to his eyes, so he couldn't imagine what it must look like for her. It didn't help that the ladder's metal rungs were strangely pitted, like they'd been etched with a strong corrosive. Some rungs had actually rotted through completely, forcing them to cling to the ladder's edge and slid down to the next solid foothold. But though Marci's breathing sped up to almost hyperventilating every time she had to skip a step, she didn't complain, and she didn't stop.

By the time they finally reached the bottom, Julius had decided he was going to regain his ability to fly if it killed him. To add insult to injury, the climb hadn't even gotten them anywhere. The ladder let out on a wide cement platform beside what looked like an artificial underground lake. Justin, who'd gotten there way ahead of them, was already pacing the edge, his growling audible even in his human form. "There's nothing here!"

"This must be the spillway overflow," Julius said, shining Marci's flashlight, which he'd carried down the ladder in his teeth, directly into the murky water in a futile attempt to see how deep it went. "Somewhere for all the excess water in the system to collect until it can be pumped out and treated."

"I don't care what it is!" Justin yelled. "It's not mages. That stupid Cosmonaut led us to a dead end!"

"*Kosmolabe*," Marci corrected sharply, snatching the aforementioned golden ball out of her bag again. "And it's *not* a dead end. According to this, our mages are right there."

She pointed at the water, and Justin threw up his hands. "What? Are you saying they've got a low-rent Atlantis down there or something?"

Marci made an irritated sound. "I *meant* on another level."

"I don't think there is another level," Julius said softly. "If this is where the water's resting, then this is probably as low as it goes."

"Well, that doesn't make any sense at all," Marci said, walking toward the water's edge with a huff. "Let me look."

Julius caught her sleeve before she'd taken two steps. Now that they'd reached the bottom of the pit, the cold, oily pressure was stronger than ever. He wasn't quite sure if it was the natural magic of this particular place or something more sinister, but there was a lot of it, and he didn't want any of them getting closer than was absolutely necessary.

"Come on," he said, tugging Marci gently back toward the ladder. "Let's get out of—"

"Incoming!"

Julius fell into an instinctive crouch, while Marci jumped a full foot in the air. They both whirled around to see Justin standing at the lake's edge with his sword in his hands, and Julius's breath caught. He'd only seen a Fang of the Heartstriker out of its sheath once before in his life, and never up close. He didn't have a chance to gawk, though, because at that moment, the water in front of Justin exploded.

Chapter 8

His first thought was that a bomb had gone off. The lake, which up to this point had been silent and smooth as a polished stone, erupted like a volcano, sending water surging up in long, black streams. It wasn't until the streams opened their mouths to reveal perfectly circular rings of razor-sharp teeth that latched on to his brother, however, that Julius realized what was actually going on.

"Justin!"

But Justin was already sweeping the curved, wickedly sharp blade of the Fang of the Heartstriker down, slicing through the mass of black, wiggling shapes like they were made of tofu. The toothed heads kept biting even after he'd separated them from their bodies, though, so Justin was forced to retreat, jumping back to where Julius and Marci were sheltered against the wall.

"What the—" His words cut off in a bellow as he ripped a clamped jaw off his arm. *"What's with the snakes?"*

"They're not snakes," Julius said, leaning over to look at the head in his brother's bloody hands before Justin flung it away. "I think they're sea lampreys."

"Ugh," Marci said. "You mean those things with the flat mouths and the rings of teeth that latch on to you and suck your organs out?"

"I never heard of them sucking organs out," he said as he helped his brother pry another severed head—which did indeed have a hinged jaw that opened to form a perfectly flat, round ring of sharp teeth—off his leg. "They're an invasive species to the Great Lakes. I'd thought Algonquin had kicked them all out, but clearly these found a way back in." He grimaced at the basketball-sized head in his hands and tossed it back into the churning water. "They're not normally this big, though."

Marci gave him a funny look. "Are you a lamprey fan or something?"

"I studied them in my New Ecosystems of the Great Lakes class," Julius explained. When this only seemed to make her more confused, he added, "I have a bachelor's degree in Applied Ecology from NYU Online."

Marci's mouth fell open. "You're an *ecologist?*"

"Try professional student," Justin said with a snort, brushing the blood off his body like another man might brush off dirt. "If it's online, undergrad, and useless, Julius has it. He also has degrees in Pop Culture, Art History, and Accounting."

"Accounting's not useless," Marci said.

Justin ripped the final lamprey head off his shoulder. "It is if you don't have any accounts."

"I like learning things," Julius said irritably, though that was only a half truth. He *did* find school interesting, but the sad reality was that online classes and gaming had been the only things that kept him sane and connected to the outside world during the years he'd spent hiding from his family's plots. Also, being in school had been a great way to keep his mother off his back, at least until she'd realized he was studying things that interested him instead of properly draconic topics like how to exploit the legal system or become a titan of international finance. "Anyway, that doesn't matter. What I want to know is why there's a lake full of super-sized lampreys below Detroit."

"Well, if there was a lake of super-sized lampreys anywhere, it would be here," Marci said. "This place is Ground Zero for weird."

She crouched down beside one of the black, slimy bodies Justin had severed. Even without its head, the snake-like corpse was easily as long as she was tall, its slick, muscular flesh barely dimpling when Marci poked it. "They must have gotten washed into the storm water system at some point, and then the magic down here caused them to change." She wrinkled her nose. "It *is* pretty thick."

'Pretty thick' didn't begin to describe the cold, pressurized magic Julius could feel pushing down on them from all directions. "I told you we should have turned around."

Marci shrugged. "Well, at least this explains why the Kosmolabe led us here. A lake full of magically altered wildlife would definitely account for the blip I was seeing." She looked around at the bodies littering the cement floor. "I wonder if they're worth anything?"

"Would you stop talking about the stupid lampreys?" Justin growled, flinging the blood off his sword with a flick of his wrist. "We're not down here for the fishing. Now let's go find those mages for real before we waste any more— OW!"

His cry was accompanied by a loud *whack* as he slapped his hand against to the back of his neck. *"They spit at me!"* he roared, whirling around to face the still-roiling water.

Julius was opening his mouth to inform his brother that lampreys didn't spit when he saw the streak of smoking black bile coating the back of Justin's neck. A second lamprey broke the water as he watched, lifting its head above the surface just long enough to spit another line of burning goo at Justin's shoulder.

His brother ducked just in time. "Oh, that is *it!*" he bellowed, brandishing his sword at the water. "I'm going to eat every last one of you slimy bastards!"

"Justin!" Julius yelled, grabbing his brother by the shoulder. "Calm down! You can't kill them all. There must be thousands in there." *Or more,* he thought with a shudder. "Let's just go before—"

Pain exploded over his wrist, and he cut off with a gasp. When he looked down, his whole lower arm was covered in the same black slime that was on Justin's neck. It burned like hot oil against his skin, but before he could wipe it off on his shirt, a full-scale volley of black goo shot out of the water, coating the wall above their heads.

At first, Julius thought that was because the lampreys had terrible aim, then he looked up and realized the truth. "They're aiming for the ladder!" he cried, ducking to cover his head. "They're trying to cut us off!"

Even as he said it, Julius knew it was already too late. He also knew how the ladder's metal had gotten so pitted. This was clearly not the first time the lampreys had sprung this trap. They'd hit the ladder perfectly, coating the entire bottom half in thick, acidic spit that smoked and hissed against the old steel.

The fumes were even worse. As if the rotted fish smell wasn't bad enough, the acidic goo also reeked of magic. Dark, fetid, oily magic that was getting thicker by the second. Julius covered his mouth and nose with his hands and looking around for Marci, but she was no longer behind him. This sparked several seconds of panic before he spotted her on her knees at the far corner where the platform met the wall, yanking something out of her bag.

It looked like a collapsible laundry basket, the kind with the plastic ribs that you could fold up into a tiny ball, but would still spring back to its original size the moment you let up the tension. That sight was absurd enough to make Julius forget the danger for a moment to wonder why she would have such a thing. He was still speculating when Marci dropped the basket on the ground.

The plastic ribs snapped open the second she let them go, flattening out in a ring, and Julius realized it wasn't a basket at all. It was a circle. A collapsible casting circle made of yellow tent cloth with layer upon layer of spell notation written around the edges in Marci's meticulous handwriting.

"Get in!" she shouted.

Julius didn't wait to be asked twice. He sprinted across the cement and into the circle just as the lampreys launched another volley of burning goo straight at their prey. It struck the wall behind them in hissing splats, but when the sticky stuff crossed Marci's circle, it burned up in a white flash, landing in a patter of harmless ash against Julius's chest.

He let out a long, relieved breath. "Nice work."

"Always pays to carry an emergency shelter," she said, nodding at Justin, who had miraculously managed to dodge every shot since the first one. "Is he coming?"

Julius had no idea. He was spared having to say as much, though, because at that moment, Justin swung his sword with a roar that shook the ground. For a second, Julius couldn't understand why. From what he could see, Justin was swinging at nothing, and then the air begin to change. All at once, the bite of dragon magic was all around them, surging up so fast and sharp, Julius thought he was going to be bitten in half. Just before the pressure became unbearable, Justin finished the strike, and the black lake parted in front of him like the Red Sea.

Thanks to the glare of Marci's magic, Julius saw the whole thing clear as a lightning flash. Justin's strike had cut the water and everything in it, slicing through the enormous, tangled mass of lampreys hiding below the surface like a laser. He saw his brother, larger than life, the bloody wounds from the earlier bites already closing. More than anything, though, he saw the sword in Justin's hands. The sword that wasn't a sword at all.

It still *looked* like a sword. It had a hilt and a wide, curved blade that was sharp on one side, like a long scimitar, but the blade itself was bone-white and slightly discolored at the tip, like an old tooth. An ancient fang of something very large and very, very deadly.

His strike finished, Justin stepped back, resting the Fang of the Heartstriker on his shoulder as the bite of the dragon magic faded and the water fell back into place, covering the bodies of the unknown number of lampreys he'd just chopped in two. "There," he said, his voice thick with self-satisfaction as he turned around to give Julius a superior look. "*That's* how it's done."

Julius sighed. It wasn't that he wasn't happy they weren't going to be eaten by overgrown sea snakes, but he wasn't exactly looking forward to the next several hours of inevitable bragging. Justin was already opening his mouth to begin when something long, black, and glistening shot out of the water and wrapped around his waist from behind, yanking him off his feet back into the water.

"Justin!" Julius shouted, almost running out of Marci's circle before he caught himself. Even if he had risked it, he would have been too late. Justin had already vanished beneath the black water without a trace.

He was still watching the waves when Marci grabbed his hand. Julius glanced over his shoulder in confusion to see her staring at him with her heart in her eyes. She looked like she was about to cry, though with everything that had happened, it took Julius a stupidly long time to realize why.

"Don't write Justin off yet," he said with what he hoped was a reassuring smile. "He's very hard to kill. But we need to make a safe place for him to come up." Or a safe place for them to take shelter in case Justin lost his temper down there. "Can you move the circle closer to the edge?"

Marci's expression made it clear she thought he was being crazy optimistic, but she played along. "No. This circle's a prototype. I haven't figured out how to make it mobile yet." She bit her lip. "I'm actually kind of surprised it worked just now. Maybe we can—"

Her voice cut off in a yelp as a wave of black, wiggling bodies shot out of the water straight toward them.

Julius moved instinctively, knocking the first lamprey away before it could smack Marci in the face. The next one made it past him, and though it began to smoke when it crossed Marci's circle, the power that had incinerated the blobs of acidic spit must not have been strong enough to cook seven feet of wiggling, magically corrupted sea parasite. The lamprey crashed into Marci's legs with a horrible, unearthly squeal before she kicked it away.

"What is going *on*?" she cried. "I thought lampreys lived *under* the water!"

Julius squinted through the glare of Marci's circle at the black lake, now boiling harder than ever. Everywhere he looked, the lampreys were in a frenzy, flinging their long, black bodies out of the water. But it wasn't until he saw the ones trying to slither up the slick, straight walls that bordered the lake like they were trying to get clear of the lake at any cost that he realized what he was actually looking at.

"They're not trying to attack us," he said, wiping the greasy water from his face. "They're trying to get away from something." *Justin*, he added to himself with a shiver that was equal parts pride and dread.

That was going to be a real problem. But when he leaned out over the edge of Marci's circle to try and get an idea of what form of his brother they should be expecting, a strange glow began to fill the room.

Up until this point, the only light in the cavernous spillway had been the flashlight he'd dropped when Justin was first attacked and the glare of Marci's magic. Now, something beneath the water was shining with a blue, ghostly light that didn't look like anything his brother could do. It was getting brighter, too, and as it grew, the cold, oily pressure that had been making Julius uneasy since they first arrived grew exponentially worse.

Julius was very young for a dragon, and undeniably inexperienced, but even he understood there were some things you just didn't want to look at. Some sights couldn't be unseen, and immortality was a long time to carry those kinds of memories. Unfortunately, he was already looking at the water when the thing broke through, and the moment the hideous shape came into view, Julius knew that even if he lived to be as old as the Three Sisters added together, he was never going to be able to forget this.

Other than their remarkable size, spitting ability, and supernatural aggression, the lampreys they'd seen up to this point had looked more or less like overgrown versions of the normal predatory sea creatures of the same name. This thing, on the other hand, was a true monster. Its skin wasn't just black; it was a void, drinking in Marci's light without leaving so much as a glimmer. He had no idea how big it was beneath the water, but what he could see above was nearly twenty feet tall, an enormous column of thick, serpentine body ending at a small, flat head ringed with snaking black feelers, almost like a mane. No part of it, however, was glowing, and Julius was starting to wonder what it was he'd seen under the water when the thing opened its mouth.

Like the other lampreys, its mouth opened to form a flat, round circle. But where the other lampreys had three or four rows of jagged teeth, this thing had endless interlocking rings of arm-length points descending all the way down its throat. Julius could see them all, too, because the monster's mouth was the source of that sickly blue light.

The glow emanated from deep in its throat, almost like dragon fire. But where dragons breathed flame in a continuous stream, this thing launched it like a shot. Their only warning was a slight hiss and the sight of the huge, slimy neck puffing up like a bullfrog before a car-sized lump of blue, luminous, deathly feeling magic exploded out of the thing's throat straight at them.

As the blast left the monster's mouth, Julius felt Marci pull in magic for a counter shot. But even though she was sucking down power so fast the air was crackling, it wasn't enough. The magic in her circle felt like a raindrop compared to the tidal wave hurtling down at them, but there was no time to gather more. There was no time to dodge, no time to flee, no time for anything. Already, the blue glow filled his vision, and Julius knew this was it. He was going to die. But even as his mind accepted this fact, he realized it didn't mean Marci had to die with him.

After that, the choice was simple. It was barely a decision at all to step in front of Marci and reach, not with hands, but with his power. The mental muscles he hadn't exercised in nearly a decade screamed as he forced them into action, giving him an instant pounding headache. Julius ignored it, digging deep into his own magic—not the physical shape his mother had cut off, but his *actual* power, the spark of internal magic that made him a dragon trapped in a human body instead of just human.

He reached as hard and as far as he could. And then, when he felt the burning pain that meant he was at his absolute limit, Julius yanked up, pulling his magic over them like a shield as the creature's magic crashed down.

***

Years ago, when he'd been a hatchling too young to even assume a human form, Julius had developed a knack for using his magic as a wall. His mother, not yet realizing what a failure of a son she'd hatched, had declared him "exceptionally gifted" for figuring out such a unique way of using their inborn power. For Julius, however, it was a simple matter of self-defense. As a small dragon already at the bottom of his clutch, learning how to make a shield to protect himself had been a vital survival skill.

Unlike humans, who drew their magic from the outside, a dragon's magic was inborn. This difference was the reason his kind had been able to scrape by when magic had vanished for the last thousand years while human mages and spirits had completely shut down. Unfortunately, it also meant that when Julius used his magic as a shield, anything that struck the barrier also hit *him*, and right now, he felt like he'd just hit the ground after jumping off the Grand Canyon.

The giant lamprey's magic slammed into his own so hard, he felt it in places he hadn't realized he'd had. Just when he thought for sure he was going to be pounded under completely, the lamprey's blast struck something heavy, dense, and immovable deep inside him, and the surging magic stopped.

For a terrible moment, that was actually worse. The impact raced through Julius's body, shaking him nearly to pieces. But then, like a tennis ball bouncing off a wall, the lamprey's spell rebounded, shooting back across the water to strike the monstrous sea snake square in the throat.

By this point, Julius was more magical than physical. He could still see, still feel, but all of his normal senses were secondary to the horrible shaking going on inside him. So when the glowing blue blast he'd sent back at the lamprey exploded in its face so hard the monster was blown back, he saw it only vaguely. It wasn't until Marci grabbed him around the chest and dragged him to the wall, away from the waves caused by the giant's frantic thrashing, that Julius realized what he'd done. He'd bounced the monster's magic. He was still wondering at the miracle of that when he saw something jump out of the water and began scaling the giant lamprey's body. Something that looked remarkably like his brother.

He sat up so fast Marci yelped. Sure enough, Justin, still human and seemingly uninjured, was climbing up the writhing monster's back, stabbing his sword into the thing to keep his hold whenever it dropped under water. But while Justin was clearly doing damage, the lamprey wasn't going down. Worse, it seemed to be recovering from the blow Julius had accidentally landed on its head.

That thought had barely finished when tentacles began flying out of the water to yank Justin off. Normally, this wouldn't have been a problem, but with his sword stabbed into the thing's back like a climbing hook, Justin couldn't fight them all off. If Julius hadn't been sealed, he could flown over and cut his brother free, but he couldn't fly. He could barely sit up after all that magic. But he had to do *something*. Justin could be a royal pain, but he'd come to help him tonight, and he was his *brother*. Julius was trying to figure out what that something could possibly be when the tentacle wrapped around Justin's waist suddenly let go.

The creature shrieked at the same time, and he looked up in alarm to see Marci standing at the center of her circle with two lampreys, one of which was still alive and wriggling, piled in front of her. He was working up the strength to help her knock them away when Marci shoved her hand out, and the two oversized black sea creatures at her feet seized up like they'd been electrocuted. At the same time, a wave of super-heated air shot out to strike the monster's face.

It screamed in pain when her spell hit, but Marci wasn't even looking. She was already yanking another snapping, terrified lamprey into her circle, kicking out the old ones to make room. It wasn't until she fired another shot, though, that Julius realized what she was doing. She was using the lampreys like batteries, sucking power out of them like she'd done with the chimera tusk back at the house.

Fresh lampreys must have been much more powerful than preserved chimera parts, because now that the shock of bouncing the creature's attack was fading, Marci's magic was all Julius could feel. Power rolled off her in waves as she launched shot after shot of her repurposed microwave spell at the monster in the water, leaving long, blistering burns across its pitch-black skin as she screamed for Justin to just kill it already.

Julius didn't know if his brother could hear her, but Justin obeyed all the same. With a speed and strength that would never pass for human, he tore himself out of the web of grasping tentacles that had gone stiff from the pain of Marci's attacks. Using his sword like a pick, he scaled the lamprey's slick side until he was right behind the monster's head. Then, grabbing the Fang of the Heartstriker with both hands, Justin slammed his sword into the creature's skull.

As always, the Fang of the Heartstriker cut clean. With a roar of rage and victory, Justin sliced sideways. The moment the sword cleared the last of the creature's inky flesh, its horrible bellowing cut off like a switch, and then it toppled so fast Justin was forced to dive back into the water before the enormous body crushed him like a falling redwood.

The lamprey landed with a crash that sent a wave washing all the way over Julius and Marci's heads. They were still sputtering when Justin hauled himself up onto the cement platform beside them. He shook his body like a dog, spraying blood and black water everywhere, and then he rolled his shoulders beneath the soaked remains of his shirt and turned to survey the now-quiet lake.

"See?" he said. "I had it in the bag the whole time."

Julius had no comeback for that, especially since his ears chose that moment to start ringing. He was trying to figure out how to get them to stop when Marci bent down and plucked his miraculously still-functional phone out his jeans pocket, the actual source of the ringing.

He expected her to hand it to him, but Marci didn't. Instead, she looked at the caller's name on the screen, lifted the receiver to her ear, and said, "Hello?"

It was like watching a horror movie. Punch drunk on magic, flat on his back, muscles useless, Julius couldn't do anything but lie there and feel his blood go cold as Marci said, in her cheerful, clearly human voice, "Oh, I'm sorry, Bethesda. Julius isn't available right now. Can he call you ba—"

Justin snatched the phone out of her hand mid-word. "It's me," he said gruffly, shoving the phone between his soaked shoulder and his dripping ear. "No, she's Julius's and he hasn't trained her properly. You know how he is. No, I'm not going to kill her. Calm down."

Marci's eyes went wide, and she turned back to Julius with a questioning look. He didn't have time to answer, though. He was too busy forgiving Justin for every childhood insult and thoughtless word. That idiot dragon had just saved Marci's life, and he was probably the only one who could have. Mother *adored* Justin. Things that would have gotten another Heartstriker gutted were deemed "cute" when he said them. Normally, the double standard annoyed Julius. Right now, though, Justin was his favorite sibling.

"Here."

He jerked as Justin's voice sounded suddenly right beside him, and then again when his phone appeared in the air above his face. "She wants to talk to you."

Julius raised a shaking hand and took the phone, pressing it against his ear, which he'd just realized was bleeding. He moved the phone back a bit with a grimace and tried again. "Hello?"

"*Julius Heartstriker,*" Bethesda roared. "What are you doing?"

"Currently? Lying on my back."

"Don't get smart with me," his mother snarled. "What has gotten into you?"

Way too much magic, Julius thought, but even that had an odd detachment. Normally, the sound of his mother's angry voice was enough to send him into instant cowering obedience. After the giant lamprey, though, Bethesda's rage didn't seem so bad. Clearly, he must be in shock.

"I'm sorry," he said, more out of habit than any real sincerity since he still didn't know why she was angry.

"You should be," Bethesda said. "What you thinking, using my magic like that? I felt that blast all the way down here. If I wasn't so shocked to discover you possessed the presence of mind to come up with such a clever trick, I'd fly to the DFZ and skin you for your presumption."

Julius closed his eyes with a trembling sigh. So *that* was what had happened. The lamprey's attack hadn't bounced off something unknown inside of *him*—it had bounced off Bethesda's *seal.* His mother's punishment had just saved his life and Marci's, and the irony was so beautiful it actually struck him dumb for several seconds. Fortunately, his mother was too busy chewing him out to notice.

"Well," she said when she'd finished, her voice scalding. "What do you have to say for yourself?"

Historically, those words were the cue for him to clam up in terror. Woozy as he was from the blast and everything else, though, Julius rolled with the first thing that came to him. "Only that I'm very sorry. I never dreamed you'd be able to feel such weak magic from so far away, but I should have known better than to underestimate your incredible powers of perception. I'm grateful for your mercy in allowing me to survive and learn from the experience so that I may never make such a stupid mistake ever again."

That was the biggest line he'd ever fed his mother. Even Justin looked taken aback. Bethesda's voice, on the other hand, sweetened noticeably.

"My my," she said. "It seems this fiasco has finally taught you how to grovel. That's a step forward, but don't you *ever* do anything of this sort to me again. Children exist to help their parents, not hinder them. And if you must keep a human, teach it some manners before it gets itself killed. Now put Justin back on."

Julius dutifully handed his phone back to his brother before reaching his hands out for Marci to help sit him up. She did so without looking, eyes glued to Justin's back as he walked away.

"What was that about?" she whispered. "And what did you do earlier? What's going on?"

Julius didn't know how to answer any of that safely. He didn't know much of anything, actually. The world had started spinning as soon as Marci had pulled him up, and as he tried and failed to focus on a single point, he wondered vaguely if this was what being drunk felt like. Dragon metabolism was so fast that actually getting sloshed took way more effort than he was willing to invest, but he'd always been curious. If this was what it was like, though, Julius was glad he'd never bothered. Not knowing whether you were going to hurl or pass out was hardly his idea of fun.

In the end, passing out won. He dropped Marci's hands and fell straight back, mercifully blacking out before his skull hit the concrete.

***

When Julius woke up again, his head was much clearer. It also hurt like hell. Groaning deep in his throat, he opened his eyes to see he was still on the platform by the lake, though he was no longer lying directly on the floor. Someone had put a folded sweater down to cushion his head, and since he was pretty sure Justin didn't wear bright purple, he could only assume it was Marci's.

"Hey, you're up!"

He looked over just in time to see her boots come to a stop right beside his head before her face filled his vision. "How are you feeling?"

He considered the question for a moment. "I've been better," he said at last. "How long was I out?"

"About ten minutes. I'm actually amazed you're conscious. That was the nastiest case of backlash I've ever seen, especially in someone who isn't supposed to be a mage."

"For the *last time*," Justin's voice echoed from somewhere beyond Julius's feet. "He's not a mage! Julius is terrible at magic."

"If you can use magic, you're a mage," Marci called back with the sullen tone of someone who's already said this numerous times, though she didn't take her eyes off Julius. "I've never seen someone just shove magic out of themselves like that. How did you do it? Can you show me? Your brother won't tell me anything."

"Because he asked me not to," Justin growled, finally stepping into Julius's line of sight. "So stop asking questions already."

Marci shot his brother a deadly glare, and Julius closed his eyes with a sigh. Not that he didn't appreciate Justin actually keeping his mouth shut for once, but would it be too much to ask that he do it in a way that didn't make it sound like Julius was hiding things?

"It's complicated," he said at last, pulling Marci's attention back to him. "I'll be happy to explain everything later"—*never*—"but this isn't really a good place or time. We're still on a deadline, and we need to find those mages."

Marci and Justin shared a look Julius couldn't make out. "I don't think that's going to be a problem."

Before Julius could ask what she meant by that, his brother grabbed his arm and heaved him to his feet, putting him face to face with the crowd waiting at the other end of the cement platform.

Even seeing it with his own eyes, Julius couldn't quite believe it. The landing beside the black lake was packed with human men and women in clothes ranging from fashionably distressed to straight-out bizarre. Still more humans were on the water in boats, fishing bits of lamprey out of the bloody lake with large nets. All of them were clearly mages, a fact made obvious both by the hum of human magic that had replaced the deathly aura of the giant lamprey pool and by the bright glow of the light spells hanging from the spillway's roof like the world's most elaborate chandeliers.

"Turns out my Kosmolabe was right," Marci said smugly, patting the bag at her side. "They *were* under the water. Their base is in an old bomb shelter that goes under the lake. That was why we couldn't reach them from the pipes. They were never actually part of the water system! The storm drain we saw is a fake they use to disguise their entrance. They actually cut a door into this spillway so they'd have a back exit, but they had to stop using it when the lampreys moved in."

Happy as Julius was that Marci had solved the mystery of their missing mages, he was only listening with half an ear. The rest of his attention was on his nose as he breathed deeply, sorting through the various horrid sewer stenches for any sign of their prey. But while he did catch a trace of a cold, wintry sea scent that reminded him of Svena, it was old. Katya wasn't here.

"Justin," he said softly.

"I know," his brother whispered back. "I smell it, too. But don't worry, I've got a plan."

That made Julius more worried than ever, but before they could discuss it, his brother yanked him to his feet and half helped, half carried him over to the edge of the platform, as far from the humans as possible. When Marci tried to follow, Justin shot her a full-on "I am predator, you are prey" glare that stopped her in her tracks. Only when she'd turned and scurried back to the mages did he finally return his attention to Julius.

"We need to work quickly," he said, his voice low and urgent as he propped Julius against the wall. "Our target's gone, but from the scent, she was with these people up until at least an hour ago, so she can't have gotten too far. Now, the dragon smell is strongest on the guy who's acting like their leader, so here's what we're going to do. I'll grab him and be bad cop since you couldn't pull it off if you tried. You be good cop and tell your mage to run interference on the others. I don't think they'll fight since they're all impressed we killed big-and-slimy, but if they do, we'll smoke 'em. Ready?"

"No," Julius said, resting his weight against the wet cement. "Justin, the only reason I'm even standing right now is because of the wall."

"Well, how much longer are you going to be?" his brother said. "Because we're in kind of a hurry."

"Do you even listen to yourself?" he said, jerking his head at the group around Marci. "There have to be thirty humans here, and that's not counting the ones in the boats. You can't actually think we can beat them all."

Justin didn't answer, but then, he didn't need to. His confident look was answer enough.

"They're mages," Julius continued, a bit more frantically now. "I'm sealed. Katya's not even here."

"She was," Justin said, adjusting the sword on his hip.

"There's no way you can do it without revealing your true nature!" he cried, playing his final card.

His brother shrugged. "So what? It's not like we'll need them again. Now, are you ready to do this, or do you need to pass out like a pansy again first?"

Julius began to shake. His brother really meant to do it. Of course, Julius had known Justin had no problem killing the humans when he'd suggested they sneak in, but he'd talked himself into believing that was acceptable since Katya would be inside. But she wasn't, and these people were just standing there. If Justin attacked, they'd defend themselves, and then he'd kill them. Even if he didn't, there was no way they'd believe he was human past the first fire breath, which meant if Justin didn't kill them, Chelsie would. Either way, every human in this room was about to be dead, and it would be all Julius's fault.

"No," he whispered.

"What did you say?" Justin asked, arching an eyebrow.

"*No*," Julius said again, lifting his head. "We're not going to attack. We're not going to fight these people."

"Well, how else are you going to get them to talk?"

"I don't know," he confessed. "But I thought I'd start by asking."

Justin rolled his eyes. "I'm serious."

"So am I," Julius growled.

His brother stared at him in utter confusion, like he couldn't believe he was hearing this. Julius couldn't believe he was saying it. He'd never directly contradicted anyone in his family before, much less *Justin*, but he didn't take it back.

He wasn't sure exactly when he'd reached his limit—when he'd nearly died fighting that lamprey, or when he'd realized they'd done all of this for *no reason*. Marci had just told him the storm drain with the ward he'd found earlier led directly into the shaman's commune, which meant that if he'd followed his instincts instead of letting Justin bully him into a more "draconic" plan, none of this would have happened. They might have even have gotten in quick enough to catch Katya before she bolted. They definitely wouldn't have almost died fighting a stupid lake monster they'd never needed to bother in the first place, and the more Julius thought about that, the angrier he got.

He *always* did this. He *always* let bigger dragons talk him into doing things he didn't want to do, because they were draconic, and he knew he should want to be like them. But he didn't. He'd been told his whole life that he was a failure, but how could he be anything *but* a failure when the thought of acting like Justin or Ian or any other successful dragon filled him with loathing? The attempts and subsequent disasters of tonight were like a microcosm for his entire existence, and Julius was sick to death of it. Sick of the expectations, sick of failing them, sick of trying to be what he wasn't. He was sick of *everything*, and he wasn't going to do it anymore.

"I'm done," he said.

Justin scowled at him. "What do you mean? Done with what?"

"Everything." The word fell so easily from Julius's lips that it startled him, but even more surprising was the weight that fell off with it. It was like he'd let go of two decades' worth of fear and expectations, and suddenly, he felt light as a feather. "I'm done," he said again, his voice full of wonder. "I give up."

"You can't *give up!*"

A bit of the backlash must still have been lingering, because the sound of his brother's anger almost made Julius laugh. "Watch me," he said, putting out his hands in surrender. "I always thought if I just tried hard enough, I could change myself, but I can't. I can't change what I am, and if I keep trying to force it, I'm just going to keep failing like I always have. But I'm done banging my head against the wall. It's time to face the truth, and the truth is I'm never going to be like you, and I'm never going to be the sort of dragon Mother wants, either."

His brother's growl grew louder with every word. By the time Julius finished, it was vibrating the puddles of water at their feet. "You can't be serious."

"Why not?" Julius said. "I can't just keep doing the same thing over and over and hope some day I'll get a different outcome. That's crazy. If I want to get out of this rut, then I'm going to have to try something new. So I'm going to do things the way I want for once and see what happens. I mean, it's not like I can fail any worse."

"You absolutely can!" Justin roared, making the humans at the other end of the platform jump. Justin didn't even spare them a look, though he did lower his voice. "Dammit, Julius, can't you see I'm trying to keep you alive here? How am I supposed to convince Mother not to eat you when your 'plan' consists of 'ask humans nicely, hope it works out'?"

His teeth were bared and sharp when he finished, but Julius couldn't help smiling. That little speech was the closest his brother had ever come to actually admitting he cared. In the end, though, it didn't change a thing.

"I'm tired of trying to be what I'm not," Julius said, pushing off the wall to stand on his own. "You were right. This *is* a test. *My* test, and from here out, I'm going to pass or fail on my own. I'm done doing things I'm ashamed of, so if you still want to stay and help, you're welcome, but we're doing this my way from here on."

Looking as scared as he felt would fatally undermine his point, so Julius held his ground with all the bluster he had. Inside, though, his heart was pounding. This was the first time he'd ever told his brother what to do, and he fully expected to have to pay for it. Justin wasn't the sort of dragon who took challenges to his dominance lightly.

But though he was braced for the retaliatory fury, Justin didn't say a word. He simply stepped back and opened his arms in a *go for it* gesture. So, with a nervous swallow, Julius went, using the wall for balance as he hobbled back across the platform toward the mages on the other side.

Chapter 9

Almost as though they could sense they were among predators (which, on some deep, instinctual level, they probably could), all the humans, including Marci, had drifted to the far side of the cement platform, as far from the dragons as possible. They were all talking seriously as he approached, their heads together, and then Marci turned to point Julius out to the large man who seemed to be the leader.

As humans went, Julius supposed he was handsome in a rough, rugged way. Tall and imposing with dark black skin and thick, tight curled hair that ran down his face to form an equally impressive beard, he looked more like an angry river god than the sort of person you'd find running a mage commune. His clothes were even stranger, a perfectly cut outfit of a long duster, vest, pants, and tall boots all made out of deep green alligator leather. It wasn't until the man stuck out his hand and introduced himself, though, that Julius understood why anyone would voluntarily dress like that. This was the human Katya had supposedly left the party with. Ross Vedder, the alligator shaman.

"So," he said as Julius took his hand. "You're the one leading the group that took out the lampreys. On behalf of all of us, thank you. We've been trying to get rid of that menace for months."

"You're welcome," Julius replied, savoring the rare words. "But we can't take too much credit. We got lost and ran into the lampreys by accident. Anything else that happened was self defense."

The man laughed. "Lost, huh? You got guts getting lost down here. So what brings you to our neck of the pipes? You three hunting bounties?"

"No," Julius said, pausing for a steadying breath. Here went nothing. "We're actually looking for a woman named Katya. Is she here?"

Ross's smile vanished the second Julius said the dragoness's name. "Why do you want to know?" he growled, standing taller. "Did her family send you?"

Julius took a moment to consider his answer. Keeping clan secrets was a habit as deeply ingrained as breathing, but whatever this human was to Katya, he clearly wanted to protect her. Julius respected that, so he settled for a half truth. "Yes," he admitted. "But I don't mean her any harm. I just want to talk to her."

The shaman looked deeply skeptical, but when he answered, Julius felt certain he was telling the truth, and he wasn't happy about it. "She's not here anymore. Lark called right after we left his party to let us know that a friend of Katya's was looking for her." He eyed Julius up and down. "I suppose that was you?"

When Julius nodded, he continued. "I was suspicious 'cause we weren't expecting anyone, but I didn't think too much of it until I went into the bedroom and discovered Katya had packed up her stuff and left. That was about an hour ago. I don't know where she is now."

Julius sighed. Of course. "Do you have any way of getting in touch with her?"

Ross's eyes narrowed in a cold, steady glare that fit well with his chosen animal. "Nothing I'd give to you. Now, if you'll excuse me, I have to get back to work."

Julius was scrambling to think of some way, *any* way, to keep the man from leaving when Marci suddenly said, "What kind of work do you do down *here*?"

Her incredulous, borderline insulting tone sent Julius into panic mode. This man was their only lead; antagonizing him was not an option. To his surprise, though, Ross didn't seem to mind the question at all.

"Service for the spiritual and magical benefit of our community," he said, puffing out his chest with pride. "Algonquin cares nothing for the lives of the people in her city. We do. We stay down here to keep the monsters from preying on folks who can't afford to move up to the skyways for safety. Take the lampreys, for instance. During the spring rains when the drains are full, they swim up to the streets of the Underground to hunt. Eight foot lamprey will strike right out of the storm drains, grabbing people and pulling them back down to their nest."

Julius shuddered. What a horrible thought. "Don't the hunters kill them?"

"When they can get 'em, sure," Ross said. "But the bounty jockeys never come down here to eliminate the problem at the source. That's where we come in." He jerked his head at the lake. "We were only a few weeks away from having the power necessary for the ritual to cleanse this place. Now, thanks to you, we can use that magic for other things. Lampreys aren't the only monsters that nest down here, and we make it our business to clean them out. That's our work—making this city safer for the people who don't have the money or pull to buy Algonquin's protection."

"Right, right, very noble," Marci said, angling in front of Julius. "How much is the bounty on those lampreys again?"

"Marci!" Julius hissed.

"What?" she whispered back. "We're broke."

The alligator shaman watched this exchange with a wary eye. "Ten dollars a head, last I saw," he answered slowly. "Hardly worth dying for, but never let it be said Algonquin overspent on something as trivial as preventing her people from being snatched off the street by wild animals." He shook his head and turned back to Julius. "Again, thank you for what you did here. Even if it was an accident, our city's a safer place now, and that's always a good thing. We'll clean up the water and put down wards to keep this area clear, and to make sure we don't draw any death spirits. In the meantime, I'll be happy to assign someone to escort you back to the surface so you don't get 'lost' again."

He finished with a pointed look that made it clear he knew perfectly well they'd been trying to sneak up on his stronghold from behind. If the alligator shaman hadn't been the leader of a seemingly selfless band of eco-mage crusaders, Julius would have almost suspected him of leaving the lamprey nest on purpose to guard his back. But all the other humans looked too genuinely relieved as they gathered the slimy lamprey bodies into piles for disposal for him to suspect Ross on that angle at least. The destroyed nest was clearly a true and loathsome menace, and everyone seemed glad to be rid of it.

Well, Julius thought with a sigh, at least something good had come out of this. For his part, he was ready to call it a night. He was filthy and exhausted and his head was throbbing. Add in his behavior toward his mother and his brother and it was clearly time to throw in the towel. He needed time to make a new plan anyway now that he'd decided to stop doing things that didn't feel right, which definitely included hunting down and chaining runaway dragons. He wasn't sure if there *was* a solution to this mess that would sit well with him, but at the moment, Julius was too relieved by the idea that he wouldn't have to put his boot on Katya's neck to care.

"An escort would be great," he said, pulling out his phone. "If you don't mind, I'd like to give you my number in case Katya comes back. As I said, I just want to talk to her, so if you could pass on the message, I'd really appreciate it."

Ross glowered suspiciously for a moment, then he shrugged and pulled out a brand new, top-of-the-line AR smartphone, the kind that kept the augmented reality field running around you at all times even when you weren't directly touching it. Devices like that were worth more than most cars, and Julius had to act fast to hide his surprise that Ross owned one. Clearly, something down here paid very well, a fact that did not escape Marci.

"Hold on a sec," she said. "If we're wrapping this up, then you need to tell your people to stop stealing our lampreys."

Ross blinked. "Excuse me?"

Marci pointed at the bloody water. "You said it yourself. Those lampreys have a bounty of ten bucks a head, and since we killed them under the direction of my employer"—she pointed back at Julius—"they belong to him. Not you."

Ross's face turned scarlet. "We're not *stealing* anything!" he shouted. "This is an eco-magical disaster area! A reflection of Algonquin's completely irresponsible attitude toward the safety of her citizens and the magical health of any land that isn't under her lakes! The whole reason we're down here is to clean up this sort of thing. These bodies need to be properly disposed of to prevent any further contamination of the natural magic. You can't just haul them up and hawk them to Algonquin's corporate stooges for a paltry ten dollars! What kind of sell-out are you?"

"The kind who likes to be paid for her work," Marci said, lifting her chin. "And ten bucks each isn't paltry when you're working with this sort of volume."

As much as Julius agreed with the alligator shaman's moral high ground, Marci did have a point. They were desperately short on money, and there were a *lot* of dead lampreys lying around. Hundreds easily, and that wasn't even counting the big one. At ten dollars a head, that added up.

"This isn't about money," Ross said, his voice underlined by a distinctly reptilian growl. "We're doing what's right for the good of everyone. I know as a Thaumaturge you have no connection to the land, but *some* of us—"

"What?" Marci shrieked, and Julius winced. He could practically see the storm of righteous indignation building around her, and Ross wasn't much better. Alligators were apparently much less laid-back spirit guides than albatrosses. If Julius didn't do something fast to defuse the situation, this was going to turn into a full-scale duel.

"I think we're getting ahead of ourselves," he said, stepping between the two mages. "Mr. Vedder, we understand and respect what you're trying to do here, but my partner"—he grabbed Marci and pulled her to his side, partially to show solidarity, but mostly to keep her from throwing any spells—"also had a valid point. That said, I see no reason we can't find an arrangement that will make us all happy. I understand your movement down here is well-funded, correct?"

That was a wild guess, but phones like Ross's didn't come cheap. Neither did a full suit of what was certainly humanely sourced alligator leather. There had to be money coming in from somewhere to keep this crusade rolling, and sure enough, Ross shut his mouth, reaching up to rub the back of his head in a way that looked almost embarrassed.

"I fund it," he said quietly. "My dad's the CEO of a mana-tech integration company. He set me up with a few million back when I was a teenager to keep me out of his hair, but that doesn't mean I'm just a trust fund kid playing around down here."

"You sure?" Marci said before Julius elbowed her.

"I got into this work precisely to fight back against the damage corporate raiders like my dad do to our communities," Ross growled. "Algonquin guards the lakes and the spirits who obey her, but she couldn't care less about what happens to the rest of us. Guys like my dad make a living taking advantage of that, abusing whomever they can to make a buck. I wouldn't touch his money if I could help it, but do you know how much it costs to keep wards running down here?"

"I'm guessing more than comes in through donations," Julius said.

"By a factor of ten," Ross replied. "We need money for our work, and if I've got it, then why not spend it doing good?"

"I completely agree," Julius said quickly before Marci could open her mouth. "It's clear to me that you and your people are providing a vital and critically underappreciated service down here. I can't tell you how glad I am to hear you're not in financial danger."

The alligator shaman seemed caught off guard by this sudden and effusive praise. "Well, thank you. I'm glad you're on our side."

"I absolutely am," Julius said. "Of course, knowing all that, I'm sure you'll understand why I can't just give you this job *pro bono*. My partner and I aren't fully funded, and we need the money. That said, I'd much rather deal with you than Algonquin's people, so how about a compromise?"

That was his best shot at making this work, and he held his breath while Ross scratched his beard thoughtfully. Then, at last, the shaman said, "What did you have in mind?"

"I was thinking rather than turn the lampreys in for the bounty, we'd sell them all to you as-is for a flat rate," Julius explained. "That way, we'll still get paid fairly for our work, and you'll get to clean your lake exactly as you like. Everyone wins, what do you say?"

Ross glanced at the bloody water. "That sounds fair to me, assuming we can agree on a price." He thought about it a second longer, and then his head dipped in a sharp nod. "I don't see why we couldn't make it work. Let me talk to my co-chair. Hold on a moment."

Grinning wide, Julius motioned for him to do as he liked. The moment the shaman was out of earshot, Marci grabbed Julius's arm.

"What are you doing?" she whispered fiercely. "Don't cut a deal with these lunatics! Especially not for a *flat fee*! We don't even know how many lampreys we're talking about yet. You could be giving away thousands of dollars!"

"I'm not giving away anything," he said, gently prying her fingers loose before he lost all feeling in his hand. "Look around. Do you know how long it would take us haul these bodies through the sewers to the Animal Control office to collect our payout? Even if we carried them up two at a time, it would take us days of non-stop hard labor to empty this place. If you calculate that out to an hourly rate, we'd make better money painting houses, and that's assuming half the lampreys didn't rot before we could get to them. If we sell to Ross, we get paid for the work we already did, and we don't have to do any more, which is actually the best part of the deal. I don't know about you, but I'm exhausted. Right now, I'd gladly *pay* several thousand dollars just to get out of here, take a shower, and never worry about touching another lamprey for as long as I live."

Marci's face pulled into into a scowl. "Okay," she grumbled. "I'll admit taking the money and running does have its appeal, but that doesn't mean we should let them rip us off. I say we hold out for forty thousand."

"Marci," Julius said with a sigh. "There are not four thousand lampreys here."

"Doesn't matter," she said, crossing her arms over her chest. "The point is that we killed something they couldn't, and now we own the bodies, which they want. That puts them over a barrel, and when you've got someone over a barrel, you have to shake them until their pockets are empty. It's the freelancer's code."

"I'm not shaking anyone," he said firmly. "I said we were going to agree on a mutually fair price, and that's what I mean to do."

"Juliuuuuuuus," she moaned. "The guy's a trust fund kid! He won't even miss forty grand. Don't be such a goody-two-shoes."

"Refusing to take advantage of people doesn't make me a goody-two-shoes," Julius said sharply, making Marci flinch. Normally, that would have made him feel guilty. Right now, though, he had a point to make. "I know you don't have much respect for shamans, but these people seem to be doing legitimate good work. They're also Katya's allies. We still need their help to find her, and I'm not going to torpedo our chances there by ripping them off for a one time gain."

"Are you nuts?" Marci said. "This isn't a kid's show, Julius. It's not like these people are going to suddenly change their minds and give you all the info on this Katya person just because you were square with them. They live in a *sewer*. We'll probably never even see them again. If we don't go for broke now, we'll be SOL forever."

"You never know," Julius said. "I'm not saying it isn't a gamble, but if I'm going to be taking risks, I'd rather take them doing what I think is right. That way, even if I do get ripped off, at least I'll know I wasn't the one being a jerk."

Marci stared at him a moment, and then she threw up her hands. "Fine," she said. "It's your money. You want to pay the good karma fee, that's your choice."

The fact that she thought it was an idiotic one was clear from her voice, but Julius appreciated the gesture all the same. "Thank you, Marci."

"Yeah, yeah," she said, looking away. "Just never try and take that good nature to Vegas. You'll get swindled down to your underwear before you can blink."

That was a risk he was willing to take. For the first time Julius could remember, he actually felt good about something. Not just okay or not bad, but really, honestly *good* about his decision not to use his unexpected superior position to squeeze Katya's alligator shaman for all he was worth. And when Ross returned with his co-chair—a stern, middle-aged Indian woman with shed snake skins woven into her hair—Julius greeted them with such a smile that the lady actually looked taken aback. This only made Julius grin wider as he settled his shoulder against the wall and dug in for some good, honest, old-fashioned haggling.

***

An hour later, all parties were satisfied, and Julius was no longer an impoverished dragon. That wasn't as good as being an *unsealed* dragon, but he was ready to call it a win.

The shamans had started out wary, but once it became clear that Julius honestly wasn't trying to rip them off, the pace picked up enormously. In the end, Ross's circle kept all the lampreys, and Julius received an immediate cash transfer of twenty-five thousand dollars, ten of which was actually for the big one, which Ross explained was full of magical components his circle needed for their wards.

"It's not enough, really," Ross admitted with a sigh. "Large, unique creatures like that are almost priceless. You could probably sell it for thirty thousand easy if you called in one of the big magical component suppliers from the Upper City. We can't afford to pay that, of course, but you've been very upfront with us, and I wanted to make sure you knew the creature's real value before you signed it over, just in case you wanted to pull out."

"Thank you, but ten thousand will be fine," Julius said, keeping his voice low so Marci wouldn't overhear and fly to his rescue. "I meant it before when I said I thought you were doing good work down here. Also, have you seen that thing?" He jerked his thumb over at the bus-sized corpse of the giant lamprey that five mages were currently weaving a spell around in an attempt to finally lift it all the way out of the water. "Not exactly something I can put in my pocket. If you count that in, I think ten thousand for a monster I don't have to pay to move is a very fair deal."

"Fair indeed," Ross said, sticking out his hand with a genuine smile. "Thank you, Julius."

"Thank *you*," Julius said, shaking his hand firmly.

As soon as he'd settled everything with the mages, Julius hurried back to Justin. He'd fully expected his brother to get bored and leave once it became clear Julius was serious about not attacking the humans. When he hadn't, Julius had started getting nervous, but his brother had actually been remarkably patient, sitting against the wall and snarling at people who got too close. From anyone else, such behavior would have been surly. From Justin, it was practically an audition for sainthood, and Julius wanted to thank him before the miracle ended.

Justin didn't look up when Julius approached, just gave his sword a final swipe with the cleaning cloth before sliding the blade back in its sheath. "Well?"

"All done," Julius said. "They're paying us—"

"Screw the money," his brother said. "What about Katya?"

Julius shook his head, and Justin lifted his eyes at last to give him a look of such deep disappointment it actually hurt.

"I don't understand you," he said, rolling to his feet in one smooth motion. "You're not stupid and you're not a coward. You can even be bold if someone pushes you. You'll never be a really good dragon, but that's enough to be an okay one if you'd just stop dicking around. But you *won't*."

"I—" Julius began, but he stopped when Justin held up his hand.

"I don't want Mother to eat you," he went on, belting his sword back onto his hip. "We've been together our whole lives, and while you can be a total buzzkill, you're also the brother I dislike the least."

Julius's eyes widened. That was the nicest thing anyone in his family had ever said about him. "Thank you."

"Save it," Justin growled. "I'm only telling you all this so you'll understand why I took Bob's ticket to the DFZ. I thought if I came myself to keep an eye on you, I could make sure you didn't screw this up too badly. But after sitting here for a hour listening to you being so, so…"

"Reasonable?" Julius suggested.

"Nice," his brother spat. "Roll over, play along, suck-up *nice*. Seriously, you were practically submissive to that human. I almost threw up." He shook his head with a sigh. "I just don't know what else I can do for you. It's like you've got a faulty connection in your brain that makes you buddy up to humans instead of dominating them."

Julius shrugged. "Is that really so bad?"

"*Yes*," Justin growled, stabbing his finger at the mages fishing lamprey bodies out of the water. "If these people knew what you actually were, they wouldn't be your friends. They'd be terrified, as they should be. Because if they weren't scared, they'd be trying to kill you and sell you for parts."

Julius shook his head. "It's not like that."

"Isn't it?" Justin asked, stepping closer until he was looming over his brother. "You might be a sheep in wolf's clothing, but never forget that, to the humans, you're just another monster with a bounty on its head. We're all monsters to them, and they will punish us for it every chance they get if we don't give them a reason to run away. In this whole world, your clan is the only thing you can trust, so if I were you, I'd worry less about pleasing a bunch of short-lived mortals who will never accept you, and more about pleasing us."

Julius longed to point out that he'd been trying and failing to please his family his whole life, but it wouldn't do any good. Justin was already turning away.

"Thank you very much for your help tonight," he said to his brother's back. "I owe you."

Those were heavy words between dragons, but Justin just shrugged. "I'll add it to your tab."

Julius had no doubt of that. From the moment he'd learned how to talk, Justin had been able to recite every debt he was owed and why. He could still do it, too, though it took him over an hour to get through the list these days. Every dragon in the Heartstriker clan seemed to owe Justin for something, but while he collected favors with a vengeance, Julius had never heard of him cashing any in. Some Heartstrikers, the ones who didn't know Justin very well, thought he was storing them up for some kind of massive power play in the future. Julius, however, was far more inclined to believe that his brother had simply never encountered a problem he didn't think he could take all by himself with one arm tied behind his back.

He watched Justin haul himself up the now-dried metal ladder without a word. Since his brother didn't even seem to be pretending at humanity anymore, it took him ten seconds to climb the thirty-foot wall and vanish into the pipe at the top. Fortunately, all of the mages were too busy cleaning up lampreys to notice. All of them, that was, except for the one who mattered.

"How did he *do* that?"

Julius looked over to see Marci standing a few feet behind him, staring up at the now-empty metal ladder with a look of pure wonder. It was the sort of thing that would take a very clever explanation to cover up. Unfortunately, the best his tired brain could do right now was, "Justin is special."

Marci gave him an odd look, and for a moment, Julius could almost feel her adding up all the impossible things Justin had done. But as he braced for what seemed like inevitable disaster, Marci just turned away, shifting her wet bag higher on her shoulder. "Let's get out of here."

Julius nodded dumbly, following her over to the water where the shaman who'd been tasked with escorting them back to the surface was waiting. But as they were climbing into the repurposed canoe that would take them across the lake, Ross ran over and stopped them.

"Wait!" he called. "I wanted to give you this before you left."

Before Julius could ask what, the alligator shaman pulled out his phone and gestured in the air. A second later, Julius's own phone buzzed, and he pulled it out to see a new entry had been added to his contacts, fronted by a picture of a smiling Katya standing in the arms of an equally happy-looking Ross.

"That's everything I've got," the shaman said quietly. "Her most recent number and all her old ones, just in case. My info's in there, too, so please call me if you find her or if there's anything else I can do."

The shaman's change of heart was so surprising, even after such a long, strange night, Julius couldn't stop himself from asking, "Why?"

Ross sighed, running a hand through his thick curling hair. "Because I'm really worried about her, and because you seem like a decent guy. She's only been my girlfriend for a week, but she's amazing, and if she's in trouble, I want to help her. I told her as much all the time, but she just kept saying she didn't want me to get involved. Now she's gone, and I can't help, so if you can, I don't want to be the one who messed it up." He blew out a worried breath. "Just promise you'll let me know when you find her, okay?"

"I will," Julius said, and he meant it. Because whatever his brother said, it wasn't as simple as dragon versus human, clan versus the world. Whether Ross knew what Katya actually was or not, his concern for her was real, as was the trust he'd just shown, and Julius was determined to make good on it. Because when Katya's shaman clapped him on the arm and waved goodbye, that warm, happy feeling from before had come back in spades. For the first time in years, maybe ever, Julius felt like he'd actually done something right, and greedy dragon that he was, he wanted more.

Once they'd crossed the underground lake, it was a short trip through the mage's compound up to the surface. As Lark had described, Ross's people did indeed have an amazing setup. In addition to the bomb shelter, they'd sealed up and converted almost a mile of old electrical tunnels, turning the dreary cement corridors into a lively warren of homes, casting rooms, and observation cages for an enormous variety of magical animals, most of which Julius couldn't begin to name. He fully expected Marci to try and wheedle a more thorough tour out of their guide, but she didn't say a word.

She'd been oddly silent for a while now, actually, but it wasn't until they got into the brightly lit elevator that would take them back up to the street level that Julius saw why. Marci was exhausted. Her dark brown eyes had huge shadows beneath them, and her normally olive skin was an unhealthy grayish color. The combined effect made her look terrifyingly mortal, and Julius suddenly felt like a heel for pushing her so hard.

Her car was right where they'd left it, parked on the curb across from the warded "storm drain" that was actually the shaman's front door. Since Marci was clearly in no shape to handle even an automated system, Julius volunteered to drive. She agreed after a token resistance, flopping into the passenger seat with an enormous yawn. By the time Julius had said goodbye to their guide and gotten in himself, she was asleep, curled up with her head tucked against the window.

The sight filled him with tenderness and surprise. Nothing, not even animals, fell asleep next to a dragon. If Justin had been here, he would have claimed this was just more proof that Julius was officially the saddest excuse for a predator to ever live. For Julius, though, it was a precious sign of trust, and the more he thought about that, the more determined he became to make sure it was not misplaced.

Moving slowly so as not to wake her, he keyed in their destination, sending the old car up the curving ramp to the brightly lit skyways. It was nearly three in the morning, but the Upper City was still hopping, and the elevated roads were crowded with sleek, driverless cars, some of which didn't even have passengers. Since Marci's ancient autodrive wasn't as quick on the pick up as the newer models, Julius ordered them to the far right. When the rusty sedan was safely locked into the slow lane, he pulled out his phone to do a little business with his newfound wealth, starting with a message to an old acquaintance.

He had plenty of time. Traffic was moving at a decent pace, but unlike the grid roads of old Detroit, the upper city skyways looped and circled in on themselves in ways Julius, and apparently Marci's GPS, didn't really understand. As a result, it took them almost forty minutes to reach their destination. Marci woke up when they turned in, blinking sleepily as the car pulled to a gentle stop in front of an absolutely massive superscraper right on the bank of Lake St. Clare.

"The Royal Hotel?" she asked, craning her head back to look up the building's cliff-like side. "Are you trying to spend all your money at once or something?"

"It's not *that* expensive," Julius said, getting out of the car.

Marci got out too, yawning as she walked around to the driver's side. "Thanks for letting me nap," she said, holding out her hand for the keys. "I guess I'll get in touch with you later, then?"

"What are you talking about? You're staying here, too."

He paused, waiting for her to be excited, but Marci was staring at him like he'd just told her she was going to Mars. "You want me to go to a hotel with you?"

"Not like that," he said quickly, face going hot. "I'm getting you your own room. My treat."

Marci's expression of frank disbelief morphed into one of cautious skepticism. "Why?"

"Because you've been invaluable to me tonight," Julius said honestly. "And because the idea of sleeping in a bed while you go back to that cat graveyard you call a house is more than my conscience can stand. Just leave the car to the valet system and let's go check in."

Marci narrowed her eyes, clearly waiting for the trap. When it didn't appear, Julius finally got the look he'd been waiting for: the beaming smile of pure delight. The sight warmed him right to his toes before Marci dashed away, tossing her trunk open and grabbing a fraying gym bag in a frantic explosion of energy. This plus her overpacked shoulder bag left her pathetically weighed down, so Julius, who had no bags, offered to carry something. After a short protest, she let him, handing him the gym bag with another smile that made him feel like the best thing on the planet.

This being a waterfront hotel, there was a real, old-fashioned check-in desk staffed by actual human clerks even at this hour of the morning. It was such an anachronistic sight, Julius was half tempted to ask them for a room just for the novelty factor. But despite her renewed energy, Marci looked worse than ever under the lobby's elegant lights. Also, their filthy clothes were already drawing the hairy eyeball from the clerks, so Julius resigned himself to checking in the normal way: through the kiosk system via his phone's AR.

By the time they walked across the marble floor to the elevators, he'd bought them two connecting rooms overlooking the water. He grabbed their key cards from the dispenser in the elevator on their way up. When the doors opened, he gently guided Marci down the hall. "I'm going to order some food," he said as he handed her the key card to her suite. "What do you want?"

"Anything," she said dreamily, opening the door and staring at the huge room with its sweeping view of the lake like she'd just opened the gate to fairy land.

He smiled and put her bag down beside her before walking one door down to his own room. As soon as he was inside, he pulled up the room service menu and ordered them breakfast. He also ordered himself a few things through the hotel's automated concierge service, including a full set of new clothes. His had been on their last legs when his mother had burst into his room yesterday, but while they'd survived the fight with Bixby's men and his dust-up with Chelsie, the trip through the sewers had completely done them in.

Fortunately, waterside hotels were famous for their ability to get anything in a hurry. The porter brought up a bag containing new jeans, underwear, and a fancy shirt made from a fabric Julius didn't even recognize before their food could even arrive from the kitchen. The moment Julius was sure everything fit, his old clothes went straight into the trash, never to be spoken of again.

Thirty minutes later—showered, shaved, dressed in new clothes, and bearing the breakfast tray that had just arrived, as well as a special package that had come up with his other purchases—Julius knocked on the door that connected his room to Marci's, opening it when she answered only to find an empty room. After a quick look around, he found her in the bathroom, cutting her hair in front of the huge mirror with the trimming scissors from the complementary shaving kit.

The gym bag she'd grabbed from her car must have been full of clothes, because she'd changed into a loose UNLV t-shirt and pajama bottoms so faded, Julius couldn't make out the original design. He could, however, clearly make out the shape of her legs underneath, and he quickly looked away before she caught him staring.

"I'll be done in a sec," she said, wrenching her neck around to get at the hair on the back of her head. "I've been dying to straighten this mess out for days."

Julius cleared his throat and walked over to put the tray down on the table by the window. "I hope you didn't pay whoever gave you that haircut."

"Trust me, this wasn't my first choice," Marci grumbled, carefully trimming the wispy trails of hair above her eyes into something like bangs. "Do you have any idea how long it took me to grow my hair out? But Bixby's mage was using it as a material link to track me, so I had no choice. I chopped my ponytail off and used it as bait to lure his goons into my house. Then, when they went inside after me, *bam!*"

Julius arched an eyebrow. "Bam?"

"Blew them up," she said fiercely, glowering into the mirror as she put down the scissors. "Trust me, it was better than they deserved for killing my dad." She grabbed a brush next, running the stiff bristles through her now mostly even short-cropped hair. This went on for almost ten seconds before she realized what she'd just said.

"Oh, wow," she whispered, going still. "I guess that counts as confessing to murder, doesn't it?"

Julius put up his hands. "I'm not judging. If someone killed my parent, I'd do the same." If anyone actually managed to take out Bethesda, getting blown up would look like a holiday compared to what the Heartstrikers would do.

Marci dropped the brush on the marble counter with a loud clatter and leaned forward, resting her head dejectedly against the mirror. "You know," she said softly, "believe it or not, I was a nice girl before all this. Never blew up anything bigger than a car, never killed anyone or went spelunking in the sewers or got in alley fights. They say people come to the DFZ to reinvent themselves, but I think I've taken the idea a bit further than intended."

"I think you're doing great," Julius said, grabbing the package he'd ordered for her off the breakfast tray. "Come over here, I got you something."

She gave herself a final shake and pushed off the sink, padding over to the table by the window. When she came around the bed, he noticed that her feet were bare. They were also adorable, her toes painted with the same glitter polish that was chipping off her fingernails, creating little flashes of sparkle as she walked.

"What is it?"

Julius blinked, startled. "Sorry," he said, quickly looking away. "Here."

He handed her the cardboard box, which she ripped open with focused curiosity. But instead of being excited as he'd hoped, her face fell into a confused frown. "But Julius," she said. "This is a…"

"A phone," he finished for her, plucking the slim, purple rectangle out of her hand and turning it on. "Here, let me show you the best part."

He flipped through the phone's small AR, fumbling a bit with the unfamiliar interface. He'd already set this part up through his own phone, though, so even with the fumbling, it only took a few seconds to find and pull up her account and put it on the screen. When he handed the phone back, he was rewarded with the sight of Marci rendered completely speechless.

"You can change the security settings to whatever you want," he said. "But as you see, it's all there. That's your half of this morning's earnings plus your fee for the hours you've worked so far, full rate."

Marci didn't say a word. She just stood there, staring at the five-digit number that was her new bank account balance. "But," she whispered at last, "How? This account's in my name. You need a DFZ Residency ID to have a phone in the city. I never got one since Bixby could use it to track me, and it wasn't like I had any money to put in it anyway, but this...How did you *do* this?"

"I used to play some pretty popular full-immersion MMOs," Julius explained. "You meet a lot of people in games, some of whom make their living doing less than legal work. It just so happens one of my old guildmates works as a data merchant, and he was happy to sell me a fake Residency ID for you at a discount."

Marci stared down at her phone again. "So this is fake?"

"The *number* is fake," Julius said. "The money is real. As for the ID, my guy assures me it'll pass any sort of routine check, though we probably shouldn't do anything that might earn you a full background scan."

He'd meant that last part as a joke, but Marci looked stricken. "You didn't have to do this."

"You earned the money," he said with a shrug. "And I needed you to have a phone. Besides, I had to talk to this guy anyway since I've hired him to help us find Katya."

He'd debated that move a lot, actually. Now that he had Katya's number, he'd been tempted to just call her and try to work something out. After much back and forth, though, he'd concluded that contacting her would be a waste of time. She probably wouldn't answer, and even if she did, a call out of the blue on a number she'd only trusted to a few people might cause her to bolt for good. But a good hacker like his guildmate could take a phone number and work backward to find the Residency ID and bank account it was attached to. And since phone enabled electronic transfers were used for everything from restaurants to car rentals, tracking Katya's movements had just become no problem.

"He's got a search going to for her ID right now," Julius explained. "The moment she uses her phone to pay for anything, the tracking program will message us with the location, and then all we have to do is drive over and say hello." And hope that Katya wasn't so spooked she ran even from a sealed dragon. Still, Julius thought it was a pretty clever plan, and he was a little let down when Marci's face remained frighteningly blank.

"So your friend did all of this for you just off a phone call?"

"Well, he's not really my friend," Julius admitted. "I don't even know his real name, actually, but I was his healer in the game, and the bond between healer and tank runs deep. And it's not like he's working for free. I'm paying him like any other client would. He just did me a favor by moving me to the front of the line."

Marci nodded, but Julius got the impression she wasn't really listening. The whole time they'd been talking, she'd been staring at her phone with a closed-off expression he didn't like at all. Clearly, it was time to break out the big guns.

"Here," he said, sitting down at the table where he'd set the breakfast tray. "Come eat. I got you waffles."

He lifted the silver tray covers with a flourish, revealing the beautifully arranged piles of sugar dusted Belgian waffles and fresh cut fruit. But when he looked up to see if he'd gotten a smile at last, Marci was still just staring at him, and then her bottom lip started to tremble. She turned away a second later, raising her hand to her face, but it wasn't until her shoulders started to shake that Julius realized she was *crying*.

"What?" he cried, jumping up. "I'm sorry, what did I do? Do you not like waffles?"

"No, no," Marci said. "Waffles are perfect, it's..." She stopped and scrubbed furiously at her face. "I'm sorry, I'm not normally this emotional. It's just, it's been a really hard week for me, and you're being really, *really* nice."

Julius flinched instinctively at the word *nice*. Before he could hide it, though, Marci whirled back around to face him.

"I can't accept this," she said, holding out the phone. "The payment for my work is one thing, but the lamprey money and the phone and getting me an ID and the room and, and..." She trailed off, swiping at the tears that were still rolling down her cheeks. "Sorry," she whispered in a shamed voice. "I don't mean to be such a fountain, but I can't tell you how nice it is to be clean and safe and not surrounded by cats or afraid the house is going to fall on my head. And I know you saved my life back in the sewer when you bounced that blue fireball. No one's ever done that for me before—saved my life, I mean—but now you've done it twice in one night, and I don't know how I can ever pay you back. I will, though, I swear, but I owe you so much already, and if I take this, I'll—"

Julius's hand landed on her shoulder, grabbing her so hard she jumped. He felt guilty immediately, but he couldn't let her say another word. "Stop," he said. "Please, just stop and listen. You don't owe me anything. There is no debt between us."

She blinked at him. "But…"

"I did this because *I* wanted to," he said firmly. "Because we're a team, and how are we supposed to work together if I can't call you? As for the money, you earned it fair and square. You were the one who found the nest, and it was you who pointed out the lampreys had value. We wouldn't have any money at all if you hadn't been there, so I'm not accepting it back. If you don't want it, you can throw it away, but you need to understand that *we are even.*"

Even as he said it, he knew he was being ridiculous. A human would never make such a big deal out of this, but Julius had spent his entire life watching dragons use debts as leverage to gain power over others. He'd been there numerous times himself, but always as the one on the bottom, the one being squeezed. Now, when he was finally in a position to be the indebted instead of the debtor, he wanted nothing to do with it. He'd told Justin he was through and he meant it. He didn't even want to pretend to be a good dragon anymore, especially not if it meant holding money over Marci.

"You are my ally," he said earnestly, filling the word with all the conviction he had so she would know just how rare such a thing was for him, and how much it meant. "Everything I do, I do because of that. Because I value your help and your company and because it makes me happy to see you happy. So please don't ever think that you have to pay me back, because you don't, and you never will."

He could have said more. He could have gone on forever until he was positive she understood. But instead of being relieved by his reassurances, Marci looked like she was going to start crying again.

The sight sent Julius into a panic. His mind whirled frantically, searching for the right thing to say that would undo whatever he'd done to cause this. In the end, though, it didn't matter, because Marci didn't cry. She did something different, something completely unexpected.

She kissed him.

Chapter 10

If Marci hadn't put her hands on his shoulders, Julius would have jumped out of his skin. But she held him in place, gently sliding her arms up to encircle his neck as she tilted her head, slanting her lips against his own. Her body followed, pressing against his, and Julius jumped again, because she was soft and warm and pretty and she was kissing him and...and that was as far as he got before his mind started fogging over and his hands sank down to rest on her hips of their own accord.

Vaguely, in a tiny, dusty corner of his brain that hadn't gotten the message to shut down yet, it occurred to Julius that this was his first real kiss. Oh, he'd had a girl's lips on his before. Thanks to Bethesda's love of attention, the Heartstrikers weren't exactly secret, and there were lots of humans who came to the town at the foot of his mother's mountain in hopes of sleeping with a dragon. Julius had been jumped several times, once in his own room while he was asleep by a girl who'd wandered in after one of his sisters had sent her away. But while other dragons accepted such attentions as their due, Julius had always found the setup extremely distasteful. He had just enough pride to resent being chased after solely because he was a dragon and for absolutely no other reason. Marci, on the other hand, had no idea what he was, but she was kissing him anyway, and it was very, very nice.

Cautiously, Julius lifted his hands to her face, cradling her head as he started to kiss her back. Her breath hitched at his touch, a little gasp of pleasure and surprise that set his heart pounding wildly. Emboldened, he leaned closer, pressing his body tighter against hers as he breathed her in. Not surprisingly, Marci smelled of human and magic, but also of soap and casting chalk and deep down, the smell that was just Marci, a warm, welcoming, feminine scent enhanced by the faintest tang of tears.

He stopped cold, fingers stuttering to a halt against her skin. What was he *doing*? Marci was upset. She'd been crying not thirty seconds before, and now he was *groping* her?

At this point, the part of him that really wanted to keep going loudly reminded Julius that she'd started it, but the rest of him knew it wasn't that simple. Marci had just lost her father and had her life turned upside down. She'd been alone, basically homeless, living off barter and whatever money she could scrounge for the last four days, and that was before he'd made her stay up all night chasing dragons. Now she was exhausted, overwhelmed, and feeling excessively grateful to him, and if

Julius took advantage of that, if he took advantage of *her*, he would be the absolute worst user in his entire family.

That thought was the kick that finally made Julius let go. He took a full step back, snatching his hands off her face. From so far away, he had an excellent view of Marci's dazed expression turning to confusion, then horror as she realized what had just happened.

"Oh," she said, looking down at the carpet as her cheeks got redder and redder. "I, um, I don't suppose you could just forget that happened? Because I'm really sorry."

"You don't have to apologize," he said lamely. When she didn't respond, he felt like kicking himself. He knew he needed to say something else, something better. Before anything came to mind, though, Marci turned away to face the window.

"I just ruined everything, didn't I?" she whispered, biting her nails.

"You didn't ruin anything," he assured her quickly, but she didn't look convinced. He ran his hand through his damp hair, scrambling to think of a way to explain his logic that wouldn't sound like he was pitying her, but his brain was a complete blank. He was exhausted, his mind still soft and stumbling from the kiss. So with no solution in sight and Marci pulling further away by the second, Julius went with the only out he could think of: procrastination.

"Let's just get some sleep," he said softly. "We'll talk about this in the morning."

He knew that was the wrong thing to say when her shoulders stiffened, but he didn't know the right thing, and she wasn't looking at him. So, with no ideas left to try, he grabbed his plate off the breakfast tray and quietly went back to his room.

Back in his suite, he sat down at his own table by the window and ate his food mechanically, shoving the eggs and bacon he'd ordered for himself down as fast as he could before drawing the blackout curtains and falling face down into the huge and strangely lonely hotel bed. But tired as he was, sleep refused to come.

He lay in the dark with his eyes open, trying not to listen for Marci moving on the other side of the wall, trying not to think about the possibilities that kiss opened, or how badly he'd bungled them, trying not to think at all. Unfortunately, his brain refused to shut up. Two hours later, he was still wide awake and buzzing with nervous energy. So, since sleep was clearly impossible, Julius got up, stripped off his new shirt and jeans, and dropped to floor in a plank position to set about trying to recover the ground he'd lost during seven years of hiding.

Thirty minutes later, he was panting like he'd never done a day's work in his life. If Justin had been there, the I-told-you-so's would have gone on for a month, but at least the lack of oxygen stopped his brain's constant obsessing over kissing Marci.

Mostly, anyway.

***

One of the nice things about being a dragon was that, with a little food and effort, you could recover just about any amount of lost ground. It would take a lot more than one morning's work to get his speed and endurance back to where it had been when Justin had moved out, taking all of Julius's motivation to stay fit with him, but six hours, multiple exercises, three more calls to room service, and one power nap later, Julius was showing marked improvement.

By the time noon rolled around, he'd actually managed to get back enough speed to pull off his favorite trick of all: pouring out a full cup of water and then dropping down fast enough to catch it in the cup again before the stream hit the floor. Of course, back when he and Justin were in their prime, they'd done two cups at a time. Justin could probably do three by now, but one definitely wasn't bad, especially considering where Julius had started, and he felt quite accomplished as he grabbed an armful of towels from the closet and set to work mopping up all the spilled water from the practice runs off the bathroom floor.

He'd started exercising as a way to get his mind off Marci. Now, though, Julius was genuinely glad he'd done it. He hadn't thought about it in years, but for a while there, he'd actually been the fastest dragon of his age group. Even faster than Justin, who'd been the undisputed king of J clutch from the moment he'd hatched. Back then, he'd actually wondered if his speed was a sign of true talent. His mother, however, had been quick to knock him back down, pointing out (correctly) that the only reason Julius had gotten so fast was because he spent so much time running away. By that point, all of his siblings had discovered other, more subtle ways to torment him anyway, so he'd traded running for hiding, and his speed had correspondingly fallen off.

Julius didn't feel much like hiding now. For the first time in his life, things actually seemed to be going his way. Not only had he gotten his reflexes back to a respectable level, but he was closing in on Katya. True, the trace he'd bought from his old guildmate hadn't turned up anything yet, but it was still early for a dragon who'd gone on the run late last night. She was probably still asleep wherever she'd gone to hide. Eventually, though, she'd wake up, and the moment she used her phone to buy anything, he'd be able to find and talk to her at last. He still wasn't sure what he was going to say, but he was absolutely certain he wouldn't use Svena's chain on her, and reckless as it was, that made him happier than he'd been in a long, long time. And then, of course, there was Marci.

His eyes flicked yet again to the door connecting their rooms. He'd practically memorized the woodgrain by this point, but while Julius knew for certain he'd made a mess of things earlier, he was just as sure now that he could fix it. After all, Marci was a reasonable, clever, practical human. Surely once Julius explained that he hadn't been rejecting her when he broke their kiss, she would understand. She might even kiss him again, which was *definitely* something to look forward to.

That happy thought was enough to send his already soaring optimism through the roof. He actually started whistling as he mopped the last of the water off the tile. When he was done, he tossed his sopping towel into the bathtub and grabbed a fresh one to dry himself. He was still toweling off his hair when his phone began to ring.

It was a sign of how crazy his good mood had made him that his first guess was that it was the tracker calling in at last with Svena's location. A hope that fizzled when he walked over to the bed where he'd tossed his phone to see Bethesda's name shining up at him from the screen.

Fast as it had risen, his optimism took a nose drive straight through to his feet. It was such an intense reversal that, for a moment, Julius seriously considered not answering. But ignoring Bethesda was practically begging for disaster, and so, wrapping the tattered remains of his good mood around him like a blanket, he grabbed his phone and lifted it to his ear with a deep breath.

"Good morning, Mother."

"Try afternoon," she said, the disdain in her voice so ingrained it was almost lazy, like this was her default setting and she just couldn't be bothered to put in the energy for anything more. "Really, Julius. Sleeping in is a luxury reserved for those of us who've done something with our lives."

"Actually, I wasn't sleeping," he said, draping the towel over his bare shoulders. "I was working on the water glass trick. You know, the one Justin used to make me do? He reminded me last night that I've been slacking, and since I'm out of the mountain now, I figured I'd better get back in shape."

There was a moment of stunned silence. "Julius," his mother said at last, drawing his name out into something between a growl and purr.

"Is this some kind of shock left over from your little adventure last night, or have you finally learned how to lie?"

"Neither, I hope," he replied. "I just thought it was time I started taking more responsibility for myself."

"Really?" Bethesda said, her tone loading the word with so much skepticism he was surprised it didn't collapse. "You'll forgive me if I have trouble believing that after the hissy-fit you threw last night, begging Ian for money and generally making a spectacle of yourself."

Julius winced. Of course his mother had heard about that. Bethesda heard *everything*. "Yes, well." He stopped to clear his throat. "I followed Ian's advice and took initiative. Justin came to help, too, and together we turned things around. Now I'm just waiting for my lead to come in and, barring disaster, this Three Sisters business should be finished on time."

He paused, holding his breath as he waited for—not a compliment, of course, since it wasn't the end of the world—but some sort of acknowledgment of his lack of failure. He might as well have been waiting for his mother to announce she was starting a charitable institution, because all Bethesda said was, "Oh, so you'll have everything tied up by tonight, then?"

Julius started to sweat. Like the rest of his family, he'd learned never to give his mother a deadline. The moment Bethesda had a date, it became an iron-clad requirement you were expected to meet, preferably beat, at all costs. But then, Ian had already demanded Julius find Katya today, a fact that his mother almost certainly knew, which meant this whole line of questioning was nothing but a tactic to intimidate him. It was a classic Bethesda maneuver, and the fact that he'd actually seen through it ahead of time for once made Julius feel almost confident.

"I told Ian tonight," he said. "Therefore, I'll have it done tonight."

His mother chuckled, a cold, light sound. "My, my, so self-assured. Did I call the right son?"

Julius had to spot her that one. Fortunately for his fledgling ego, however, a reply was not required.

"I know this is asking you to play against character," she went on. "But do try not to mess this up. It's such a simple task, finding one little runaway dragon, and I can't tell you how unhappy I'd be if Ian's chance with Svena, and, thereby, my chance at becoming a grandmother, fell through because of your incompetence."

"Grandmother?" The word popped out before Julius could stop it, and he bit his tongue. He *had* to get better at this poker face stuff before he blurted out something that got him killed. Thankfully, his mother only chuckled.

"Don't sound so surprised. Those ice snakes are as stuck-up as they come, but Ian is so handsome and takes so much after myself that I think he has a real chance at this, provided he's not undermined by underperforming siblings."

Julius swallowed.

"Just think what a triumph this would be for us," his mother continued. "I've mated into every important dragon clan on the planet over the last thousand years. Those three old fossils were the final holdouts. They always thought themselves so far above me. I can't wait to see the looks on their faces when they finally wake up to discover one of their precious daughters has slept her way onto the winning team. And not just any daughter, but the White Witch herself!"

She cackled after that. An honest-to-God cackle, and Julius began to sweat. He couldn't imagine cold, vicious Svena condescending to touch a Heartstriker, let alone agreeing to something as serious as a mating flight. But while he privately considered his mother's plan to be wishful thinking bordering on delusion, Bethesda the Heartstriker wasn't stupid, and she wasn't the sort to drop information thoughtlessly over the phone. If she was telling him her hopes for Ian, there had to be a reason, and it wasn't just so he'd know the stakes. After all, for Julius, the stakes for this job were already life and death. Telling him about a potential mating flight wouldn't change his motivation one way or the other, so why was she doing it? And why phrase it so that it sounded like Ian's chances with Svena hinged entirely upon *Julius's* success? Surely his mother wasn't really pinning her hopes on—

Julius's breath left him in a rush. "You're setting me up."

"Pardon?" his mother replied sweetly.

"You don't actually care about finding Katya," he said. "This whole job was just a ploy to give Ian a chance to seduce Svena."

"Naturally," she purred. "Why else would we help them?"

"But we're not," Julius said. "You're baiting them. Svena's one of the oldest and most revered dragons in the world. Bob would barely have a chance with her, much less Ian. If Svena plays with him and dumps him, it makes our whole family look bad. You'd never let anyone gamble with Heartstriker pride like that, but Ian's one of your favorites, and he's ambitious enough for two dragons. You wanted to let him try, but you needed a safety measure, someone else who could take the fall if things went bad."

The whole puzzle was coming together as he spoke, and with every piece that snapped into place, Julius got angrier and angrier.

"That's why you had Ian give me the job, isn't it? I was the excuse he used to involve himself in Three Sisters politics and get closer to Svena. But you never even meant for me to find Katya, did you? That's why the deadline is so ridiculous. You *want* me to fail. That way, if Ian can't land Svena, he can just blame it on me for not getting the job done." His hand clenched so hard on the phone he nearly cracked the glass. "I'm nothing but your fall guy!"

"Why, Julius," Bethesda whispered tearfully. "What a terrible thing to imply about your mother."

He didn't buy it for a second. "It's true, isn't it?'

"Of course it's true," she said, dropping the hurt mother act as easily as she'd picked it up. "But I don't see why you're so upset. It's not like you were doing anything with your life. Ian, on the other hand, is already a success, and any good player knows you always sacrifice the lower-value piece to support the higher."

Her casual words made Julius's stomach clench with a sharpness that surprised him. It wasn't that he was shocked his mother was using him—that was the only reason Bethesda had children—but he hadn't realized that she considered him quite so...disposable. "If you never meant me to succeed, why the big setup? Why even bother sealing me?"

"Come now, Julius. You're a weakling and a coward, but you're not usually an idiot. Try to keep up. Sealing you wasn't just necessary to make Svena buy Ian's story that we had the perfect tool to nab her skittish sister, I also needed it for *you*."

"For me?" Julius repeated, disbelieving. "But I thought I was the lesser piece you were throwing away?"

"You are, dear," Bethesda said. "But I'm your mother. I understand your weaknesses better than anyone, and I knew right from the start that if I didn't build a proper fire under your feet, nothing would get done at all. The seal was the easiest way to keep you desperate and hard-working while also conveniently making it highly unlikely that you'd get into any real trouble in DFZ. Plus, it kept you from flying away, which I felt was pertinent. You always were a runner."

She finished with a chuckle, but Julius didn't know what to say. His mother had played him utterly, saying and doing exactly what was needed to make him jump at her command. She'd only been wrong about one thing so far: he *was* an idiot. An idiot for thinking that by giving up his freedom and hiding in his room, he could also hide from his mother's plans. What a joke. The only thing he'd managed by sticking his head under the sand was to miss the trap closing around him, and now it was too late. If he ran, he was dead. If he failed to get Katya, he was dead. Even if he did find her before the deadline, if Ian's power-grab didn't work, Julius was still the fall guy. Bethesda would figure out a way to make it his fault, and then he was dead. Anyway he looked at it, he was dead. Anyway, that was, except one.

He cleared his throat. "Do you know how successful Ian has been with Svena so far?"

"I have it on good authority they slept together last night," she said, too smug to take offense at the tactless question. "Though I'd rather you didn't poke your snout into Ian's business. He's fighting an uphill battle with the Three Sisters pride as it is. The last thing he needs is you mucking it up in some misguided attempt to save your life. Really, Julius, I'd think the fact that your ultimate survival is in Ian's hands would be a relief. He's a much better dragon than you are."

That went without saying, but Julius wasn't about to sit back and wait while his brother, who *also* considered him disposable, played dice with his life. But while it was far too late to wiggle out of his mother's trap, that didn't mean there was nothing he could do. If he couldn't avoid being Ian's fall guy, then he'd just have to make sure there was no fall to take.

"Well, Mother," he said stiffly. "Not that this hasn't been a delightful call, but I'm afraid I have to get moving if I'm going to get Katya back before your deadline."

"See that you do," Bethesda said. "I'll be expecting a full report. Oh, and Julius?"

He fought the urge to sigh. "Yes?"

"Don't do anything stupid," she said, her voice curling into a deadly whisper. "You've had years to prove you were more than a pawn. You didn't, which means you've surrendered your right to balk when I use you as one. I've spent a great deal of time and effort getting my pieces in line for this. It would be very bad sport of you to try and buck the system this late in the game just because you're upset you didn't do more with your life here at the end, don't you think?"

Julius couldn't begin to respond to a statement like that. Fortunately, it didn't seem to matter. Bethesda took his obedience as a given, no confirmation needed.

"Good boy," she cooed. "I'll talk to you tonight."

"Yes, Mother," he whispered, but she'd already hung up, leaving Julius alone with his growing panic.

He forced it down with a deep breath. Panic was a luxury he couldn't afford right now. His only chance to survive was to dig up the calm, plotting dragon that lurked somewhere inside him and figure this out. But as he was sitting down on the bed to do just that, his phone rang again.

Julius swore under his breath, but when the AR threw the name up in front of him, it wasn't his mother. It was the Unknown Caller, which was almost worse. With a surge of longing for the days when the powerful members of his family couldn't be bothered to look his direction, much less call him, Julius brought the phone back to his ear. "Hello, Bob."

"Wrong."

The cold female voice chilled him to the bone, and Julius almost hung up right there. The only reason he didn't was because he knew it wouldn't do any good. "Hello, Chelsie."

He could almost hear the Heartstriker family enforcer giving him her famous deadly smile before she ordered, "Go to the window."

Julius obeyed at once, standing up and walking over to the suite's enormous window overlooking Lake St. Clare. He was wondering if Chelsie was going to tell him to jump out of it when she said, "Look down."

He did, and found her at once.

Thanks to its location up on the skyways, the Royal Hotel was perched high above the lake it overlooked. It also boasted an impressive elevated boardwalk that extended almost fifty feet out over the water below. It was the middle of the day, and the bright white boards were packed with tourists and other wealthy people getting lunch from the numerous restaurants and cafes that ringed the edges of the cliff-like dock. From his high window, the crowd looked more like an undulating mass than a group of individuals, but even so, Chelsie was impossible to miss thanks to the ten-foot ring of empty space the colorful river of humanity was giving her.

No matter how civilized people became, some instincts never really went away. To the casual observer, Chelsie would look completely human, just another woman enjoying the summer sun on a bench by the water. Julius couldn't even tell what she was wearing from so far away, but it wouldn't be anything crazy. A dragon's predatory aura didn't rely on trappings or appearances, and Chelsie's was a mile wider than most when she chose to let it show. Even safely tucked inside his hotel room a dozen stories up, Julius could feel the bite of her attention like an icy claw on his spine, and his heart started pounding all over again.

"I have more important things to do with my time, so I'll be brief," she said. "I know Mother just called you."

The obvious question had barely formed in Julius's mind before Chelsie answered it. "I've lived with her for a long time. I know how she thinks. I also know that you are likely a mess right now. I don't blame you for feeling that way, but I do want you to look out at the water."

Her tiny figure turned toward the lake as she said this. Julius's eyes followed, but all he saw was the white pillar of Algonquin's tower.

"That's right," Chelsie said, her voice barely more than a whisper even over the magically augmented speakers. "*That* is who rules this city. I know you're feeling backed against the wall at the moment. You might even be considering doing something reckless, so this is a courtesy call to remind you of the price of acting out in a city where the slightest failure in judgment could bring the Lady of the Lakes down on all our heads."

"Wait," Julius said, confused. "You want me to watch out for *Algonquin*? You're not calling to tell me not to act out against Mother?"

Chelsie scoffed. "My job is to keep the Heartstriker clan alive and in line, not babysit her plans."

There was a note of ingrained frustration in her voice that Julius had heard a thousand times in his own, and for a moment, he felt a whisper of empathy for the sister who'd had to deal with their mother far more and far longer than he had.

"I'm not telling you not to crack," Chelsie went on, her voice flicking back to its normal sharpness like it had never left. "I'm just asking that you do it in a way that won't cause trouble for the family. I'd hate to have to come down on you for something as stupid and preventable as making a scene in Algonquin's city."

"I have no intention of making a scene anywhere," Julius said. "But I appreciate the warning."

"Everyone gets one," his sister replied. "And for what it's worth, I wish you good luck. You'll need it."

Julius placed his hand on the cold glass, unexpectedly touched. "Thank you, Chelsie."

"I'm not doing it for your sake," Chelsie snapped. "I'm doing it for mine. I *hate* killing dragons under fifty. You're barely more than hatchlings, and it's just depressing. So don't make me do it. And don't forget I'm watching."

Like Julius could. But before he could say anything else, the call cut out. He lowered his phone with a sigh, watching his sister's tiny figure far below as she got up from the bench and vanished into the colorful, swirling crowds that mobbed the boardwalk. When he could no longer see her, he sank back down on his bed.

It was nice to know Chelsie didn't relish the idea of killing him. That wouldn't stop her, of course, but his sister's unexpected warning had made him feel slightly less alone in the face of Bethesda's plots. But while it was comforting to know he wasn't the only one, his sister had been absolutely right. He *was* up against the wall, and his only hope of getting down again was to find Katya as soon as possible. He'd just started typing a message to his old guildmate to see if his tracking program had found anything when he heard a soft knock on the door that connected his suite to Marci's.

It was a sign of how flustered he was that he went ahead and told her to come in before he remembered he wasn't wearing anything but his boxers. Thankfully, he'd been working on his speed all morning, and he managed to grab his pants and shove them on before she opened the door.

"Hey," she said as she came in, "I just—" Her voice cut out as she stopped short, eyes flicking to the bathroom full of soggy towels, then to the bed torn up by his tossing and turning, and finally to him, standing shirtless and sweaty in front of the window. "Rough night?"

"Sort of," Julius said, wiping his face with the towel around his neck so she wouldn't see his embarrassed wince. When he looked up again, Marci's eyes were locked on his bare chest. She stared just long enough for Julius to see her cheeks turn bright pink before she whirled around and walked swiftly to the doorway that led into the relatively untouched living room portion of Julius's suite.

"I'm sorry to bother you," she said when she got there. "But I heard you talking, so…" She stopped with a frustrated sound, drumming her fingers on the door frame. Then, like she'd come to a decision, Marci turned around again and looked him straight in the eye. "I wanted to tell you I'm very sorry about what happened earlier."

After the horrors of the last twenty minutes, it took Julius several seconds to figure out what Marci was talking about. By the time he remembered, she'd already blazed ahead.

"My actions were completely out of line," she said, folding her hands in front of her. "I breached the bounds of a professional relationship, and I sincerely apologize. My only excuse is that I was exhausted and making bad decisions, but I'm feeling much better now, and I promise I'll never put you in that position ever again. So, if it's okay with you, I'd like it if we could just forget about the whole thing and move on with our business together."

Julius stepped forward, mouth already opening to tell her she had nothing to apologize for. That what had happened in her room was actually the best thing that had happened to him in years, and he wouldn't forget it for the world. In the end, though, he just looked away again with a bitter sigh, because while she had the why of it all wrong, Marci was still absolutely right.

She'd been the one to kiss him, but Julius had had no business enjoying it. She was human, and—as his conversation with his mother had so pointedly reminded him—he was most likely a dead dragon. Even if he did somehow manage to survive, he liked Marci too much to drag her into the snake pit that was dragon politics. He really should go ahead and tell her goodbye right now, before he got her into any more trouble, but he didn't feel right leaving her alone while Bixby was still at large.

That was grasping at straws and he knew it, but Julius grasped gladly. His mother's call had turned a fire hose on the new spark of confidence he'd been nurturing all morning, and Chelsie's follow-up had stomped on the ashes. If he lost Marci, too, he might go out entirely.

"I'll do whatever you want," he said finally, grabbing his new shirt and pulling it over his head so he wouldn't have to look her in the eyes. "Consider it forgotten."

"Oh." He couldn't see her expression, but Marci's voice sounded surprised and a little disappointed, though that last part might have been Julius's imagination. "Well, that's settled then. So what's the job for today?"

"Same as yesterday: find Katya." And fast, he added to himself, checking his phone again on the off chance he'd missed something in all the chaos, but he had no more messages than he'd had this morning. Frustrated, he sent a quick inquiry to his contact and got a near instant reply. Everything was working; there was just nothing to report.

"Julius?" He looked up to see Marci watching him, her face worried. "Are you okay?"

"Yeah," he breathed, determined to make sure that wasn't a lie. He would be okay, he decided. He would be calm and rational and figure out how to make Ian's courtship of Svena an unquestionable success with absolutely no need for a scapegoat, because if he didn't, he'd be dead.

That thought filled him with just as much dread as always. This time, though, he managed to get through it a little better, sliding his phone back into his pocket as he turned to Marci. "Do you have anything you need to do today?"

She blinked. "I thought you were in a hurry?"

"I will be once the trace comes back, but until she actually uses her phone, we're stuck in limbo." And if he had to sit around waiting with nothing to do, the worry would destroy him. "Can I help you with something in the meanwhile?"

Marci still looked pretty skeptical, but she nodded anyway. "I'd like to swing back by my house, if that's okay. I didn't exactly pack for a long trip last night, and I need to grab some stuff." She paused, her face suddenly brightening. "All of it, actually. Now that I have some money, I'm never spending a night there again."

She sounded so excited at the idea of finally getting out of her cat-infested basement that Julius couldn't help smiling back. Helping Marci move actually sounded like exactly the sort of steady, mindless work he needed to calm back down to a functional level while he waited for Katya to make a move, and who knew? Maybe if he chilled out, he could come up with the sort of brilliant, outside-the-box plan he needed to save his life.

"Let's go, then," he said, tapping over to his phone account to leave a large tip in the room's AR for the maids who'd have to deal with the fallout of his water-catching practice. "I'm ready when you are."

Marci ran back to her room. "Just give me a moment to pack!"

Julius nodded and shut the connecting door behind her. When he was alone again, he grabbed Svena's silver chain from where he'd hidden it inside the nightstand and slipped it into his pocket.

***

It was a truly glorious afternoon. The late summer sunshine was bright and clear, and the DFZ skyways were crowded with beautiful people out enjoying the fine weather. Even Marci's car was running better thanks to a complementary battery charge and software update from the hotel's valet system. Marci seemed recharged as well, keeping up a steady stream of conversation as she touched up the marker on the inside of her chunky spellworked bracelets.

Julius said nothing. Even though they'd agreed it was forgotten, it was painfully obvious that Marci was covering up her discomfort over what had happened in her hotel room with an impenetrable shellac of cheerfulness. He wanted to tell her she didn't have to pretend, but he had no right to call out her deception and nothing to offer her even if she did admit she was hurt. He could only handle so many crises at a time, anyway, and so though it made him feel like a coward, he took the out she offered and pretended along with her, nodding where appropriate as the car took them down the ramps from the rich Upper City and into the desolation that was the DFZ's north side.

The sunlight dimmed noticeably when they drove into the old University District. It had been dark the last time they'd driven through, so while Julius had noticed the dilapidated buildings, strange magic, and giant fence that marked the edge of Algonquin's spirit land, he hadn't been able to see the haze that hung over the old neighborhood like a greasy film. Just trying to read the street signs through that muck gave him an instant headache, but what really got him was the strange feeling of being watched that only seemed to get worse as the streets got emptier. No wonder no one wanted to live out here. This place was creepier than the Underground.

His feelings of foreboding only got worse when Marci took over the car and turned them off the main road into the hoarded mansion's driveway. This struck him as odd, because the brick house's wildly overgrown garden and sagging overhangs actually looked much less scary in the bright afternoon than they had at night. But the intense sunlight did nothing to stop the chill that crept up Julius's spine as the car pulled them around to the back of the house.

He squinted up at the sagging eaves as they rolled to a stop in front of the collapsing garage, trying figure out what was making him so uneasy, but he saw nothing. There was no movement at all, actually. Even the vines that covered the rear of the house like a parasitic colony were still, but it wasn't until he looked through the equally quite, dust-caked windows that he realized he hadn't seen a single cat.

Fear shot through him like a spear, and he whipped back to Marci, who was already getting out of the car. He'd already sucked in a breath to tell her to stop when he saw it. There, in the wall of privet that separated the yard from the next one over, the sunlight was glinting off the long, silenced barrel of a pistol.

After that, he didn't bother with a warning. Even if he could have yelled something that made sense, Marci wouldn't be able to react fast enough. But Julius had been practicing being fast all morning, and he moved before he could think, launching over the driver's seat to tackle Marci around the waist just as the shot went off.

Chapter 11

The bullet passed so close, Julius felt the heat of it on his back as he tackled Marci to the ground. They landed together in the overgrown grass hard enough to knock Marci's breath out. He was moving again before she caught it, yanking her back toward the car. But just as he grabbed the edge of the driver's seat to haul them both inside, a second gun barrel poked through the tangled wall of vines and bushes on the other side of the car.

The moment Julius saw it, instinct took over completely. He rolled without thinking, whirling with obviously inhuman speed as he dropped them back to the ground. Just in time, too. They'd barely hit the dirt before the next shot shattered the passenger window, cutting through the stuffing of the driver's seat to lodge in the steel frame of the front wheel well not a half inch from Julius's shoulder.

By this point, Marci had recovered from her shock enough to realize what was happening. The stifled *whiff* of the second silenced shot was still fading when she grabbed Julius's hand and took off for the house, dragging him behind her as a third shot whizzed over their heads to blast a chunk off the sagging mansion's brick foundation.

Marci jumped down the basement stairs and hit the ward on the rickety old door with both hands. The magic flashed, and then the basement door flew open as they both ran inside. As soon as they were over the threshold, the ward snapped back into place, covering the doorway in a glowing barrier while the door itself hung open, listing on its rusty hinges. Since the wood was half rotted anyway, Julius didn't even bother kicking it shut. He simply spun to the side and slammed his back against the bare stretch of wall between the open door and the wardrobe in the corner. Marci followed suit, plastering herself against the house's foundation as she gasped for breath.

"What is going on?" she panted.

"Not sure," Julius said, arching his neck back in an attempt to look through one of the little ground-level windows that pierced the wall above them. "I think—"

What he thought was cut off by an explosion of gunfire. Apparently, whoever was attacking had completely given up on subtlety. Bullets began hitting the house like hail, shattering the window above their heads and shredding the basement door to splinters.

"I thought this place was warded!" Julius cried, pressing himself even tighter against the brick wall as bullets flew through the empty doorway to land in the piles of trash that filled the far end of the basement.

"Against *living things!*" Marci yelled back, covering her head with her arms. "Not bullets! Why would I ward against bullets?"

As though in answer, a second rain of shots came in from the side of the house, shattering the single ground-level window on their left. But while the bullets were quickly making powder of Marci's couch and mini-fridge, nothing hit them, and Julius realized that they'd taken refuge in the one spot that wasn't in line of sight for any of the basement windows. Before he could celebrate this fantastic stroke of good luck, though, someone outside yelled an order, and the gunfire stopped.

In the sudden silence, Julius could hear heavy shoes rustling through the undergrowth as their attackers checked the windows. One man even walked down to the door to push on the ward and got zapped for his trouble. Marci looked a little smug about that, but it didn't last long, because while the ward kept the enemy out, it also kept the two of them *in.*

"Is there another exit?"

Marci nodded and pointed at the sea of trash that filled the non-warded half of the basement. "There's a stairway up to the main house somewhere over there."

Julius grimaced. Even if they could battle their way through all the debris, they'd expose their backs to the open door. Not a valid option. "What did you do to Bixby, anyway?" he grumbled, leaning out as far as he dared in an attempt to catch a glimpse of the driveway.

"Oh, no, this can't be Bixby," she said, shaking her head frantically. "I mean, yeah, he wants me dead, but there's no way he'd send an army like this all the way to Det—"

"Novalli!"

Marci froze, her eyes going wider with stark, naked terror as the deep, booming voice bellowed her name. "Come on out, sweetheart," the man continued. "We've got you surrounded, and this time we *know* you're in there. Don't make us torch the place."

Marci threw her head back, squeezing her eyes shut as she mouthed a string of silent curses.

"Do you know that guy?"

"It's Oslo. He's Bixby's freaking *second*. What is he doing up here?"

Julius had no idea, but at least that answered the Bixby question. "See if you can stall them," he whispered, pulling out his phone.

"Why?" Marci whispered back. "What are you doing?"

"Calling the cops. They'll run when they hear sirens." And so would he and Marci, but she was already shaking her head.

"That won't do any good. This is the DFZ, remember? The police are all contractors. Even if we paid their fees in advance, it would take a riot to get them to take a job this close to the Reclamation Zone."

Julius rolled his eyes. Of course. Why should he expect anything else from this capitalist dystopia of a city? He supposed he could call Justin, but his brother would have to fly to get out here fast enough to save them, and there was no way anyone could miss a dragon flying over the DFZ during the *day*. With his brother out of the picture, though, Julius was rapidly running out of ideas, and Oslo seemed to be running out of patience.

"Last chance, Novalli!" Bixby's second yelled. "The boss gave orders that you weren't to be killed, but he didn't say anything about you not being shot. We even brought along a medic, just in case. Of course, that means we can be as rough as we want and you'll still pull through, and my boys and I are mighty pissed about having to come all this way on short notice. So if you want to keep your limbs intact, you should stop wasting my time and get out here now."

The color had completely drained from Marci's face by the time he finished, but her jaw was set as stubbornly as ever. "*You're* pissed?" she shouted at the open door. "*I'm* pissed you idiots can't take a hint and shove off! But feel free to keep yelling at my ward. I've already called the cops. We should be hearing helicopters any second!"

Julius stared questioningly at her, and Marci shrugged. "What? If you didn't know, they might not either."

Oslo, however, did not seem to take the threat the way it was intended, because his reply was, "Break it down."

The order had barely finished when the glowing wall of Marci's ward flashed bright as the sun. Marci gasped at the same time, doubling over like someone had just punched her in the gut. "They have a mage," she whispered through clenched teeth when Julius reached out to steady her. "They're going to brute force the ward."

He grimaced. "How long have we got?"

"Don't know," she said, her face pained. "Whoever they hired has some serious weight behind him. Bastard must be pulling off a small fortune in magical materials." Another blow landed, making Marci's whole body clench so hard it took her several seconds before she could speak again. "If I keep holding it up like this, I'd say two, maybe three minutes?"

Julius shook his head. Even if he'd had a plan, three minutes wouldn't be enough to pull it off. His eyes darted over the trash, looking for something he could use when the time came—a gun, a shovel, even a baseball bat would be better than nothing. He was debating the weapon potential of the rusty rake in the corner when he felt something soft and freezing cold brush against his leg.

He looked down with a start to see Ghost sitting beside him, twitching his semi-transparent tail back and forth across the glass-strewn cement floor. Considering their situation, the sight of a death spirit, even one for cats, was enough to thoroughly creep Julius out. Marci, however, looked delighted.

"Ghost!" she cried. "Perfect! Get out there and do your thing. Jump on them! Eat their souls!"

The transparent cat gave her a look of absolute disgust and started bathing its paw.

"Oh, come *on*," she pleaded as another hit landed on her ward. "You're my death spirit. Go be scary!" Ghost started washing his other paw, and Marci slumped against the wall, defeated. "I don't get it. I thought bound spirits had to obey their masters."

"Well, he is still a cat," Julius pointed out. "'Obey' isn't exactly in his vocabulary." Still, Ghost's appearance had given him an idea. He actually liked it less than the attack-gunmen-with-a-rake plan, but at least this one had a chance of actually working. "Marci," he said quietly. "If you had a strong source of magic to pull on, could you beat these guys?"

"If you mean Ghost, it won't work. Bound spirits are at equilibrium with their masters. He can pull on my magic just as hard as I pull on his, so the net return—"

"I'm not talking about Ghost," Julius interrupted. When she gave him a funny look, he took a deep breath. "What if you used me?"

Marci's face went blank in surprise. "You?"

Julius nodded grimly. This wasn't how he'd wanted her to find out the truth, but he didn't have much choice. If they didn't do something, they were going to die in a hoarded cat house to a bunch of human thugs, and after everything he'd survived since being dumped in this city, that end was too pathetic to stomach. "Do it," he said, putting out his hand just as Bixby's mage hit her ward again, sending sparks flying. "Quickly."

"No!" she cried, horrified. "I can't do that!"

Now it was his turn to be surprised. "Why not? You pulled on those lampreys last night just fine."

"Those were *animals*," Marci said, her voice frantic. "Drawing off another human's soul is *blood magic*! It's the mage equivalent of cannibalism, and it's illegal even in the DFZ. Also, that stuff taints you for *life*. My magic would be ruined forever!"

Considering they were in a life-or-death situation, Julius thought that sounded like an acceptable price. Since he wasn't human, though, it was also an irrelevant one. "Marci," he said gently. "It won't be blood magic. Trust me."

Her panic faded as she stared at his face, and then her expression shifted to something he couldn't quite put a name on. Cracks were already appearing in her ward above them, but Julius didn't try to rush her. It wasn't like he could force her to take his magic, anyway. All he could do was sit and hope that the trust that had allowed her to fall asleep beside him was still there.

Finally, she raised her own hand until her fingers were hovering right above his outstretched palm, but she didn't touch him yet. Instead, she looked at him again. *Really* looked at him, like she was searching his face for the final bit of evidence that would convince her this was the right decision. She must have found it, because a second later, her hand slammed into his, fingers wrapping around his palm like a clamp.

Julius relaxed his guard at once, opening his magic wide to let her in, and Marci jumped like she'd been electrocuted. Seconds later, her shock faded, and then her face broke into the most beautiful smile he'd ever seen. "I *knew* you weren't human," she whispered, her voice humming through him like it was his own.

"We'll talk when we get out of this alive," he replied, breathing deep as he adjusted to the incredibly strange feeling of having someone else inside his magic.

Marci nodded, squeezing his hand even tighter. "Ready?"

He nodded, and then nearly fell over as Marci yanked his magic so hard he saw stars. Julius almost broke the connection after that, but stopped himself at the last moment, clutching her tighter instead. This had been his idea. He'd asked her to take a chance and trust him, and she had. Whatever happened, he couldn't pull the rug out from under her now, so he breathed through the pain, keeping his magic steady as Marci pulled and pulled and pulled until she was shining bright as a spotlight.

That was all the warning he got before Marci's ward exploded.

***

Aside from the time he'd spent with Marci, Julius hadn't seen a lot of human mages at work. He had, however, seen enough magic to know when he was witnessing something amazing.

The dust from her exploding ward had barely settled when Marci walked away from the shelter of the basement wall and into the open doorway, pulling Julius behind her. She grew brighter with every step, her body saturated in a golden haze of magic so thick, she looked like she'd been dipped in sunlight. Even for a dragon, it was an awesome sight, though Julius would have appreciated it more if she hadn't been sucking him dry in the process.

Her hand was still clamped around his like a vise, drinking his magic down with impossible strength. He hadn't realized a human could take so much, though he should have known better than to underestimate Marci. But though he was quickly going lightheaded, he refused to cut off the power he'd offered her, especially since it seemed to be working.

Now that she'd pulled him to the open door, he was able to get his first real look at their attackers. From the amount of gunfire, he'd expected ten guys, maybe fifteen. What he saw was a small army.

Thirty men were crowded in the overgrown driveway behind the house. Still more had fanned out to the sides of the property. Their weapons were a mix of assault rifles and automatic pistols, and most of them were clearly muscle augmented, their dark suits straining over their technologically enhanced physiques. All of them had the hardened, seen-everything look of professional criminals. Or, they would have, if they weren't all currently gaping like fish at Marci's sudden and spectacular appearance.

Their shock lasted only a second, but for Bixby's men, it was a second too long. As soon as she cleared the door, Marci's arm flew up, her plastic bracelets vibrating wildly on her wrist as she pushed Julius's power through. Attached to her as he was, he could actually feel his magic flowing through her spellwork, the raw power twisting and folding like paper into a new shape. It was wondrous and terrible, and he was still trying to make sense of it when a shimmering wall of super-heated air exploded from Marci's fingertips and slammed into the men in front of them.

Her spell hit the thugs like a freight train, the modified microwave spell cooking their skin even as the explosively expanding hot air knocked them through the bushes and into the neighboring yard. The thunderous boom of her first attack was still echoing when Marci sent out the next, this time blasting the goons off her car. The old sedan was too heavy to be thrown by air pressure, but the heat of her attack blistered the fading paint on the driver's side and cracked the half of the windshield that hadn't been shot.

Marci didn't seem to notice the damage. Even when the men on the side of the house recovered from their shock enough to start shooting again, she didn't flinch, not even when a bullet grazed her cheek. She just kept going like a one-woman army, yanking power out of Julius as she launched wave after wave after wave, scorching the grass black and blasting everyone she saw until, at last, there was only one person left.

The moment Julius saw him, he understood why this human alone hadn't been burned or thrown back. The young man standing in the middle of the cracked driveway was so covered in magic, Julius could smell it even over Marci's. With so much blatant power, he didn't need the blood trickling down the man's face from Marci's backlashed ward to know he was looking at Bixby's mage. Marci knew it, too, and she yanked her hand back, muttering under her breath as a different bracelet began to vibrate.

The other mage responded by raising his own hands, which were encased in very expensive looking gloves worked all over with sparkling silver spellwork, and Julius felt a stab of panic. He would bet on Marci any day, but mage duels were famously deadly, often in horrific ways. He was trying to catch enough breath to suggest that Marci stand down before the situation got out of hand when she bared her teeth like an animal and pulled on Julius's magic so hard he nearly blacked out.

If he hadn't been fighting to stay conscious, the sight of the enemy mage's cocky expression collapsing as he realized just how much power he was up against would have been comical. Marci was shining like a supernova now. The heat of the trapped power was so intense, smoke was starting to curl up from her bracelets, filling the air with the smell of burning plastic. But though she was holding enough magic to blow the whole place sky high, she didn't release it. She just kept turning the power over on itself, folding and sharpening and honing the pressure until Julius's ears were popping and the air itself felt tight.

The other mage was building something, too, but they never got to see what. He'd barely started pulling on the various magical sources Julius could feel in the pockets of his long vest when Marci threw her fist out like a punch, sending the ball of power she'd built through the pink bracelet containing the telekinetic choke she'd used back in the alley. But there was no choking now. Instead, Marci's magic bit down like a bear trap, and the whole world seemed to shudder as the mage's building power snapped.

The scream that split the air made Julius's blood run cold, but with her choke spell going, the mage couldn't fall until Marci let him. When she released him at last, he collapsed onto the driveway, clutching his silver gloved hands to his chest like they'd been broken. It was such a pathetic sight, Julius would have felt sorry for him, but that was impossible with Marci's satisfaction coursing through him.

There was so much of her in him now, it was hard to tell where she ended and he began. He could actually feel the rush of joy and vengeance as she wrote the mage off and started looking for her next target. Considering what she'd been through, he didn't actually begrudge her that, but when he felt her make the decision to pull more power off him in preparation to go hunt down the survivors, Julius knew it was time to end this.

Fast as he'd opened to let her in, he snapped his magic shut. If he'd ever bothered to train his power, he probably could have done it more elegantly, or kept Marci from taking so much in the first place. He hadn't, though, so he had no choice but to cut her off cold.

She jerked when the connection collapsed, snatching her hand out of his as though she'd been burned. Without her support, Julius dropped like a stone, landing hard on his back in the grassy embankment beside the basement's dug-out stairs.

"Julius!"

Marci was beside him in an instant, but though he could see her clearly, she sounded a million miles away. He didn't have the presence of mind to listen in any case. He was too busy trying to breathe.

Now that he'd cut the connection, the emptiness she'd created when she'd sucked out his magic felt like a yawning cavern, and his whole body seemed to be collapsing into it, starting with his lungs. No matter how hard he tried, he couldn't get them to expand. But then, just when he thought he was going to black out for good, his lungs thundered back to life.

Breath exploded into his body so hard, he arched off the grass. He'd never tasted anything so sweet in his life as that first gulp of air, but the next burned like fire, sending him into a full body coughing fit.

He curled over in the grass, his body folding into itself as he tried to breathe through the coughing spasms. Finally, after what felt like ages, the attack passed, and he slumped into ground with a groan, twitching as he tried to find some part of his body that didn't hurt to rest his weight on.

It was a hopeless quest. Between the magic and the coughing, he felt like he'd been run through an industrial crusher. It was all he could do to just lie still and keep breathing. But this was one of those times when being a dragon was actually a blessing. A human would have been motionless for hours after something like that, but Julius was able to roll over after just a few more deep breaths, grimacing through the pounding in his head as he looked around for Marci.

He found her a few feet away, staring down him with a look of absolute, horrified guilt. "Julius," she whispered when he met her eyes.

"I am so sorry. I am so, so, *so* sorry. I didn't mean to take that much, I swear. I—"

She cut off when Julius raised his hand. After a second's hesitation, she took it, helping him sit up. Now that his body had realized it wasn't going to die, he was finally calming down enough to actually take in their surroundings. Or what was left of them.

Marci couldn't have been pulling on him for more than a few minutes, but the area around the house was now completely empty. The only exception was the mage, who was still lying in a whimpering ball in front of Marci's car. Julius could vaguely hear the moans of the other men from beyond the disaster area of broken bushes and shattered yard statues where Marci's blasts had thrown them, but those who were still alive seemed more concerned with pulling themselves to safety than retaliating. By all accounts, it looked like Marci had just beaten Bixby's force hands down, which was why Julius was so surprised when he heard the sound of a pistol cocking just a few feet away.

"Don't move."

Marci's head snapped up at once, but it took Julius a few seconds to turn far enough to see a large, heavily augmented man with a bald head and a very nice, though now very dirty, gray suit step out from behind the trunk of Marci's car. He must have used the vehicle for cover during the fight, Julius realized, which made him the only one of Bixby's hirelings with the presence of mind to do something clever. But while that was unexpected and unlucky, what really caught Julius's attention wasn't the man's unexpected survival or his gun; it was the golden ball he was clutching like a trophy in his left hand.

If Julius had had any lingering doubts, Marci's horrified gasp would have ended them. The big man was holding the Kosmolabe, the priceless magical tool Marci carried in her bag at all times... the bag she'd left in the car when they'd run for the house.

"Put it down gently, Oslo," Marci ordered, holding out her hands, though her fingers didn't glow this time. A fact that didn't escape Bixby's second.

"You shouldn't leave such valuable things lying around," he said casually, tossing the Kosmolabe and catching it one-handed. "Anyone could just pick them up."

He tossed it again, and Marci made a strangled sound. "You're messing with things you don't understand," she warned. "That Kosmolabe is irreplaceable."

"So I've been told," Oslo said, tossing it again. "But I'm not in the antiquities business, and I'm getting mighty tired of chasing a ball like a dog." He snatched the Kosmolabe out of the air as he finished, fingers curling menacingly over the thin glass as he leveled his gun at Marci with his other hand. "The only reason you're not dead right now is because Bixby wants to do it himself, but just because I can't kill you doesn't mean you're safe." Before Julius could even wonder what that meant, Oslo turned the gun on him, aiming the barrel straight between his eyes. "Hands up, or pretty boy here says goodbye to his head."

Marci's hands shot up at once.

Julius followed more slowly and with far less obedience. He might be drained, beaten, and unable to stand, but that didn't mean he was ready to roll over. He'd spent his whole life cowering before real monsters. This human didn't even come close.

"I'm sorry you've had a bad day, Mr. Oslo," he said calmly, resting his hands on top his head. "But if you'd asked nicely instead of opening fire, maybe we could have found an arrangement that didn't end with your men getting toasted and scattered all over the block. I'm sure we can still come to a compromise, however, if you'd just explain what this is all about."

"It's about you about to get shot," Oslo snarled. "I don't know what kind of line she fed you, buddy, but your lady friend there is a thief. Mr. Bixby doesn't take kindly to thieves. Novalli here is about to discover exactly what happens to bad girls who steal from us, but there's no reason you have to suffer, too."

Julius snorted. "You don't think I'll just abandon her."

"That wasn't what I had in mind," Oslo said, tightening his finger on the trigger.

The soft click of metal made Julius go still. He hadn't been taking Oslo's threat seriously up to this point. He was only a human, and Julius had been shot before as part of his training. It hurt like all get out, but a single shot was almost never fatal for a dragon. As the concept of a bullet ripping through his skull shifted from threat to incoming reality, though, Julius suddenly realized he had nothing to defend with. He couldn't change shape, and his magic was drained dry. He was a shadow of his true self, practically human, and humans got killed by bullets all the time. But just as it occurred to him that he should probably try to dodge, or at least keep the man talking until he could come up with a better plan, Oslo let out a blood-curdling scream.

The gun and the Kosmolabe both fell to the grass as Oslo's hands flew up to grab at his neck where Ghost was hanging with his claws latched in the soft flesh beneath the large man's jaw. Unfortunately for Oslo, there was nothing to grab. His hands passed right through the cat's transparent body as Ghost's talons sunk in deeper, cutting deep into his flesh without wound or blood. And then, with a silent hiss, Ghost's head snapped forward, biting deep into the big man's neck with his small, sharp, vividly white teeth.

As the bite landed, Oslo's scream faded to an echo, like he'd fallen down a well. Seconds later, the sound vanished completely, and Bixby's second pitched forward, landing face-first in the trampled grass. Ghost released him before they hit, nimbly climbing over the big man's shoulder as he collapsed on the ground. When Oslo's body relaxed into its final rest, Ghost was sitting on his back between his shoulder blades, lashing his tail and looking very pleased with himself. He also looked slightly bigger, Julius noticed with shiver. Bigger and more solid, his body shimmering brighter than ever under the hazy sunlight.

"I don't think that was a good thing."

"What are you talking about?" Marci cried, jumping up to grab the Kosmolabe. "That was a *great* thing." She grabbed Ghost next, hugging his glowing body to her chest. "Who's my good kitty?"

Ghost gave her a nonplussed look and dropped out of her hold, passing through her arms like his namesake to land again on the dead man's back. He opened his mouth when he hit, showing his teeth in a silent yowl, and Julius heard a rustle behind them as the cats began to appear.

They poured out of the hoarded house like a furry tide, hopping down from the collapsing roof and running up the basement stairs and wiggling through the shot-up windows. They came out of the garden as well, appearing from the underbrush like they'd popped out of thin air. Within seconds, the driveway was carpeted with hundreds of sickly, bony cats of every color, all riveted on the dead body Ghost was lording over like an emperor. They covered the downed mage as well. The broken man barely had a chance to cry out before he was buried under the hungry, meowing wave.

The sight was horrific enough to push Julius to his feet. But when he tried to take a shaky step toward where Marci was still standing next to her spirit cat in the middle of the mass, Ghost's head snapped, his pale, glowing eyes locking on Julius's as a soft, purring voice whispered in his mind.

Ours.

Julius jerked liked he'd been punched.

Ghost sat up a little straighter, swishing his fluffy white tail back and forth over Oslo's enormous body. *Our kill,* the voice whispered again. *Our feast. Leave.*

"Marci," Julius said, slightly frantic. "I think we'd better go."

"What?" She looked up from the Kosmolabe she'd been cuddling and wrinkled her nose at the cats. "Oh, right. Just let me get my stuff."

Julius glanced at the shot up house. "I don't think there's anything left to get," he said, hobbling forward to grab her arm. "And I think we need to leave *now*."

He couldn't even see the bodies anymore. The part of the backyard where the men had fallen was now a solid mass of cats with Ghost looming over them like a specter. Just the sound of their eating was enough to make Julius want to gag, and the revulsion gave him the strength he needed to pull Marci away, skirting the edge of the cat feeding frenzy until they reached her car.

The old sedan now sported several new bullet holes and a killer burn mark from bumper to bumper on the driver's side. The heat spell had actually melted through the headlight's plastic cover in places, and the seats were full of glass from where the windows had either cracked or been shot out. But while the windshield had a huge crack running across it and a perfect bullet hole in the upper right corner, it was still mostly intact. Even more miraculous, the engine started when Julius hit the ignition, and he let out a breath of relief.

"Drive," he said, brushing the glass out of the driver's seat before plopping Marci down.

"Come on, Julius," she said as he circled around to the passenger side. "They're just cats."

"That was *not* just cats," he snapped, barely pausing to sweep the broken glass out of his own seat before jumping in. "Go."

She glanced back at the house. "But my—"

"*Go*, Marci."

She heaved an enormous sigh, but she obeyed, gunning the engine manually and pulling them out onto the street past the waves of cats that were still arriving.

***

"*Gone?*"

Mr. Bixby stood in the corner of his office, hunched over his phone like a boy hiding contraband. "What do you mean they're gone?"

"I mean your team got trashed!" the young man on the other end of the phone cried. "But boss, you never saw anything like this. She was tossing guys around like they were nothing. Everyone she hit's got third degree burns or worse, and we're the lucky ones who got away. Oslo's just dead. I don't know what happened to the mage, but—"

"Stop."

The kid shut up at once, and Bixby used the opportunity to take a calming breath and reminded himself that young guns could be as hysterical as teenage girls when they got spooked, and hysterical kids tended to exaggerate. "Let me make sure I have this right," he said, calmly now. "You're telling me that Oslo, my mage, and all the men I sent up to Detroit were beaten by *one girl*? Is this really the story you want me to believe?"

"I swear it's the truth," the kid said. "But the girl ain't alone anymore. She's got some kind of other weird mage with her, and they were doing all kinds of I don't know what. And then a bunch of cats appeared, and it was super creepy, so the rest of us turned tail and—"

"Enough," Bixby growled, rubbing his hand over his face. "So Oslo's dead, my mage is unaccounted for, and everyone else just ran?"

"Yes, sir," the boy said.

"And I suppose you want a medal for being the only one to report in?"

"Maybe not a medal, sir. But I wouldn't be opposed to—"

Since the young man clearly had nothing else of value to add, Bixby hung up and called Oslo. When he got no response, he called his mage. Nothing. None of his field lieutenants were answering either, or his old hands. When he'd gone through his entire contact list without a single pick-up, he hurled his phone across the room with a curse, shattering the blown glass vase he'd won from his ex-wife in the divorce.

That made him curse louder still. He didn't even like the ugly thing, but she had, and so he'd taken it as a trophy, a monument to the fact that he always won in the end. Now it was broken, and the symbolism was so fitting it made him want to punch someone.

Instead, Bixby glanced at the clock as he walked over to retrieve his phone from the glass-strewn carpet. As much as he didn't want to, there was nothing else to do now but accept that the boy had been telling the truth. Still, Bixby wasn't screwed yet. It was just after eleven in the morning in Vegas, which meant it was only one in Detroit and seven hours before his buyer was supposed to check in. Since Bixby's seer always called two hours late, that gave him nine hours total to figure out a new battle plan for catching a girl with the devil's own luck in a city that was two thousand miles away. It wasn't impossible, just expensive and obnoxious, but at this point Bixby didn't care about money. So long as got the Kosmolabe and the Novalli girl under his control before midnight tonight, and everything would be—

His phone buzzed in his hand, and Bixby looked down at once, praying to the god he only remembered at times like this that it was one of his men reporting in. When the AR popped up, though, it wasn't a call at all. It was a message from the Unknown Caller.

Looks like you lose.

The words made Bixby want to throw his phone again, but he didn't. He couldn't. He wasn't about to accept that his life was over because of something that happened on the other side of the country, and he wasn't going to let this punk of a glorified fortune teller make him sweat.

"So fix it," he snarled, typing the words so fast they would have been gibberish if his phone's autocorrect hadn't fixed them for him. "You see the future. Tell me what to do."

I did, came the reply. *You had a ninety-two percent chance of capturing the girl and my Kosmolabe this afternoon, but you couldn't even manage that. I'm afraid your number's up, Bixby.*

No, he thought frantically. He was supposed to live. The whole reason he was doing this was because the damn seer had promised he would *live.*

He hadn't even finished typing that when the seer's reply flashed in the air.

I didn't tell you you would live, it read. *I told you you would die, and then I told you how to prevent it. That was the service I rendered in exchange for the Kosmolabe, which you have yet to deliver. Since I remain unpaid, I don't see why I shouldn't just leave you to your death.*

"You were the one who told me to capture her," he typed back. "If we'd done things my way and had her shot, we wouldn't be in this situation."

There is no future I can see where you kill Marci Novalli and I get my Kosmolabe.

Bixby's eyes went wide. "I thought you said there was no future where Novalli died and *I* lived!"

Whatever, the seer typed. *You're dead now, or good as. I don't even know why I'm bothering to reply, really.*

Bixby's breaths began coming in short pants. Part of him, the skeptical businessman who survived by never taking anything at face value, was sure the seer was bluffing. Vegas was his town. There was no way he could die here, safe in his stronghold surrounded by security, because some idiot girl was alive and running around loose in Detroit. It was impossible.

But the rest of him, the man who wanted to live at all costs, refused to accept that logic. Everything the seer had predicted had seemed impossible, and yet it had all come true. He'd been doubling his empire for months now on impossible long shots. Did he really want to count on dodging the one that was aimed right at his head?

He was still going back and forth when the phone in his hand buzzed again, and a new message appeared in his AR, the letters glowing like cinders in the air.

I should just let you die. It would be a fitting end to your arrogance to let you kill yourself ignoring my advice, and I always did enjoy seeing mortals done in by their own pride. But I have seen my own future, and the only way I get my Kosmolabe is through you, so I have no choice but to keep helping you.

There was a short pause, and then the seer's messages began arriving rapid fire. *I have made arrangements that open up one last chance for you to save your life,* it read. *The odds for success are not as favorable as I usually prefer, but if you do nothing, it is absolutely certain you will die tonight. Therefore, if you ever want to see another sunrise, you will follow my instructions to the letter. No questions, no backtalk, and no deviations. Do we have an understanding?*

Bixby took a long breath, fingers hovering over the virtual keyboard. He actually typed the word "No" before he erased it with a defeated sigh. "What do I have to do?"

The answer arrived almost before he hit reply. *Give me unfettered access to all your accounts, contacts, and operatives. I'll be running the show from here out, and if you want to survive, you'll run along behind me like a good little dog.*

Bixby's eyes went wide. Oh, hell no. He didn't care what was going to happen, he didn't care if the Novalli girl was destined to draw and quarter him on the floor of his own office, there was *no way* he was going to give a stranger unfettered access to anything involving his businesses. Not a dime, not a contact, nothing. But when he went to tell the bastard exactly that, another message was already waiting.

Breaking our agreement so soon? I just said no backtalk. You must really want to die. Now send me everything you've got. Time is already ticking away, and you have very little left to waste.

Bixby closed his eyes with a string of curses that would have made his mother roll over in her grave if she'd been dead, the old bat. In the end, though, Bixby was a practical man. He knew when he was beaten. It took a while for his sense to beat back his pride, but eventually, he sent the seer everything. Two minutes after that, he received his reply.

I've secured you a place on the next low-orbit flight to Detroit, it read. *Check in at Gate 5 in precisely eighteen minutes. Bring no luggage. When you find your seat, trade places with your neighbor on the left. Do not let him know your name and do not fall asleep. Further instructions will be waiting upon your arrival.*

The list of instructions sent him into a rage all over again, but he didn't bother trying to argue. He just grabbed his coat and marched out the door, cursing seers and phones and planes and mages and Kosmolabes and everything else he could think of as he made his way down to the garage where his car was already waiting to take him to the airport.

Chapter 12

After driving nearly ten minutes with no sign of pursuit, Julius motioned for Marci to pull over. She did so immediately, coasting to a stop next to the remains of a curb long since crumbled by the roots of an ancient oak tree. Julius checked one last time for pursuers as they slid into the tree's shadow, but the street was empty, the condemned houses on either side listing like low country tombstones. There was no sign of Bixby's men—no sign of Chelsie either, not that he'd see one. Still, the emptiness was enough to make him finally release the breath he'd been half holding since Ghost had spoken in his mind as he turned to face Marci.

"Before we run into another hit squad. I think it's time you told me what's really going on."

Marci winced. "I'm super sorry about all that. I never thought Bixby would send a real force all the way up here."

"You stole a priceless object," he replied irritably. "Of course he's going to come after it."

"I didn't steal it!" she said. "My *dad* stole it, and he only took it because Bixby was illegally withholding his money."

"Fine," Julius snapped. "But why did *you* keep it after he died? I would have thought one death would be enough to prove that thing isn't worth messing around with."

Marci shot him a hurt look, and Julius instantly felt like a jerk.

"Sorry," he said, rubbing his hands over his face. "It's just…stealing a magical relic from a vengeful mobster seems like a pretty stupid move for a smart girl like you."

"I didn't set out to take it," she said, petting the Kosmolabe in her lap. "I didn't even know what it was until Dad told me, and after everything went down, it seemed kind of pointless to try and give it back."

Julius let out a long breath. "I just wish you'd told me everything back at the restaurant. If I'd known from the beginning you had something Bixby wanted, we might have been able to avoid all this. We could have used the Kosmolabe as a bargaining chip and negotiated—"

"Negotiated?" Marci shrieked. "Those people killed my *father*! They nearly killed us just now. The only negotiating they do is at gunpoint." Her eyes narrowed. "And anyway, if there's anyone in this car who should have come clean earlier, it's *you*. You're not even human!"

Julius didn't try to deny it. He just sat still while Marci eyeballed him like he was a wild animal she'd discovered in her car.

"So what are you, anyway? Skinwalker? Vampire?"

"Vampire?" Julius repeated, glancing pointedly at the dappled sunlight falling across his legs.

She shrugged and kept going. "Wendigo?"

"Why are you only guessing the *worst* things? Maybe I'm a kind and benevolent spirit of nature?"

"No reason to hide being a spirit in Detroit," Marci said, shaking her head. "Besides, I've felt spirit magic plenty of times before, and it's nothing like—" She stopped, eyes lighting up in sudden recognition. "Oh my God, you're a *dragon!* That's it, isn't it?" When he didn't say no, she started bouncing up and down in her seat. "You *are* a dragon! This is amazing! I've never met one. Can you breathe fire?"

Julius's spirits sank lower with every breathless word. "Ix-nay on the agon-dray," he grumbled. "I'm not legal here, remember?"

"Oh," Marci said, dropping her voice, though not her excitement. "So *can* you breathe fire?"

"Yes," Julius said heavily. "But before you ask, I can't right now. My dragon form is sealed at the moment."

Marci snapped her fingers. "I *knew* you were under a curse. So how old are you? A hundred? A thousand?"

"I'm twenty-four," Julius said before she tried to check his teeth.

She gaped at him. "Twenty-four what? Years?" He nodded, and Marci collapsed back in her seat. "I can't believe it. I *finally* meet a dragon, and he's a year younger than I am. I have the worst luck *ever*." She heaved an enormous sigh and sat up again. "So how did your dragon form get sealed? Did you try to eat a great and powerful mage or—"

"Can we not talk about this?"

Marci flinched as though he'd struck her, and Julius immediately feel awful.

"Sorry," he muttered. "I was sealed under complicated circumstances, and I'm not really up for an interrogation right now."

"I understand," Marci said, lowering her eyes. "I don't mean to be pushy, but I've wanted to meet a dragon all my life. Though I guess I've actually met two now. Your brother's a dragon, too, isn't he?"

Julius nodded, and Marci's face split right back into a grin. "That explains a lot. I knew nothing human could survive in that lamprey pool."

He fought the urge to growl. Of course *Justin's* actions would be explained. He was bold, arrogant, everything a dragon should be, whereas Marci hadn't even been able to guess what Julius *was*.

"So why didn't you tell me what you were earlier?" she asked, leaning toward him between the seats. "If I was a dragon, I'd tell *everyone*. Is it because we're in the DFZ?" She gasped. "You weren't afraid I'd turn you in for the bounty, were you? Because I'd *never* do that. I mean, who in their right mind would pick money over having their own *dragon*? You can't buy that sort of access! So do you really make your own magic?"

By the time she finished, Julius's stomach was clenched in a tight little knot. He'd been warned that humans took the dragon reveal badly, but he'd never expected this from Marci. She was leaned all the way over into his seat now, staring at him with gleaming eyes like he was her prize catch, and suddenly, Julius had to get away.

He couldn't take this, not today. He couldn't sit here and listen to the person who'd become the closest thing he had to an actual friend badger him for *access.* Especially since he couldn't give it to her without getting her killed, which was what *always* happened to humans who learned too many dragon secrets. Marci wasn't the sort who'd give up before she knew everything, and Julius didn't have the strength to tell her no over and over again. But as he threw off his seatbelt and opened the door, Marci's hand landed on his shoulder.

"Wait! I'm sorry."

It was the tremor in her voice that stopped him more than her words or her touch, and Julius looked over his shoulder to see Marci staring at him with real fear in her eyes. That would have been appropriate for a human who'd just learned she was sharing a car with an immortal predator, except Marci's hand was still latched onto his shoulder. Hard. Because she wasn't afraid *of* him, she was afraid he would *leave.*

"I'm sorry," she said again. "Don't go, please. I messed that up. I get overly excited and talk before I think. I didn't mean to insult you."

The urge to run was still there, but Julius couldn't go when she was looking at him like that. "It's okay," he said quietly.

Marci shook her head so fast her short hair flew. "It's not okay. I was being stupid. I'm sure you had your reasons for not telling me, and it was rude of me to push. Especially since the only reason I found out at all was because you let me pull off you back there to save our lives."

"The life-saving was all you," Julius said, but Marci would have none of it.

"No way. I couldn't have done a tenth of that on my own. I mean, I've pulled off strong sources before, but touching you was like…" Her voice trailed off as she searched for the words. "Plugging into the sun," she said at last, her lips curling into a wondrous smile. "It was absolutely amazing. So much concentrated power, and it was *right there*, right at my fingertips. I've never felt that strong in my life, and I'm afraid I might have gone a little overboard."

Remembering the surge of righteous vengeance that had bled into him when she'd crushed the other mage, Julius wasn't sure overboard was the right word. He would have picked "mad with power." He didn't say so, though, because Marci already looked guilt stricken enough.

"I'm so, *so* sorry, Julius," she said, letting go of his shoulder at last. "Not about what I did—I would have burned them all if I could—but because I hurt you to do it. I'm sorry for all of it, actually. I'm sorry I sucked you into my mess of a life, I'm sorry I didn't tell you the truth about the Kosmolabe earlier, and I'm *very* sorry I went crazy with the questions just now. I've been curious about dragons forever, and finally getting to talk to one was more than my brain could handle. But I've got it together now, and I promise I don't think of you as my own private dragon resource center. I'll never ask you another question again if you don't want me to, just don't go. You're the nicest, most considerate person I've ever met. You deserve much better than I've treated you, but I promise I'll be better. Just give me another chance. Please?"

The *please* pulled him right back into the car. He closed the door and sank back into his seat, rubbing his eyes with the heels of his palms. It wasn't a question anymore of whether he would stay—there was no way he could do otherwise after that—but he didn't know what to do about the rest of it, especially the part at the end. Because when she said *nice* and *considerate* like they were the best compliments she could give, he wanted to *be* those things. He wanted to be the person she thought he was, the one who deserved that warm, sparkling look in her eyes, and that was a serious problem. It was one thing to tell Justin he was done pretending to be a good dragon, but if Julius started actually trying to be what she said, he wasn't sure he'd be a dragon at all.

He sighed and shifted his fingers to peek at Marci, but she was still staring at him like her whole life hinged on his next words. His did too, he realized, because whether or not he managed to sort out his own mess, staying with Marci meant he was going to have to tell her the truth, and Julius wasn't at all certain she'd feel the same way after she heard it.

"I'm not going to go," he said, dropping his hands to face her at last. "And I'm not mad at you, either, just overwhelmed. I should have told you what I was before now, but I was afraid to, and not just for the reasons you think."

Marci frowned. "What do you mean?"

"Our two species don't exactly have the best history together," he said, trying his best not to fidget. "Most humans see dragons as either a threat to be eliminated or a power to be tamed and used, and with good reason. We deserve all the fear and mistrust aimed at us. Dragons see humans as pets at best, and you don't want to know about the worst."

Marci arched an eyebrow, and Julius scrambled to add, "Not that *I* see you like that, of course, but I'm a little different from the rest of my family. I'm also in a lot of trouble with them right now, and I don't know if I can protect you if they find out you're with me."

"You don't need to protect me," Marci said, pulling herself straight. "I'm—"

"A very good mage," Julius finished with a smile. "Believe me, I know. That's not what I meant."

She still looked miffed, and he blew out a breath, trying to think how best to explain this. "Dragons think of things in terms of tools and ownership," he said at last. "So long as you were just some random mage I hired, you were a tool, which is the safest thing to be. You don't kill someone and then go break his hammer out of spite. Now that you know what I am, though, things are different. Even if I claim otherwise, my family will see you as *my* human from here out, which means when they target me, they'll also target you."

She nodded. "And since you're in trouble, you think that's going to happen."

It was practically guaranteed seeing how Justin had already told their mother that Marci was Julius's. "That's why I didn't tell you. Just knowing that I'm a dragon is enough to make you a liability, and I'm not a big enough threat to keep others away if they decide not to tolerate it. It would have been a lot safer for you if we'd broken the contract as soon as I realized Katya wasn't at that party, but I needed your help, and I—"

"And you didn't want to leave me to face Bixby alone," she finished, grinning.

He'd been about to say that he liked her, but if she wanted to see it that way, that was fine with him. "I'm afraid I've only made things worse now. You think Bixby's bad? He doesn't even touch the Heartstrikers."

Marci gasped. "You're a *Heartstriker*?"

He blinked, confused. "You've heard of us?" Most humans didn't know one clan from another.

"Of course I've heard of you!" she cried. "I was a little girl who grew up obsessed with magic and magical creatures in Nevada. The entire southwestern US is Heartstriker territory. You guys were my home team. Wait, so if you're a Heartstriker, does that mean the Bethesda I talked to on your phone last night was *the* Heartstriker?"

When Julius nodded, she sucked in a breath so fast he worried she'd hyperventilate. "I talked to a *great dragon!*"

"You were almost *killed* by a great dragon," Julius snapped, grabbing her hands. "This is what I'm trying to explain. Even among dragons, my mother is considered ruthless and prideful. She's had humans killed for wearing the same dress as her to a party. If Justin hadn't grabbed the phone last night, she probably would have ordered me to kill you just for daring to speak to her. I'd have had to do it, too. I can't disobey a direct order from my mother."

Marci didn't look cowed in the least, and Julius let out an enormous sigh.

"See? This is *exactly* what I'm talking about. Dragons and humans don't mix. Dragons and dragons barely mix."

He glared hard as he said this, trying his best to frighten her into accepting just how dangerous this game was. Apparently, though, he was bad at this, too, because Marci's face melted into a warm smile.

"It's really sweet how you're working so hard to scare me into backing off," she said. "Pointless, but very sweet. You know, you're nothing like how I imagined a dragon would be. I'd always heard you guys were cold and calculating, the sort who would stroke your hair while stabbing you in the back."

"Most dragons are."

"But not you."

She grinned wider as she said this, and Julius took a deep breath. "No, I'm not. And that's why we're both in trouble."

Marci's smile faded, and Julius breathed deep again, building up his courage. Here went nothing.

"I'm a failure," he confessed. "I'm not ruthless or cunning or any of the things dragons are supposed to be. That curse you saw on me? It was put there by my mother to seal my true form, sort of a combination test and punishment. That's why I'm on this job, actually. I'm supposed to be proving myself as a dragon so I can earn my wings back, but seeing how I'm explaining all of this instead of just threatening to turn you over to Bixby unless you swear to serve me for eternity, I'm clearly messing it up. That's okay, though, because I don't *want* to be like that, but it's important that you understand I'm a really, really *bad* dragon. The others aren't like me at all, and when they come, I won't be able to stop them."

His heart was pounding by the time he finished. It felt good to finally tell Marci the truth, but that didn't make it hurt any less. He hadn't realized just how much he cared about her good opinion until it was time to ruin it. But as he was bracing for her tell him she had no interest in risking her life to help such a miserable failure, Marci opened her mouth and turned his world on its ear.

"What are you talking about?" she said, utterly incredulous. "You're a fantastic dragon."

Julius gaped at her, momentarily speechless. "No," he said at last. "No, no, no. You don't know what you're saying. I don't have any ambition or guile, and if someone gave me the world to rule, I'd probably try to give it back. I've spent my entire adult life hiding in my room playing video games and earning online degrees as an excuse to avoid my family, and if my mother hadn't threatened to eat me, I'd still be there right now. Trust me, I am awful."

Marci arched an eyebrow and lifted her hand, counting off on her fingers. "You came into town last night with nothing. Now, not twenty-four hours later, you've earned more money than I saw in the last six months, beaten up everything Bixby has thrown at us, and saved my life at least three times. Oh, and this was all while you were *sealed,* which I can only assume means you're operating under a serious handicap, correct?"

When he nodded, she spread her arms wide. "There you go. I can't claim to be a dragon expert, but in what world does that add up to awful?"

Julius was mortified to feel his cheeks heating. "That's not really—"

"I mean, God, you're a much better dragon than *Justin,*" she went on. "No offense to your brother, but he's more charging bull than cunning lizard. Frankly, I'm amazed he's still alive."

"Justin is very hard to kill," Julius said, but he was only half paying attention. His mind was still reeling from the fact that someone thought he was a better dragon than *Justin*. Fish would start raining from the sky next. Not that Marci's opinion would matter to a dragon, of course, but it mattered to him. An astonishing amount, actually. "You really don't think I'm terrible?"

"Of course not," Marci scoffed. "I mean, sure you're a little shy, and you probably could stand to be more assertive so people don't take advantage of your good nature, but you're also clever and brave and pretty charming when you want to be. You don't have to threaten to get what you need. People want to help you because you're a nice guy. *I* want to help you, which is why I'm not charging you another cent from here out."

Julius blinked in surprised, and Marci's grin turned bashful. "I think the last day has made it pretty clear that we're a lot more powerful together than we are apart, and I'm definitely not going to abandon you to your family just because things might get rough. I mean, you didn't abandon me to Bixby's men just now, and that was amazingly dangerous. You could have easily tossed me out the door and been on your way."

His eyes widened in horror. "I would never do that!"

"Exactly. So why should you expect less from me than you expect from yourself? You saved my life back there. The least you can do is let me try to return the favor."

"I told you," Julius said, slightly frantic. "You don't owe me for—"

"I'm not doing this because I owe you," Marci said, sitting up straight. "I'm doing it because I *want* to. And because there is absolutely no way I'm letting the only dragon who'll actually talk to me escape."

Julius didn't know what to say. He'd never encountered anything like this before. Loyalty to the clan was expected, but this sort of loyalty, personal loyalty, was completely beyond his scope of experience. "You're sure?" he said. "Absolutely sure? Because unless I pull off a miracle, I'm probably going to die tonight."

"Well, then I'm definitely not leaving," she said, crossing her arms over her chest with an insulted huff. "Honestly, Julius, what kind of friend would I be if I left you to pull off a miracle on your own?"

Julius didn't answer. He couldn't. No thanks seemed big enough for the person who was offering to stand by his side against his family. He tried to tell himself that Marci couldn't really know what she was getting into and he should send her away for her own good, but that argument never even had a chance, because she was right. They *were* much stronger together than he could ever be alone, and if he was going to have a prayer of surviving until tomorrow, he needed all the help he could get.

"Thank you," he said at last.

"You're welcome," Marci replied. "And now that we're officially partners in this, I think you should answer some questions. We have a much better chance of making it through whatever this is alive if one of us isn't in the dark, don't you think?"

Her transparent digging made him laugh out loud. "You never give up, do you?"

"When I've got a primary source trapped in the car with me?" she cried. "Never! Now, why are you in danger of dying tonight?"

Keeping family secrets was far too ingrained for Julius to risk revealing what he'd discovered about his mother's plan to use him as the fall guy for a long shot gamble at mating her son into the Three Sisters, but he figured he could probably explain the basics. He was opening his mouth to do just that when his pocket began to buzz.

The sound made him jump nearly out of his seat. The second he recovered, he was scrambling, digging out his phone so fast he almost dropped it. The AR came up as soon as his fingers touched the mana contacts, and his heart leaped into his throat.

It was a short, automated message. Just an address, a time stamp, and a picture snatched from a security camera of a beautiful blond woman sitting down at a booth in a diner. A woman whose face Julius now recognized almost as well as his own. "It's her," he whispered.

"Katya?" Marci asked, but Julius was already putting the address into the car's GPS. The route popped up a few seconds later, and Marci's expression grew skeptical. "Are you sure that's right? I mean, I know she was shacking up with a shaman in the sewers, but he was still a trust fund kid. That's not a part of town you go to if you have money."

"Probably why she's there," Julius said, breaking into a grin as the reality of what had just happened finally started to sink in. He *had* her. He'd found Katya, and it was only two in the afternoon. He had practically the whole day left, and while he wasn't sure if that was enough time to pull off the plan that was beginning to piece itself together in his mind, it was way more than he'd hoped for.

He glanced over at Marci, who was busy redrawing their route manually to avoid as many of the really bad neighborhoods as possible, and his grin got wider. A lot of things were more than he'd hoped for. But thinking too much about his good fortune felt like tempting fate, so he forced himself to be serious, turning around to sit properly in his seat as he strapped himself in. "Let's go before she changes her mind and leaves."

"Aye-aye, captain," Marci said, tapping the autodrive to set the car in motion. "Now, you were telling me about dragons."

"I was?"

"That would be great," she said innocently.

Serious as he'd tried to make himself, he couldn't help chuckling. He knew better than to think Marci could be put off, though, so he gave in, sticking to the safe, practical matters—yes, he could fly, yes, dragons generated their own magic, no, he'd never eaten a person and never would, humans were horribly carcinogenic—and avoiding any of the family politics and clan secrets that could land her in real trouble.

He basically pretended Chelsie was sitting in the back seat and answered every question accordingly.

Thankfully, the basics were more than enough to keep Marci interested. Good thing, too, because Julius was only half paying attention to what he was saying. His real focus was on the plan that was now taking final shape. Furtively, he slipped his hand into his pocket to check Svena's silver chain. Even after all the rolling around during the fight, it was still there, the enchanted links as cold and magical as ever. He clutched it tight, letting out a long, steadying breath as they drove back toward the hulking shape of the double layered city and the dragon hiding somewhere beneath it.

***

Despite Marci's warning, the neighborhood the address led them to caught Julius off guard. When she'd said it was a bad area, he'd imagined something like the housing blocks that surrounded the commuter deck Ross's people lived under, only with more trash and drug dispensaries. This was like entering another world.

The first thing he noticed was the dark. Thanks to a quirk of skyways above, two enormous support pillars had been placed directly in the middle of the main road that ran through this part of the old city, cutting off all street traffic for eight blocks. Adding insult to injury, the two pillars had also been placed in the exact right position to block out the gaps in the Upper City that would have let sunlight down into this part of the Underground, leaving the eight-block span black as a cave even in the middle of the afternoon.

This combination of oppressive darkness and blocked streets had destroyed any chance the neighborhood had of rebuilding. Even though someone had carved out a driveable path around the north-most pillar, breaking through an abandoned garage in an effort to let in traffic, the alternate route clearly hadn't caught on. There were no shops here, no flashing advertisements or vending machines or vibrant crowds, just a ghost town of boarded-up brick buildings that still bore the high water marks of Algonquin's flood on their upper stories. The only building that bucked the trend was the one they were driving to.

Like everything else here, the one story diner was a relic of the days before the flood. Unlike the rest of the rotting city around it, though, this one was relatively kept up. It stood on the corner of what must once have been a busy intersection before the road had been cut off. But though its windows were clouded with dirt and the residue from decades of wax-based glass marker specials, the light that shone through them was yellow and cheerful, and more than enough for Julius to make out the slender blond woman sitting in the red vinyl booth in the corner, staring into her coffee mug like it held the mysteries of the universe.

After searching so long, finally spotting their target felt a little like seeing a ghost. Julius had gotten so nervous during the drive over, he'd half convinced himself that Katya would be long gone, yet there she was, sitting just as she'd been when the tracking program had yanked her picture off the diner's security camera.

He held his breath as Marci parked the car on the curb right by the diner window, but Katya didn't even look up. Tapping his pocket to make sure the silver chain was still there, Julius got out of the car and leaned down to speak through the shot-out passenger window. "Wait here. This shouldn't take long."

"I hope not," Marci said, eying the empty, pitch-black street. "Call me if you need me, and good luck."

He flashed her a tight smile and turned away, walking into the diner as casually as he could. An ancient string of bells on the door announced his arrival, and a voice from the kitchen yelled for him to sit wherever he wanted. Julius ignored them both, keeping his eyes locked on the diner's only other customer.

From the moment he'd entered the building, the dragoness had given no sign she noticed his existence, but as he walked past the rows of empty booths, he could see the tension building in her shoulders. By the time he'd reached her table, she looked ready to bolt. She hadn't done so yet, though, and Julius took his chance. "May I sit?"

She glanced up, looking at him head on for the first time, and Julius took an involuntary step back. In the pictures he'd seen, Katya's kinship to Svena had been obvious—same white-blond hair, same snow-pale skin, same ice-blue eyes—but now that they were face to face, the differences were all he could see.

Where Svena had been perfect, poised, and deadly, everything he expected from a daughter of the Three Sisters, Katya looked awful. The pale skin beneath her eyes was marred by bruise-dark circles, and her long hair was a tangled, ratty mess pulled back in a sloppy pony tail. Sitting in the faded booth in a long sleeved t-shirt and sweat pants, clutching her coffee mug like a lifeline, she didn't look dangerous or ancient or magical. She looked hunted and exhausted, and more than a little afraid. She was still a dragon, though, and she made him sweat through a long, weighing look before finally nodding at the seat across from her.

Julius didn't wait to be asked twice. He slid into the booth, placing both hands on the table where she could see them. "I'm—"

"A Heartstriker," she said, her softly Russian accented voice as weary as the rest of her. "The eyes always give it away."

He nodded, waiting for her to go on, but Katya just turned back to her coffee, swirling the black liquid in slow, thoughtful circles.

"I must admit it hurts," she said just when Julius thought the silence would go on forever. "I never was the pride of our clan, but I hadn't thought Estella's opinion of me had sunk so low that she would outsource my defeat to one of the feathered serpent's baby lizards."

"I'm not here to defeat you."

Katya snorted. "I'm not worried about *that*."

Considering his lowly, non-threatening status was the reason Ian had picked him for this job in the first place, Julius wasn't insulted by her dismissal. He did, however, have a point to make, so he reached out his hand, resting it palm down on the table right next to where hers were cupped around her coffee. "You should have been," he said, turning his hand over to reveal the enchanted chain hidden in his palm.

She'd been so certain of his inability to hurt her, she hadn't even bothered to get out of the way. Now, she snatched her hands back with a gasp, knocking over her mug in the process. Julius caught it before the coffee could spill, setting the chipped mug safely back down beside the silver chain, which he'd left on the table. Katya watched him warily, her eyes flicking from him to the chain and back again, and then, in a tiny voice, she whispered, "Why?"

"Because your sister wants you to come home."

"I know that," she snapped, her soft accent sharpening to something much closer to Svena's. "You think I can't recognize Svena's magic? I meant, why didn't you do it? You had it right there next to my fingers. All you had to do was twist your wrist and I would have been chained. So why didn't you? Why not put me to sleep and be done with it?"

"Because I don't work that way," Julius said with far more confidence than he felt.

Her eyes narrowed. "What is your name, Heartstriker? How did you find me?"

"I'm Julius," he said. "And I found you by tracing the number Ross Vedder gave me."

Her expression turned equal parts betrayed and furious when he mentioned her human lover's name, and Julius raised his hands at once.

"He didn't sell you out or give in to threats," he assured her. "I didn't do anything to him, actually, and it wouldn't have worked if I'd tried. That man would have fought me to the last breath rather than give up any information about you. He didn't even tell me you two were together until I'd convinced him I meant you no harm, and the only reason he gave me your number then was because he was out of his mind with worry."

"Well, I wasn't worried about him," Katya said, though the lie was so bad even she winced. "I appreciate you not putting that chain on me," she said quietly. "And I'm happy you didn't hurt Ross. He's a very good human. But I can't go back. You don't know what it's like for me at home."

"You might be surprised," Julius said, resting his elbows on the cheap Formica table.

Katya shook her head. "You can't understand. You're a Heartstriker. You have, what, a thousand siblings?"

He chuckled. "Not a *thousand*."

"There are twelve of us," she went on, ignoring him. "Twelve daughters, all born of magic one at a time."

Julius stared at her, uncomprehending. He'd heard that none of the Three Sisters had ever engaged in a mating flight, but he'd always assumed it was a myth. Even the most powerful dragons had to obey the basic rules of biology, but Katya was shaking her head.

"My mothers are the most powerful dragons to ever inhabit this plane," she explained, her voice more bitter than proud. "No one was considered worthy to father their children, and so they scorned all suitors, creating eggs between themselves one at a time using their power alone. Each daughter took centuries to create. I was the last, hatched just before the Earth's native magic dropped too low to support such an enormous ritual. Our mothers went to sleep immediately after. I've never met them, actually. Svena raised me."

She finished with a shrug, but Julius could only stare. No wonder the Three Sisters considered Bethesda an upstart. If Katya had hatched back before Earth's magic dried up, she had to be at least a thousand years old, which meant their youngest daughter was almost as old as his mother.

"Well," he said, clearing his throat. "That explains why Svena asked me to find you. She must be very worried."

Katya rolled her eyes. "If she's worried about anything, it's that I'll embarrass her. I'm a failure, you see. All of my sisters are great mages, Svena especially, but I could never manage more than the simplest magic. It was so bad that my eldest sister, Estella, deemed me an incurable disgrace before the end of my first century. I've been locked away in our glacier in Siberia ever since so no one would find out that the daughters of the Three Sisters aren't uniformly perfect."

He winced. "I can see why you ran away."

"This is my twenty-third escape, actually," Katya said bitterly. "You can't imagine what it's like up there. Nothing but ice and snow and the constant echoes of my mothers' troubled dreams. None of my other sisters will stay for more than a few days at a time, but I'm expected to live there forever simply because Estella decided I didn't fit our family image." She tilted her head toward the dark window beside her. "I came to the DFZ because I thought if I went to a place where dragons couldn't move freely, I could buy some extra time. But it's barely been a month, and here you are."

"Well," Julius began. "I—"

"I'm not going back," Katya snarled, bearing her sharp, too-white teeth. "I refuse! And if you try to make me, I will kill you!"

She said this as viciously as any dragon, but Julius had a lot of experience with death threats, and there was a lack of surety in her tone that made him suspect that Katya of the Three Sisters had never actually killed anyone in her life. Voicing his suspicions would be an unforgivable insult, however, so he made a show of looking properly cowed, lifting his hands and exposing his neck in a display of surrender.

"I wasn't planning on making you do anything," he said meekly. "Believe it or not, I understand you completely, and I'm on your side. I'm not a thousand yet, but I know what it's like to be trapped by your family's expectations. My mother actually threatened to eat me just this morning if I failed to bring you back to your sister."

"So why don't you?" Katya demanded. "What game are you playing with me?"

"I'm not playing at all," he said. "You're right. My life would undoubtedly be a lot simpler if I'd taken my chance and chained you a few minutes ago. But if I had it to do over, I'd make the same decision, because putting you to sleep and returning you to your family against your will isn't something I feel right doing."

Now she just looked confused. "What does that have to do with anything?"

"I've recently had cause to reevaluate my life," he explained. "You see, my family thinks I'm a failure, too."

"I guessed that much from the seal," she said, giving him another appraising look, though a curious one this time. "What's wrong with you?"

"Everything, according to my mother," he said with a laugh. "Let's just say I don't fit her vision of what a dragon should be."

Katya chuckled. "I can see that. Any dragon who didn't take the chance and chain me when he could is clearly a few scales shy of a full coat." Her eyes dipped to his chest. "Or is it feathers with you?"

"A mix," he admitted.

He hadn't meant it as a joke, but she began to smile all the same. "I think I see Bethesda's problem. You're much too nice to be a dragon."

Julius smiled back. "Thank you."

"I don't understand why you're letting that hold you back, though," Katya went on. "I'm a failure because I *can't* use my magic, but your problem sounds more like an attitude issue than a true handicap. Have you tried just gritting your teeth and pushing through?"

He sighed. "Several times. Most recently last night when I let my brother convince me to try and break into your old sewer compound through the side and ended up stuck in a lamprey pool. That's how we met Ross, actually."

Her eyes went wide. "You went into that horrid place and lived?" and then, "Wait, *two* Heartstrikers attacked Ross?"

If Julius had any remaining doubts that Katya really did care about her human shaman, her violent hiss at the end of that last question would have put them to rest. "No one attacked Ross," he assured her. "My brother was going to, but I stopped him."

She lifted her chin. "And you tell me this to curry my favor, I suppose?"

Julius's eyes went wide. "No! That's not it at all! Really, I didn't even think about that angle until you pointed it out just now. That's how bad I am at the 'conniving dragon' stuff, and honestly, I'm fine with that. I don't want to be someone who saves people just to get leverage on their lovers."

"But that's life," Katya said flippantly. "Use or be used. You can frown on it all you like, but if you want to survive, you'll do what you have to just like the rest of us."

Julius shook his head. "I don't think so."

She gave him a sharp look, but she didn't cut him off, so Julius hurried to explain. "When you treat everyone you meet as either an enemy or a pawn, you give others no choice but to hate and fear you."

"So?" Katya said. "It's better to be feared than loved."

"Maybe in the short term," he admitted. "If you're strong enough to take it, but no one's strong forever. No matter how good a user you are, when you treat others like tools, you're setting yourself up for an endgame that inevitably leaves you outnumbered and alone with no one but resentful pawns for backup. That doesn't sound like victory to me."

"What would you do instead?" she scoffed. "Be so nice that all the dragons have a change of heart? Teach us the power of friendship like some sickening moral tale?"

"No," Julius said. "But I am going to try being *your* friend. Because I think if you stop dismissing this out of hand and actually consider what I'm saying, you'll find we make much better allies than enemies."

That stopped her cold. "You would ally with me against your own clan?"

"That's just it," he said, leaning over the table. "We're not *against* anyone. This doesn't have to be a fight or a war or a game or any of those terrible dragon metaphors for life. Just because everyone is expecting us to be at each other's throats since you don't want to go back and I'll die if I don't make you doesn't mean that's our only option. Because we're *not* thoughtless pawns with artificially limited moves, we're *dragons*, and if we combine our efforts, there's a good chance we can turn a lose-lose situation into a victory for everyone."

He finished with a hopeful grin, but Katya was still scowling, her white teeth chewing on her pale lip. The longer she stayed silent, the more Julius worried. Maybe he'd come on too strong? He'd tried to be as honest as possible, but if Katya didn't believe him, if she still thought his vulnerability and confessions were just a show to gain her trust, there was nothing he could do. He'd gambled everything on this. If she bolted now, he had no way to stop her.

Seconds ticked by like hours, making Julius sweat. But then, just when he was sure he'd lost, Katya sighed. "I'm not agreeing to anything," she warned. "But I am very tired of being cloistered by my sisters, and even more tired of running. So tell me, Julius the Nice Dragon, what would this proposed alliance entail?"

Julius very nearly fell over in relief. The only reason he didn't was because there was no time. He was already explaining the plan he'd come up with, laying it out for her just as it had formed in his mind while he was talking to Marci. Within minutes, Katya was nodding, and though she didn't look convinced, she wasn't rejecting him either, and that was enough.

Chapter 13

Marci sat in her car, watching through the cloudy diner window as a smiling Julius leaned closer to the woman sitting across the booth from him. The amazingly, spectacularly, inhumanly beautiful woman he'd been searching for. The woman who was obviously another dragon, and not one from his family.

No wonder he didn't want to kiss you.

She scowled and pushed the unwelcome thought out of her head. She'd already made up her mind that she wasn't going to dwell on that. She should be happy she hadn't blown their friendship with that stupid slip-up, not mopey because she'd been rejected by a man she'd known was out of her league from the moment she'd spotted him sitting at the bar, *especially* now that she knew he was actually a dragon. They were an entirely different species, probably with a completely different standard of beauty. Being upset a dragon didn't want to kiss you was like being upset a horse didn't want to kiss you, and Marci definitely didn't want to kiss a horse. Though, of course, if the horse was as good-looking as Julius, maybe she'd have a different opinion.

Still, the situation wouldn't have been half as depressing if Julius and Katya hadn't looked so good together. The way his black hair and sharp features emphasized her fair skin and delicate beauty was so perfect it almost looked fake, like some artist had set the whole thing up just for that effect. And then there was Marci, safely tucked away outside so her ugly haircut, shabby clothes, and mundane humanity wouldn't ruin the moment.

That thought was melodramatic in the extreme, and Marci forced herself to look away. She needed to stop being stupid and focus on her own future, like finding somewhere to sleep now that she had money. She couldn't afford another night at the sort of hotel Julius seemed to prefer, but the last few days had been humbling enough that anywhere with a real bed and no cats sounded like paradise. She'd just grabbed her new phone to look up reviews for extended stay motels when she felt something icy brush against her leg.

She lowered her phone to see Ghost sitting on the floorboard between her feet, his transparent tail swishing back and forth as he looked up at her with that smug cat smile. *Back,* he purred in her mind.

"So I see," she grumbled. "I'm surprised. I didn't think you'd leave your adoring fans."

Ghost blinked and leaned on their connection, reminding her that staying away wasn't an option for a bound spirit. Suddenly guilty, Marci put down her phone and patted her lap in invitation. Never one to pass up the gift of warmth, Ghost hopped up, though he took his time about it to make sure she understood that this lap business was nothing special.

"You freaked Julius out good with that little display back there," she scolded when he'd settled down at last, his soft body like a bag of shaved ice across her thighs. "We're lucky he didn't run away screaming."

Ghost gave her a disgusted look.

"I know, I know, you saved us," Marci said dutifully, petting him as much as her cold-stiffened fingers could stand. "And thank you for that. But do you think you could try to be a bit less dramatic next time? We don't want to get a reputation."

Her voice was cheerful, but inside, she just felt empty. As much as she liked to pretend otherwise, Marci knew perfectly well there wouldn't be a next time. Julius had found his dragoness, which meant the job was done, and even though she'd promised to help him with whatever it was he had to do tonight, she wasn't naive enough to think it would last. There was a reason humans knew so little about dragons. Julius had let her in this afternoon because he'd had no other choice, but the moment this crisis was over, he'd say goodbye. Not cruelly—Julius didn't have a mean bone in his body—but he'd made it clear there was no place for a human in his life. As soon as he got out of whatever trouble he was in, he'd take his beautiful dragoness and go back to their world, and Marci would go back to being alone. All alone, without her father, without her home, no school, no friends she could call without endangering them. Just a girl and her death spirit on the run in a strange city.

Her vision started to go blurry after that, and her hands flew to her eyes. "Don't cry," she whispered angrily, scrubbing at the wetness gathering on her lashes. "Don't you *dare* cry."

But the tears wouldn't listen to reason. They just kept coming in big, ugly drops. Soon her whole face would be red, which wouldn't do at all. If Julius saw her like this, she'd have to explain why she'd been crying, because of *course* he would ask, probably in front of the beautiful dragoness, leaving her no choice but to die of shame on the spot.

Since stopping her stupid tears was now a matter of life and death, Marci threw open the door and leaped out of her car, toppling Ghost to the floor in the process. He yowled his displeasure in her mind, but Marci ignored him, clinging to the car as she gulped down breath after breath of dank, musty, Underground air.

She just needed some space, she thought, looking down the dark street. Space and perspective, and maybe a tissue, and… and…

And there was a man sitting on her car.

Marci jumped straight up, banging her knee on the car door in the process. But even the sudden, smarting pain couldn't tear her attention away from the stranger who was now sitting cross-legged on the hood of her dad's sedan.

Oddly enough, her first thought was that he must be absurdly tall. Since he was sitting, Marci couldn't tell if that observation was factual, or if his long, slender limbs merely created the illusion of remarkable height. Either way, it wouldn't be the strangest thing about him.

From the waist up, the man was dressed like he was going to a dinner party in a blue silk jacket with black piping and a Mandarin collar over a cream-colored shirt. From the waist down, though, he looked like a hobo. His paint-stained jeans were so old they'd lost all color, and he wore no shoes at all, though his blue-black hair, which he wore in a thick braid that hung all the way down to the small of his back, was tied off with a bright pink shoelace. He also had a pigeon on his shoulder—a live one that was currently tilting its head curiously at Marci. The strange man himself hadn't even glanced at her, however, and Marci decided she'd better make her presence known before this situation got any weirder.

"Excuse me," she said, quite politely, she thought, given the circumstances. "What are you doing on my car?"

"I couldn't possibly explain," the man replied, never looking away from the diner window where Julius and the dragoness were still deep in conversation. "But don't worry. I'll only be a moment."

Marci bristled at the curt dismissal, but she didn't yell at the crazy man to get off her hood. Rude as he was being, this was the DFZ. For all she knew, he was a spirit of some sort, and it never paid to insult spirits. "Can you tell me who you are, at least?"

She'd barely finished before the man spun around to face her, and Marci stifled her gasp just in time. And here she'd thought Julius and Justin were handsome. This man was something else entirely. He was so good-looking it was actually off-putting. Even in the dark, it was impossible not to see that his skin was bronzed and flawless. This, combined with his ruler-straight black hair, high cheekbones, and sharply beautiful face, made him look too perfect to be real. He reminded Marci more of an ancient artifact than a living thing, something sacred and powerful preserved from a more mysterious, magical time. After all that, the familiarity of his impossibly green eyes was almost a relief.

"You're Julius's brother."

The dragon flashed her a brilliantly white smile. "I'm Julius's *favorite* brother," he corrected, his deep voice rich with humor and secrets. "But he won't realize that until next year, so don't spoil the surprise."

He winked and turned back to the window, humming to himself as he resumed watching Julius like nothing had happened. Marci, however, was not so easily put off.

"What happens next year?" she asked, stepping around the car door to stand right behind him. "And why would it be a surprise?"

The dragon growled, making her shiver. Apparently, she was asking too many questions, but it wasn't every day a dragon landed on the hood of her car. Once Julius left, it would probably never happen again, and she was determined to make the most of the opportunity. "If Julius is your favorite brother, does that mean you're here to help him?"

"You've got that backward," the dragon said without turning around. "I'm *his* favorite brother, and helping him would defeat the point entirely. This is a test, you see."

Marci frowned. "A test for what?"

The dragon arched his shoulders in an elegant shrug, forcing his pigeon to flap in order to stay on. "That depends on Julius. The poor boy was going nowhere. I had to do *something*, so I gave him a little shove, just to shake things up."

She arched her eyebrow. "A shove?"

"You know," he said. "Trial by fire, adversity as crucible, et cetera, et cetera. He's in the middle of a make it work moment, and between you and me, I hope he pulls it off. I need him for a project I've been working on, and it's a little late in the game for me to start over if he flubs things and gets himself eaten."

The dragon rattled all of this off so quickly, Marci had trouble keeping up. What she did catch, though, she didn't like at all. "Does this trial by fire have to do with the seal that's on him?"

"*That* was Mother's idea," he said. "Though I will admit, the seal has made things easier. Put his back against the wall quite nicely, which always leads to results. And trauma. But really, what's a dragon without a little trauma?"

He laughed like this was hilarious, turning back to flash Marci what would have been a devastatingly charming smile if she hadn't been too angry to notice.

"Hold up," she said. "*You're* the one who did this to him?"

The dragon sighed. "I'm afraid you're going to have to be a little more specific. I've got a lot of pots on the stove."

Marci began to sputter. "This!" she cried, flinging her hands out at the dark buildings. "Shoving him into Detroit! Leaving him alone with no money, no power, and no support in a city where he can be shot just for being what he is!"

"Oh, *that*. Yes, that was me. Mother needed someone to throw at this Ian nonsense, and I thought Julius would be just the ticket. All it took was a few oblique suggestions at the right time, and Mother thought the whole thing was all her idea." He beamed at her. "Isn't that brilliant?"

"It's terrible!" Marci said. "What kind of brother are you?"

The dragon looked confused by her outburst, and then he spun all the way around again to face her head on. "Why, little human," he said softly, resting his long arms on his raised knees. "Are you attempting to call me out for being cruel to baby Julius?"

The soft mockery in his voice sent Marci's fists clenching so tight, the spellmarked bracelets on her wrists began to glow. The dragon's green eyes glittered in the light, but she didn't let the magic fade. She *wanted* to slam a spell into his smug, beautiful face. She had no idea what game this dragon was playing, but Marci knew exactly what it felt like to be kicked out of your home, and the thought of Julius—sweet, kind, thoughtful Julius who'd never had a harsh word for anybody—being dumped into this crisis by his own brother was more than she could stand.

"I'm not attempting," she said, stabbing her finger at the dragon's perfect nose. "I *am* calling you out. I'm sure you're powerful and ancient and could probably eat me in one bite, but I've had a terrible week, and what little I have left to lose, I owe to Julius. He's the best thing that's happened to me since I came to this city, and I am *not* going to stand here and listen to you brag about making his life miserable!"

The dragon's eyes flashed as she finished, and Marci felt a strange, sharp magic building in the air. She drew her own power in as well, filling the small circles of her bracelets and wishing she'd thought to draw a proper-sized one on the street before she'd started this, but she didn't try to backpedal. Her father might have had the business sense of a piggy bank with a hole in the bottom, but he'd loved her and supported her in every way he knew how. *That* was family to Marci, and she didn't care if it was her business or not. She was not going to stand silently by while this dragon made a mockery of it.

Almost as though he could hear her thoughts, the dragon chose that moment to slide off the hood of her car. Sinuous as a cat, he landed in front of her without a sound, straightening to his full height with a lazy roll of his shoulders.

Now that he was on his feet, Marci saw his remarkable height was no illusion. He was so tall, she had to crane her neck back just to look him in the face. His striking green eyes were waiting when she got there, staring down at her like he was trying to look straight through to her feet, and for a breathless moment, Marci could actually feel the presence of something larger looming over her. Something much, *much* larger.

"You're a presumptuous little creature," the dragon said, the words coming out in a deep, cruel rumble that was decidedly not human. "You really think you could attack me, don't you?"

By this point, every instinct Marci had was screaming at her to run. But her pride had made her bed, and Marci lay in it belligerently, refusing to yield an inch. "I am a mage," she replied with every ounce of haughtiness three years in a competitive doctoral program had taught her. "We bend the rules of the universe on a daily basis. Presumptuousness is the base line for entry."

The dragon's green eyes widened, and then he burst out laughing.

The sound broke the tension so sharply, Marci wavered on her feet. The dragon reached out to steady her at once, slapping his hand on her shoulder so hard she almost fell for real.

"Oh my," he said, wiping his face with a gold-embroidered handkerchief from somewhere in his pockets. "That was not the reply I expected at all. I'd forgotten how nice it is to be surprised." He looked her over one more time, and though it didn't seem possible, his smile got even wider. "For the record, Little Miss Mage, that was a test, too. Whatever Julius's dooming and glooming might have led you to believe, loyalty is very important in our family. It wasn't what I picked you for, but I welcome it all the same. You will do marvelously. I only hope my brother can keep up."

Marci blinked, her anger slipping in the face of her confusion. "Picked?" she said, and then, "Wait, keep up with what?"

"Everything," the dragon said with a sigh, replacing his handkerchief with one hand while the other pulled an ancient keyboard phone out of his back pocket and began typing a message. "Now, not that this hasn't been a lovely visit, but I'm afraid I have to go get ready to give someone a ride. Would you be a dear and tell Julius to buckle up for me?"

"Buckle up," she repeated slowly. "You mean, like, in the car?"

The dragon nodded gravely, returning his phone to his pocket. "The near-complete adoption of self-driving cars over the last quarter century has made road accidents statistically unlikely, but my baby brother has recently developed a dangerous knack for bringing in long shots, and I'd hate to lose him to a variable I don't control."

That seemed like pretty innocuous advice, so Marci promised she'd pass it on. The moment he'd secured her cooperation, the dragon gave her a winning smile and set off down the sidewalk, his pigeon riding comfortably on top of his head. He'd nearly reached the end of the block before Marci realized she'd never found out his name. Before she could yell after him, however, he turned on his heel and vanished into an alley. She was still staring at the place where he'd been when a flash of movement through the window brought her eyes back to the diner just in time to see Julius wave for the check.

***

"I will admit, it's a clever plan," Katya said as she gathered her things from the booth. "I just don't think it's going to work."

"It doesn't have to work," Julius said, paying the check when it popped up on his AR. "It just has to *look* like it's working long enough for us to get out of our mutual predicaments."

"But that's the problem. It's one thing to dally with a Heartstriker for an evening, but anything more, even the appearance of such, is completely out of the question for a daughter of the Three Sisters. *Especially* for Svena. Other than Estella herself, she's the most famous of us by far, and she's never agreed to a mating flight in her life. She certainly wouldn't start with a male so far below her, whatever your mother dreams. No offense meant to your brother, of course."

Julius shrugged. "Offend him all you want, it won't stop Ian. I don't doubt you're right about your sister, but Ian's ambitious and persistent even for a dragon. Even for a *Heartstriker*. An elder daughter of the Three Sisters is *exactly* the sort of prize he'd risk everything to go after. All we have to do is harness that ambition, and suddenly he's working for us."

Katya still looked unconvinced, so Julius laid it out for her again. "Look, you want to stay here in the DFZ with your shaman boyfriend, right?"

She glowered at his word choice, but she nodded all the same.

"But your sisters won't let you loose on your own, so you keep running away," he continued. "And it drives your sisters crazy."

She nodded again, and Julius spread his arms. "So tell me how this doesn't work? You know Svena best. How badly does she want you to stop running?"

"Bad enough to go to a Heartstriker when she failed to corner me herself," Katya admitted.

"Exactly," he said. "You have what she wants, which means you have the power to negotiate. So here's what we're going to do. We'll go to my brother and let him in on the plan. That way, when Svena arrives, Ian and I will both be there to give you backup while you explain to her that you won't run from your family again on the condition that, rather than being locked up alone in Siberia, you're allowed to confine yourself to the DFZ under her watch instead."

"So you keep saying," Katya replied with a sigh. "And *I* keep saying she'll never agree."

"I don't think you're giving your sister enough credit," he said. "It's true I don't know Svena nearly as well as you do, but everything I've seen of her tells me she's not the sort of dragon who wants to waste her time incarcerating an otherwise fully functional sister if there's a better option on the table. All we have to do is convince her that the DFZ is that better option, and I don't think it'll be a hard sell. First, we're on Algonquin's turf, which negates Estella's primary complaint that your lack of magic is an embarrassment to the clan since you can't do big dragon magic here anyway. Second, you actually *want* to stay in the city, which means Svena won't have to worry about you running away. And if those reasons aren't enough to sway her, I'm sure Ian will think of twenty more. He's good at that sort of thing."

Katya scowled. "You seem very sure your brother will help us. I thought you were considered a failure in your family?"

"Ah, but he won't be doing it to help us," Julius said. "He'll be doing it to help *himself*. That's why we're specifying Svena as your guardian here in the DFZ. If we make keeping you in the city synonymous with keeping Svena inside his reach, my brother will probably take care of the rest all on his own."

"And he'll know he owes that to you," Katya finished. "Since this was all your idea."

"Exactly," Julius said, breaking into a grin. "*Everyone* wins! I come off looking like the miracle matchmaker who found a way to keep Ian and Svena together against all odds. You don't have to go back to Siberia or spend your days hiding in dives like this. Svena doesn't have to worry about you running away anymore, and Ian gets a long and lengthy courtship to try and convince your sister to throw in with him. And if he fails after all that, there'll be no way my mother can possibly say it was my fault. It's *perfect.*"

Katya drummed her nails on the table, brows knit as she thought it over. "I thought you were pulling my tail at first, but now I'm starting to think this might actually work. I still can't believe Svena would go for a Heartstriker, but I know she hates the glacier as much as I do. She'd love any excuse to stay away for a while, especially if she'll have your brother to play with. Heartstriker wiles are not to be underestimated."

Julius cleared his throat. "Heartstriker wiles?"

"Oh come on. You can't be ignorant of your family's reputation."

"Believe me, I'm not," he said, blushing. "But 'wiles' is a much nicer word for it than I usually hear."

"It's a much nicer word than I usually use," Katya said with a coy smile, brushing her fingertips lightly over his folded hands. "Perhaps you are rubbing off on me, Julius the Nice Dragon?"

He must have looked like a deer in the headlights, because Katya erupted into a peal of laughter. "Relax, I'm only teasing," she said, still giggling. "You are so ridiculous. I can't figure out if you're just too young to be jaded or if you're actually shy."

Julius decided it was time to change the subject. "Are there any remaining issues you'd like to discuss?"

She thought for a moment. "No," she said. "No, I like this very much. It's a cunning plan that ties our victory to our enemies', making them fight for us instead of against. Quite an impressive bit of draconic guile from someone who claims to be a terrible dragon."

He couldn't tell if Katya was being sincere or not, but that didn't stop her praise from lighting him up from the inside. After years of feeling like a fish out of water, a failure in his own skin, he'd finally done something right. And though he still couldn't fly or eat properly or breath so much as a lick of flame, at that moment, Julius felt more like a real dragon than at any other point in his life, and it felt *good.*

"Thank you," he said, standing up.

Katya stared at him like she'd never heard those words before. Of course, considering her family, maybe she hadn't. "Thank *you,*" she replied, drawing out the phrase like she was testing it in her mouth. She must have liked the way it sounded, because she finished with a smile, reaching down with a napkin to pick up the spelled silver chain and drop it in her purse. "There," she said, snapping the red clutch closed. "That's done. Let's go."

Her eagerness made him chuckle. "Ready to get back to your shaman?"

"I am at no man's beck and call," Katya said with a toss of her hair. "Though I will admit I have become rather fond of him. Humans in love can be so adorably earnest, and he's a mage as well."

She said that last part with such a breathy sigh, Julius couldn't help himself. "What's so special about mages?"

Katya stared at him in wonder before breaking into a wicked grin. "You are so innocent I cannot believe you are real. Where have you spent your twenty-four years? In a monastery?"

Julius's answer was to shove his hands in his pockets with a sullen glower, which only made Katya's grin wider.

"Do yourself a favor, little Heartstriker," she said as they walked together to the door. "Don't rebel too hard against your family's nature. Some parts of being a traditional dragon are very nice indeed, especially when it comes to humans."

She gave him a wicked smile, and Julius looked away, cheeks flaming. Not because he was embarrassed by her words—or, at least, not only because of that—but because as soon as she put the idea in his head, his mind had gone straight to Marci. Lovely, talented, magical Marci, who knew he was a dragon and didn't mind. Marci, who'd stood by him more in one day than anyone else had in his entire life, and whose soft lips he could still recall in perfect detail…

But these were thoughts he had no business having, and he put them firmly out of his mind. Life was hard enough without tempting himself with what he couldn't have. He was too entangled with Marci as it was, but at least he could still claim their relationship was strictly business. If he took things further, she'd end up a weakness other dragons would exploit just because they could, and that wasn't a fate he'd wish on anyone, much less someone he liked as much as her.

But all of this perfectly sensible reasoning couldn't quite squash the surge of delighted happiness he felt when he opened the diner door to find Marci waiting for him. Katya, however, didn't spare her a look.

"I can drive," the dragoness said, pulling a cheap, disposable phone, the kind they sold at airport vending machines, out of her pocket. "My rental still has fifty miles before it locks down, and I don't want to leave it in a place like this. Just tell your servant to follow."

Marci's eyes went wide, and Julius leapt to her defense. "She's not my servant," he said quickly. "This is Marci Novalli, my business partner, and I'll ride with her if you don't mind." He needed to bring Marci up to speed before they got to Ian's.

Katya looked her up and down before turning back to Julius. "Seems I'm not the only one with plans to stay in the DFZ," she said, her singsong voice laden with innuendo.

"We'll lead the way," he said quickly before she could make Marci any more uncomfortable. "Just follow us. I'll call Ian right now and let him know we're coming."

Katya shrugged and started down the street toward a dirty but otherwise quite nice baby blue luxury sports car parked around the corner. Julius waited until he saw her open the door and get in before pulling out his phone to look up Ian's number. He was about to hit the call button when Marci tapped him on the shoulder.

He turned to find her bouncing nervously on her toes. "I need to talk to you."

"Can it wait a moment? We're heading to my brother's, and if I don't give him advanced warning, he's going to skin me alive."

He'd opened the passenger door of her car without looking as he said this, and as a result, he nearly sat on Ghost. He jumped out again when the cat hissed, glancing down just in time to see the death spirit vanish through the seats into the trunk. "Was that what you wanted to talk to me about?" he asked, settling into the now empty seat.

"No," said Marci as she hurried around the car. "Your brother was just here."

"You mean Justin?"

Marci shook her head, dropping into her own seat. "It was—"

A horn cut her off as Katya's coupe pulled up beside them. "Where are we going?" the dragoness called through her open window.

Julius sent her phone the address for Ian's penthouse. He sent it to Marci's ancient GPS as well. The route took them straight down the dark, blocked off street Marci had directed them around on the way here, but she didn't bother correcting the map this time. She just sat in her seat, biting her nails, and Julius decided Ian could wait a few more minutes.

"Okay," he said, putting his phone down. "What happened?"

"I told you," she said, her voice tense and angry as the car pulled itself out onto the dark, crumbling road. "Your brother showed up."

"Which one?"

Marci sighed. "He didn't give me his name, but he was tall with long black hair."

That described most of his brothers. "Anything else?"

"He was very weird," she said. "He just appeared on the hood of my car like he'd fallen out of the sky, and he didn't even try to hide that he was a dragon. He also had a pigeon on his shoulder, like a pet or something."

Julius's stomach sank so fast, he thought it would fall right through the seat. *Bob.* The Great Seer of the Heartstrikers had been *here,* talking to *Marci.* "What did he say?"

"Oh, a whole bunch of nonsense about tests and crucibles and how it was too late to start over. He also told me to tell you that you should buckle up, because people die in traffic accidents."

The words were barely out of her mouth before Julius was fumbling for his seatbelt, snapping it into place so fast he pinched his fingers.

Marci watched him warily. "Is that significant or something?"

"I have no idea," he admitted. "But when Bob tells you to do something, you should always do it, no matter how stupid it sounds." He glanced pointedly at Marci's seatbelt, and she grabbed it with a sigh. "Did he happen to say what he was testing me for?"

"He claimed he didn't know yet," she replied, clicking her belt into place with a frustrated huff. "Honestly, it didn't make a lot of sense."

"Bob usually doesn't," Julius said. "He's a—"

A crash cut him off mid-word, jolting the car and throwing him hard against his seatbelt. For a second, he felt like the world had stopped around him, leaving him to fly forward alone, and then reality came back with an explosive crash as Marci's entire car tipped sideways.

It came down again with a jolt that cracked his teeth together, fortunately landing back on its wheels as opposed to its side. As soon as they were down, Julius turned to Marci, grabbing her shoulder. "You okay?"

She must have been, because she wrenched out of his grip immediately, leaning out her shattered window in an attempt to look down the street. *"What the hell was that?"*

Julius was wondering the same thing. The dark street was empty as ever in front of them. He was trying to figure out how that could be when he spotted the wall of metal in Marci's rear view mirror.

He wrenched around in his seat. The back of Marci's car was completely totaled, crushed like a can under the bulk of an armored van so large, he couldn't see the edges of it from inside the car. But even that glimpse was enough for him to know that something was off. The armored van was stuck at an awkward angle, almost like it had spun into them after hitting something else...

And that was when he realized they weren't the ones who'd actually been hit. Their accident was just the remainder of the truck's momentum after slamming through the car *behind* them. The car *Katya* had been driving.

That was as far as Julius got before he tore off his seatbelt and dashed into the street.

Chapter 14

All he saw was smoke.

Huge, billowing clouds of black smoke poured off the front end of the enormous van currently stuck catty-corner through the back of Marci's car. He couldn't even see the driver between the smoke and the dark and the van's heavily tinted windows, so he stopped trying, running instead toward Katya's car. Or, rather, the place where her car was supposed to be.

Julius skidded to a stop, staring at the empty street in utter confusion. She'd been right there, right behind them, but now there was nothing. Just Marci's sedan and the giant, smoking van, which was already roaring back to life.

The smoke pouring out from under its hood must have been from something non-vital, because a second after the engine gunned, the van rushed straight at him. If Julius had been human, he would've been run down. As it was, he managed to jump out of the way just in time, dodging the van by inches as it shoved Marci's car out of the way like the old sedan was made of cardboard and surged down the empty street.

By the time it occurred to Julius that he should do something to stop it, or at least look for identifying marks, the armored van was already flying through the abandoned intersection ahead of them, tires squealing as it took the turn on two wheels and vanished around the corner.

He didn't even try to chase it. Even with his speed, there was no way he could run down a van over a long chase. He had more important things to do at the moment in any case, so he put the van he couldn't possibly catch out of his mind and shifted his focus to finding Katya.

This proved more difficult than he'd expected. They were only a few blocks away from the diner, which meant they were directly under the heavy shadow of the towering monolith of the support beam that had cut this area off from the rest of the city. Still, it wasn't so dark he shouldn't be able to find a *car*. But everywhere he looked, the road was deserted. He was almost ready to believe she'd vanished into thin air when he spotted the huge hole in the condemned building across the street.

Now that he'd seen it, Julius didn't know how he could have missed it. The old storefront on the ground floor was smashed in like it had taken a direct hit from a wrecking ball. Smoke and dust were still pouring out of the breach, but through the thick clouds, he could just make out a pair of dimly flickering headlights.

Julius didn't waste another second. He ran for the wrecked building, vaulting through one of the broken windows to land inside what must have once been a retail sales floor. Now that he was inside, he spotted Katya's car at once. He also realized why he hadn't been able to find it earlier. The impact had thrown the little blue coupe clear through the building, taking out a line of old sales counters and at least one support beam in the process. It was now lying against the far wall of the building, but it wasn't until he got past the wreckage of the old registers that Julius realized the blue sports car was actually lying *upside down.*

The sight was enough to turn what was left of his stomach into an icy ball. Just as he was starting to fear the worst, though, he saw movement in the wreckage, and relief hit him like a punch in the gut.

"Katya!" he yelled, tripping over his feet in his rush to run forward.

No answer.

Panic returned immediately, and not just because of the silence. Julius was halfway through the building now, close enough to see that the movement he'd spotted was not actually in the car, but beside it. Three large, man-shaped shadows were running down the back wall of the building toward the old emergency exit where an armored van—a *second* armored van that looked exactly like the one that had just crashed into Marci's car—was waiting for them in the back alley.

By this point, Julius was running full tilt through the debris, but he still wasn't fast enough. By the time he reached the emergency door, the men had tossed themselves and Katya's unconscious body into the back of the van. It lurched forward the moment their feet left the ground, roaring down the alley and around the corner into the street beyond. He ran after them on principle, but the van was already gone, vanished into the dark, decaying grid of old Detroit.

"Julius!"

He glanced over his shoulder to see Marci running up behind him. Or, rather, he assumed it was Marci. The alley was so dark, he wouldn't actually have been able to tell it was her if she hadn't called his name.

"I heard another car," she panted when she reached him. "Did they get away?"

He nodded before he remembered she couldn't see him. "Yes. They got Katya, too."

"What?"

"It was a trap," Julius said, hands shaking. "A setup. They were waiting for us."

He could almost hear Marci staring at him, and then she let out her breath in a huff.

"Oh come on," she said. "I mean, that doesn't make any sense. There's no way someone could have known we'd be driving this direction in time to set something like this up. *I* didn't even know we'd be driving through here until a few minutes ago. And even if they did somehow psychically know where we'd be before we did, there's no way they could have set up a situation this specific. I mean, lining up a van to hit a car at just the right angle to throw it through a building on the other side of the street where another team is waiting to grab the driver and make a getaway? I don't care if you had a year to plan, there's not enough luck in the world to pull off a stunt that. It's a miracle they didn't kill her." She stopped short, breath hitching, "Um, they *didn't* kill her, right?"

"No." Katya hadn't been moving, but she'd clearly been all in one piece, and it took more than a car wreck to kill a dragon her age. Julius was far more worried about the rest of what Marci had said, because she was absolutely right. There *wasn't* enough luck in the world, because it wasn't luck at all. This was the work of a seer.

The moment that thought crossed his mind, everything else fell into place: Bob's sudden interest in his life, the perfectly timed text with Katya's location, his appearance to Marci just minutes earlier. This was his eldest brother's doing. It had to be. The only way anyone could make something like this work was if they had knowledge of the future, but when you added a seer into the mix, everything became perfectly clear. Everything, that was, except *why*.

Julius closed his eyes. It was so dark in the alley this hardly made a difference, but it still helped him think, and he'd never needed to think faster than he did right now. Katya was the youngest daughter of their clan's greatest enemy. What had just happened wasn't technically his fault, but if he didn't find Katya before Svena discovered she'd been taken, the White Witch of the Three Sisters wasn't going to sit patiently and listen to explanations. She was going to blame *him*, and then probably kill him, which would start a clan war for sure. It didn't matter that his mother considered Julius the least of her hatchlings—no one killed a Heartstriker except Bethesda and Chelsie. Bob *knew* that, so why would he put Julius in this position? Surely even he wasn't crazy enough to involve a clan as powerful as the Three Sisters in his schemes, right?

Julius scrubbed his hands through his hair, sending a rain of dust spattering across his shoulders. Trying to figure out seer logic was a quick route to madness. For all he knew, Bob was having tea with Katya in the back of that van right now. But while he had no idea what was really going on, or why, one truth was crystal clear. "We have to get her back," he said grimly. "Tonight."

Marci nodded and turned around, her steps picking up as she starting back down the alley. "Let's get going, then."

Thanks to Katya's headlights, it was much brighter inside the crumbling building than it had been out in the alley now that the dust had settled. Marci was already on her hands and knees beside the upside-down car by the time Julius came in, her head stuck through the shattered driver's window.

It was the only place she could have stuck her head in, Julius realized with a lurch. The passenger side of Katya's car was completely crushed where the van had struck it, leaving the roof of the upside down car strewn with glass and the tattered remains of the deflated airbags. Only the driver's side was still intact, though there was a bloody dent on the dash where Katya must have knocked herself unconscious. The driver's side seatbelt was still neatly in its place, clearly unused, which only made Julius even more certain that his brother had been behind this.

That thought made him angry all over again. He didn't want to scare Marci, though, so he took a deep, calming breath. Unfortunately, this actually made things worse.

Now that the initial rush of panic had faded, the smell of the wreck was overwhelming. The stench of burning rubber and plastic mixed with the reek of fresh blood was nauseating. There was quite a lot of blood, actually, which was strange. Other than the splatter on the dash, he hadn't though Katya was so injured. It smelled odd, too, not like dragon blood at all. It wasn't until Marci ducked back out of the shattered window, though, that he realized the truth.

Marci's shirt was soaked in blood. There was so much, he thought she must have been stabbed at first. On the second look, he saw the blood was actually coming from her neck, not that that was any better. "Why didn't you tell me you were hurt?"

He didn't realize how sharp his voice was until she winced. "It's not as bad as it looks," she said, but Julius was already reaching for her. When he examined her neck, though, he saw she was right.

Though the bloody stain down the front of her shirt had made it look like she was dying, the cut on Marci's neck wasn't actually that deep. It was more long than anything else, a shallow slice that ran from just below her right ear down to the soft skin covering her trachea. Minor as it was, the cut had still bled like a faucet, which accounted for her horror-movie appearance. But while her face looked deathly pale in the glare of Katya's halogen headlights, she was clearly alive and functional, a fact that helped Julius drag his panic back down to a more or less functional level.

"How did this happen?" he said, tearing a strip off the bottom of his shirt. "You seemed fine before."

"I *am* fine," she protested, wincing as he pressed the cloth against her wound. "I keep telling you, it's just a cut. I didn't even know I was bleeding until I noticed my shirt was wet. Really, though, I'm okay. It doesn't even hurt that much."

She clearly meant this to make him feel better, but Julius barely heard it. Now that he'd seen her wound, all he could think about was how close she'd come to having her throat cut. If the slice had been just a little deeper, or a bit farther to the left, it would have gone through her windpipe. A few centimeters' difference, that was all it would have taken, and Marci wouldn't be here complaining about his fussing. She would be dead.

His body began to shake, though whether it from was fear or anger, Julius couldn't say. He tried to keep calm by focusing on the rise and fall of Marci's breath under his fingers, the undeniable proof that the worst hadn't happened, but it didn't work. No matter how hard he tried to ignore it, Julius couldn't shake the feeling that, unlike the rest of this ridiculous situation, Marci's survival *had* been luck. She was only human, and to dragons, human meant disposable. Bob probably hadn't even considered her a factor. Her death would have been a throwaway, a meaningless detail in the larger draconic scheme, and that made him angriest of all.

"Julius?"

He blinked and glanced up to see Marci watching him with a worried frown. "Are you okay?"

"I'm fine," he grumbled. "You're the one who's hurt."

"It's *really* not that bad. I was going to bandage it up, but I wanted to secure a material link before the trail got too cold. See?"

She held up her hand, and Julius saw three of Katya's gleaming, white-gold hairs pinched between her fingers. That was what she'd been doing inside the wrecked car, he realized. She must have pulled them off the headrest.

"I can't claim to be an expert tracker," she said, winding the long hairs around her fingers. "But any idiot can follow a trail this hot. Unless that van is warded, this should be more than enough to take us right to her, especially since she's a dragon. Not that I've tracked dragons before, of course, but you guys are so magical I could probably follow you from space."

Julius froze. "You knew Katya was a dragon?"

Marci gave him an *oh, come on* look. "It was kind of obvious. Humans don't look like that."

"Like what?" Because he'd thought Katya had looked remarkably *undraconic*.

She ducked her head, and he was relieved to see a bit of color come back to her cheeks. "Never mind. Just let me go so I can start on the tracing spell."

Julius stilled her with a firm push. "Not until I'm done."

Marci froze, but it wasn't until he saw how wide her eyes had gotten that he realized he was growling deep in his throat. He stopped at once, keeping his attention on his work as he carefully wiped the blood from Marci's neck. Still, it was hard to keep his hands steady. He was just so *angry*, angrier than he could ever remember being, and he didn't know how to handle it. But there was nothing he could do while Marci was bleeding, so he poured himself into the present, tearing off another piece of his shirt to bandage the cut. He was trying to think of the quickest way to get her to a real, sterile bandage when he heard the faint rumble of a car on the road outside.

He stilled, bracing for fight or flight. Since it was unlikely their enemy would be returning to the scene of the crime so soon, he was betting on flight. This might be a nearly abandoned section of a terrible neighborhood in the Underground, but the wreck had been *loud*. That sort of thing was sure to draw human attention. Not cops, of course, this was still the DFZ, but nosy humans of any sort were the last thing Julius wanted, and when he saw an ancient Crown Victoria drift to a stop behind Marci's totaled sedan, he knew it was time to go.

"Do you need anything from your car?"

Marci stared at him like he was stupid. "Of *course* I need the stuff in my car. Do you have any idea how expensive casting markers are?"

"I'll buy you new ones," he said, grabbing her arm. "Come on, we have to—"

The blare of a horn cut him off. In the street, the Crown Victoria's driver was beeping out a *Shave and a Haircut* pattern, and Julius's poor stomach clenched again. He turned around, watching in stunned silence as the antique car's tinted window rolled down to reveal the smiling, too-handsome face he really should have been expecting all along.

"Hello, little brother! I had an inkling you could use a ride."

When Julius didn't answer, Bob climbed out of the car. "What? No hello for the loving brother who came all this way just to offer his assistance?"

He was never able to say later what part of that had been the last straw. He couldn't even explain his thought process, most likely because he hadn't been thinking at all. He was furious and frightened and the smell of Marci's blood was all over him. Bob, on the other hand, was standing there grinning like this was all a hilarious joke, and something inside Julius just snapped.

Before he knew he was moving, before he realized he'd even made the decision, Julius was standing right in front of his brother with his hands fisted in the seer's midnight blue jacket. "*You,*" he snarled. "I *know* you did this!"

Bob didn't answer, just stared down at his little brother with his all-knowing green eyes, and in the silence, the magnitude of what he'd just done hit Julius in a rush. He'd grabbed his brother, his *eldest brother*, a dragon nearly forty times his age who could swat him like a fly.

This dawning realization must have been plain on his face, because Bob's lips pulled into a smug smile. "Ah, there it is," he whispered. "There's the *fear*. I was beginning to worry I'd lost my touch."

By this point, Julius's hands were shaking so badly he could barely grip, but he still didn't let go of his brother's coat. He was in for it now, he reasoned. The hammer of retribution was going to fall no matter what, so he might as well speak his piece.

"I don't know why you did this," he said. "I don't know what you think you're going to gain from using me or stirring up trouble between the clans, but whatever convoluted mess of a game you're playing, you had no right to drag others into it."

"Others?" Bob's bright green eyes narrowed to dangerous slits. "How *interesting*. Why don't I believe you're talking about the tragically kidnapped Katya?"

His narrowed gaze slid pointedly over Julius's shoulder to where Marci was standing across the street, but he needn't have bothered with the dramatics. Julius knew perfectly well that he'd revealed his hand, he just was too angry to care. "Marci is *not* your pawn," he growled. "I can't stop you from using me, but you leave her out of this or I swear I'll do everything in my power to wreck any of your plans I can reach."

As threats went, it was a pretty weak one. For all Julius knew, that was exactly the response Bob wanted. It was the only retaliation he had, though, and at that moment, Julius fully intended to follow through however he could. But his brother was looking at him strangely, sagging against his hold in a way that forced Julius to support his weight as the silence stretched thinner and thinner.

Julius's nervousness stretched with it. The longer his brother went without answering, the more certain Julius was that those rash words would be his last. But then, after almost thirty seconds of horrible, empty quiet, Bob's face broke into a wide smile.

"I think that little speech might just be the most draconic thing that's ever left your mouth," he said, easily breaking out of Julius's hold. "Territoriality, possessiveness, aggression, threats of reprisal..." He shook his head in wonder. "Why, baby Julius, could you be growing into your fangs at last?"

Julius had no idea how to respond to that, or how to react when Bob reached down to slap him on the back.

"Don't get your feathers in a fluff," he chided. "I'm here to help! I can't let you have all the fun, can I?"

Julius gaped at him. "What's *fun* about almost dying?"

"But that's the best sort of fun," Bob replied. "The kind you can look back on centuries later and laugh about. Of course, since I'm always centuries ahead, I can laugh about it right now."

And then he did, loudly.

Julius watched with growing apprehension, reminding himself not to read too much into Bob's antics. Seers were famously mad, after all, and he'd always suspected Bob had a bit more fun with that than he really should. Since his brother showed no signs of pulling himself together anytime soon, he looked around for Marci instead, spotting her poking through the ruins of her car. He was about to go help her when Bob's arm suddenly wrapped around his shoulders.

"Don't bother her yet," he warned, his laughter gone as quickly as it had come. "She's about to get a phone call."

Julius attempted to tug out of Bob's grip only to find that he couldn't. "What phone call?"

The words were barely out of his mouth when a jangly electronic tune rang out across the street. Marci jumped at the sound, her hands flying for her shoulder bag, which had never left her shoulder and had gotten rather bloody as a result. She fumbled with one of the wet front pouches before pulling out the phone he'd given her. Rather than answer, though, she looked at Julius. "Should I take it? No one has this number."

"That's never stopped me," Bob said before Julius could open his mouth. "Just answer it already. The suspense is almost as obnoxious as your ringtone."

Marci shot Bob a surprisingly nasty look, but she touched the screen to accept the call all the same, putting it on speaker. It wasn't much of a speaker since Julius had been forced to get her one of the cheaper models, but the result was still plenty loud enough for dragons to hear from several feet away.

"I've got your girl."

Julius had never heard that deep, angry voice before, but Marci clearly had, because her whole face flushed with rage. "Bixby," she spat.

"Hello, Miss Novalli," Bixby crooned. "Long time no see."

If Marci had been a dragon, Julius would have expected her to start breathing smoke at this point. "What do you want?"

"You know exactly what I want," Bixby said, his voice so smug Julius could actually hear the sneer that must have been on his face. "I want my property, and you're going to bring it to me. And before you get any ideas, let me say right off that I know exactly what sort of company you're keeping these days, so if you don't want the Lady of the Lakes to add a pretty blond dragon head to her collection, you'll shut up and do exactly what I say."

There was a pause while Bixby waited for Marci to protest. When she didn't, he continued.

"In one hour, I'm going to send you an address. You come alone with the Kosmolabe, and I'll let your little friend slither off none the worse for wear. You don't show, or you decide to bring along that new boyfriend I hear you've picked up, and we'll toss Sleeping Beauty into the lake faster than you can say 'I miss my daddy.'"

The sound that came out of Marci when he said that last part was closest thing to a growl Julius had ever heard from a human. Bixby must have heard it too, because he sounded smugger than ever. "Good to know we have an understanding. See you in an hour."

The call had barely cut off before Marci grabbed the screen like she was going to crush it between her palms. "That, that, *ooooh.*"

Julius swooped in just in time to rescue her phone. He plucked it out of her straining hands and hit the icon to trace the number. Naturally, the results came back blank, and Julius made a mental note to talk to his hacker about putting real tracing programs on their phones, because he was getting mighty sick of this Unknown Caller nonsense. He huffed in annoyance and turned to hand the phone back to Marci only to find her staring at him, her face stricken.

"Julius," she said, voice shaking. "I'm sorry. I'm so, *so* sorry. This is all my fault. I never meant to get you involved in my drama, and now I've messed everything up. You were right, I should have left that stupid golden softball in the desert. I—"

Julius put a hand on her shoulder. With gentle but firm pressure, he steered her farther down the street, away from his brother. Real privacy was impossible when a seer was involved, of course, but that didn't mean he wanted a live audience for this.

"Marci," he said when they were more or less alone. "You have nothing to apologize for. This trap was not your fault, and I've been waiting for a chance to get my hands on Bixby."

She shook her head. "But—"

"But nothing," he said, looking her in the eyes. "We're going to handle this together. You help me, I help you. That's what makes us a team, right?"

She stared at him for a long time after that, biting her lip in a way that made him worried she was going to cry again. Thankfully, she didn't, but he could hear her heart in her throat when she whispered, "Thank you."

"No thanks needed," Julius said, but he coveted her words all the same, hoarding them in his memory like precious stones. If she kept this up, it was going to take more fingers than he had to count all the times someone had thanked him and meant it. He liked that idea very much indeed, and he couldn't keep the smile off his face as they walked back to her car to salvage what was left of her stuff.

Sadly, it didn't take long. The wreck had crushed her trunk, destroying everything breakable and burying everything that wasn't inside a twisted mass of metal. Ghost, being non-corporeal, was the only survivor, if a death spirit could be said to have survived anything. He seemed to be giving Marci a piece of his mind, though, so Julius left her arguing with her cat and returned to Bob, who was watching from the hood of his car like this was the best show ever.

He smiled as Julius approached, patting the spot beside him on the freshly waxed hood, which his weight was already denting. Julius ignored the invitation and leaned on the bumper instead. "So how long have you been playing Bixby?"

Bob's eyes widened, and then his hands flew up to grip to his chest like he was having a heart attack.

"What?" Julius cried. "What's wrong?"

"Nothing," Bob said, dropping his hands. "It's just the shock of seeing you acting so stern and dragon-esque. If I'd known getting you kicked out of the mountain would have such immediate positive returns, I'd have told Mother to do it years ago." He paused. "Oh wait, I *did* know! Must have been a timing thing. That's the problem with being all-knowing but not all-remembering. After a while, you just can't keep up." He frowned and started fumbling with his pockets. "I really should start leaving myself notes."

He *did* leave himself notes. They were hidden all over the mountain, sometimes for years. Finding them was a favorite game for young Heartstrikers, but Julius had no time or patience for his brother's antics right now. "Wait a second. *You're* the reason I was sealed?"

Bob rolled his eyes. "As I pointed out to your human earlier, the seal was Mother's idea. She'd been fretting over who to use as a scapegoat for this Ian situation for months. I merely gave her a nudge in your direction."

"A nudge?" Julius repeated, his anger coming back in a rush. "You *nudged* me right out of my home!"

"Don't act all put out," Bob said. "This little jaunt to the DFZ has been the best thing that's ever happened to you. You were miserable hiding in your room, and it made me miserable to look at you. At least now you're actually living up to your potential."

Julius opened his mouth to argue, but he closed it just as fast, because Bob was right. The last few days had been terrifying and painful, but also completely life-changing. Just because he was enjoying the results didn't mean he approved of his brother's methods, though, and he shoved his hands into his pockets with a surly harrumph. "Well, you could have gone about it in a nicer way, or at least a less dangerous one. Last I checked, a car wreck didn't count as a nudge."

"Oh, Julius," Bob said sweetly. "You're all the nice we've got. And as much as it pains me to admit, you're giving me a shade too much credit in all this. This Bixby person is indeed a pawn, he's just not mine."

The confession came so quickly that Julius, who was still stewing over the fact that he'd actually benefited from Bob's meddling, robbing him of his right to be upset, almost missed it. "Wait, what?"

"I didn't arrange this little incident."

"But it had to be you," Julius said before he could think better of it. "There's no way this could have happened without a seer."

Bob rolled his eyes. "I never said a seer wasn't involved, only that it wasn't me. If *I* was going to nab your dragoness out from under you, I'd find a classier way to do it. Being hit by a car is so *pedestrian*."

Julius winced as his brother broke into hysterical laughter at his own terrible pun. In a way, though, the break was good, because he needed to think. Bob's claim that he wasn't behind this was a huge relief, *if* it was true. He didn't think his brother was lying, though, because the idea of Bob kidnapping Katya so Bixby could use her to get the Kosmolabe when Marci had it in her possession not ten feet away just didn't make any sense, even for Bob. But if the Heartstriker's seer wasn't behind this, who was?

"That's a good question."

Bob's laughter cut off like a switch. He was now sitting perfectly still on the hood of his car with his legs crossed in lotus position, studying Julius with a serene expression. "Your face is very transparent," he explained. "Tell me, Julius, how many seers do you think are alive in the world right now?"

Before Julius could even open his mouth, Bob broke into a grin. "Trick question! The answer is three. There are *always* three, and only three, seers in existence at any given point. At this moment, the roster includes myself, Estella the Northern Star, and the Black Reach."

Julius shuddered at that last name. The Black Reach was a legend from the Golden Age of dragons, that mythical time a thousand years before the disappearance of magic when power had been plentiful and great dragons had flown freely. He hadn't known the old menace was still alive, or a seer, though the latter would explain the former nicely. Still, "I thought the Black Reach lived in China."

"That doesn't mean anything," Bob said with a shrug. "The Black Reach doesn't have to be in the same hemisphere to meddle in your affairs. He didn't get his name for having unusually long arms, you know. But while the Black Reach certainly could have arranged this particular act of automotive tragedy, I don't believe he would. Far too unsubtle. This is lazy seer tinkering, real last-minute stuff. The Black Reach would never stoop to such sloppiness."

Julius shook his head. "But if he didn't do it, and you didn't do it, that only leaves Estella, which doesn't make any sense. She's the acting clan head of the Three Sisters, isn't she?"

"Indeed."

"So why would she do this?" Because even by dragon standards, arranging to have your little sister hit by a car and kidnapped by humans was a bit much.

Bob sighed. "Oh Julius, not all clans value family as highly as the Heartstrikers."

He grimaced at the thought. "So what's Estella up to, then?"

His brother lifted his shoulders in a helpless shrug. "I have no idea. I can't see a thing. This is why seers normally stay away from each other. We block each other's sight. It's highly annoying, which is why I've been blocking Estella's at every opportunity."

Julius gaped at him. "So you've just been antagonizing her?"

"You make it sound like a bad thing," Bob said. "Come now. I know you've spent most of your adult life hiding in a cave, but even you must be aware that our clan's not winning many popularity contests at the moment. Mother stepped on quite a few scaly toes in her rush to the top, including Estella's, and the Northern Star never could learn not to take things personally. She'd eat our whole clan for breakfast if she ever got the chance, and part of my job is to make sure she doesn't. Now pay attention, this next bit is important."

Julius nodded, and Bob slid off his car to pace in front of it, his hands moving dramatically as he spoke. "For reasons I haven't figured out yet, Estella is using this Bixby fellow to go after your charming pet mage and her Cosmopolitan."

"Kosmolabe," Julius said.

Bob dismissed the correction with a flick of his wrist. "Whatever. I'm not even sure if the Kosmo-thing is her endgame or just another step, but it warms my heart to keep her from getting it. That's half of why I'm here: interference. If Estella's taking a personal hand in this, it must be very important, and making sure Estella's important plans fall through is one of life's little joys."

He pressed a hand to his heart with a satisfied sigh, but Julius was more confused than ever. "Only half? What's the other part?"

"You, of course."

Julius blinked in surprise, and Bob rolled his eyes. "Please. I know your little human told you about our delightful conversation. This is a test, by me, for you. Though I have to admit it's a much better one now that Estella's come into the game. I never would have thought to wreck your car."

Julius was sure he'd regret asking, but this was already the longest conversation he'd ever had with his eldest brother, and he wasn't about to waste what might be his only opportunity. "What are you testing me for?"

"Ah, ah, ah," Bob said, wagging his finger. "If I told you that, it wouldn't be much of a test, would it? Let's just say I learned the hard way to always stress test my tools before I use them. Now, go help your human. It seems my lady love has finally woken up, and I need to get her opinion on a few matters before we begin."

He tipped his head toward the Crown Victoria, and Julius looked back to see Bob's pigeon perched on the giant steering wheel, her beady eyes blinking as if she had, indeed, just woken up. Bob walked over to the driver's door and leaned through the open window to drop a loving kiss on top of the pigeon's head. It fluttered happily in reply, cooing rapidly. Bob cooed back, face beaming, and Julius quickly turned away, walking over to join Marci before he saw something that ruined the last remaining vestige of hope he maintained for his brother's sanity.

Chapter 15

"So let me make sure I've got this straight," Marci said. "The three great dragon seers are the Black Reach, Estella the Northern Star, and *Bob?*" When Julius nodded, she arched an eyebrow. "One of these things is not like the others."

"Bob's just his family name," Julius explained. They were hunched together in the enormous back seat of Bob's Crown Victoria as he drove them away from what he'd termed the 'Scene of Interest.' It wasn't the most private place to have a discussion he really, *really* shouldn't be having, but Marci had refused to stay behind, and Julius couldn't bring himself to let her step into a mess like this without some basic information. "He's actually Brohomir, Great Seer of the Heartstrikers, but he only answers to that on formal occasions or when he's booking tables at restaurants."

"I can't address an ancient, supposedly future-seeing dragon as *Bob*," she said, shooting a look at the back of Bob's head. "It's undignified!"

"Trust me, it's better this way." He'd seen his brother put aside his goofy, slightly insane Bob persona and become Brohomir only once, and it wasn't an experience he wanted to repeat, especially in front of a mortal. That thought sent his eyes drifting back down to the makeshift bandage on Marci's neck. The bleeding had stopped, thank goodness, but the smell of blood still lingered, reminding Julius just how close the miss had been.

"Are you even sure he's really a seer?" she whispered, leaning closer. "Because every paper I've seen on the subject concluded that true clairvoyance is a myth."

"A century ago, your kind considered dragons to be myths," Bob said, making them both jump. "Why are mortals always so eager to declare things impossible, anyway? It's not like things do or don't exist just because you say so."

She straightened up again. "So you're saying you actually see the future?"

Marci's question sent Julius into a panic. You did not just *ask* elder dragons to spill their secrets. But before he could think of a way to cover for her before his brother took offense, Bob did the unthinkable. He answered.

"Only very occasionally," he said, tapping his fingers on the steering wheel. "Mostly, I see what will *probably* happen based on decisions people make: whether you eat lunch now or later, whether you decide to fake being sick or go to work, whether you kill a man or spare his life, that sort of thing. Every decision made creates a fork in the future, and a seer's power is the ability to read ahead down those forks to find the path that leads to the outcome we want. Once we find it, we simply nudge the players as needed to make sure all the critical decisions come out in our favor." He paused, frowning. "This isn't to say I don't also have true visions of things that cannot be changed, but they're not my bread and butter."

By the time he finished, Julius's jaw was on the floor. He'd never heard Bob talk about his seer powers like this to anyone. Of course, he'd never heard Bob talk much at all since he'd always made it a point to avoid the upper alphabet members of his family. Marci, however, didn't seem to appreciate the gravity of what she was learning. She just asked another question.

"What's the difference between things you nudge and things you can't change?" she said, leaning as far forward as her seatbelt would allow. "From your explanation, it sounds like the future is made from our decisions, which suggests it's all free will. But if there are also things that can't be changed no matter what, that sounds like destiny. So which is it?"

"Is light a wave or a particle?" Bob replied with an elegant shrug. "Really, Miss Mage, you need to keep a more open mind to the inherent dualities of nature if you ever want to understand the higher workings of magic."

That was clearly not an answer that held water with Marci. Before she could object, though, Bob turned around to look at Julius. "Where to?"

Julius blinked. "You're asking *me*?"

"It's *your* future," Bob reminded him. "And in case you missed the point of that impromptu lecture, your decisions are kind of a vital element in all this. Now, where do we go?"

Julius bit his lip. He hated making snap decisions. He especially hated making them when Bob was looking at him instead of the road while operating a manually driven car. He *especially* especially hated making decisions under the implication that whatever choice he made would influence his entire future. "Can I think about it?"

Bob rolled his eyes. "See, this is exactly why I don't normally tell people how the game works. You start overthinking and double-guessing and everything gets tangled in knots. Just pretend I'm not here and do whatever you think is best."

That was kind of hard to pull off with Bob staring straight at him, so Julius turned to the window and set about working things through logically. "The last time Bixby attacked, he went big. I doubt he'll do any less this time, especially if he thinks Marci might bring help even after he told her not to, which I'm sure he does." He glanced back at Marci. "Do you think he could put together another army like the one at the house?"

She pursed her lips, thinking. "Not of his own men, but he's rich and apparently dead set on making this happen. *And* he knows he's dealing with dragons now, so yeah, he's probably going to roll something pretty big."

"Which means we're going to need help," Julius finished, because there was no way he could play magic battery again today. When he looked hopefully at Bob, though, the seer shook his head.

"I'm here on a strictly observational basis. Pick again."

Julius blew out a long breath. He hadn't been too keen on the idea of relying on Bob, but without him, their options were limited. Singular, really, but as much as he hated the idea, he couldn't think of anyone else, and he dropped his head with a sigh. "I'm going to have to ask Justin."

"Excellent choice," Bob said, turning back to the road at last. "And where is Justin at the moment?"

Julius snapped his head up again. "You mean you don't know?"

"I'm a seer, not a directory," Bob replied testily. "Though if I had to guess, I'd say the family safe house."

"We have a safe house in the DFZ?"

"Of course we have a safe house here," Bob said, smiling in the rear view mirror. "Mother keeps safe houses in all the major cities as protection for those she feels deserve protecting."

Which would explain why Julius had never heard of it. "That's probably where he is, then. Unless he got a hotel?"

Bob shook his head. "Justin's not allowed in hotels anymore. Too many incidents."

Marci snorted. "I can *totally* see that."

Both dragons looked at her, but she just looked back totally unrepentant, and Julius sighed. "Fine," he said, dragging his hands through his hair, which was already standing on end after a full day of such abuse. "Safe house it is."

"Heartstriker Safe House, coming up," Bob said cheerfully. "Hold on."

Before Julius could ask why, or to what, his brother floored the gas, sending the car shooting forward. Marci grabbed Julius with a yelp as the momentum launched Ghost, who'd spent the impromptu car trip hiding in Marci's bag, straight through her chest and into the trunk. But if Bob noticed the chaos in his back seat, he paid it no mind. He just leaned over the wheel, dodging the late afternoon traffic like he was playing a racing game while his pigeon clung to his shoulder, flapping her wings for balance whenever he took a particularly sharp turn.

***

Svena stood in front of the mirrored vanity in the white dressing room of the penthouse suite she'd secured for her stay in the DFZ, ignoring her sister as she put on the diamond earrings Ian had sent over this morning. As bribes went, jewelry was unsubtle and a clear sign of his youth, which might have been why Svena found it thrilling. Estella, on the other hand, thought it was tacky, and she said so. Repeatedly.

"He treats you like a human," Estella spat, not even looking up from her phone, which she'd been typing on frantically all afternoon. "Like some mortal paramour. It's insulting and vulgar, but what more could you expect from the children of Bethesda the Broodmare? She is trash, and trash breeds true."

"So you keep saying," Svena replied, turning her head side to side to set the strings of diamonds glittering in the brightly lit mirror. "But if you would look beyond your superiority for a moment, you might notice that the world has changed. The Heartstrikers are no longer a minor power we can ignore. And besides"—she smiled at her reflection—"*I* am the elder dragon. That means Ian is *my* paramour, and if he wishes to shower me with gifts, who am I to stop him?"

"Your paramour," Estella scoffed, glaring at her phone as she slid deeper into the cushions of the dressing room's silk sofa. "The whelp son of an upstart whore whose only talents are luring more powerful dragons into her bed and breeding like a barnyard animal."

"And yet with those two talents, Bethesda the Heartstriker has made herself the undisputed matriarch of the largest dragon clan on Earth," Svena said, calmly adjusting the bust of her strapless dress before turning to face her sister at last. "You are a fool if you ignore that simply because you don't approve of her lifestyle."

"It is you who is being a fool!" Estella shouted, dropping her phone at last as she shot up from the couch. "Defending our enemies and primping in the mirror like an idiot girl for a dragon so far beneath you, I cannot even acknowledge his presence without debasing myself!"

"Who else could I choose?" Svena said, staring her sister down. "To hear you tell it, *everyone* is beneath the daughters of the Three Sisters. Has it never occurred to you that I might be tired of being all-powerful, dreadful, and alone?"

"Better alone than to roll about in the mud with pigs!" Estella snarled, drawing herself up to her full height. "At least *I* remember the fear and respect our bloodline demands. Our mothers were worshiped as gods!"

Svena turned away with a growl, snatching her hairbrush off the marble counter. This was an old argument, and it was no more likely to be settled tonight than the hundreds of other times they'd clashed over the years. "You're overreacting," she said, dragging the brush through her already perfect hair. "Ian is nothing but an amusement. Something to pass the time while I wait for his idiot brother to find Katya, which, I might remind you, was *your* idea to begin with."

"Yes," Estella said. "To *set up* the Heartstrikers! If I'd foreseen you behaving like such a tasteless harlot, I would have scrapped the entire venture and returned Katya to the mountain myself."

"Then I guess you don't see as much as you claim," Svena said, slamming the brush down again. "Enough. I've got better things to do than stand here and listen to this. I'm going out. Don't wait up."

"Svena."

Svena had already decided to ignore her, but there was an edge on Estella's voice that made her look back. When she did, her sister was standing in front of the dressing room door, imperious as a queen. "You will not go."

The command was sharp as cracking ice, and it called forth a rage Svena hadn't felt in many years. "You may be acting head of our clan," she said slowly, drawing herself up to her full height as well. "But this is not clan business, and you are dangerously close to overstepping your authority."

"All business is my business," Estella replied haughtily. "Especially yours. Other than myself, you are the greatest of us. Your actions echo through the entire family, and I cannot stand by while you permit yourself to be used in such a fashion."

"It is *I* who am using," Svena growled. "Ian is *my* amusement, and I will keep him for however long I like."

Estella laughed then, a sound as beautiful and cold as the arctic sea they ruled. "Ian? Ian is a tool, a puppet too young and blind to even realize he's dancing to someone else's tune. I was referring to the one who pulls his strings. The dragon who plays all the Heartstrikers like a symphony while allowing that shallow peacock Bethesda to take the credit."

Svena rolled her eyes. If this was about the Seer of the Heartstrikers again, she did *not* want to hear it. She opened her mouth to tell Estella as much, but before she could say a word, she noticed her sister had that odd gleam in her eye that warned she was no longer in the present, but lost in the hazy maze of possible futures that only seers could see.

"He taunts me," Estella whispered, her voice shaking with frustrated fury. "He blocks me at every turn and takes what I hold dear purely out of spite. Even you." She looked up, her blue eyes suddenly focusing as they locked with Svena's. "Katya was always weak. Her loss is nothing, but you are our prize. I sent you here because I thought you would be untouchable, a mountain too great to even notice his foolish nudging, but no sooner did you arrive in this horrible city than your future began to vanish." She closed her eyes with a little sob that cut right to Svena's icy heart. "He is taking you away from me."

"Oh, sister," Svena said, her anger forgotten as she hurried to Estella's side. "You are upset over nothing. I've never even met the Heartstriker's seer."

"You think that matters?" Estella said, her voice thick with a hatred so old and deep, Svena couldn't begin to imagine how long it must have been growing. "He cannot defeat me, and so the coward strikes at you, tempting you through his brother's whispers of power. They are all his pawns, and now he seeks to add you to his game as well. But he shall never have you." She reached up to grab her sister's shoulders, digging her nails into Svena's flesh. "You are *my* pawn!"

Svena's sympathy for her sister died in a freezing rush of rage. "*I am no one's pawn!*" she roared, ripping out of her sister's hold with a thrust of power that shattered the mirrors and sent frost spreading across the carpet.

Estella's eyes widened at the blatant display, and for a moment, it almost looked like she would back down. Instead, she breathed out an icy breath of her own, and as the air left her body, the thin veneer of her humanity vanished along with it.

Svena gasped as the full weight of her sister's power landed on the room with the force of an avalanche. Estella hadn't changed completely—the dressing room was much too small for that—but the image of her dragon hovered over her like a specter, a pure white shadow of glistening scales and wings as thin and beautiful as frosted glass. Looking up at the ice-blue eyes she knew so well, Svena realized with a pang that she was no longer speaking to the older sister who'd taught her how to fly over the glacial seas. This was not the Estella she'd burned villages with so many centuries ago, laughing together as the little humans fled before them. This was the Northern Star, Seer of the Three Sisters and acting head of their clan, and the words that fell from her lips were law.

"You will not leave this room."

The command landed like a blow. It had been years since Svena been ordered so directly, or so forcibly, and the shock was enough to make her consider fighting back. She was larger, her magic stronger. If it had been any other dragon, that would have been enough. But a seer always had the weight of the future on her side, and Svena knew better than to start battles she wasn't certain she could win. She was proud, yes, but not stupidly so, and in the end, she dropped her eyes. "I will not leave."

Estella smiled, and the power roaring through the room vanished as quickly as it had come. "Good girl," she murmured, reaching up to brush Svena's hair away from her face just as she had when they were young. "You will see, lovely, this is no loss. These Heartstrikers are nothing but grasping fools. They seek to divide us, to topple our clan and make room at the top. But we are ancient magic, as far above them as stars above the sea. We shall remain long after Bethesda's lust for power has doomed them all, and you will thank me for my wisdom today."

Svena said nothing. She simply stood and waited while Estella checked her phone again. Whatever she read there, it must have been good news, because her face lit up at once. "I must go. Everything will fall into place soon, you will see. All I need from you is that you stay here. Do that, and I promise I will have Katya back to us before midnight. Then, my dear sister, we will deal with these foolish Heartstrikers together. When we are finished, Bethesda and her horde won't even be a memory."

Svena smiled and held her tongue, allowing herself to be kissed before Estella walked out of the room. When the seer's soft footsteps finally vanished down the hall, Svena walked across the suite to the window that overlooked the hotel's front entrance. It was nearing sunset, and the glare off the skyway's white buildings was blinding, but if she squinted, she could see the human doorman escorting Estella to her waiting limo. The moment her sister was safely ensconced in her car, Svena marched back into her dressing room and snatched her phone out of the litter of broken glass on the vanity.

As usual, Ian picked up before the second ring. "Changed your mind about dinner?"

Any other time, Svena would have happily strung him along. Tonight, however, she was in no mood for games. "Be at my hotel in thirty minutes."

Ian didn't answer at once, giving Svena time to ponder how he would react. A younger, less secure dragon would object to being commanded to appear, while a more experienced one would expect a trap and proceed with caution. As usual, though, Ian was a pleasant surprise.

"I'll be there in twenty," he said with all the confident ambition that had drawn Svena to him in the first place. "See you then."

Svena ended the call and sank onto the couch Estella had vacated with a smirk. She might have no choice but to obey her eldest sister's edict not to leave her suite, but that didn't mean she couldn't do as she pleased inside it, and Svena was suddenly very inspired to do *exactly* as she pleased. Because no matter what Estella said, the White Witch of the Three Sisters was no one's pawn, and if her sister could no longer see Svena's future, that just meant she was free to make of it what *she* wanted for once.

And as she looked out the bedroom window at the glass and steel towers of the DFZ shining like torches in the evening sunlight, Svena was surprised by how very much she wanted.

***

Julius wasn't sure what he'd thought the Heartstriker safe house would look like, but the building Bob stopped in front of definitely wasn't it. Positioned at the southwestern corner of the Upper City, as far from the water as you could get and still be on the skyways, the modern three-story mansion looked more like an upwardly mobile couple's urban showcase home than a dragon clan's emergency lair. It didn't even seem to have walls, just windows and brushed steel accents. It was, however, very conveniently located right off an exit ramp, and the enormous faux-cedar porch that wrapped around the house's western face to poke off the edge of the skyway made an excellent emergency landing spot for a dragon.

Bob dropped them off at the front gate, though he refused to actually go inside with them. When Julius asked why, Bob had declared he was the servant of "Great and Important Matters" and driven off, yelling out the window that he'd be back to pick them up "before the fun started."

Since it was now go inside or hang out on the curb, Julius walked up the stairs to the red-painted front door with Marci right behind him. The house was locked, of course, and when no one responded to the doorbell, he knocked as loudly as he could. He was about to knock again when the door flew open to reveal a sweaty, shirtless, and barefoot Justin with a slice of pizza in one hand and the Fang of the Heartstrikers in the other.

His eyebrows shot up when he saw who was at his door, and he lowered his sword, taking another bite of his pizza before asking, "What happened to her?"

Marci's hand instantly went to her throat, and Julius sighed. "Car wreck. Can we come in?"

Justin shrugged and stepped aside. "Your safe house, too," he said, still chewing. "The human has to wait outside, though."

"No, she doesn't," Julius said, lowering his voice. "Marci knows all about us now. Bob was the one who drove us over."

He'd expected Justin be impressed by that last bit, but his brother just rolled his eyes. "Don't tell me the Pigeon Whisperer dragged you into one of his stupid schemes." When Julius nodded, Justin shook his head. "Fine, the girl can come in, but if anyone asks, it was your idea."

Julius pulled Marci inside before Justin could change his mind, closing the door quickly behind them.

The safe house's interior was just as nice as its exterior, full of tasteful furniture that managed to look both modern and timeless, a sure sign that someone other than Mother had chosen the decor since Bethesda's taste in interior design ran more to gilded skulls than designer tables. But while the vestibule and plant-lined back porch were immaculate, the living room was a disaster area of trash and beer bottles. Clearly, Justin had made himself at home.

"How long have you been here?" Marci asked, staring wide-eyed at what had to be fifty empty pizza boxes stacked against the sliding glass door to the back patio.

"About ten hours," Justin said, walking to the open pizza box currently sitting in the middle of what had once been a pristine ecru couch. "I slept eight of those, though."

Marci's eyes went wider still. "You ate all of this in two hours?"

"Please," Justin said, dropping down on the floor to start a set of one-armed push-ups. "Haven't you ever seen a dragon eat? This took me ten minutes. I actually thought you were the pizza guy with my second order when I heard the door."

Marci made a little choking sound and looked at Julius with new understanding. Justin, however, seemed to have written them off entirely. Clearly, it was time to stop making small talk and get to the point.

"Justin," Julius said solemnly. "I need your help."

Justin stopped mid-push-up, arching his neck back to stare at his brother. "My help," he repeated. "You're asking *me* to help *you*?"

"Yes," Julius said. "Please."

Justin thought about it for a second, and then he pushed off the ground, popping himself back onto his feet like a cork. "Okay."

Julius blinked. "That's it? You don't even want to know what we're doing first?"

"I told you I'd help last night," Justin said, walking into the bathroom. "And anyway, how much trouble can you be in?"

Marci and Julius exchanged a silent look. "I think your brother has a chronically underdeveloped sense of danger," she whispered.

Julius couldn't argue with that. "Remember that dragoness I was trying to find?"

"The Three Sisters girl?" Justin said, his voice muffled by the towel he was using to dry the sweat from his hair. "You still haven't found her?"

"No, we found her. That's sort of the problem. We were taking her back to Ian's when Katya's sister Estella, the seer, arranged for her to be kidnapped by a human named Bixby in exchange for Marci's Kosmolabe. He's going to be contacting us in an hour, and if we don't meet his demands, he'll kill her."

"The dragon or the human?" Justin asked, tossing the towel on the floor before walking back out into the living room.

"Both, probably," Julius replied. "We've had one shootout with Bixby's men today already. I wouldn't be surprised if he had a full—"

Justin nodded. "Got it."

"How can you get it if I haven't said it?" Julius snapped.

"What's to get?" his brother asked, combing his short hair back into order with his fingers. "Kill humans, rescue dragon, done. Do we need to save this Kosmo-whatever, too?"

"Yes," Marci said before Julius could answer. When he looked at her, she shrugged. "What? If Estella wants it, it must be important. We can't let it fall into the wrong hands."

By which she clearly meant any hands other than hers. "I don't want to give anything up that we don't have to," Julius said. "But Katya is our first priority."

Justin was grinning by the time he finished. "Good to see you taking the initiative for once," he said, smacking Julius on the back. "Never thought I'd see the day. Now, let's get you a weapon."

"A weapon?" Julius coughed, trying to get his lungs working again after his brother's punishing hit.

"Of course," Justin said, kicking the trash out his way as he walked across the living room to a maglocked door on the other side. "What, did you think they'd just surrender if you asked politely?"

Julius shot him a dirty look, but his brother was too busy punching a code into the door's keypad to notice.

"You ask for my help, we do it my way," Justin said when the door clicked open. "That means assault, and assault means you have to stop being a wuss and come get a sword."

"No offense, Justin," Marci said. "But I'm pretty sure Bixby's men are going to have guns. Last I heard, you don't bring a sword to a gun fight."

"Then you haven't heard of swords like these," he said, pushing the door open.

Marci gasped, and Julius felt a little overwhelmed himself. Behind the door Justin had just unlocked, a small room glittered like an ancient hoard under tastefully recessed lighting. Though clearly meant to be a bedroom, the walls and windows had been been replaced with reinforced cement slabs lined with metal shelving, and on those shelves was a display of wealth greater than anything Julius had seen outside his mother's throne room.

"You've got to be kidding," he whispered. "That's not…"

"Of course it is," Justin said, stepping high over a bag of gold coins stamped with the faces of long-dead kings. "You remember how Chelsie was always going on about how keeping all your treasure in one place was risky and stupid?"

Julius nodded. Even locked up in his room, there was no way he could have missed the fit his mother threw every time anyone suggested moving so much as a coin of her hoard.

"Well," Justin continued. "Last year, Mother finally gave in and agreed to start redistributing some of her less valuable objects. Most of the safe houses have rooms like this now, alternate treasuries just in case something happens to the main hoard in the mountain, and they are *not to be touched.*"

This last bit was directed at Marci, who was rushing the door in her hurry to get to all the sparkly, shiny beauty.

"I'm not going to take anything," she protested as she stepped inside. "I just want to look."

"So look from there," Justin snarled, picking her up bodily and setting her firmly back on the other side of the door. "Minor treasury or not, this is all property of Bethesda the Heartstriker, and even a human should know how serious dragons are about their treasure. She'll know the second you touch so much as a dust bunny, so if you don't want your mortal life to be even shorter than usual, you'll keep your sticky fingers to yourself."

Marci huffed with disappointment, casting Julius a pleading look. When he spread his arms helplessly, she pointed at the far corner of the treasure room where an amber carving of an owl in flight had been propped haphazardly on top of a pile of velvet jewelry boxes. "Can you at least tell me what that one does? I can feel the magic pouring off it from here."

Justin's answer was a low growl, and Julius decided it was time to move things along before Marci got herself in real trouble. "What did you want to show me?"

"Not show," Justin said. "Loan." He reached up to grab an enormous jeweled sword off the weapon rack on the far wall. "Here, give this a try."

Julius stared at the six-foot-long bar of sharpened metal and magical ornamentation with a sinking weight in his chest. "Justin, I can't even lift that."

"Oh, right," his brother said. "I forgot you have baby arms." He returned the large sword to its bracket and took down a pair of ancient looking jade hook swords instead. "What about these?"

"No," Julius said again. "It's not that I don't appreciate the effort, but I haven't touched a sword since we were teenagers, and I wasn't even good then. If you want to give me a weapon, how about a shotgun? Or a taser? You know, something point-and-click I can use without years of training?"

"Like Mother would ever keep anything so mundane in her hoard," Justin said with a snort. "Don't worry, I'm sure your training will come back once your life is on the line. Even if it doesn't, you're a dragon. We're naturally good at killing stuff."

"*You're* naturally good at killing stuff," Julius grumbled, leaning over Marci to look around the room for a weapon that would shut his brother up while still being light enough for him to actually carry. Unfortunately, everything in the corner by Justin was either huge or overly complicated. He was about to tell his brother to forget the whole thing when he spotted a familiar-looking golden hilt sticking out of a vase on the top shelf.

"There," he said, pointing. "Get me that one."

Justin looked deeply skeptical, but he got the sword down as requested. The moment the slender red leather scabbard came into view, Julius's face broke into a huge grin.

"That's it," he said, holding out his hand. "That's the one I want."

"You can't be serious," Justin said, holding the weapon with his fingertips like he thought it might be contagious. "This isn't even a sword."

It *was* a bit short. The golden handle was large enough to fit comfortably even in Justin's big hands, but the sheathed blade was barely more than a foot long. For Julius, though, that was a mark in its favor, and he opened and closed his palm in a grabby hands motion until his brother relented and handed the sword over.

"What are you going to do with that pocket knife anyway? Chop onions?"

"I could chop you," Julius said proudly, unsheathing the short, razor sharp blade. "For your information, this is Tyrfing, forged by dwarfs for Odin's own grandson to never miss its mark."

Justin rolled his eyes. "You are such a nerd. How do you even know that?"

"Because I looked it up years ago," Julius said with a sly smile. "Remember those knife tossing competitions when we were kids?"

Justin's eyes went wide. *"That's* how you beat me?" When Julius nodded, his brother's face contorted in fury. "I *knew* you cheated!"

"There was no rule against using enchanted weapons," Julius said, smiling at his reflection in the sword's mirror-bright surface. "I wonder how it ended up here, though? It might not be pretty, but Tyrfing is *old*. Even if she was redistributing her treasure, I'd have thought Mother would keep all the really good stuff back at the mountain."

"She did," Justin said, still scowling. "She just doesn't consider swords to be 'good stuff.' Why else do you think she let us play with them? Jewelry's another matter. Remember the time Jessica tried to touch one of her diamond tiaras?"

Julius remembered it fondly. "I thought her hair would never grow back."

They both snickered. Marci, however, was still staring at the sword in Julius's hands like he'd threatened to kill her with it.

"What I want to know is how a relic like that ended up with you guys at all," she said, pointing at Tyrfing. "That's an honest-to-God ancient artifact! A girl in my History of Lore class gave a freaking presentation about how the Tyrfing legend was a prototypical example of a cursed weapon cycle." Then, like she'd just realized what she'd said, Marci took a quick step away from the naked blade. "Wait, isn't Tyrfing cursed to kill a man every time it's drawn?"

"Oh, that was broken ages ago," Julius said, sheathing the sword again to prove it. "Mother would never let something as valuable as a still-functional cursed weapon out of her private hoard. I'm pretty sure she took it from another dragon during the centuries she spent in Europe preparing to kill her father the Quetzalcoatl and take his lands. Considering how plain it looks, though, I'm pretty sure the only reason she bothered to keep it is because it's famous."

"I don't care if it's a sharpened stick, so long as you actually use it," Justin grumped. "You *are* going to use it, right? Because I'm not risking Mother's stuff if you're just going to stand around talking to everyone again."

"I don't think talking's going to be an option this time," Julius said sadly, undoing his belt and sliding it through the loop on the sword's red scabbard. "But this should be good enough. Tyrfing might not be as powerful as it used to be, but it still never misses. So long as I know what I'm aiming at, all I have to do is swing and the sword will do the rest." He grinned. "Sounds about right for my skill level."

Justin made a disgusted sound and walked out of the small treasury, locking the door behind him, to Marci's evident dismay. "So," he said when they were all out in the living room again. "What's the plan?"

"We haven't gotten the location yet," Julius said. "But we know it's a trap. One for Marci specifically, set by a seer."

"You pissed off a seer?" Justin gave Marci a scathing look. "That was dumb."

"I didn't do it on purpose!" she cried. "And she's not pissed at *me*. She wants the Kosmo—"

"Well, if a seer's pissed, I don't know if there's anything we can do," Justin said over her, walking across the room to grab his shirt off the back of the couch. "They command the future. We might as well try to beat back the ocean."

Julius frowned, thinking back to what Bob had told them in the car. "I don't think that's right. They don't command the future any more than we do. They're just able to see what's coming."

"And push you in front of it," Marci added, crossing her arms over her chest. "You know, as much as I hate to say this, I think I might actually have to agree with Captain Bring Down. If seers really do work like Brohomir says, I can't see how we're going to win. If this Estella lady can see all our decisions before we make them, then it doesn't matter how great a plan we come up with—she's already seen it and thought up a counter."

"Unless she knew we'd know she knew," his brother added, pulling on his shirt. "Then she'll have counters for both our best plan and the one we're going to come up after that because we know that she knows the first one." He stopped, frowning like he'd just confused himself. "This is too complicated. It's probably best to just assume she has a counter for every contingency and leave it at that."

"I think we're getting ahead of ourselves," Julius said gently. "First, even a seer can't plan for *every* outcome. There are millions of variables, it's just not physically possible. Second, Bob said specifically that Estella was rushed, and therefore being sloppy." And the more he thought about that, the more he realized that Bob's seemingly random seer crash course in the car wasn't random at all. He'd been feeding Julius the information he needed to make a decision, a decision a seer could see. And then he'd promptly *left*, probably so Julius could make his decision where Bob wasn't blocking him, which meant whatever Julius decided, Bob had wanted Estella to see it, and…and…

And this was where seer plotting got to be too much for him. "Give me a second," he muttered, pulling out his phone. When the AR flashed on, he pulled up the last message he'd received from Bob and began typing. *Can Estella see us right now?*

The reply was immediate. *No. My brothers = my turf. This decision is purely for my own edification. Just try to forget I'm watching your every move while silently judging you and make the decision as you normally would based on the information provided. Thank You! <3 <3*

Julius didn't think the hearts were strictly necessary. Of course, he didn't think any of this was necessary. This situation was hard enough without his brother getting all cryptic on him. Doing nothing wasn't an option, though, and he turned back to Justin and Marci with a heavy sigh.

They'd been bickering about something he hadn't been listening to while he'd been on the phone. When they saw him looking, though, they both went quiet, turning to him expectantly. That threw Julius for a moment. Marci he could understand—unless the subject was magic, she was generally happy to listen to his ideas—but Justin *never* looked to him for orders. Then again, the parts of being a dragon that required skills other than smashing had never had been Justin's forte. He was probably just letting Julius do all the work of planning before he tried to take over. Whatever the reason, though, Justin was listening, and that made Julius more determined than ever not to mess this up.

"Estella's moving quickly," he said. "And no one, not even dragons, not even *seers*, can move fast without sacrificing something. She simply does not have the time to cover every contingency, and if we want to break her trap, our best bet is to take advantage of that. We need to do something she won't have bothered to prepare for, something completely unexpected."

His brother frowned. "You mean like crashing in through the roof?"

"Crashing in from any direction is *exactly* the sort of thing she'll expect," Julius said. "So is just going along and giving up Marci for Katya."

"Does that mean we're not doing that?" Justin asked, eying Marci, who'd gone very still. "Because trading a human for a dragon sounds like a pretty good—"

"No," Julius snapped. "We're absolutely *not* going to sacrifice Marci. In fact, I don't plan to sacrifice anything. We're just going to *look* like we have." The first wisps of a plan were already taking shape in his head, and he turned to his mage. "Do you think you can make yourself a full body illusion and a strong ward in"—he checked the time—"twenty minutes?"

"The illusion shouldn't be a problem if it's just me and I can find a good source to pull off," she said. "But what kind of ward are you talking about?"

Julius smiled. "One against bullets."

Marci pursed her lips in an O and began digging through her bag for her casting chalk, dislodging Ghost in the process.

Justin jumped back with a curse as the see-through cat landed on his feet. "What is going on?" he cried. "Why does she need a ward against bullets? And why does your human have a *dead cat* in her purse?"

"I'll explain everything in a second," Julius said, clapping a hand on his brother's shoulder. "But Justin, you're a strong dragon, right?"

"Fifth strongest in the clan," Justin said instantly.

Julius had no idea how he'd come up with that number, but it served his purposes nicely. "Wow," he said. "That's even better than I thought. Would you mind sparing some of that power, then? Just to speed things up?"

"What are you talking about?"

Marci, who knew exactly what Julius was talking about, looked up from the pizza boxes she was clearing off the floor with a wide smile. "Oh, he'll do *great!* Bring him over."

"Great for what?" Justin asked suspiciously. "What am I doing?"

"Helping Marci," Julius replied. "I did it earlier today, but I wasn't strong enough, and she really knocked me for a loop. I still haven't recovered enough to do it again, so I was hoping you could step up. If you think you can handle it, of course."

And just like that, an entire childhood's worth of living with Justin paid off. "Of course I can handle it," his brother snapped, puffing out his chest. "Anything you can do, I can do better. Now where do I stand?"

Julius stepped back to let Marci take over, grinning as she ordered his brother into the center of the spellworked circle she was drawing on the newly cleared stretch of floor in front of the couch.

Chapter 16

"**I** can't believe you let a human do that to me," Justin grumbled, glaring across the room at Marci, who was happily putting the finishing touches on the ward she'd built from his magic. "I feel used."

"Nonsense," Julius said, checking his phone yet again for some sign of Bob. Their hour was five minutes from being up, but the seer still hadn't returned. "She didn't pull a quarter as much magic out of you as she pulled out of me. You're not even winded."

Justin lifted his chin stubbornly. "It's the principle of the thing. My own brother, ordering his human to yank out my magic like I was nothing but a battery, and now I can *feel* her using it." He shuddered. "It's degrading. How did I let you talk me into this?"

Fortunately, Julius didn't have to answer that. His brother hadn't even finished talking when Marci's phone buzzed in her pocket. She pulled it out at once, holding it awkwardly between her hands to avoid getting chalk dust all over the screen.

"Bixby," she said gravely, glancing at Julius. "We ready?"

"I should hope so," Justin snapped. "Considering how the magic you sucked out of me like a—"

A blaring horn outside cut him off, and Julius pounced on it. "There's Bob!" he called, opening the door. "Let's go."

Justin was still grumbling, but he went, claiming the front seat of Bob's car while Julius and Marci piled into the back. The 1971 Crown Victoria was too old to have a GPS, but Bob said he knew where the address was when Marci told him. She was trying to show him the location on her phone anyway when Bob peeled back out into traffic, driving down off the skyways just as crazily as he'd driven up.

Unsurprisingly since dragons and kidnapping were two of the only things that actually counted as illegal in the DFZ, Bixby had arranged for the trade off to be in the Underground. That suited Julius just fine. He hadn't spent much time in the Upper City, but after two full days of being chauffeured all over by Marci, he was feeling pretty familiar with the underbelly of the DFZ. Or, at least, he thought he was, until Bob drove him into a part of the Underground he'd never seen before.

The meeting spot was in the north of the city, under the skyways that lined the shores of Lake St. Clare. The fancy hotel where he and Marci had stayed last night was actually right above them, but though they were beneath some of the most expensive real estate in the DFZ, the Underground was darker and emptier than ever. At first, Julius thought this was because the side of the skyways bordering the lake had been walled over for some reason, closing in the Underground until it looked like a cave in truth, darker even than the eight block blight where they'd found Katya. Even that place had had a diner, though. This place had *nothing*, no new construction, no shops, not even any lights. Just crumbling old houses that didn't look like they'd been touched since the flood, which made no sense at all. How could the space directly below one of the most affluent financial centers in the world just be…empty?

It was a mystery, and since Julius didn't want to meet the enemy on anything less than the firmest footing, he pulled out his phone to look it up. A few searches later, though, he was beginning to wish he'd stayed ignorant.

Back before the return of magic, this area had been known as Grosse Point, an affluent suburb of Detroit. Unfortunately, the same proximity to Lake St. Clare that made the city so desirable was also its undoing. The night Algonquin had woken in fury to clear her waters of a century and a half's worth of pollution, the lakeside community Grosse Point had been Ground Zero for her rage. Now that Julius knew what he was looking at, he could actually see the darker shadows of old boats and rusted oil barrels littered among the collapsing houses, but what really got him was the forbidding chill in the air.

Between Algonquin's wave and the chaos caused by the return of magic, no one knew for certain just how many people had died the night of the flood, but all sources agreed that the Grosse Point was the hardest hit. That much death changed a place, an effect that was only amplified by the waves of magic rushing back into the world like water into dry desert sand. The combination left a residual aura of magic so thick, even non-mage humans reported feeling it. Being a dragon, Julius was almost choking on it. Even sixty years after the fact, it was just as thick as the magic surrounding the Reclamation Area. But where that magic had felt like woods and wild places, this darkness felt like fear. Fear and cold and a sorrow so intense, he could actually feel it pulling him down like gravity. He also understood why Grosse Point's original name had been abandoned for a new, more accurate title on the DFZ maps: The Pit.

The others must have felt the magic, too, because by the time the lights of the normal Underground behind them vanished, all conversation in the car had stopped. Even Bob was uncharacteristically silent as they made their way down the empty, silted over streets past the washed out remains of houses and shops. He cut his lights a few blocks later, rolling through the dark on superior dragon eyesight and probably no small amount of seer's intuition before finally pulling to a stop in what appeared to be a parking lot strewn with old nets and other lake bottom garbage. Julius wasn't actually sure why Bob had chosen that particular lot until he caught a glimmer of light across the street.

His head jerked up immediately, but it still took him several seconds of squinting before he realized that the large, strangely rectangular shape in the dark was a high school—one of those mid twentieth century reinforced cinder block monstrosities built to double as fallout shelters, which explained why it alone was still standing. Mostly, anyway. The light he'd spotted was shining through the cracks in the double doors of what must have been the gym, and, oddly, out of the roof. Julius wasn't sure why light was shining through the roof, but it suited his plans nicely.

"Justin," he said. "Do you—"

"Way ahead of you," his brother said, getting out of the car. "Let's move."

Julius opened his own door to follow, but before he got out, he turned to Marci. "Are you still okay with this? The magic here is a bit unpleasant."

From the expression on her face, she clearly thought that was the understatement of the century, but she nodded all the same, meeting his eyes with a determined stare. "I've got my end," she said, clutching her bloody shoulder bag. "Just be ready to back me up."

"We will," he promised, flashing her a final reassuring smile before running after his brother into the dark.

The strange blackness of the Pit was even worse outside the car. Even knowing it was just a magical echo, Julius would have sworn the air clung to him, leaving an oily sheen of loss and foreboding that made him want to weep and look over his shoulder at the same time. That last part was actually good since he and Justin were going to have to sneak past any lookouts, but even with the magically induced paranoia, they didn't see a soul. Whatever backup Bixby had hired for this job must not have been willing to brave the Pit alone, because though the school's lot was filled with cars, they didn't spot so much as a doorman standing watch as they snuck around the side of the gym and up the crumbling wall to the sagging metal roof.

The flood had apparently dropped multiple large objects on the school when the wave passed over, punching massive holes in the gymnasium's steel roof, the source of the light Julius had seen earlier. Between this and the three story elevation at the roof's peak, Julius would have expected a lookout up here for sure, maybe even a sniper. But Bixby must really have been putting his eggs in one basket, because the roof was just as empty as everything else. Julius was starting to worry this whole thing was even more of a set up than he'd anticipated when his brother gave a soft whistle and motioned for Julius to join him at the edge of one of the larger holes near the roof's center.

"Gotta hand it to your human," he said as Julius crept over. "She sure knows how to stir up the hornet's nest."

Julius could only nod, staring down in horror at the massive crowd of humans standing in the dusty basketball court below.

"I don't believe it," he whispered. "I mean, I knew he'd have a bigger force than the one he sent to the house, but that's just ridiculous. There must be a hundred guys down there!"

"Eighty-one," Justin corrected, breathing deep through his nose. "No mages, and no heavy ordinance." He sniffed again. "Mostly smells like assault weapons and semi-automatic side arms—Glocks, Desert Eagles, Beretta Twenty-Fifties—that sort of thing. Someone down there definitely has a taser, though, so watch out for that. Getting electrocuted sucks."

By the time he finished, Julius was staring at his brother with his mouth hanging open. "How is your nose that good?"

Justin gave him a haughty look. "If it's important, I'm good at it."

"So if you're not good at it, it's not important?"

"Exactly," Justin said, leaning down. "You see Katya?"

Julius didn't, and that was a problem. He could smell her—a sharp, ancient, icy scent that rose over the haze of gunmetal, human sweat, and cheap cologne—so he knew she was here, but even though he could see the whole of the dust-covered basketball court and most of the fold out wooden bleachers beside it, he didn't see a single person in the crowd of heavily augmented muscle who could possibly be their dragoness. He did, however, see Bixby.

Marci had never actually described him, but there was no one else the man standing under the portable floodlights clipped to the remains of the home basketball goal could be. If the flashy suit and slicked-back mobster hair hadn't been a big enough tip-off, the way he was ordering the battalion of hired guns around, despite being the only non-augmented person in the building, was a dead giveaway.

"There's one at least," he whispered, inching closer to the torn, rusted edge of the hole. "But we have to find Katya. If we can't get a bead on her, this won't work."

Justin shrugged. "Fine with me. If your overly complicated scheme falls through, we'll just go back to my original plan of 'beat up humans, take dragon.'"

"I don't think even you can beat up that many humans."

"Then you clearly haven't seen me fight in a while," Justin said, shifting his weight as he scowled up at the dark. Something he'd been doing a lot since they'd gotten up here, Julius realized with a start.

"What are you looking at?"

"I don't know," Justin said. "That's the problem. I'm normally great in the dark, but I can't see a thing." He shifted his weight again. "I don't like it."

That was the closest Julius had ever heard his brother come to admitting he was nervous. Then again, this place would make anyone uneasy. The creepy, depressing magic wasn't actually as bad up here on the roof, but thanks to the light coming up from below them, the rest of the Pit was darker than ever. Even trying to see across the street to where Bob had parked felt uncomfortably like staring into the abyss, and Julius grimaced, returning his gaze to the gym full of hired murderers, which suddenly seemed like a much safer thing to look at.

"I wish Bob would stop being so cryptic and just help us for real," he grumbled. "He's older than all of us put together and multiplied by ten. He could take that whole room without breaking a sweat."

"Then it's better that he's waiting in the car. He's got enough glory already, we don't need him here hogging ours. Besides, we still don't know why Estella's actually doing all of this. It could be this whole setup is just a ploy to lure Bob out and assassinate him."

Julius froze. He hadn't even thought of that angle, and he was even more surprised that his brother had. Of course, Justin *was* a knight of the Heartstriker. It was a knight's job to think about things like assassinations. When he turned to ask what else his brother thought might be important, though, Justin was no longer beside him. He was standing several feet away, glaring up into the dark like he was trying to clear the air with the force of his disapproval.

"Justin!" he hissed. "Stop that! It's almost—"

His phone buzzed in his pocket, and Julius ground his teeth. "There's the signal," he whispered, waving his hand. "Get over here, we're about to start!"

Justin ignored him entirely, holding up his hand for silence before cupping it to his ear like he was listening.

Julius was about to get up and drag the stupid dragon back into position when a crash echoed through the Pit's eerie silence. Forgetting about his brother, he whirled back to the hole, almost falling in as he leaned down to see the gym's double doors slam open, and then Marci strode into the room.

Even though they'd planned her entrance together, actually seeing it happen sent a surge of pride all the way to Julius's toes. She marched out into the gym like she owned it, stopping at the old basketball court's free throw line to stare down the wall of guns that had immediately locked onto her with all the self-possession of a queen. Not a flicker of fear showed on her face as she eyed the army that had been hired to trap her, and when she spoke, her voice was so calm and confident, Julius didn't even catch the illusion she'd woven to hide her nervousness until he realized Marci sounded almost nothing like herself.

"I'm here," she announced. "Alone, as requested."

Not wanting to be outdone, Bixby pushed out of his circle of guards and stepped forward. Unlike Marci, though, he had no magic to hide behind, and he couldn't keep the telltale quiver out of his voice. "*All* alone?"

"As you see," she said, gesturing back through the doors at the empty dark behind her.

Bixby didn't look convinced. "And the Kosmolabe?"

Marci reached into her shoulder bag and pulled out the glistening golden ball that had started this whole mess. "Right here," she said, holding it up for all to see. "Let's get this over with."

"Fine by me," Bixby replied, jerking his head.

At the signal, one of the goons walked behind the ancient bleachers and picked up a long, wrapped bundle tucked against the wall that Julius had initially dismissed as trash. Now, though, he saw that the thing inside the black plastic tarp moved and slumped like a body. Sure enough, when the goon reached his boss, Bixby reached over and yanked the dusty plastic away to reveal Katya's unconscious face.

"No funny business," he warned, pulling a big, old-fashioned revolver out of his jacket pocket and aiming it at Svena's little sister. He pointed his other hand at a folding card table that had been set up on the old basketball court's center line. "Put the Kosmolabe there and step back. Once I'm sure you're not cheating us, we'll bring the girl over."

Marci shook her head. "You first."

Bixby cocked his gun and pressed the barrel to Katya's temple. "You're in no position to make demands. I've told you what to do, now do it, or kiss Blondie the Magic Dragon goodbye."

Julius winced at the casual mention of Katya's true nature. What was Estella thinking, playing so loose with their identities in the DFZ? Still, so far, Bixby was acting exactly as predicted. Likewise, Marci was playing her part to the hilt, putting on an almost too dramatic show of thinking it over before slumping her shoulders in apparent defeat and starting toward the table.

She placed the sparkling Kosmolabe on the square of blue jeweler's velvet Bixby had provided and stepped back again, raising her hands as she went. At the same time, a pair of men stepped in to shut the gym doors behind her, blocking her escape. Only then, when the trap was seemingly closed, did Bixby re-holster his gun and walk to the table, leaving Katya in the care of the giant human who'd picked her up.

"Julius," Justin said.

Julius waved for his brother to shut up. It was almost their cue.

"Julius."

"What?"

"You know how the Underground is supposed to have all sorts of nasty creatures since it's super magical spirit land or whatever?"

"Yes," Julius said, keeping his eyes locked on Bixby as he approached the Kosmolabe. Just a few more steps. "What about it?"

"Can any of them fly?"

That question was just odd enough to make Julius risk a look. He tilted his head back, staring up into the dark, but he didn't see a thing. He couldn't even see the bottom of the skyways he knew must be above them, just blackness. But as he turned to ask Justin what on earth he was talking about, something enormous, heavy, and full of jagged teeth fell out of the dark right onto his head, knocking Julius straight through the rusting roof and into the gym below.

***

Marci was ninety percent sure she was going to mess something up. She'd played it off to Julius back at the house, but now that she was actually here, wrapped in so many wards and illusions her hands were shaking from the effort of keeping them all up, she knew, just *knew* she was going to blow it.

If she'd been alone in the gym, there wouldn't have been a problem. She'd held down this many spells plenty of times before, but those had always been in practice rooms back at the university, usually to win bets against her fellow doctoral candidates. Field experience, she was learning, was a completely different animal.

Even with her anti-bullet ward roaring around her like a furnace thanks to the enormous bank of power she'd siphoned off of Justin, she'd underestimated just how terrifying it would be to have an entire room full of guns pointed at you. But even that might have been tolerable if it wasn't for the toxic ambient magic of the Pit itself.

Any mage with even a year of formal training had heard of the Pit. It was one of the most famous magical fallout zones in the world. Everyone studied it whether they were going to be working with magical ecosystems or not. Again, though, academic knowledge was letting her down. Reading about the magical pollution left by so much death was one thing, but actually being in the middle of all that cold, empty, stagnant power was quickly becoming more than she could take. Even loaded up on Justin's clean, high-grade magic, just standing in the filth made her feel dirty from the inside out. Add in the Bixby situation, and all Marci wanted to do was run away as fast as she could. But while her instincts were in complete agreement that fleeing was the best course of action, she didn't move, because Julius's plan was working perfectly.

So far, everything had gone exactly as he'd predicted: Bixby's over-the-top setup, the army of hired thugs, his demand to inspect the Kosmolabe himself, everything. The only detail he'd gotten wrong was his assumption that Bixby would have a mage. But, unless he was keeping someone in reserve, Marci didn't even feel the presence of another ward. A suicidally stupid oversight on their enemy's part, and a very lucky break for her.

With no mage to worry about, all she had to do was hold on until Bixby reached the golden ball on the table, the illusionary Kosmolabe she'd spent twenty minutes putting together in the safe house with all that wonderful dragon magic. When Bixby's fingers touched the false surface, Marci would backlash the spell right in his face. With so much power behind it, the shock would kill him instantly, at which point Justin and Julius would drop down and grab Katya while Bixby's men wasted their bullets on Marci's ward.

She'd been a bit skeptical about that last part, but Julius had reasoned that Bixby's hired guns would be much more interested in protecting the man who paid them than the thing they'd been paid to protect. His hope was that by the time the goons realized their shots weren't doing the job, the two Heartstrikers would be out the door with Katya. Once they were clear, Marci would dump the rest of her hoarded magic into her microwave spell for one final heat blast, opening a window for her to GTFO with the *real* Kosmolabe, which was safely hidden at the bottom of her bag.

That was the detail she'd argued with Julius about the most, actually. She would have felt much safer leaving the actual Kosmolabe in the car with Ghost and Bob where there was no chance if it being damaged in the chaos, but Julius had refused to back down. The Kosmolabe was the highest value target, he'd said, which meant Marci should have it on her to ransom for her own life if something went wrong.

Given her own misgivings about her ability to pull off the operation, she had to admit it was nice to have a backup. But they were nearly halfway through now, and everything was running smoothly. Bixby was almost to the table already, and she hadn't messed up yet.

She wouldn't, either. Even though the cut on her neck stung like crazy and the stress was making her sweat so badly she was worried the spellwork she'd painted around her body would start to smudge, Marci just clutched her illusion of perfect calm tighter and waited for her chance. Bixby was almost in position. Six more steps and she would finally be able to pay him back for all he'd done. All she had to do was hold on. Just five more steps and it was done. Four more. Three—

A crash exploded trough the room, followed by an animal roar that turned her blood to ice.

No, she thought frantically. Not yet. It was too soon. But Bixby had stopped in his tracks a good three feet away from the fake Kosmolabe to look for the sound, and he wasn't alone. Everyone's heads were jerking toward the roof, and Marci knew with crushing certainty that it was all ruined. There was no way she could draw the room's fire now. All she could do was look up with the rest as Julius hurtled down from the roof to land on the dusty gym floor…

With an enormous creature right on top of him.

The sight drove all thoughts of ruined plans from Marci's head, replacing them with pure, frozen panic. Julius had hit the ground so hard, part of her mind couldn't accept that he was still alive even after he rolled over and started fighting the thing on his chest. The thing Marci couldn't actually put a name to.

Even with the glaring floodlights Bixby's people had set up, the monster on top of Julius was unrecognizable. The best she could make out was a roughly eight-foot-long mass of black leathery wings, hooked claws, and teeth that seemed to be getting brighter every time they snapped. Whatever it was, Julius didn't seem to be able to get out from under it, and the fear on his face was what finally broke Marci out of her shock and into action.

In the space of a heartbeat, she dropped every illusion she had, pulling the magic back into her like she was sucking in a breath. The power burned as it returned, a pointed reminder of why you were always supposed to release and redraw magic instead of reusing, but even in her scramble, she wasn't about to touch the awful stuff in the Pit. She only had to bear the pain for a second, anyway, just long enough to bring up her arm and shove the power through the circle of her bracelet, sending a scorching spear of super-heated air straight at the creature that was currently trying to bite out Julius's throat.

And that was when things got weird.

Generally speaking, when Marci cast a spell, that was it. She'd been holding Justin's magic for a long time at this point, though, and her connection to it lingered longer than it should have. As a result, part of her went along with the magic as it slammed into the monster's side. But just as she felt the heat begin to scorch the creature's hide, the spell vanished.

The loss was so sudden, she actually stumbled. Her body rebalanced itself instinctively, which was good, because her brain was no help at all. It was too busy trying to comprehend what had just happened.

Any way she approached it, it made no sense. She'd *felt* the spell work, felt it hit, and then the magic was just *gone*. But that was impossible. Magic obeyed the same laws as energy. It changed forms and lost quality, but it didn't *vanish*. Apparently, though, no one had told the spell that. She'd thrown enough power at that monster to boil it alive from the inside out, but it didn't even seem to notice her in its frenzy to dig its talons into Julius's ribs.

After that, Marci forgot about impossibilities. She reached out desperately, swallowing her revulsion as she yanked in the cold, heavy magic of the Pit. Before she could gather enough to start on a movement spell to save him, though, a second shape plummeted through the hole in the ceiling like a shot.

Justin must have done something more than simply jump down, because the gym's ancient rubberized floor cracked when he hit. The resulting wave of dust and debris sent the men, who until this moment had been standing around like gaping statues, scrambling to cover their faces. Justin ignored them completely, turning instead to Julius, his unsheathed sword flying at the winged creature's head.

By the time the monster realized it had a new opponent, it was too late. Justin lopped its head off in one clean stroke, sending an arc of blue-black blood flying all the way to the back of the broken bleachers. For a shocked second, the wet splatter was the only sound, then Bixby shouted something unintelligible, and all hell broke loose.

The air filled with the pop of gunshots as the entire room full of hired thugs turned and fired on Justin. He grunted when the first shots hit, but though Marci could see the impact of the bullets rippling over Justin's body, not a drop of blood appeared on his white shirt as he took up a defensive position over Julius, who was still on the floor. It was such an astonishing sight, Marci didn't realize the thugs were also shooting at *her* until her ward, which she'd drained nearly dry in her attempt to save Julius, started to buckle.

She shored it up as best she could, pulling in more of the heavy, repulsive power of the Pit and forcing it through the spellwork she'd written in casting marker on her skin under her clothes. But the magic here wasn't just disgusting to touch, it also wasn't nearly as concentrated as the power she'd siphoned off Justin, and she simply couldn't keep up.

A ward that was tuned to only stop bullets shouldn't have taken so much magic. The general rule was the more specialized the ward, the more efficiently it worked. But there was a practical limit to everything, and there were a *lot* of people shooting at her. The ground at her feet was already carpeted with crumpled slugs, and the work of canceling all that force had left the protective bubble of magic around her dangerously dim. Another ten seconds and it would go out entirely, which would have been enough time if she'd been running for the door. But she couldn't run. Not until she got the others out, too.

Swallowing against her fear, Marci glanced back at Julius to see what she could do to help. Not much was the answer. Obnoxious as his arrogant bragging could be, Justin was guarding his downed brother like a wall. There were actually more spent slugs around his feet than hers, but the dragon didn't even look winded.

That sight did more to calm her panic than anything else, and Marci was finally able to move past Julius's immediate danger and focus on the next most important thing: salvaging the job.

By this point, her ward was in serious danger. It hadn't cracked yet, though, so Marci forced herself to ignore the bullets and look for Katya. The man who'd been guarding her earlier must have had other things to do, because when she finally spotted the dragoness, Katya was lying on her side against the gym's far wall, alone and miraculously untouched by the violence around her.

Target in sight, Marci darted across the gym, dodging the gunmen who tried to grab her. She lunged for Katya the moment she was in range, yanking her out of the black tarp Bixby had wrapped her in. But as the covering came off, Marci saw there was something else hidden beneath it. A dark, padded band had been wrapped around Katya's waist, almost like a weightlifter's belt with wires sticking out of it, each one of which was connected to a sewn-in compartment filled with a gray, clay-like substance that reminded her of—

"Enough!"

The enraged shout cut through the racket, making Marci jump. She whirled around as the gunfire died to see a panting Bixby standing by the card table where the illusionary Kosmolabe had rested before Marci had been forced to drop it. His hand was out in front of him, his fist wrapped around something that looked like an old-style joystick.

There was even a red button at the top that he was currently mashing down with his white-knuckled thumb as his wild eyes slid over the room to stop on Marci.

"Hands up!" he bellowed. "She's wrapped in enough C4 to take this whole place out. One false move out of any of you, and I blow us all sky high."

Marci snatched her hands away from Katya, raising them instantly over her head. All around the room, Bixby's men were lowering their guns and regrouping, but even though the shooting had stopped, it was hardly quiet. A horrible sound was coming through the broken roof, a mix of flapping wings and shrill, inhuman shrieking. The combination made Marci shake from her toes to her fingers, but while she was desperately trying to get a hold of herself, Bixby began to laugh.

"Well, well, well," he said, looking from Marci to Justin, who was still crouched protectively over a bleeding Julius. "Life just gets weirder and weirder, doesn't it? But it all came together just like the seer said. Even them."

He jerked his head up to the dark shapes fluttering around the hole in the roof, and despite the ridiculousness of her situation, Marci's curiosity immediately got the better of her. "What are they?"

"Magic eaters," Bixby said, his face breaking into a wide, slightly unhinged smile. "A little known local specialty. I'm told they don't usually flock in numbers like this unless there's wounded prey to be had, but magical predators aren't so different from the normal variety. All it takes is a little blood in the water to start them circling."

His looked pointedly at Marci's feet as he said this, and she looked down to see something red coating the ground where Katya had been lying. It was on her arms, too, staining the dragoness's white shirt crimson. But while the color suggested blood, the liquid was much too shiny, and there was a rainbow sheen on its surface, almost like gasoline floating on water…

And that was when Marci realized that dragon blood looked very different from human.

"Oh yes, Miss Novalli," Bixby cackled as her expression turned horrified. "It's done. Just listen to those wings. It's only a matter of time before we're up to our necks in those bastards, especially with all the new blood your little surprise attack there is dumping on the ground."

Marci supposed he meant Julius, and scared as she was, that just made her mad. "You don't know what you're messing with, Bixby!" she yelled. "It never pays to piss off things bigger than you."

"Save your threats," Bixby said. "I'm perfectly safe. The magic eaters don't care about humans—at least, not about ones who aren't

239

mages. That would normally put you in a lot of trouble, but you're in luck tonight. There's better meat to be had." He jerked his head at Justin and Julius. "Your rescue squad is about to be the main course of a monster-on-monster feeding frenzy, and if you want them to have a prayer of escaping with their lives, you will shut up and do exactly as I say."

"Don't do it," Justin barked, making Marci jump. When she turned to him, though, the dragon wasn't even paying attention to her. He was glaring at Bixby, growling with a rumble Marci could feel through her shoes. "Don't do a thing he says. I will not be used as a bargaining chip by a human!"

"You do *not* want to push me today, buddy!" Bixby snarled, brandishing the C4 remote in his fist. "Now shut up and back off before I turn you into dragon salsa."

His finger began to lift off the trigger as he said this, and Marci gasped. "Wait!" she cried, pulling the Kosmolabe out of her bag. "Here it is. This is the real one. I'll roll it to you right now, just don't be stupid."

That must have been what he was waiting for, because Bixby's face lit up in a triumph. "Oh, no," he said slowly. "You bring it to me, nice and easy."

Marci swallowed and glanced at Julius. He was always the one with the plan. Surely he'd thought of something. But Julius was still down on the floor, his bloody chest rising and falling in shallow, pained gasps. Overhead, the shrieks were getting louder as the magic eaters grew bolder. A few had already come inside, crawling upside down along the ceiling like spiders.

Now that she knew what to look for, Marci could actually feel their presence sucking the magic out of the air, leaving an emptiness even more awful than the Pit's creepy death magic. From the set of Justin's shoulders, she knew he felt it too, and that only made things worse. If *Justin* was getting nervous, they were *really* screwed, and it was that more than anything that made Marci's decision.

"Okay," she said quietly, standing up and walking across the shot-up gym with the Kosmolabe held out in front of her like an offering. "Here. Just take the stupid thing and let us go."

Bixby grinned as she closed the distance. "Oh, they can go at any time," he said, snatching the golden sphere out of her hand and shoving it into a warded bag tied to his belt under his jacket. "But you? You're staying right here."

Marci was about to tell him exactly where he could shove that idea when his other hand, the one that wasn't holding down the trigger, shot out to press something large, square, and black straight into her stomach.

Intense pain flared in every part of her body. It was like getting a massive charley horse cramp, only instead of just her leg, it was everywhere. The shock was so intense, Marci didn't even realize she'd gone down until she was on the floor. But it wasn't until the spasmodic pain forced her to drop every magical protection she had—the last of her anti-bullet ward, the remnants of her illusion of calm, even the low-level safeties that warned her when other mages started fiddling with her magic—that she finally understood what was going on. Bixby had *tased* her.

"Don't move!"

Considering none of her muscles currently worked, Marci had no idea how he expected her to follow that command. A few seconds later, though, she realized Bixby hadn't been yelling at her. He was shouting at the dragons.

"You stay right there!" he screamed, his voice high-pitched and frantic as he lifted the bomb trigger high with one arm and reached down to grab Marci's still-twitching body with the other. He must have traded out his taser for a gun while she'd been on the ground, because when he yanked her into a choke hold against his chest, Marci felt the chamber of a revolver digging into her cheek. But even the warm pressure of gunmetal wasn't enough to rouse her tasered body to fight as Bixby started dragging her backward toward the rear of the gym.

"Don't worry, sweetheart," he grunted, panting with effort as he hauled her across the floor. "I'm not going to kill you, not quite. See, I know my future. My seer told me I'd die the moment Aldo Novalli's daughter did, and my seer is never wrong. So once I hand off the Kosmolabe, you and me are getting on a plane back home to Vegas where I've got a doctor lined up to put you in a coma. A nice little sleep with nothing to bother you, because we're both going to live a long, long time together."

By the time he finished, Marci was so angry she could barely breathe, but she couldn't do anything about it. The taser had left her whole body locked up and unresponsive, and her magic was an absolute mess. Even if she'd been herself, though, she couldn't have cast anything. The air was so empty of magic now it felt shriveled, like a bit of fruit left out in the sun. She couldn't even feel the dragons anymore.

They must have already left, she realized dimly. Well, good for them. Running was their only chance of escaping the epic disaster she'd dragged them into. She only wished she'd had a chance to tell Julius how sorry she was.

She was still contemplating this when she finally managed to get her muscles working enough to turn her head. She used this newfound power to look back down the gym on the off chance of catching a final glimpse of Julius's back. When she got her head around at last, though, her still-stuttering body stopped working all over again, because Julius wasn't fleeing. He was standing beside his brother, who had Katya over his shoulder.

The sight sent Marci into a panic. But as she fought desperately to get herself together enough to scream at Julius to just run already, he did.

Straight toward her.

Chapter 17

When Julius had fallen through the roof and into the gym, he'd learned two important facts. First, falling is much scarier when you can't fly, and second, there were things in this world that ate dragons.

On the way down, he hadn't been able to properly appreciate just how big the thing trying to kill him was. After they'd hit, though, he could see every inch of it thanks to Bixby's floodlights, and the sight made him wish he couldn't. Monsters were supposed to be scarier in the dark, but at least up on the roof he hadn't been able to see just how big the multi-faceted spider eyes staring down at him were, or how the jagged fangs currently snapping at his throat were perfectly fashioned to puncture and rip. He could see it all now, though, and the sight of teeth flashing right under his chin sent instincts Julius had never known he possessed surging into action.

All at once, his body felt wrong, too small and too weak, his throat empty and cold without a flicker of fire. If his mother's seal hadn't been in place, he would have changed spontaneously for the first time in his adult life, but he couldn't. He was blocked. He had no protections, no flame, just soft human flesh that the creature's barbed talons cut into like knives through clay.

As the youngest, most bullied member of a violent family, Julius had been through a lot of pain in his life. Even in his worst fights, though, he'd never experienced anything like this. He could actually feel the tips of the creature's claws *inside* his chest, holding him down while its teeth snared his neck for the deathblow. The shock of the bite was so intense, he couldn't even get his hands close to the sword on his belt. But then, just when Julius was sure he was one heartbeat away from being just another stain on the floor, the whole building shook.

Even through the pain, the sudden jolt made him jump. The impact must have startled the monster, too, because it let go of his neck and looked up, raising its head just in time to lose it. The thing didn't even get a final scream before its body went stiff, and then Julius felt hard hands slide under his arms to yank him to safety as the now-headless monster toppled over.

"You all right?"

Julius had never been so happy to hear his brother's voice in his life. He was trying to stay as much when the roar of gunfire filled the room, a great deal of which seemed to be focused on Justin. That was wrong. The whole point of the plan was that the goons would waste their shots on Marci's ward, but the bullets just seemed to be going everywhere. He should probably be concerned about that, but Julius couldn't work up the energy to care. The moment Justin had yanked the monster off him, all the pain in his chest had vanished. He wasn't even scared anymore, just empty, like he was floating in a void. He was about to say screw it and go to sleep when Justin shouted in his ear.

"Pull yourself together!"

His eyes shot open to see his brother looming over him with a scowl on his face and the Fang of the Heartstrikers naked in his hand. Bullets were bouncing off his shoulders and chest like hail, and though Justin didn't actually seem to mind, Julius felt he should probably say something, just in case.

"You're being shot."

"Better me than you," Justin said, dipping his sword down to bounce a stray bullet before it could land in Julius's head. "Just stay still. That thing almost sucked you dry."

It took Julius a good five seconds to understand what his brother meant. He'd been so glad for the lack of pain, he hadn't even realized he was missing magic. Now that Justin had pointed it out, though, the gaping hole in his essence was all he could feel. The emptiness in his head was no longer a floating, happy sort, but a sucking wound far more terrifying than the gashes on his chest, and he closed his eyes in panic.

"It'll come back."

His eyes popped open again just in time to see Justin flash him a reassuring smile. "I've taken much bigger hits to my magic and been perfectly fine five minutes later," his brother said, turning back to the chaos going on all around them. "You're just in shock and stuck as a human, which makes everything harder. Focus on breathing. Your power will fix itself."

Julius nodded and closed his eyes, ignoring the bullets whizzing over his head as he tried to follow his brother's instructions, because if there was anything Justin had experience with, it was recovering from damage. Sure enough, after a few quiet breaths, his magic began to expand again, creeping back to fill the void the monster had left.

The empty-headed feelings of detachment and weakness faded along with it, bringing back the sharp, immediate pain of his shredded chest. Even that was comforting, though. Pain he could work with, pain he understood, and while the ache was bad enough to bring tears to his eyes, Julius couldn't help sighing in relief. Exceptionally short-lived relief, it turned out, because when he was finally stable enough to start paying attention to his surroundings again, the first thing he saw was Bixby tasing Marci.

He shot to his feet before he could think. Just rolled right up only to fall right back down again when the dizziness hit. But he was recovering with every breath, and the second time he got to his feet, he stayed there, looking around for Justin, who was no longer beside him.

After a few frantic seconds, he spotted his brother again on the other side of the room, kneeling down to scoop something onto his shoulder, but it wasn't until he saw her pale hair that Julius realized it was Katya. The sight hit him like all the shots he'd avoided. Justin had Katya, which meant they'd done it. They'd gotten her back. They'd *won*.

Julius sucked in a victorious breath. Even with all the failures, his plan had worked. They had Katya! He wasn't going to be eaten! Now all they had to do was save Marci from Bixby and—

His thoughts cut off when Justin turned and charged straight for him. For a moment, it looked like his brother was going to run him over, but Justin stopped just in time. "Good, you're up," he said, grabbing his arm. "Come on, we gotta go."

"What?" Julius cried, eyes going back to Marci's slumped body, which Bixby was hauling toward the gym's rear door. "No! You have to rescue her!"

"Can't," Justin said, yanking him back toward the main door, which was currently packed with fleeing goons. "Bixby's rigged Three Sisters here like a suicide bomber, and we've got magic eaters coming down our necks."

Julius glanced up at where Katya was slung over his brother's shoulders. Sure enough, a homemade bomb of plastic explosives was wrapped around her waist, but that didn't explain the rest of it. "Magic eaters?"

His brother snorted. "Look up."

Julius did…and immediately regretted it.

The hole in the roof where he'd fallen was now completely swarmed by more of the giant, winged monsters that had attacked him. They were crawling over the ceiling like roaches, hissing at the lights as they tried to get closer to the dragons in the middle. "What *are* those things?"

"I just told you," Justin snapped. "Magic. Eaters."

"Right," Julius said, mentally rubbing the place where the chunk had been bitten out of his own magic. "But where did they come from?"

"They're predators that eat magic, you're a wounded dragon who's bleeding all over the place. Do the math. Now let's get out of here before things get worse."

He turned to go, but Julius didn't follow. He was too busy looking for Marci.

What he found wasn't good. The taser must have been turned to max, because she still wasn't moving. Bixby had dragged her almost all the way to the rear door by this point, one arm wrapped around her neck in a choke hold while the other clutched the bomb trigger against his chest. The rest of his men were in full retreat, throwing themselves at every available exit in their panic to escape the leathery winged monsters crawling down from the ceiling. A smart move on their part, and a stroke of luck for Julius, because with all his men jumping ship, Bixby was now alone.

"Hey!" Justin said, stomping back over. "Are you deaf? I said let's *go*."

"Not without Marci."

His brother stared at him for a second like he couldn't believe what he'd just heard, and then his face got scary. "This isn't the time to be stupid," he growled, shifting Katya's body higher on his shoulder. "We got what we came for. Dragon secure, clan war averted, mission accomplished, now let's scram before we lose it."

Julius held his ground. "I'm not leaving her."

"Oh, come on!" Justin yelled. "She's a mortal!"

"She's my friend!" Julius yelled back.

"*We don't have friends!*" his brother bellowed. "You want to play nice, you do it on your own time, but this is family business, Julius."

He stopped, waiting for a response, but Julius had already turned away, and Justin cursed loudly. "Is this really the story you want me to bring back to Mother? That you had a clean escape with the Three Sisters' girl in your hands, and you threw it away to save a *human*? There are nine billion of the bastards running around! I'll get you another one. Now let's *go.*"

"*No!*"

The word came out so loud, even Julius jumped. He didn't regret it, though. He'd already made up his mind, and he'd had about enough of this. "It doesn't matter what she is," he said, staring Justin down. "Human or dragon or anything else. She's my friend and my teammate, and I will not leave her behind." He dropped his hand to his sword and turned back to face Bixby. "You don't have to help me," he said softly. "You don't even have to stay if you don't want, but don't get in my way."

Justin snarled in frustration and reached out to grab him, but Julius was already gone, racing across the gym with his hand wrapped tight around Tyrfing's worn grip.

The sprint wasn't his fastest. Even though he'd thrown everything he had at it, after the magic eater's attack and this whole crazy day, there just wasn't enough left to go around. He was still faster than the human Bixby, though, and that was what mattered.

The mobster swore as Julius appeared right in front of him. This close, he could see the panic in Bixby's eyes, the absolute, up-against-the-wall, survival-at-all-costs battle going on inside him as he dropped Marci to turn his gun on the new threat. Another time, when he wasn't so injured or out of practice, Julius could have dodged. Now, though, he didn't have a prayer, so he ignored the gun and stayed on target, fixing his eyes not on the detonator clutched in Bixby's hand, but on the hairy stretch of wrist between the mobster's suit cuff and his gold-plated watch as he yanked Tyrfing out of its sheath.

Like it had been waiting for this moment, the short sword leaped into his hand. It flew up so fast, Julius wasn't even sure it was flying in the right direction, but he didn't try to correct its momentum. He simply kept his eyes on the mark, swinging his arm as hard as he could and trusting the cursed blade to do the rest.

A well-placed trust, it turned out. The moment the short blade was free of its sheath, it flashed and turned in Julius's palm, jerking his swing up and sideways to land a perfect strike on Bixby's exposed wrist. The ancient sword cut through bone and flesh without a whisper of resistance, slicing Bixby's hand—and the detonator clutched in it—clean off.

The strike was barely finished before Julius lunged forward, catching the trigger as it tumbled from Bixby's now lifeless hand just like he'd caught the falling water this morning. The moment his fingers made contact, he stabbed his own thumb down on the detonator button, pressing it back into place before the bomb could go off. It was such a marvelous save, such a perfect catch, he didn't even realize he'd been shot until he heard the bang.

Julius dropped like a stone. His chest, already ripped to ribbons by the magic eater, was on fire all over again, though this time the pain was focused just below his left lung. He supposed he should be grateful that the shot hadn't gone *through* his lung, but he was in too much pain to think about anything except holding on to the detonator. *That* he clung to for dear life. He was trying to roll over and curl himself into a protective ball around it when someone grabbed him unmercifully by the shoulders and laid him flat again with a snap.

"Of all the—" Justin growled, snatching Tyrfing out of Julius's hand before the exposed blade could stab anyone. "It was *one* bullet, Julius!"

His brother's bedside manner left much to be desired, but at least Justin's scathing appraisal helped to remind Julius's panicked body that it wasn't actually dying. He was, however, in a great deal of pain, not to mention bleeding like a hose. But neither of these things would kill a dragon, even an awful one, and he was certainly doing much better than Bixby.

The mobster had collapsed after Julius sliced his hand off. He was now lying on the floor, gripping the stump at the end of his arm and screaming at the top of his lungs. Marci was down right beside him, coughing on her hands and knees. Any other time, that would have been a sorry sight. Right now, though, the relief of seeing her alive and whole was almost enough to make Julius forget the horrible pain in his chest, especially when she looked over at him and asked, "Are you okay?"

"He's fine," Justin snapped before Julius could open his mouth. "He's just being a baby." He kicked what was left of Bixby's severed hand away with practical ambivalence before kneeling down to glare right into Julius's face. "Honestly, who ever heard of a dragon going down to one bullet? All that big talk about not leaving anyone behind, and then you go down like a leaf at the first shot. You should be ashamed. I'm ashamed *for* you."

"If anyone should be ashamed around here, it's you!" Marci cried, yanking herself up on pure indignation. "What were you thinking, letting your injured brother get shot like that?"

"How was I supposed to know he'd be stupid enough to try and save you?" Justin roared.

Marci sucked in a furious breath, but Julius cut her off. "Can we talk about this later?"

Both of them snapped their heads down toward him, and Julius nodded at the ceiling, which was now crawling with magic eaters. A fact he had an excellent view of, being on his back.

The visual reminder worked as intended. Justin and Marci gave each other a final glare, and then they put their argument on hold as they burst into action. But while Justin leaned down to get Julius, Marci went for Bixby. The mobster made a few feeble attempts to keep her away, but he was too busy going into shock to run any real interference as she plunged her hand into the bag on his belt and pulled out the Kosmolabe.

"Really?" Justin said as he hauled Julius to his feet.

"Waste not, want not," Marci said, shoving the golden orb into her bag. "Besides, the Kosmolabe is the whole reason Estella did this. I'm not just going to leave it here for her to scoop up."

Justin rolled his eyes. "Well, if you're done collecting, can we go?"

"One last thing," she said, reaching down to pick up the gun Bixby had dropped. Before Julius could ask what she meant to do with it, Marci turned the barrel on Bixby and shot him in the heart.

There was no warning, no hesitation. Even Justin jumped when the crack of the shot filled the room. The bang was still echoing when Bixby's thrashing stopped, and he let out a last, gargling breath before falling still forever.

Marci let out a breath as well, bending over to set the gun back down on the now very bloody gym floor. "There, now we can go."

Everyone was staring at her when she looked up again. "What?" she cried. "He killed my dad! He tried to kill Julius, *and* he was going to put me in a coma. He deserved that."

"No argument here," Justin said, hoisting Katya's still-unconscious body back onto his shoulder from where he'd put her down to tend to Julius. "You're a better dragon than he is."

Marci didn't seem to know quite how to take that. Julius wasn't sure either, but he was very, very glad when she stepped in to support his other side. "Thank you," he whispered, leaning on her. "I'm glad you're okay."

"That's my line," she grumbled, sliding her arm around his waist to support his back. "You're the one who got shot."

"It was just one bullet."

Marci shook her head and leaned closer, supporting more of his weight as the four of them—Justin carrying Katya on one shoulder and supporting Julius with the other—half ran, half hobbled to the gym's main doors.

"All right," Justin said when they got close. "This whole situation is FUBAR, and if you don't want it getting more so, do exactly what I say. The magic eaters are predators. They'll go for the wounded first, so we're going to stay close and move fast. Marci, you keep Julius up. I'll get everything else."

"Right," Marci said, pulling Tyrfing back out of the sheath on Julius's belt.

Justin arched an eyebrow. "Can you even use a sword?"

"Nope," she replied. "But that's kind of the point of a sword that never misses, and it's not like I can use magic at the moment."

Now that she'd mentioned it, Julius realized he couldn't feel any magic in the air at all. The dark, heavy aura of the Pit had vanished completely, leaving only a void that was somehow worse. No wonder his family complained so much about the days before the magic returned. The unnatural emptiness felt *terrible*. It also brought to mind a pertinent question.

"How many magic eaters do you think are here?" he asked as Justin lifted his foot to kick the press bar that opened the gym door.

"Not enough to take me," his brother said confidently, smashing the exit open. "Just stay close and there won't be any troub—"

He stopped short, causing Marci to bump into him. This, in turn, bumped Julius between them, jostling his wound hard enough to make him see spots. He was still blinking them away when Justin said, "Okay, this is a bit more than I anticipated."

'A bit' didn't begin to describe it. Back in the gym, Julius had assumed the magic eaters who'd come in through the ceiling had been the boldest, or at least the hungriest. Now, he was starting to wonder if they hadn't just been pushed in by the rest. The area outside the gym was a solid carpet of magic eaters. The ground was literally black with their crawling bodies, and the beat of their wings in the air above was so constant, it actually raised a wind. Everywhere Julius looked, the darkness was moving, and he didn't need his brother's unusually serious scowl to know that they were in very real trouble.

Marci swallowed. "Should we—"

"No." Justin swung Katya's unconscious weight into a fireman's carry across his shoulders to free his right arm to draw his own sword. "We're going to do this quick, so keep that kitchen knife up. Julius, you hold tight to that detonator until we can tie it down. And try to stop bleeding so much. You're only drawing more."

Julius sighed. "I can't just stop—"

"I'll carry the girl and go offense," Justin went on, rolling over him. "Ready?"

Julius started to say no, but Justin was already out the door. Marci dragged Julius after him a second later, sticking to Justin like glue as he raised his sword to cut a path.

Cut turned out to be the wrong word. Justin's Fang of the Heartstriker never actually made contact. Apparently, he'd been right about the magic eater's unwillingness to attack. Despite their exponentially superior numbers, they were clearly not eager to take on an uninjured dragon like Justin. They scrambled to avoid his blade whenever he swung, filling the dark with their horrible screeching as they flew out of reach, but not away. They would always land again a few moments later to rejoin the circling mass, their spider eyes glinting in the dark.

Despite Justin's orders, it was slow going. Even with Marci's support, Julius could barely walk. By the time they'd made it to the end of the sidewalk, he was ready to lie down and never get up. The only reason he didn't was the magic eaters. He could almost feel their eagerness as they watched him limp past, and the memory of those sharp, cold claws digging into his chest was awful enough to overcome his exhaustion. Fortunately, they didn't have much farther to go. They were already crossing the street to the parking lot where Bob was waiting for them, and none of these overgrown scavengers would dare mess with a dragon like Brohomir.

Holding that promise in his mind like a beacon, Julius made himself keep moving. One step at a time, he forced his feet up and down, ignoring the pain in his chest, ignoring the monsters snapping their teeth right behind him, ignoring how they seemed to be walking forever. He put all of it out of his head and pushed forward, keeping his eyes firmly on the dirty, broken ground in front of him, which was how he almost ran into his brother when Justin suddenly stopped.

"What?" he panted, slumping into Marci.

Justin shook his head. "He's not here."

Julius blinked, uncomprehending. "Who's not here?"

"Bob!" Justin snarled, swinging his sword at the circle of magic eaters around them. "We've walked over the whole damn lot now, and the car isn't here." He bared his teeth. "Bastard left us."

"I'm sure he wouldn't do that," Marci began, but she went quiet again when Julius and Justin shot her matching looks of disbelief.

"You *had* to stop and save the human, didn't you?" Justin muttered, adjusting Katya on his shoulder. "Fine. Doesn't matter. We can get out on our own, it'll just be a walk."

Julius couldn't stop his grimace at the idea of more walking. "Isn't there another—oof!"

His surprised gasp turned into a pained one as Justin was thrust into him, nearly sending them both to the ground. His brother recovered instantly, whirling around with his sword up, but the magic eater who'd shoved him had already scurried away. But one success leads to others, and a few seconds later, another magic eater worked up the courage to take a snap at Katya, actually cutting off some of her hair before Justin drove it back.

"We have to keep moving," he growled. "The longer we stop, the bolder they'll get. Now go."

"Go where?" Marci said, bracing against Julius's weight. "We can't walk ten blocks like this."

"We have to," Justin said. "Just—"

His words transformed into a roar as a long, barbed claw shot out of the dark to hook his leg and yank it out from under him. Justin went down with a crash, taking Marci and Julius with him. For a second, he lay prone on the cracked asphalt, and then he came up swinging, lopping off the barbed claw—and the leg it was attached to—in one smooth strike. But the damage was already done.

The monster had barely scratched him, but the small stain of blood on Justin's jeans sent the magic eaters into a frenzy. It didn't help that the fall had reopened Julius's wound, either. The double dose of fresh scent combined with the fact that all the dragons were now injured drove the creatures insane. Within seconds, their screeching had gotten so loud it was physically painful, and then, as though a signal had been given, the whole mass attacked.

Justin attacked back, dumping Katya on Julius as he swung his sword in a huge arc in front of them. The Fang of the Heartstriker sang through the air, cutting the magic eaters like paper wherever it touched them, and it wasn't alone. In the confusion, Marci had thrown up Tyrfing with a squeak, closing her eyes as she waved the enchanted sword wildly.

The blade took things from there. Lighting up like a flare in the dark, Tyrfing turned expertly in Marci's clumsy grip, slicing straight through a magic eater above her to cut it in two. It took out the one on her left next, sending that half of the attacking mob skittering back in terror, and Julius felt a rush of relief. *Finally,* something was going right.

"It's not even dulled," Marci said breathlessly, examining Tyrfing's glowing edge. "They must not be able to consume imbued magic locked in through the enchanting process! I wonder if we could—"

A roar cut her off. While Marci had been fighting, a second rush of magic eaters had tried to swarm Justin. He'd broken free immediately, but not without cost. His shirt, already full of holes from the bullets, was now gone completely, and his bare chest was riddled with tiny cuts. He was breathing heavily, blowing out puffs of smoke with every pant, and Julius felt a fresh surge of dread rise up to join the ocean already roiling in his stomach.

"Justin," he said softly, trying to go to his brother only to realize he couldn't. He was still on the ground from his first fall with Katya in his lap where Justin had dumped her. He couldn't even grab her to roll her over because his right hand was still wrapped around Bixby's stupid detonator and he needed his left to keep his wound together. The situation was so ridiculous, he would have laughed if it hadn't been happening to him. But it was, and if he didn't want things to get even worse, he had to calm his brother down. Right now.

"Justin," he said again, biting the name out with a snarl. The challenge got his brother's attention at last, and he whirled around, eyes flashing dangerously. Julius dropped his own in reply, lowering his head

in an attempt to look as meek and nonthreatening as possible, but that didn't stop him from reminding his brother, "You can't change here. This is the DFZ."

Justin wiped the blood off his neck, flinging it away in a savage gesture. "I don't give a—"

The rest of his words were drowned out by a scream Julius would never be able to forget for the rest of his immortal life. He didn't know what had caused it, his own show of submission or Justin's careless blood-flinging, but all at once, the magic eaters rose up with a high-pitched wail that echoed to the skyways and attacked as one.

In the space of a second, the whole world became a confusion of snapping teeth and clawing fangs. Julius didn't even try to defend himself. It was all he could do to keep a hold on both Katya and the detonator trigger as the magic eaters began sucking his magic right out of him. The only good part was that the magic eaters didn't seem to care about Marci. Julius was trying to figure out how he could get to her and his sword when the ground began to shake.

His first thought was an earthquake, followed by an explosion, and then a foolish hope that it was Bob coming to help them at last. The truth, however, was none of these. It was much worse, because by the time Julius realized the shaking was connected to his brother's deep, bellowing roar, it was too late to do anything about it.

Flames burst through the darkness, and the magic eaters screamed, scrambling over each other in their panic. But there was no escape. Fire was everywhere, clearing a ring around them as Justin rose from the ashes that had been a pile of magic eaters.

He raised the Fang of the Heartstrikers at the same time, bringing the bloody edge of his sword to his mouth and biting down with a bone-chilling *clang*. The flash that followed was so bright that even Julius, who knew what to expect, had to close his eyes. When he opened them again, the human Justin was gone, and in his place stood an enormous, and enormously pissed off, dragon.

Something sharp dug into his shoulder, and Julius jumped before he realized it was Marci's fingers. She'd scrambled to his side during the fire and was now gripping his arm like she meant to rip it off, staring at Justin with eyes so wide, they looked ready to fall out of her head. Julius didn't blame her. If Justin had been his first dragon, he probably would have had the same reaction.

The Heartstriker clan was known for its beauty, not its size. Justin, however, was the exception to the rule. Even at twenty-four, he was already nearly forty feet from nose to tail, a heavy, winding snake of a dragon with a viper's head crowned by a feathered crest. A pair of enormous, gloriously colored wings in blue, green, and gold extended from his feathered back, and his tail was a long whip of trailing plumage. All of this was supported by four thin, scaly, but enormously strong legs that ended in raptor-like feet tipped with curving talons, which were currently digging into the scorched parking lot like the asphalt was freshly turned dirt. But while his claws were definitely not to be messed with, it was his brother's fangs that made Julius shiver.

Now that Justin had cast all illusions aside, his sword had followed suit. The Fang of the Heartstriker was a blade no longer, but a bone-like shell encasing Justin's front fangs. Magic poured off them, filling the empty air with the sharp, biting fury of the Heartstriker's power. Any wounds Justin inflicted with those teeth would never fully heal, and when the fire spewing out of his mouth passed them, the blaze changed from yellow to the brilliant green flame that had once made their grandfather the most feared dragon in the Americas.

By this point, the magic coming off Justin was so intense it was almost dizzying. But when he turned that green fire on the magic eaters, they did not feast as they had on Julius's blood. They fled, surging into the air with a chorus of terrified wails.

Justin followed with a roar that cracked the blacktop, launching off the ground with a flap that nearly blew Julius over. By the time he'd righted himself again, Justin was high overhead, burning the magic eaters out of the air with gouts of green flame until the ashes fell like snow over the three remaining figures huddled together in the now-empty parking lot.

"Julius," Marci whispered, her face lit up by fire and wonder. "He's a *dragon.*"

"Yes," Justin said, looking down to check on Katya, who was still somehow asleep. "We've established this."

"A *real* dragon," Marci clarified. "With *fire.*"

"He's a dragon flying around and breathing fire inside the Lady of the Lake's city," Julius said heatedly, bracing against the pain as he tried and failed to pick Katya up. He tried again anyway, growling in fear and hurt and frustration and a thousand other things. Chelsie was going to kill them all for this. "We have to find some way to wake Katya. There's no way we can move fast enough with her like this. Can you see if she's under a spell? That's the only thing I know of that could keep a dragon unconscious this long." He paused, listening for a reply. When he heard nothing, he looked over to find her still staring at the sky. "Marci," he snapped. "This is kind of important."

She nodded absently, eyes never leaving Justin. "Do you have feathers like that?"

Julius sighed. Clearly, she was going to be no help at all until her curiosity was satisfied. "Yes," he said quickly. "All Heartstrikers have feathers. It's why we're called feathered serpents. I look like Justin, but much smaller and with a different coloration and no green fire. Now, can you *please* check to see what's making Katya sleep?"

Marci blinked like she was hearing him for the first time, and then, to his relief, she dropped down to examine Katya. A few seconds later, she pulled up the dragoness's sleeve to reveal a silver chain wrapped around her bicep. "Here, there's a spell on this."

Julius wanted to slap himself. Of *course* Estella would know about the chain. For all Julius knew, this was the reason Svena had given it to him in the first place. The only question was what kind of a moron was he for not figuring it out earlier? When he grabbed the chain to yank it off, however, a wave of drowsiness swept over him, nearly taking him under as well before he snatched his fingers back. Apparently, the spell was now activated. He was about to ask Marci to give it a try when he heard the squeal of tires in the distance.

He froze, listening. Considering the show Justin was putting on, his guesses were evenly split between bounty hunters, a news crew, or, if they were really unlucky, one of Algonquin's anti-dragon task forces. When he didn't hear any shots, sirens, or excited screaming, however, Julius dragged himself up on his knees to try and see what was actually coming, and was subsequently nearly run over when Bob power-slid his Crown Victoria around the corner and into the parking lot.

"*Bob!*" Julius cried, clutching his chest, which felt in danger of collapsing under the combined weight of injury and shock. "What are you doing?"

"Helping," Bob said cheerfully, hopping out of his car. "Or didn't you want help? Because I can go."

That was enough to nip Julius's anger in the bud. "I'm always happy to receive any help," he said humbly. "Yours most of all. Thank you."

Bob sighed. "So beautifully said, but why isn't Katya awake yet? She's supposed to be awake. We're on a tight schedule."

"Working on it," Marci grumbled, ripping off the duct tape Bixby had used to secure the chain to Katya's arm.

"We need to get the vest off her, too," Julius said, showing Bob the detonator he was still clutching in his hand. He'd been holding it so tight for so long now, his fingers had started cramping. Before he could explain the bomb to his oldest brother, though, Bob leaned down and yanked out one of the wires seemingly at random.

Julius felt like he was having a heart attack. "What did you just *do*?" he cried. "That could have—you would have—how did you know that was the right one?!"

"I don't know!" Bob cried back, slapping his hands to his face in an exaggerated expression of horror. "It's almost as though I can *see the future!*"

"Oh," Julius said quietly, shoulders slumping as he looking down at the detonator in his hand. "Right. So I guess I can let go of this, then?"

"Only if you want to," Bob said, scooping Katya up and stripping off the bomb vest before tossing her into the Crown Vic's back seat like a sack of potatoes. "Right, then! Let's get going, because between you and me, this place is about to get very crowded."

He looked pointedly at Justin, still flaming in the sky, but Julius didn't need the hint. He was already turning to tell Marci to get into the car...and found only empty space.

At this point, Julius would have thought it impossible to panic any more than he already was, but the sudden lack of Marci sent his brain into overdrive. "Marci!" he shouted, whirling around. *"Marci!"*

"Just a second."

Her voice was like a balm, sending relief running through his body. The feeling was short-lived, though, because when he finally spotted her, she was crouching on her hands and knees all the way back at the edge of the blackened circle where Justin had first shifted.

"What are you doing?" he yelled, running over to grab her by the shoulders. "Come on! We have to go."

"But it's gone!" she said frantically, yanking out of his hold. "It was in my bag back in the gym, and now it's gone."

He stared down at her, uncomprehending. "What's gone?"

"My Kosmolabe!" she cried, pressing her cheek against the ground so she could look along the asphalt at foot level. "It must have fallen out when the magic eaters jumped us. Just give me thirty seconds to find it and—"

She cut off as Julius pulled her up, spinning her around to face him. "We don't have thirty seconds." he said, forcing his voice to be calm. "We'll come back later and look together, I promise, but we're going to be up to our necks in serious trouble if we don't leave *right now*. So please, Marci, *please* let it go. For me. Because I'm not going to leave you here, and if you stay, we're all in danger."

She stared at him for a long moment, her whole body shaking with urgency, and then she went limp under his hands. "Okay," she whispered, sliding her bag back onto her shoulder. "Okay."

Relief flooded into Julius so fast, he almost fell into Marci in his rush to hug her. He didn't think it was possible to properly process all the emotions stomping through him like a herd of elephants, so he didn't take the time to try. He simply squeezed Marci tight before tugging her back toward Bob's car, almost yanking her over in his rush to get them both inside and out of danger. But then, just when he was starting to believe they might actually all make it out of this alive, Justin's flaring green fire that had been illuminating the Pit from above suddenly snuffed out.

Julius stumbled, his head snapping up, but he couldn't see a thing. The Pit was once again as black as its namesake, and there was no sign of his brother at all. Not a flame, not a roar, not a flap of his wings, not even the squeals of the magic eaters as they died. Nothing. It was like he'd just vanished.

He was still staring up at the silent void where Justin had been when something whooshed by in the blackness—something enormous and incredibly fast. The only reason he spotted it at all was because he was already looking up, and even then, he didn't catch more than an impression of power and speed before the thing was gone, vanishing into the dark like a hunting owl. He was still staring after it when his phone began to ring.

He answered it without really thinking. By this point, the pain and repeated shocks had rendered his brain nearly useless. He barely noticed when Marci grabbed his arm and pulled him into Bob's back seat between herself and the now-stirring Katya. As luck would have it, the call picked up just as Bob hit the gas, knocking them all backwards and sending Julius's phone clattering to the floor. This turned out to be a blessing in disguise, because the roar that came through the cell phone's speaker would have deafened Julius otherwise.

"Do you idiots listen to nothing I tell you?"

The feminine voice was so furious, he almost thought it was his mother, but that wasn't quite right. It wasn't high-pitched enough, and there was a brutal edge on the words that Bethesda could never manage. It wasn't until Bob drew a *C* in the air, though, that Julius was able to put a name to it. Not that that made things any better.

He scooped the phone off the floor with a sinking heart, leaning back into the Crown Vic's padded cushions for strength as he raised it to his ear. "Hello, Chelsie."

"I specifically warned you not to do anything that would bring the Lady down on us," his sister snarled, making him wince. "That includes letting your *moron* of a brother run rampant breathing fire over a city like some throwback from the dark ages!"

Julius swallowed. "I can't exactly control what Justin—"

"I know that!" Chelsie shouted. "And it's the only reason you're still alive. Justin might not be so lucky."

Her voice had turned into a growl by the end, and Julius began to sweat. "Is, um, is he okay?"

"At the moment, yes, because I snatched him out of the air before he could get himself killed. But I can't vouch for his wellbeing from this point forward. I have very little patience for *idiots*"—there was a sharp crash over the phone, followed by a pained bellow that sounded a lot like Justin's—"who *lose their tempers*"— another crash—"and use the power they were given for the *defense of the family*"— another bellow of pain—"to make a spectacle of themselves in the *Algonquin's front yard!*"

Justin's pained cries went through Julius like spears. "Please don't be hard on him," he begged. "It's my fault. I asked him to help. He would never have—"

"Justin doesn't need your permission to be a fool," Chelsie said, her voice wavering back toward human, but only just. "He has been warned *numerous times*, but his head is like a rock. Now, he's going to learn the hard way why we do not break the rules, and *you* are going to keep your snout out of it. The only reason I'm even calling you is to make sure you're running. The Lady of the Lakes would have to be deaf, dumb, blind, and asleep to miss a display like that, so if you don't want the family to disavow all knowledge of your existence, you will get your lousy carcass out of the Pit this instant."

"We're running," Julius assured her.

"Good," Chelsie said, slightly calmer. "Let me talk to Bob."

Julius looked up to see Bob frantically shaking his head. "Uh...he's not—"

"I *know* he's there," Chelsie growled. "Put him on *now*."

Bob's shoulders slumped in defeat, and he reached back for Julius to give him the phone. When he got it, he pressed it between his shoulder and his ear, answering in a voice so falsely cheerful, it put Julius's teeth on edge. "What a delight! A call from my favorite sister. How are you, Chelsie love?"

Julius couldn't make out Chelsie's answer from the back seat, but her tone didn't sound nearly as pissed as he would have expected given Bob's greeting. Then again, Chelsie had known Bob much longer than he had. Maybe she was too used to his antics to care? He was wondering if he shouldn't take a page from her playbook when he felt Katya stir beside him.

He turned just in time to see her sit up in a rush. Her blue eyes popped open, looking around the car in frightened confusion, and then in horror when she spotted Bob in the front seat. "What is going on?" she whispered, turning to Julius. "Why are we in a car with the Great Seer of the Heartstrikers?" Her eyes dropped as she spoke, and she recoiled, pressing her back against the door. "What *happened* to you?"

Between the dark and the constant panic, Julius hadn't actually had a chance to look at his wounds properly. He did so now, tilting his head down to study the shredded bloody mess that, this morning, had been a brand new shirt. The longer he looked, though, the more he realized that wasn't quite right. Most of his shirt had been ripped away during the fighting, which meant the torn-up, far-too-bloody thing he was looking down at was actually his *chest*.

With that awful realization, the world officially became too much. After all the shocks, attacks, and blood loss of the last hour, he simply had nothing left to pull on, and Julius passed out on the spot, slumping back into the seat with Marci's frightened shout ringing in his ears.

Chapter 18

Estella the Northern Star, Seer of the Three Sisters, stood behind a rusted-out dumpster at the end of what had once been a high school parking lot, waiting. Above her, the magic eaters she'd lured with her sister's blood were still swarming, but they gave her a wide berth. Estella paid them no mind in any case. She simply stood, waiting patiently until, at last, she heard the beautiful *clink clink* of antique glass rolling over decaying asphalt.

She leaned down, pressing her fingers to the broken ground just in time to catch the golden ball rolling across it. The priceless treasure the human mage had lost in the chaos. The Kosmolabe. Estella stroked the smooth, cool glass with her fingers. *Her* Kosmolabe, at last.

Tucking the beautiful orb carefully into the warded box she'd brought along just for this purpose, Estella hurried back to her car. This whole operation had been a mess. Thanks to the young Heartstriker's antics, there wasn't even the remotest possibility the Lady of the Lakes wouldn't notice what had happened here, which meant Estella needed to leave. The idea irked her—she did not run from anyone—but her mothers had taught her early that it was best to give Algonquin a wide berth, and Estella always listened to her mothers.

Fortunately, her limo was waiting just around the corner. She slid into the back seat, commanding the autodrive to take her back to her hotel. She'd barely made it a block before her ears caught the muted blare of sirens approaching at top speed, and the thundering hooves of a horse.

A minute later, she passed a convoy of DFZ heavy weapons teams going the opposite direction, led by an enormous man riding a horse made of crashing waves and carrying a spear the size of a telephone pole. His magic was so potent, Estella caught the scent of him even inside her car: ocean spray and blood, dragon's blood to be precise. But then, whom else would you send to a situation like this but a dragon slayer? She was only sad the overgrown Heartstriker whelp had vanished before Algonquin's hunter could spear him.

In an ironic twist, the wasteland created by the Lady of the Lakes' emergence was located directly below the DFZ's Financial District. This meant it was barely a five-minute drive from her hotel, yet another reason why she'd chosen it as the stage for Bixby's final act. She had hoped he'd beat the odds and survive since he was the only human she had in Vegas, but then, that was why she'd made him give her all his information before sending him in. Estella never bet on long odds.

She'd avoided touching the Kosmolabe the whole drive over, but once she reached her hotel, a massive superscraper luxury development directly across from Svena's, Estella gave in, digging out the golden ball the moment the elevator doors closed. As a dragon, she'd always coveted beautiful, rare, powerful things, but it was the seer in her who treasured the Kosmolabe's true gift. With this as her guide, she could find her way straight to any of the outer planes, no matter how hidden. The one she sought was the most hidden of all, but when she looked into the Kosmolabe, there it was, nestled in among all the others like a little star in the heavens, and all she had to do was follow her new compass right to it.

But while Estella finally had what she'd set out to acquire, the cost had been higher than she'd reckoned thanks to Brohomir's interference. Katya's loss was negligible—the girl had always been more of a liability than an asset—but Svena was a blow from which their clan could not recover. Estella had seen the possibility building for years now, but even so, she'd held on to hope. She'd even broken her rule against betting on long odds by ordering Svena directly in a desperate attempt to change their fate, but it had all come to nothing. Despite her best efforts, everything had turned out exactly as she'd foreseen. Now, the only thing left to do was to make sure the last chance she'd paid so dearly for came through.

When she reached her hotel suite, Estella locked the door and started clearing a space in the front room. When she'd pushed all the matched furniture to the walls, she stepped into the middle of the now open floor, clutching the Kosmolabe between her palms. Peering down into the twitching, interlocking gold patterns, she fixed on her target and pulled her magic tight, honing her power to an edge sharp enough to slice through the fabric that separated this world from the worlds beyond. She was almost done when the phone in her purse began to ring.

The noise made her jump. She hadn't foreseen getting a call now. She didn't recognize the number, either, but her surprise plus the Chinese country code at the front was as good as an engraved calling card, and by the time Estella answered, the voice on the other end was as expected as it was deep.

"Do you know what time it is here?"

Estella sighed. Only the Black Reach would call you to complain about the time where he was. "What do you want?"

There was a rain-like sound as the elder seer stretched, his scales clicking together like a cascade of jade beads. "Actually, this is a courtesy call. I promised the last time we spoke that I would say something if I saw you setting foot down an irrevocable path. Of course, if I'd known you were going to do so at seven-thirty in the morning, I would never have agreed."

"You didn't foresee that as well?" Estella said. "And here I thought you were supposed to be the greatest of us all?"

"The greatest and the oldest," he agreed. "And the most patient with overwrought young seers like yourself who don't stop to think things through."

"Your concern is noted," she said briskly. "But my decision is already made. I refuse to live in a world where that tacky whore and her upstart brood become more powerful than us."

"So I see," the Black Reach replied, his smooth, deep voice turning serious. "But a promise is a promise, Estella. I swore to warn you, though it's up to you to listen."

Estella sighed and sat down in a richly upholstered chair. "Get on with it, then."

"You're beginning your fall, little star," the old dragon said. "For over two thousand years, the Three Sisters have been the unquestioned queens of the dragon world; their magic unmatched, their seer unparalleled. But no queen rules forever. The wheel of fortune turns on all levels, and the old must always make way for the new."

"You think I don't know that?" she snapped. "You act as though you're the only seer in this conversation. I foresaw the Heartstriker's rise perfectly well. Unlike you, though, I wasn't content to drink tea and watch the world fall apart around me. I've worked tirelessly for decades now to prevent this catastrophe."

"And lost your favorite sister in the process."

Estella closed her eyes with a sharp breath, and in the silence that followed, the Black Reach continued. "Brohomir has done his job exceptionally well for one so young. The Heartstriker's ascent cannot be prevented. If you wish to survive, you must adapt."

"You're wrong," she said, looking down at the Kosmolabe shining in her hand. "There is one last way."

"Perhaps," the Black Reach said. "But know this, Estella. If you start down this path, you will find the weapon you seek, but it will be your death as well. You have lived longer than any seer in history save myself. Are you sure you're ready to give that up for a revenge you will not live to enjoy?"

"Of course," she said at once. "You might see more than any seer, Black Reach, but seeing isn't the same as understanding. There is more to life than mere survival. It is because I've lived so long that I can say without doubt that I would rather die tomorrow with my teeth lodged in the Heartstriker's throat than live forever in a world where the daughters of gods are forced to bow to Bethesda the Broodmare."

The phone vibrated against her ear as the Black Reach let out a long, deep sigh. "So be it," he said. "My warning is delivered. With this, all debts between us are answered, which means I will see you soon."

"Soon?" Estella repeated, scowling. "Why?"

There was soft click of sharp teeth as the Black Reach smiled. "Because the next time we meet will be the day you die. Have a nice trip, Estella."

The phone went silent as he hung up, and Estella stared it for a long moment before flinging it away. She was not afraid. She was a seer, the Northern Star, and she had set herself down this path long ago. Death was just another price, and if it could be used to buy the destruction of her enemy, she would count her life well spent indeed. With that thought ringing in her mind and the Kosmolabe as her guide, Estella reached out and tore the world apart.

Her honed magic sliced through the fabric of the universe like claws through cloth, ripping a six-foot-wide hole in the air above the hotel suite's tasteful Ottoman carpet. On the other side, a black desert stretched out like an endless sea, lit only by a blood-red moon trapped eternally at its zenith by powers so old even Estella could not name them. There was no movement in this world, no howling wind, no water. Only dust and the distant clink of chains from the black mountain at the desert's center.

For the first time since she'd decided to embark on this journey, Estella hesitated. There was no future on the other side of that hole, no river of possible choices for her to look down. All she could see was what she perceived with her physical eyes, and for the first time in many years, Estella the Northern Star felt a twinge of fear.

Like all her weaknesses, though, it was fleeting, because on this side of the portal, she could see just fine. For example, she knew if she looked out the window behind her, she would find shadows moving against the drawn curtains of Svena's hotel room. *Two* shadows, caught in an embrace…

That horrid thought was all she needed. With a furious snarl, Estella stepped through the portal, casting off her humanity as she went. When her feet landed in black dust of the other world, they were white claws, and they only touched down for an instant before she took flight, her delicate, frost-traced wings moving in powerful beats as she flew up into the still, empty, eternally night sky. By the time the portal sealed behind her, she was following the bright gold beacon of the Kosmolabe straight toward the mountain of chains at the center, the black prison even seers could not foresee, throbbing like a beating heart beneath the light of the blood-red moon.

And back in the hotel room, discarded and forgotten beneath the silk damask couch, her phone began to ring.

And ring.

And ring.

***

Marci crouched in the back seat of Bob's car, one hand pressing the scarf she'd found at the bottom of her bag against the wound on Julius's chest, the other pinning Ghost behind her just in case the death spirit got any ideas. On the opposite side of the seat, Katya watched nervously from a safe distance, which actually made Marci like her a great deal better. Julius had warned her that dragons were calculating and manipulative, but anyone who looked so legitimately worried about his welfare couldn't be all bad. Bob, on the other hand, was no use at all.

He'd slowed down when they hit the skyways, but he was still driving like a maniac, watching his phone instead of the road despite the fact that he was driving a manually operated antique. He'd finished his conversation with whoever Chelsie was a few minutes ago, and now he just seemed to be dialing the same number over and over again. With no luck, apparently.

"What's wrong?" Marci asked.

"There's been a great disturbance in the Force," Bob said gravely. "As if millions of voices suddenly cried out in terror and were suddenly silenced. I fear something terrible has happened."

Her eyes widened. "Really?"

"No," Bob said, dialing the number again with an irritated growl. "How's our fainting flower doing? Still breathing?"

Marci's jaw clenched, but things were much too serious to bother with a comeback, so she let it go and just answered the question. "Shallowly," she reported, pressing her makeshift bandage harder against the deep wounds that were still sluggishly bleeding. "Is he going to be okay?"

"Outlook hazy," Bob replied. "Try again tomorrow."

Now it was Marci's turn to growl. "How can you be so flippant about this? Your brother might be dying. Who are you calling, anyway?"

"An old girlfriend," he said, meeting her eyes in the mirror. "Do you always ask so many questions?"

"Are you always so cryptic and annoying?" Marci snapped back, earning her a gasp from Katya.

"Mortal," she warned softly, casting a nervous eye at the front seat. "Perhaps you are unaware, but the dragon you are addressing is Brohomir, the Great Seer of the Heartstrikers. You should not speak to him like that. You are making Julius look bad."

"Oh, Julius does that all on his own," Bob said, dropping the phone on the seat beside him with a sound of defeat. Hands now free, he grabbed the wheel and turned the car hard, flinging Marci against the door as he took them around a corner on two wheels. She righted herself with an annoyed sigh, but she'd already learned it was pointless to try to correct Bob's driving, so she decided to focus on making sure Julius didn't get any worse.

He already looked awful. The sun had sunk while they'd been down in the pit, but there was still plenty of light up here on the skyways, enough to see that the amount of blood in the car was staggering. If it wasn't for the fact that he was still breathing, Marci would have sworn Julius was already dead.

"Don't worry. He's a dragon."

Marci's head snapped up to find Katya watching her with a little smile on her face.

"He won't die from this," she said. "It's only one bullet."

The gentle words made Marci want to wring the dragoness's lovely neck. "It's not just the bullet. He also got bitten by the magic eaters, *and* he's sealed. He shouldn't have been in there at all!"

She hadn't meant for that last part to come out quite so hysterical, but to her surprise, Katya was nodding. "I know this was my family's doing," she said. "I smelled my eldest sister while the humans were putting the chain on me. I'm not sure what sort of play she was making with this—I could never claim to know the workings of a seer— but your clan was hurt in the process, and I would offer amends." She straightened up, looking Marci dead in the eye. "I offer your master a life debt in payment for my rescue and to make things even between our clans."

Marci blinked. "Master?"

"You are his human, are you not?" Katya said, nodding at Julius. "I'd offer it to him directly, but he's not exactly in a position to make a decision at the moment, and I would like this settled quickly."

Marci bit her lip, brain racing. For the sake of accuracy, she felt she should own up to her own part in the Bixby/Kosmolabe fiasco. On the other hand, if Katya wanted to blame her sister and give Julius a life debt to settle the score, who was Marci to screw that up? There was only one problem; Julius hated debts. If Marci accepted one on his behalf, he'd probably be really upset. Then again, it *did* sound like a pretty sweet offer.

"I don't know," she said at last. "I don't think Julius would—"

"Nonsense," Bob interrupted, making her jump. When she looked up, he was staring straight at her through the rear view mirror. "A life debt between dragons is a power that can balance clans. It is not tendered often and should never be squandered. Julius, of course, is too young and too nice to understand this because he would never dream of going to war. But he's indisposed at present, so the question is, how nice are *you*, Marcivale Novalli?"

"Not *that* nice," she said, turning back to Katya. "We accept the debt."

With remarkable lightness for someone who'd just given up something of such vaunted value, Katya smiled and offered her hand. After cleaning the blood off her own, Marci took it, but the bite of icy magic she felt through the dragon's fingers almost made her let go again. She had pride to maintain, though, so she held her ground, gritting her teeth as the magic swelled and burst, falling over all of them like snow before Katya finally let go.

"There," she said, folding her hands in her lap. "That's settled."

"And just in time, too," Bob said, whipping the car around another corner and down a ramp into a parking deck set into the skyway itself. "Fancy that."

Marci looked up in alarm. With everything that was going on, she hadn't been paying attention to where they were driving. Judging by how nice the parking deck was, though, she could only imagine it was somewhere very expensive—a hypothesis that was further supported by the pair of armed and augmented security guards who tried to stop Bob when he parked his car directly in front of their elevator.

The guards had barely taken their first menacing step forward before Bob hopped out with a huge, friendly smile. "Gentlemen, gentlemen," he said warmly. "No cause for that. We're expected. Just call up to apartment fifty-three and tell Jessica that her brother Bob is here to see her."

The guards looked skeptical, but they obeyed, the bigger one hanging back to keep an eye on Bob while his partner made the call on his headset. Whatever answer this Jessica person sent, though, it must have been a doozy, because by the time Marci got Julius to the edge of the seat, the guards were falling all over themselves to help. One even offered to drive Bob's car around to a more secure location that wasn't in the middle of a loading zone. Bob's reply was to smile sweetly and announce that anyone who touched his baby would lose a hand. This threat was further reinforced by Ghost, who chose that moment to hop up into Crown Victoria's back window and splay his fluffy, transparent body out in the shadows like a normal cat would in a sunbeam.

After that, the guards didn't say a word. Not about Bob's parking or the apparent dead body he dragged out of his back seat and tossed over his shoulder like a bloody sack of flour. They didn't even comment on the trail of ashy dirt the three of them tracked into the fancy elevator, or the pigeon that quietly swooped out of the car to land on Bob's head. It was a mark of just how surreal Marci's life had gotten that riding in an elevator in one of the nicest buildings she'd ever seen with three dragons didn't even strike her as notable anymore. She was mostly worried about Julius, who was starting to look terrifyingly pale.

Bob stopped them at the fiftieth floor, leaving a little trail of blood on the carpet behind him as he carried Julius down the tastefully appointed hall to one of the building's corner units. The door opened before he got there, revealing yet another fantastically beautiful woman with perfectly dyed blond hair and striking green eyes, giving Marci pause. Just how many Heartstrikers were there, anyway?

"Brohomir," the new dragon said breathlessly, ducking her head in a little bow. "This is such an honor. I was not expecting the Great Seer of the Heartstrikers. What can I do for..." She stopped suddenly, eyes flicking to the body on Bob's shoulder. "Is that *Julius?*"

"Indeed it is," Bob said, shoving his way into the immaculate apartment behind her. "Hello, Jessica! No need for pleasantries. We're just here to borrow your medical degree."

"For Julius?" she said skeptically.

"An excellent medical deduction, seeing how he's the one bleeding on your carpet," Bob replied. "Now are you going to tell me where to put him, or should I just choose a spot?"

He looked at her for an answer, but the dragon seemed to have lost her ability for speech. Her green eyes had turned as round as cue balls as they traveled from Bob to Marci and then to Katya, where they got stuck. When the silence had stretched on too long, Bob shrugged and started for the white, incredibly expensive-looking couch in the middle of her living room.

He was about to drop a very bloody Julius on the cushions when Jessica cried, "No!" The threat to her furniture seemed to have woken her up, because she burst into motion, marching quickly through the living room and down the hall that led to the rest of the apartment. "This way. I'll look at him immediately."

Smiling, Bob followed his sister, Julius's body bouncing on his shoulder. Marci hurried after them, leaving Katya to shut the door, blocking the view of the curious neighbors who'd come out to see what all the fuss was about.

***

Julius woke up slowly, easing into consciousness like he would into a too-hot bath. Fortunately, coming back wasn't nearly as bad as he'd feared. He felt clean and dry, and there was something on his chest that, though itchy and constricting, was much better than the painful mess he'd passed out to.

Encouraged, he slid his hand under the sheets to investigate and immediately encountered the familiar softness of medical gauze. Bandages, then. Also sheets, which meant he was probably in a *bed*. That was a definite improvement over the back of Bob's car, worth checking out, and so, with a deep breath, Julius cracked his eyes open.

He was in a bedroom. That much wasn't surprising, given the bed, but what *was* surprising was that he recognized it. The elegant beige and white room was one of Jessica's guest bedrooms. Bob must have brought him to their sister for medical treatment after he'd passed out. That would explain the expert bandage job, and why he'd been upgraded from the couch. Seers always got the best stuff.

After a few groggy tries, Julius managed to sit up with relatively little pain. He was contemplating giving standing a go when the door opened and Marci burst into the room.

"Oh, thank goodness," she said. "You're finally awake."

He smiled at the clear relief in her voice, but before he could ask any of the pertinent questions—how he'd gotten here, what had happened, was she all right—Marci flung herself onto the bed and hugged him tight.

She kept her arms on his shoulders to avoid his injuries, but Julius wouldn't have cared if she'd crushed them. The feel of her around him would have been worth the pain. This was still lovely, though, and after a few seconds, he tentatively returned the gesture, putting his arms loosely around her waist as he breathed her in.

There were no tears this time, thankfully, just Marci and the distinctive scent of Jessica's fancy soap. She'd showered and changed since he'd last seen her, but the pale lemon sundress she was wearing must have been Jessica's, because it didn't fit Marci at all in size or style. She was beautiful in it, though. Beautiful and alive and soft with her body pressed against his so firmly, he could feel the racing thrum of her heartbeat. And reckless as it was, Julius really, *really* wished that she would kiss him again. Right now. Instead, she pulled away.

"Sorry," she muttered, dropping her eyes. "Got carried away. The others kept acting like your injuries were nothing, but I swear you almost died a few times back there, and..." she trailed off with an emotional sigh. "I'm just really, *really* happy you're okay."

"Me too," Julius said softly, fighting the urge to sigh himself. That was quite possibly the nicest, most beautiful thing anyone had ever said to him, and he took a moment to revel in it while she checked his bandages.

"Wow, you *do* heal fast," she said, tucking the gauze back into place. "Your skin's already closed over. How are you feeling?"

Not nearly so good now that she wasn't hugging him. "Not bad," he said. "Almost normal, actually. Where's Bob?"

"He left half an hour ago," Marci replied, glancing nervously over her shoulder at the door. "I really wish he'd stuck around, though. Things are getting tense out there."

That put Julius on alert. "What's going on?"

"I couldn't explain it if I tried. You'd better come see for yourself. Can you stand?"

Between the two of them, they managed to get him to his feet. Once he was up, the remaining grogginess cleared quickly, and he started looking around for something to wear. Unfortunately, his shirt was now nothing but bloody scraps, and he wasn't about to ask Jessica for a spare. Going out bare-chested felt crass, though, so he settled for draping one of Jessica's decorative throw blankets over his shoulders like a shawl.

When he was decent enough to face company, he let Marci help him into the hall, breathing deep to try to get an early warning for whatever was waiting. He caught the scent just as they turned the corner into the living room, and swallowed his groan just in time.

The apartment was full of dragons. Ian and Svena were sitting on the couch, the former watching with carefully veiled interest while the latter glared ice-cold daggers at Katya, who was standing by the window like she wanted to jump out of it. Jessica was in the kitchen, making drinks and looking like she wanted to throw the lot of them out the window, or at least out of her apartment. Her head snapped up when she heard Julius coming, and she went straight for him like a charging shark, yanking him away from Marci and back into the hall.

"What were you thinking, bringing all these dragons to my doorstep?" she hissed. "That's the White Witch in there! Are you trying to get me killed? And you'd better teach your human some manners before—"

"Don't speak that way about Marci," Julius said, calmly removing his arm from his sister's grasp. "I'm sorry for the inconvenience, but I didn't ask them to come. Bob brought me here, so if you have problems, take them to him. Now, I'm going to go try my best to get these dragons out of your living room." His eyes darted past her to the tray of gin and tonics she'd been in the middle of preparing. "I'll also take a drink. And one for Marci, too, please."

With that, he patted his shocked sister on the shoulder and walked back into the living room to see what was going on.

Katya was waiting for him when he got there. "I'm so glad you're up," she said, pulling him over to stand before the dragons on the couch like he was a prisoner facing his parole board. "This is the one who saved me."

Julius froze, eyes wide. Svena was staring at him like she was contemplating just how slowly she wanted to gut him while Ian's face was perfectly blank and unhelpful. "Well," he said, scrambling to pick words that might best encourage Svena not to do anything permanent. "Justin did most of the work. I—"

"Because you asked him to," Katya said firmly, glaring at her sister. "You see? It's just as the human reported. Julius Heartstriker rallied his human and his brother Justin, a Blade of Bethesda, to come to my aid. They fought valiantly to save my life, which Estella would have thrown away. This is why I vowed a life debt to him, and I will not revoke it."

Julius almost choked as she finished, looking desperately between Katya, who was standing with her chin lifted defiantly, and Svena, who looked ready to murder them both. "I think there's been a misunderstanding," he said. "I didn't—"

A flash of movement caught his eye, and he glanced at the kitchen to see Marci waving her hands in a frantic *play along* gesture.

"What I mean is, Katya is telling the truth," he corrected. "I found her this afternoon and convinced her to come home, but then she was abducted by humans—"

"Who were working for Estella," Katya cut in. "She was using me as a pawn to breed war between our clans. You know she will stop at nothing to—"

"Enough!" Svena yelled, shooting to her feet. "You will not speak so of our sister in front of outsiders!"

"I'll speak however I like!" Katya yelled back. "I am a daughter of the Three Sisters same as you, and it was these *outsiders* who saved my life when our *sister* endangered it!"

Svena lifted her lips in a deadly snarl and began speaking rapidly in Russian. Katya responded in kind, getting into her sister's face so aggressively, Julius worried it would come to blows. Apparently, the youngest daughter of the Three Sisters took being kidnapped by humans on the orders of the eldest very personally. The defeated, tired girl he'd seen at the diner had vanished completely, leaving behind a dragoness who was absolutely determined to get her way and more than ready to drag Julius into battle with her if necessary.

"I am through being thought of as the failure of the clan!" Katya cried, in English now. "And I am done being kept like a prisoner by my own family! My debt is mine to give, and if I choose to give it to the one who risked his life to save mine, you cannot stop me."

Svena shot Julius a nasty look. Or she would have, but Katya got in the way, growling loud enough to rattle the coffee table's glass top. This got Svena's attention as nothing else had, and the dragoness flopped back down on the couch with an angry sigh. "Fine," she snarled. "I acknowledge your stupid debt. But you are still coming home."

"No," Katya said, her face breaking into a wicked smile. "You just acknowledged my debt."

"So?" Svena said. "What does that have to do with anything?"

"It has to do with everything," Katya said proudly. "By your own words, I am now honor bound to answer the call of Heartstriker, and I can't do that if I'm locked up in Siberia, can I?"

Svena's ice blue eyes widened in surprise before narrowing to dangerous slits. "Very well," she said slowly. "If you aren't going home, then where would you live?"

"Here," Katya said, standing tall. "I wish to remain in the DFZ."

Julius's breath caught. *That's* what she was doing. This wasn't actually about life debts or gratitude or any of that. Katya had just used the circumstances surrounding her kidnapping to modify their original plan to keep her in the DFZ. She'd also upped the ante enormously. Now that Svena had formally acknowledged the debt Katya owed to the Heartstrikers, not allowing her to stay and honor it was as good as refusing to pay. She was using her own capture to force Svena's hand, turning her defeat into her means to victory, and the whole thing was such a beautiful twist on dragon politics that Julius couldn't have stopped grinning if he'd tried.

Svena, however, was far less impressed. "You think I can't see what you're doing?" she said, her voice an icy threat. "You think to make a fool of me?"

"I don't have to," Katya said. "You're making a fool of yourself if you let pride stand between you and such a good outcome for all involved. Come on, Svena. Do you really want to have to keep going back to Siberia every month to check on me? I've always thought that a sister who's constantly running away is a much greater embarrassment than one who can't use magic. This is a far superior arrangement for both of us, especially since I'll be in a city where I shouldn't cast anything flashy even if I could. And since I don't want to run, you won't have to worry about chasing me. Everybody wins."

As Katya spoke, Svena's expression had turned from furious to conflicted. Now, she was openly thinking it over, tapping her sharp nails on the arm of Jessica's couch. "Estella will never permit you to live on the Lady's lands."

"She won't," Katya agreed. "But Estella isn't here, is she?"

Julius didn't understand the significance of that statement. Of course Estella wasn't here. If she'd been in the apartment, a clan war would probably be breaking out right now. But physical nearness clearly wasn't what Katya was referring to, because Svena gave her sister a cross look. "That is *definitely* not talk for outsiders."

Katya shrugged. "It's no secret that she's not around right now," she said. "Surely you don't mean for us to sit around waiting on a seer's convenience when it would be so much easier for you to step up in her absence and make the call yourself,"—she broke into a coy smile—"clan head?"

Svena raised a warning finger, but Julius didn't miss the flash of interest in her eyes. Clearly, Svena liked the idea of being clan head very much. Ian seemed to like it even better, because his face lit up like a young dragon seeing his very first pile of gold before he masked it.

"I think your sister makes an excellent point," he said casually. "The DFZ's strategic advantages are unparalleled if you're going to be managing your clan's assets in Estella's stead. Just until she comes back, of course. In the interim, I would be more than happy to offer you a place to stay as a token of good will between our two clans. It just so happens that I own all three of the penthouses in my building. You could have your pick."

Julius held his breath. Even though turning Ian into their advocate had been his plan from the beginning, he still couldn't quite believe it was actually working. Better still, Ian wasn't even paying attention to him. His eyes were on Svena, waiting for her to take the bait, and from the sour look on her face, she knew it. At the same time, though, there was no question that this arrangement worked enormously in her favor. Now, everything depended on what she decided was more important: pride, or getting what she wanted.

That was always a tricky call with dragons, and Julius began to sweat as the seconds dragged on. In the end, though, ambition won. "It would certainly make my life easier if you stopped running away," Svena said, leaning back on the couch and generally making a great show of being highly put out. "Oh, very well. So long as you stay out of trouble and obey me as you would our mothers, you may remain here."

"Thank you, Svena!" Katya said, running to hug her sister.

Svena sighed and waved her away, but even her cold dragon routine wasn't quite enough to keep the smug smile off her face as she leaned over to whisper something in Ian's ear. Whatever she said had him smiling, too, and they exchanged a meaningful look before Svena announced she was going to inform the rest of her clan of the new arrangement and walked off to the rear of the apartment.

Katya followed right on her heels, taking two drinks off the tray Jessica had just finished preparing as she passed. Being treated like a waitress in her own home was apparently too much for Jessica, however. She slammed the tray down on the counter and stormed off as well, leaving Ian, Marci, and Julius alone in the living room.

Ian glanced at the drinks and then at Julius. Getting the message, Julius grabbed the tray and set it on the coffee table in front of his brother, who helped himself.

"I understand you're the mind behind all this," he said, taking a slow sip.

"Partially," Julius said. "Katya was the one who sold it, though."

"Modesty ill becomes dragons," Ian said, no longer bothering to hide his grin. "Svena told me just now that her sister named you as the instigator during that rather delightful bout of Russian. It seems I must reevaluate my opinion of you, Julius Heartstriker. You got the job done."

"Thank you," Julius said, taking a careful sip of his own drink. "Though if you want to tell someone, I'd appreciate it if you'd tell Mother."

"I will," Ian said, studying him. "I'm not quite sure how you pulled it off, but whatever you did, it was clearly effective. You got Brohomir on your side, prevented a clan war, solved Svena's little sister problem *and* kept them both in the city, which makes my life much easier. *And* you got rid of Estella."

"That wasn't me," Julius said quickly.

"Who cares?" Ian said with a shrug. "The point is that everything turned up roses for Heartstriker, especially *this* Heartstriker. So yes, I'll be telling Mother a great deal. I can't make her unseal you, of course, but if she doesn't, it won't be for lack of positive reporting on my end. You are absolutely wasted as a scapegoat."

"Thank you," Julius said, but it was more out of habit than anything else. He was still trying to wrap his brain around the fact that he'd actually pulled it off. The long shot plan he'd thought up in the car and then sold to Katya had actually *worked.* And while Ian's good opinion wasn't the same as their mother's, he was reasonably certain she wouldn't kill a dragon her current favorite son considered useful, which meant he might actually *live.*

Considering the number of times he'd squeaked past death tonight, that shouldn't have come as such a shock, but Julius had lived in fear of his mother for so long, the idea that he'd wiggled out of one of her traps barely seemed possible. He was still wondering at it when he realized Ian had asked him a question.

"Sorry," he said, shaking his head. "What was that?"

Ian gave him a cutting look. "I said, what are you going to do now? And *don't* say go back to your room in the mountain. This Katya business has bought you a reprieve, but mother's still going to expect you to do something with your life. So, what is it?"

Julius had no idea. Hiding had been his life for so long, he'd never actually put much thought into what else there was to do. The only thing he knew for certain was that he definitely wasn't going back to the mountain, but beyond that, he had no clue. It must have shown on his face, too, because Ian sighed.

"Let me put it another way," he said, setting his drink down on the table. "What do you *want* to do? I have several businesses that can always use someone competent. I'd be happy to start you out somewhere in my organization in exchange for a few favors."

That didn't sound like something Julius wanted to touch with a ten foot pole, but his brother had still given him an idea. "Actually," he said. "I think I'd like to start with the payment for this job."

Ian smiled as he reached for his phone. "Now you're thinking like a dragon. Very well, how much do I owe you?"

"We didn't actually agree on a specific amount." Which was a mistake Julius would *never* be making again. Right now, though, the oversight actually worked in his favor. "I was wondering if I could ask for a different kind of payment, though. You own a lot of properties in the city, right?"

"A few hundred," Ian replied casually. "Including our family safe house, which I presume is still standing after its recent Justin infestation?"

"Last I saw," Julius said, though the mention of Justin's name made him wince. Overbearing as his brother could be, Justin had come through for him in spades tonight. He was trying to think if there was any way he could get back in touch with Chelsie and ask her to be lenient when Ian cleared his throat and snapped Julius back to the conversation.

"Sorry," he said quickly, smiling at his brother, who was looking dangerously bored. "I was just thinking that, instead of paying me money, you could let me use one of your buildings instead. I'm thinking of starting a business."

Now Ian looked flat-out shocked. "What would *you* do with a business?"

"Make something of myself," Julius said, pulling himself a little straighter. "You and Mother were right, I wasn't going anywhere hiding in my room. I'd like to change that, but I need a base to operate out of, preferably one without a human landlord to worry about. So if you're offering me payment, that's what I'd like. Please."

Ian tapped his phone, thinking it over. "That's highly suspicious," he said at last. "But I don't see any reason why such an agreement wouldn't work. Come by my office tomorrow afternoon and we'll go over your options."

"Thank you, Ian," Julius said, but his brother was already turning away, lifting his phone to his ear to take a call Julius hadn't even heard go off. Leaving him to have his conversation in private, Julius got up and went to the kitchen in search of Marci.

He found her standing by the sink, emptying something out of her purse into one of Jessica's stainless steel colanders.

"Hey," she said when he came over. "I hope your sister doesn't mind me using her strainer. I tried to find an older one, but I swear everything in this place is brand new. It's like a show apartment or something."

"That's Jessica," Julius said, looking over her shoulder at the half dozen long, sharp, black objects Marci was now rinsing in the colander under a scalding spray of water. "What are those?"

"Magic eater teeth," she replied, moving her hands so he could get a better look at the blade-like fangs. "I found them on the ground when I was looking for my Kosmolabe. I figured they were probably worth something, and since I'm going to need money to fix my car, I picked some up. Really glad I did, too. I looked them up while you were asleep, and according to the Thaumaturgy forums, these things have all kinds of unique properties, not to mention the bounty."

Julius looked at the teeth with new interest. "They have a bounty?"

She nodded. "A big one. Since wounded dragons aren't exactly common here, magic eaters in the DFZ prey primarily on spirits, and this being a spirit's city, the money on them is off the charts. Justin probably burned a few million's worth while he was rampaging." She sighed sadly. "I *really* wish I'd thought to grab a head. There were several lying around that weren't too badly scorched."

Julius's lips quirked in a smile. "Actually, that's kind of what I wanted to talk to you about." He moved around to her side, leaning on the marble counter so he could look her in the face. "What are your plans now?"

"I was just wondering that myself," Marci confessed. "I'd like to go back to school, but I've got no money and this semester is pretty much a bust. Honestly, even with Bixby dead, I'm not comfortable going back to Vegas. He and my dad screwed over a lot of people, and it's not a very friendly town for me at the moment, if you get my meaning. I guess I'll just look for a job here."

"I'm happy to hear you say that," he said. "It so happens that I need a job as well, one that's *not* for my family, and I was thinking, if we're both free, why not work together?"

Marci blinked at him. "Doing what?"

"I haven't quite figured out the details yet," Julius said, reaching over to pick up one of the magic eater teeth. "But I think we've established that this city is full of nasty things that are worth a lot of money if you're willing to take them on. Considering how awful the civic services are here, I bet there are also people who would be willing to pay us handsomely to clear said animals off their property. That plus the bounties and the magical parts we could collect adds up to a pretty nice income, so I'm thinking about starting a business to take advantage of it. Sort of like magical pest control. I've already got a building lined up and everything."

Now Marci just looked impressed. "A building? How'd you manage that so fast?"

"I'm not a *complete* failure as a dragon," Julius said, flashing her a confident smile to hide how nervous he actually was. "So what do you think? You said yourself that we make a good team. Want to help me keep it rolling?"

Her eyes lit up so fast, he could almost see her forcing the excitement back down. "Could I have my own lab?"

"You can have whatever you want," he said, spreading his arms. "I'll make you co-owner, just come help me. Please?"

"Deal," Marci said immediately, her face splitting into a glowing smile as she stuck out her wet hand. Julius took it gladly, grinning back just as wide as they shook on it.

"Oh, man," Marci said, turning back to the sink. "A dragon and a mage doing bounties in the DFZ! We are going to make *bank*."

"Hopefully," he said. "But, please, no more getting people over barrels and shaking them. I don't like it."

She sighed dramatically. "Fine, I'll be *nice*. It might not be so bad, though. After all," she flashed him a smile, "it worked out pretty well for you."

"I suppose it did," he said slowly, reaching down to help her pick up the freshly scrubbed teeth.

Marci laughed, an excited, happy sound that thrilled him right to his toes. And as he basked in the glow, Julius couldn't help thinking that she was right. At this moment, being nice, being himself, was working out very well indeed.

"Come on," he said, dumping the clean teeth into her bag. "Let's go get dinner. My treat."

"Dutch," Marci countered. "It's a business dinner. Before we go, though, I think you need to work on your business attire."

Julius blinked in confusion, and Marci reached out to tap her damp finger against his naked chest, making him shiver even as his face began to burn. "Maybe a little." he admitted, looking down at his bare feet to hide his blush.

That must have been the right thing to say, because Marci burst out laughing. Julius joined her a few seconds later, the two of them raising such a racket that Jessica came out of the back bedroom to see what was the matter.

Epilogue

Hours later, Chelsie, Bethesda's Shade, returned to Heartstriker Mountain. After securing and disarming her idiot brother, and taking a brief shower to get the ash out of her hair, she strapped two Fangs of the Heartstriker to her hips and went to report to her mother.

Bethesda was in her usual spot, lounging on her favorite piles of gold in all her feathery, rainbow-hued glory. She was staring off into the middle distance, dragging her manicured claws through the seemingly empty air in front of her as she worked the enormous custom AR interface required to run her empire. "That's it," she announced when Chelsie walked in. "The world's gone mad. Do you know what I just received?"

"A declaration of war from Algonquin?" Chelsie guessed.

"You're not still upset about that nonsense in the DFZ, are you?" Bethesda said. "I told you, it wasn't Justin's fault. He's young—overly energetic and aggressive, you know how boys get. You shouldn't be so hard on him."

Chelsie let out a silent, angry breath. It was her job to be hard on them so Bethesda could be free to play the doting mother. They both knew this, but for some reason, Bethesda enjoyed pretending her role wasn't just that: a role. But Chelsie had played this game with her mother for a long, long time, and she'd learned the hard way to keep her anger to herself. "What did you receive?"

"Hmm?" Bethesda said. "Oh, that. I got a message just now from Ian praising Julius to the rafters. Julius! You know, the runty one?"

"I know who Julius is," Chelsie said. "What did Ian say?"

"Oh, some nonsense about Estella and rescuing some Three Sisters dragon," she answered blithely. "Nothing you'd be interested in." Which Chelsie understood was Bethesda-speak for 'things you should already know about that I don't want to explain.'

"Anyway," her mother went on. "Apparently Ian believes little Julius pulled off quite the coup. He even suggests that I unseal him. Says I should make a big show about it for the others, too. Something inspirational like 'hard work brings reward' and 'even the lowest of us can achieve,' that sort of thing."

Chelsie nodded. "Sounds reasonable. Will you do it?"

"I haven't decided," Bethesda said. "I just don't see what's in it for me. Julius is doing so well being sealed. Why should I mess with what works? I don't want to unseal him and give him an excuse to go right back to slacking." She tapped a gilded claw thoughtfully against her fangs. "No, I think I'll let him stew a bit longer, see what else he can pull off now that he's properly motivated."

"Then I'll be going back to the DFZ," Chelsie said. "Brohomir's up to something."

"Brohomir's always up to something," Bethesda replied proudly. "It's the seer in him. That and he's a *genius*."

Chelsie shook her head, but her mother was already reabsorbed in the invisible display in front of her, and she took the opportunity to make a quiet escape. As soon as she was in the hall, she pulled out her phone, tapping the screen as she tried to remember how to get to the actual phone part of this particular model.

She got a new phone every week, and never saved her contacts. Phones were too easily lost or compromised to trust with something as important as her list of Heartstriker private numbers. She did keep a secret backup on an old-style data stick hidden in her boot, but she didn't need it for Bob. Her eldest brother had had the same number for over a hundred years, and Chelsie knew it by heart.

She dialed quickly, and then settled against the wall to wait while she went through the four full cycles of rings and voicemail Bob always put her through when she called. Finally, just before his voicemail picked up for the fifth time, the phone clicked, and a bright voice said, "I feel so popular."

"Do we really have to go through this every time? One of these days, it's going to be really important."

"Nonsense, Chelsie-lamb," Bob said. "That's the thing about being a seer: I *always* know when it's important."

She frowned. To the casual listener, the words would sound flippant, but Chelsie knew her brother, and to her, Bob sounded distracted. Distracted and worried. "What are you doing with that boy?"

"Julius?" Bob said. "Oh, just helping him grow, reach his full potential, providing a good male role model, all that big brother stuff."

Since the hall was empty, Chelsie permitted herself an eye roll. "Seriously."

Bob sighed. "I'm going to need someone soon," he admitted, his voice deepening and darkening to its real tone. "There's a storm coming. I can see it, but I can't see through it, or beyond. All I know is that we are approaching a crux, and one of us is going to have to make a choice that will either doom or save the entire clan."

"And you chose *Julius*?" Chelsie cried. "Why not me? Why not Amelia? There are ten clutches worth of Heartstrikers. Surely one of them is more qualified than Mr. Nice Dragon."

"It's precisely Julius's failure that makes him so perfect," Bob replied. "Most dragons have absolutely no idea what to make of him, but I have, through rigorous testing, discovered that Julius is, in fact, remarkably predictable if you understand his thinking."

"And you do?"

"Of course not," Bob said, chuckling. "Do I look nice? But the point is that Julius's actions are internally consistent, and yet he is such an atypical dragon, none of us can reliably predict what he's going to do. He's both unpredictable and entirely predictable at the same time! And that, little sister, makes him the best chance we have. Trust me."

"I do," Chelsie said, leaning hard against the stone wall. "I just wish you'd make it a little easier."

"That would be no fun at all," Bob said. "See you in a month!"

She went stiff. "What happens in a month?"

But Bob had already hung up, leaving Chelsie alone in the hall with only her worries and the distant echo of Bethesda's cackling laughter for company.

Thank you!

Thank you for reading *Nice Dragons Finish Last*! If you enjoyed the story, or even if you didn't, I hope you'll consider leaving a review. Reviews, good and bad, are vital to any author's career, and I would be extremely thankful and appreciative if you'd consider writing one for me.

Would you like to know when my next book is available? Sign up for my new release mailing list! You can also follow me on Twitter @Rachel_Aaron or like my Facebook page for up-to-date info on all of my novels.

The next Hearstriker novel, ***One Good Dragon Deserves Another***, will be available in 2015. If that's too long to wait, I hope you'll check out my other completed series. You can find all my books, plus free sample chapters, at **www.rachelaaron.net.**

Thank you again for reading, and I hope you'll be back soon!

Yours sincerely,
Rachel Aaron

Want more books by Rachel Aaron?
Check out these completed series!

THE LEGEND OF ELI MONPRESS
The Spirit Thief
The Spirit Rebellion
The Spirit Eater
The Legend of Eli Monpress (omnibus edition of the first three books)
The Spirit War
Spirit's End

"Fast and fun, The Spirit Thief *introduces a fascinating new world and a complex magical system based on cooperation with the spirits who reside in all living objects…Fans of Scott Lynch's* Lies of Locke Lamora *(2006) will be thrilled with Eli Monpress. Highly recommended for all fantasy readers."*
- ***Booklist****, Starred Review*

PARADOX (written as Rachel Bach)
Fortune's Pawn
Honor's Knight
Heaven's Queen

"If you liked Star Wars, if you like our books, and if you are waiting for Guardians of the Galaxy to hit the theaters, this is your book."
- ***Ilona Andrews***

"I JUST LOVED IT! Perfect light sci-fi. If you like space stuff that isn't that complicated but highly entertaining, I give two thumbs up!"
- ***Felicia Day***

To find out more about Rachel and read samples
of all her books, visit
www.rachelaaron.net!

About the Author

Rachel Aaron is the author of nine novels as well as the bestselling nonfiction writing book, *2k to 10k: Writing Faster, Writing Better, and Writing More of What You Love,* which has helped thousands of authors double their daily word counts.

When she's not holed up in her writing cave, Rachel lives a nerdy, bookish life in Athens, GA, with her perpetual motion son, long suffering husband, and obese wiener dog.

Made in the USA
Middletown, DE
21 December 2020